ALSO BY MARK A. HENRY

Lacking Evidence to the Contrary
A Lowbrow Novel of Questionable Necessity

AGENT ONE

Mark A. Henry

OPERATION DODECAHEDRON

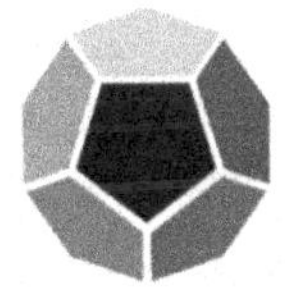

This is a work of fiction. All of the characters, organizations and events portrayed in this work are products of the author's imagination or are used fictitiously. For the record, I called the US Customs and Border Protection Office in Honolulu to ask them some very innocent, very hypothetical questions about their standard responses regarding shipping container-related breaches of national security and they made it quite clear that any protocols or procedures *do not* include discussing them with randos on the telephone at 4am (I forgot about the time zones). Thus, a lot of this shit is made up. I'll say it again: fiction.

THE HONOLULU SITUATION

For more information, please visit

operationdodecahedron.com

facebook.com/markahenrybooks

To bloviate poorly punctuated nonsense, please tweet

@markahenrybooks

Cover artwork by Maura McGurk

Library of Congress Control Number: 2023913411

Operation Dodecahedron Hardcover ISBN 978-1-7363446-6-8

Operation Dodecahedron Paperback ISBN 978-1-7363446-7-5

Operation Dodecahedron Ebook ISBN 978-1-7363446-5-1

For my boys.

I stumble to the floor and only then see that I'm climbing
I can fall right up a staircase
Just as easily as down
'Cause hope can flip a building on its end and in the timing
Needs a hand
Or else it lands
Within the sand
Without a sound

—Blues Traveler, "Ode From The Aspect"

A few long years ago…

PROLOGUE

United States currency. Legal tender. Banknotes. Dollar bills. Foldin' money. Straight cash, homie.

It's made from rags, you know. According to the US Bureau of Engraving and Printing, rag fibers of cotton, linen and "versatile synthetic fibers" are used. The federal government feels that the vague description of that third component is necessary to thwart would-be counterfeiters looking to recreate their secret recipe. Also, it makes it sound like the government has invented some cool proprietary supercloth when the truth is that it's probably just rayon or some shit.

The rag fibers are used because they're much more durable than paper alone. Bills need to survive an average lifespan of four to ten years, during which time they may be folded up to 4,000 times before finally tearing.

Three days off the printing press in Washington DC, the ten-dollar bill serial numbered PA06273612A was folded for the first time at the 1st Gateway Credit Union in Fulton, Illinois. A bank teller named Barbara Lange handed PA06273612A, along with a pinch of other minty fresh bills, including PA06273611A and PA06273613A, to a farmer named Gerry Garrison. Garrison pulled them out of the 1st Gateway bank envelope, slid the envelope back and said, "Save this for the next guy, Barb." He bent the cash square and zipped the square into his jacket.

An hour later, PA06273612A changed hands again over a tank of Grade D acetylene in the dull light and showering sparks of Tommy Casey's welding shop. For generations, the Casey family has offered a discount for cash and Garrison was looking to repair his snowplow, not pay sales tax.

One thousand folds later, PA06273612A had long since parted from its mintmates -11A and -13A and had circled the Midwest for nearly a year when it was handed back as change to Hudson News customer Brad Ostrowski, who was on his way to Insurance-Con Las Vegas. Ostrowski settled into a chair at Gate 28 of Chicago Midway Airport and opened his new book, a novel about a ring of Ivy League card counters. Quite a bit later that evening, PA06273612A was folded under a Lucite paddle by a dealer named Gene and shoved down a slot in a blackjack table at the Tropicana.

One thousand folds after that, PA06273612A, now cured in ABC,* was mailed in a birthday card to Cassie Green from her Nonna in Scottsdale, Arizona. Cassie folded the bill four times and tapped it into a piggy bank that was also a gift from Nonna, come to think of it.

*Abject failure, booze, cocaine.

Another thousand folds and PA06273612A was now nestled comfortably in Sunapee Ellis's bra when it was extracted to pay for a copy of *The Murmur of Bees* from the guy selling used books off a tie-dyed blanket on the sidewalk of Boston's Boylston Street, who said his name was François, but when he's working at Whole Foods, his apron says Frank. François/Frank added PA06273612A to his day's receipts, which is to say he put it in his right sock.

Eighteen months later, seven years down the line from Washington, PA06273612A, now limp and weary, but still worth exactly ten dollars, was folded for the four-thousandth time and concealed in the zippered pocket of Sam Leonard's red fanny pack as the young economist packed for a trip to Central Asia.

CHAPTER 1

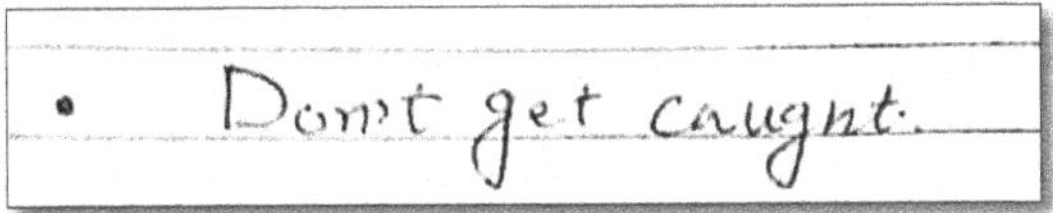

"Which of you shall be our hero?" asked Jefir.

None of the melons spoke up to answer.

"This one," Rahim said, palming a purple melon of perfect size and heft from the cart hitched behind their Honda moped. "He is our hero." He tossed the melon to Jefir.

The "hero melon" was the melon that Jefir and Rahim Zaqq juggled back and forth in order to catch the eyes of the customers at the East Station Market in Taboor City, Zazaristan. Their boss, Mrs. Khan, was skeptical of the practice at first. In her day, fruit was presented in a basket. But Jefir and Rahim had assured her that if any melon should so much as touch the ground, she shall be recompensed, fully and promptly. She agreed, but assured *them* that she still didn't like it. "But thanks for the money," she said.

Mrs. Khan began to like it when the Zaqq brothers started returning the cart emptier and emptier, earlier and earlier. They were good boys, well worth the four zazar price they paid her for each melon.

Each morning, Jefir and Rahim filled their cart to capacity (105 melons) and mopedaled to the market where they sold the melons for ten zazars apiece. They ate four melons a day. Cart rental was fifty. They each netted Z262 per cart. They hadn't dropped a melon in months. The hero melon flies but the hero melon never hits the ground, as the saying went.

And don't for a second think that Jefir and Rahim were just listlessly handing the hero melon back and forth. They had pretty much perfected a move where Jefir (a good thrower, but better catcher) would approach a customer, hold his hands out and say, "Excuse me, would you like a melon?" At this point, Rahim (the slightly better thrower) would launch a melon skyward, caber-toss style from behind the cart. When the timing worked right, the customer would say, "What melon?" just as the hero melon dropped into Jefir's hand and he would smoothly say, "This one."

As Jefir inspected the day's first hero melon, Rahim saw a young man with a red fanny pack wandering through the market gate from the station. "Jefir. An American devil, straight from the den. With the red pack."

Jefir looked up and found Sam Leonard, his American movements somehow both slower and quicker than the other shoppers around him. "Yes. But it will take him a moment. Be patient."

"I know," Rahim said. "Say what's up bro," he advised in return.

"No. I'm going to try hot-enough-for-you."

The brothers' English was decent, but there weren't a lot of Westerners who passed through the market and Jefir and Rahim liked to practice the various idioms and expressions when the chance presented.

"What's up bro has worked three out of four times," Rahim said. "Analytics. Bro."

Jefir slid into the slow-flowing market traffic and stepped in front of Leonard. "Hot enough for you?" he said.

"It is very hot," Leonard said. "This sun is no joke."

"Would you like a cool melon?"

Rahim crouched near the cart, cradling the hero melon. Waiting.

Leonard said, "What?"

Jefir cupped his empty hands. "Would you. Like. A melon?"

Leonard said, "Uhh..."

Rahim launched the melon.

"Melon," Jefir repeated.

"Sure," said Leonard. "Sure. A melon sounds good."

Jefir's eyes flicked upward. He held out his right hand and an eggplant-colored melon smacked into the center of his palm, seemingly out of the hot sky. "This melon?"

"What the fuck?" Leonard said, looking up. "Sorry. Sorry. Holy shit. Sorry. That's a melon? What kind is it?"

"You've never had our country's rainbow melon?"

"I've only been in Taboor City an hour," Leonard admitted. "I just came from the train station."

"Welcome to Zazaristan." Jefir tucked the melon into the crook of his arm. He took Zoey, his prized Swiss Army knife, from his front pocket and clicked open her biggest blade.

"My name is Jefir Zaqq," Jefir said.

Jefir *jabjabjab*-ed a triangle into the melon, then in a flash of practiced motion, retracted the big blade and flicked Zoey's corkscrew into position. He motioned to Rahim. "This is my brother, Rahim."

Leonard grinned a big Western grin. "What up, Jefir, what up Rahim," he said, without the s. "I'm Sam Leonard."

Jefir gave the screw a turn into the scribed triangle so that the knife became a T-shaped handle sticking out of the melon. He tilted the handle toward Leonard, rather than pull the free sample out himself. In Zazaristan, like pretty much everywhere else actually, it is considered rude to point one's blade toward another's face.

Leonard gently, almost daintily, pulled Zoey's handle.

There's a satisfying discovery that is drawing a prismed core sample from a rainbow melon. Jefir and Rahim always let the customer do it for themselves. Tell someone about a melon, and they walk right by. Show someone a melon and you may have their interest for a moment. Allow them to *discover* a melon and you've got a sale.

The rainbow melon never fails to delight anyone seeing it for the first time. They grow only in Zazari soil, in the foothills of the Pir Mountain range. In the 1930's National Geographic published an article about Zazaristan that included a photo of a split rainbow melon, but it was in black-and-white and didn't really do the melon justice. They have a violet outer skin, which gives way to a blue, then green rind, which in turn becomes flesh that grows from tart yellow to mild orange to sweet red center.

"I've never seen anything like that." Leonard said, examining the glistening section of fruit. He snapped a photo, #rainbowmelon #taboorcitylife.

"Wait until you taste it," Jefir said.

Leonard worked the glistening sample loose from the corkscrew and bit into it. "Wow," he said. "How much?" He dug into his fanny pack.

"Ten," Jefir said.

Leonard tugged ten-dollar bill PA06273612A out of his fanny pack. He unfolded it and handed it over. "Thank you," he said in rudimentary Zazarish. He walked off into the market with a melon and that grin.

America might be a den of devils, but this one guy seemed OK, at least.

The market was closing up for the evening. A slivered moon hung low above the still-warm streets.

"Let me see that American bill again," Rahim said.

As older brothers will do, Jefir turned out of Rahim's sight and tucked the folded bill into his right fist. He turned around and offered both fists to Rahim. "Choose."

Rahim considered, then tapped the left. He received a short punch to the solar plexus as a penalty for guessing incorrectly.

Jefir opened his right hand. He unfolded the bill and studied Alexander Hamilton's portrait in the pale moonlight. "Who is this guy, do you think?"

"I think he wrote a play or something," Rahim answered, taking the ten for closer inspection.

This made sense. That puffy cravat and all.

Rahim handed the bill back. "I'm hungry. Can we get kebab? Tariq's is still open."

Sales had been good that day. Only four runty and misshapen melons remained in the second cartload.

Jefir smiled and checked his watch. "Not for long." Tariq's kebab stand was a dozen blocks away.

"You don't think you can make it there before he closes?" Rahim asked. "I thought you were supposed to be a fast runner."

Jefir laughed. He quickly counted out a few bills, including the US ten, and pocketed them. He said, "Here's what we're going to do, little brother." He handed the rest of the money to Rahim. "I am going to run to Tariq's. You are going to go pay Mrs. Khan and return the cart. Then, you can ride as fast as you like to Tariq's. When you arrive *and I have already ordered*, you are going to pay for our kebab. If, by some slim chance you beat *me* there, I'll give you the American bill and WHAT IN THE NAME OF GOD IS THAT?" He shot his finger over Rahim's shoulder.

Jefir was already accelerating away by the time Rahim turned back around. Rahim shouted, "Get me chicken!"

Running at night made Jefir feel like a ghost. Flowing and cool, barely visible. Through the market, past the shuttering stalls of electronics, tea, vintage clothing. Out the west gate. Jump to touch the swinging sign. Cut a diagonal across the intersection and through the darkening city blocks like a shapeless phantom. Three dogs with eleven legs between them fell in with Jefir for a block or two, but they soon lost interest and trotted off just south of Suvi Street. Jefir made a right on Girra. Past the arena. Half a block up and cut left through the alley behind the barbershop. Victory Square just ahead. Headlights splashed against the wall of the alley.

Jefir slowed before exiting the alley so as not to get flattened by what looked to be surprisingly robust Sunday evening traffic.

He skidded to a halt when he saw two technicals parked across the mouth of the square, nose-to-nose, one of the truck's tailgates backed right up against the base of the old Ghachii statue. For the thousandth and final time, Jefir wondered whatever possessed the city to build that statue there. Two armed men were standing on either side of the first car of a small but building traffic jam. A third armed goon roved around the end of the line because armed checkpoint goons have a strict policy of no backsies.

A checkpoint. Not unusual in the city. Police, military, occupying force, militia, street gang, warlord, the only difference was the brand of gun they pointed at you and maybe the kind of kebab they ordered after they were done taking your money. Jefir, knowing Northeast Taboor City as he did, and traveling by either fleet foot or nimble moped, could usually sniff out or avoid these pinches, but everybody gets jammed up now and then and tonight his mind was on kebabs.

A spotlight in the cab of the closer technical swung away from the line of cars onto Jefir.

"STOP! STOP RIGHT THERE!"

Jefir threw up his hands to block the blinding light. The armed man near the first car was facing him. The black barrel of the man's AK-47 reflected a glint of light from the truck. He wore a loose green vest over a white tunic. With his weapon still trained on Jefir, he shook a finger at the first car idling at the checkpoint, bidding the driver to wait.

"What's the hurry?" Green Vest asked Jefir, walking toward him.

Jefir kept his hands up. To shade his eyes from the glaring light as well as to prove himself not a threat.

Silhouetted against the truck lights, Green Vest approached and stopped two paces away.

"The kebab stand closes in a few minutes," Jefir answered. There was no sense in lying. This wasn't his first time being shaken down for a few zazars. The price was the price. And you don't ask questions. Never is the phrase, "If you have to ask, you can't afford it" more apt than when the asker is staring into the blinding lights and gun barrels of a nighttime checkpoint.

"This is a toll road now," Green Vest said. "Show me your ID."

Typically, there was a sliding scale when it came to roadside extortion. One's identity factored in heavily. Hapless Westerners or Quudis, for example, would be expected to cough up much, much more than Zazaris, who in turn had a whole subset of the shakedown rate card unto themselves. For example, if the extortee happened to be from the same hometown or sect as the extorter, he might even be sent on his way with an untouched wallet and a hearty wish for a good evening. Jefir was Taboor City for life. He'd never roamed more than twenty kilometers from where he stood at that moment. Green Vest's flat accent suggested he was southern foothill country.

Jefir produced his Zazari ID card and held it into the light. Green Vest stepped forward and snatched it. "Jefir Zaqq. Taboor City," he read. "It's a thousand z, Jefir Zaqq. And then be on your way, you're holding up the queue." Jefir glanced back. It was true. When he had emerged from the alley, he had inadvertently cut to the front of the line. The line of cars and now a couple scooters stretched even further down the street. One of the scooters beeped its horn irksomely.

Thankfully, Jefir had given most of the day's income to Rahim to give to Mrs. Khan, who took the biggest bite of the melon, so to speak. Jefir carried only his and Rahim's cut: just over a thousand zazars. Paying Green Vest's toll would pretty much clean him out. Except. There *was* the American ten. But Jefir wanted to avoid spending that immediately, especially at Tariq's, who was known for his unfavorable exchange rate as much as his secret kebab sauce.

Jefir hoped to make it quick, at least. He would really have to truck it if he wanted to beat Rahim to Tariq's now. He withdrew his modest knot of cash.

"What's that?" Green Vest said, eyeing the greenback.

"What? This— OW!" Jefir exclaimed as the barrel of the AK jabbed his shoulder, knocking him back a step.

Green Vest called out. "Baba! I've got an infidel-lover over here!"

"What? Hold on," Jefir said, rubbing his shoulder. "Someone gave me that."

"And you took it, didn't you, young man?" said a gravelly voice with the same southern accent as Green Vest's." A big man emerged from the cab of the closer technical. The truck's spotlight threw a tight corona around his gray beard. "Bowing to the American devils, just as they wanted." The big man made his way over. "Good work, son," Graybeard said as he stopped at Green Vest's shoulder.

Graybeard was Bashir Hallazallah, one of Taboor City's wardens. Jefir had seen him a few times patrolling through the neighborhood in his truck, heard the sound of the .50 caliber in the back a few times. Once, Hallazallah walked right past the melon cart.

Jeff heard the slippery click of an automatic pistol cocking. "Get on your knees, young man. You know how, don't you?"

"Wait, Sheik Hallazallah!" Jefir said. "Just listen, you can have it all—" The rifle barrel flashed down Jefir's forehead, knifing open a fiery gash and dropping him to the ground.

"On your knees, he said!" Green Vest yelled.

"Just like your American friends, always trying to buy their way out of trouble," Hallazallah said. He chuckled and grabbed Jefir's money. "Of course, it's not as if you'll be needing it." He separated the zazars and tucked them away in his jacket. Jefir flinched as Hallazallah fired two pistol shots into the air. With the eyes of the roadblocked traffic upon him, he held the ten dollar bill over his head. "Behold, my Zazari brothers! The cause of our nation's suffering! The meddling and oppression of the West. The weak and intemperate among you fall prey to it, but God will judge you. This traitor's blood will mix in the gutter with the torn rags of an empire!"

That same blood running down his face, Jefir looked up at Green Vest. "Hey," he said quietly, as the older man raged on, waving the bill. "Hey. I've got some more. You might as well have it, too."

Hallazallah was ripping bits off the ten dollar bill and tossing them to the street. "...And the idolatry! And the hubris…"

Hallazallah Jr. had heard this speech before. He glanced away from his father and took his left hand off the chipped wooden handguard of his rifle to motion *give it here* to Jefir.

Jefir indicated the cash would be in his left pocket and slowly reached for it.

He felt the familiar shape of Zoey. Her corkscrew was tacky with semi-dried melon juice and that gave Jefir's thumb the extra purchase it needed. He flicked the corkscrew open. It locked into place, extended between his second and third fisted fingers. Jefir drove it between the loose flaps of that green vest.

Shirt or skin resisted just a bit before giving way with a tiny pop that belied the giant howl of pain Green Vest let out when Jefir sunk knuckle-deep and wrenched the screw into the man's liver. The flesh tore wetly. Blood flooded over Jefir's hand, splattered on his leg. He sprang to his feet and grabbed the business end of Green Vest's AK with his free hand, twisting the weapon up and away. He felt three hot rounds pulse through the barrel and a concussive *BOPBOPBOP* as Green Vest/Red Shirt clenched the weapon's trigger. Jefir yanked Zoey back. Green Vest shrieked and Jefir pushed him to the ground. Green Vest's weapon continued to fire as he spun to the pavement and his companions scrambled for cover.

Jefir ran for the technical. The modified pickups were parked diagonally, nose-to-nose, across the narrow end of the square. Jefir darted behind them, turning the tables on Hallazallah's men, who could now only fire blindly into the headlights. 7.62 millimeter bullets and unkind epithets flew by Jefir as he bolted into the night, no longer a ghost. He was alive.

Jefir ran. Full sprint. What he lost in blood from the gash on his forehead, he gained in adrenaline. He felt as though he might have been out*running* the bullets. Whatever the story, none of them found Jefir's rapidly disappearing ass as he crossed the square away from the armed roadblock in a single, short breath.

He ducked around the first corner he came to. He had to disappear before the armed goons mounted up in the technicals and came after him.

Behind him, he heard the truck's engines roar to life. Angry gunfire echoed off the city's walls. Jefir tore through a narrow alley and down a flight of stairs. At the bottom, he burst into the next street, and turned right, away from the sound. Jefir knew where he was. Just north of Hana Street. Taboor Square Park, poorly lit and closed to vehicle traffic, was just a few blocks away. He could lay low there for a while, then try to make it back to Tariq's where Rahim would hopefully still be waiting. With the phone.

Jefir and Rahim shared a cell phone because they worked and lived together and why would both brothers need their own costly phone? In the rare cases when they separated, the rule was that the phone stayed with the moped. If Jefir could get to a phone tonight, he could call Rahim for a pickup, but it's not like there was a payphone on every corner anymore. And it wasn't as if Jefir could pay if there was. Every last zazar and dollar had been taken.

Jefir took a wide turn and sprinted up Dalazak Avenue.

A man wearing Adidas Sambas, bluejeans, and a light blue shirt was sitting on the stoop of an apartment building eating a wide-sticked, chocolate-shelled vanilla ice cream bar.

"Excuse me!" Jefir called breathlessly. "Sir! Do you have a phone? It's an emergency!"

The man bit into the ice cream bar. The chocolate armor *cracked* with a tiny report. "What kind of emergency? Be specific, my friend."

"Some men are trying to kill me! Bashir Hallazallah was running a checkpoint in the square and I was carrying some American money and he got mad and I stabbed another guy and I think the guy was his son. Please, do you have a phone? They're probably after me." Jefir looked over his shoulder.

"Mm. I thought I heard gunfire," said the man. *-crack-*

"Will you help me or not?" Jefir said. He touched his head and came away with red fingertips. "I have to get out of here."

"Relax," said the man. "If there were two men and you hurt one of them, they'll be on their way to a doctor right now. No one's after you, friend." *-crack-*

"There were four or five of them!" Jefir says. "Two technicals!"

"Why didn't you say so?" The man sounded annoyed. "That's important, no?" He regarded Jefir for a moment, then stood up and said, "Come with me." He climbed the stoop and led Jefir into the apartment building's tiny foyer. He closed the door behind them to a crack. He daintily held his ice cream out behind him and pressed himself into the corner to peer out to the street. A drip of vanilla hit the floor. The foyer had seen far worse. There were no windows in the cramped space, just a slatted vent above the door and a row of battered mail bins screwed to the wall.

"How much American money?" the man said.

"What?" Jefir asked.

"You said you had some American money. How much?"

"Ten dollars."

"Do you speak English?"

"Yes. Some."

"Do you read poetry?"

"What?"

A faint but clear megaphone squawked and crackled somewhere in the neighborhood, "Jefir Zaqq… Jefir Zaqq... Jefir Zaqq…"

The man put his eye to the crack. "Jefir," he said.

"What?"

"Do you have any of that money left, Jefir?"

"No. But, please—"

"It's OK," said the man. *-crack-* "You can owe me. Stay here."

He slipped outside and re-took his seat on the stoop. He strategically let a drop of melted ice cream fall over a drop of Jefir's blood on the sidewalk.

The megaphone squawked louder: "Jefir Zaqq… Jefir Zaqq... Jefir Zaqq…"

Inside the foyer, Jefir quietly closed the door and listened.

A voice shouted, "You! On the stoop!"

Jefir heard the man answer, "What can I do for you, my friends?"

Two voices said simultaneously, "Did you see a man run past here?" and "Where did you get that ice cream?"

The man said, "The Ice Cream Whenever truck came by a few minutes ago. I find it the best truck in the city, don't you agree?"

There was a murmur of agreement from the two men.

The man continued. "At any rate. The truck took off when we heard gunfire and it drove away toward downtown. A man with a bloody head ran out of the alley a minute or two later." *-crack-* "He also headed downtown."

One of the voices either got on a radio or was just very annoying to his partner because Jefir heard him yell out, "He headed downtown!"

The three voices outside then lowered into conversation. Jefir couldn't make out everything that was being said, but he thought he picked out "toasted almond bar," and the man on the stoop saying, "It's on me."

A truck roared up the street and a new chorus of voices shouted, "Get in! Let's go!"

The truck gunned away, and the man could be heard calling, "Good luck! Enjoy the ice cream."

A moment later, the man slipped back into the foyer. He turned his stick sideways and gulped off the last glossy bulb of ice cream.

"Was that them?" Jefir asked.

The man paused as he suffered a mild brain freeze.

Jefir asked again, “Two blue techs? Bashir Hallazallah and four or five men? One had a green vest and blood on his shirt?”

The man recovered, looked around and slipped his spent stick into the mail bin marked “Office.” “That was them, all right,” he said. “I gave them some ice cream money and sent them downtown.”

“Thank you,” Jefir said.

“It’s the least I could do, Jefir.” He pulled out his phone. “Now, did you need to make a call to someone?”

“Thank you,” Jefir said. He took the phone. “I’m calling my brother.”

“What’s his name?”

“Rahim.” Jefir began tapping out the familiar number. “But don’t worry, I won’t have him come here. I’ll let him know what happened and have him meet me somewhere.”

“There’s nothing to worry about here,” the man said. “It’s Rahim that I’m worried about.”

Jefir stopped dialing. “Why are you worried about Rahim?”

“Those men knew your name. You showed them your ID, didn’t you?”

“Yes.”

“If they don’t find you soon, Jefir, Hallazallah and his men are going to pay a visit to your address. It’s not safe there. I hope Rahim isn’t home when they arrive.”

“He’s not home,” Jefir said. “By now, he’s probably waiting at Tariq’s.”

“The kebab place?” the man asked. “Do people know him there?”

"Probably. Tariq does, at least."

"He can't stay there either. It's more dangerous for him if he's out in public as Jefir Zaqq's brother. Hallazallah will be putting the word out that he's looking for you. Someone will point Rahim out as your brother to Hallazallah himself or one of the other wardens and they'll ask to see his ID. It won't be good. There's only one place that's safe for you two right now, Jefir. There's only one person in the city who knows where you are." The man thumbed his own chest. "Tell Rahim he can come here. But first, he should get kebab for us." The man glanced at his watch. "Before Tariq closes. I want lamb. Then, tell Rahim that he should say to Tariq that he's going to meet two friends and head off down Nuniz Street. Then, have him cut back around Jabbo and take Phandu up to Dalazak Avenue and come in around behind my building. Tell him I'll meet him back there."

"Why you? He doesn't know you. He might not trust you."

"You need to stay out of sight. Rahim will trust me if you tell him he can."

"How do I know I can trust you?"

"You can trust me because I'm going to trust *you,* Jefir. I'm going to let you stay alone in my apartment while I wait for your brother."

"I don't even know your name," Jefir said.

"It's Shwarma. Wahiri Shwarma. Let's not shake, my hands are sticky."

CHAPTER 2

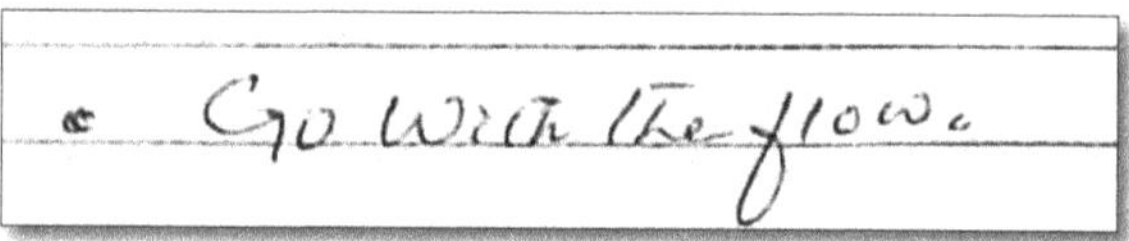

FIVE WEEKS LATER

In the cool Quudian midnight, in a well-lit and spotless alley, a road-dusted but otherwise nondescript van rolled to a quiet stop.

"It's time," Shwarma said.

Jefir rolled down the dirty passenger's side window to look into the side mirror. Behind the van and across the street, sodium lights glowed in the sky above the two-meter high wall that ringed The Islamic Republic of Quudia's International Logistics Hub Port. There was a palm tree on the other side of the wall, its fronds stirring in a light breeze.

"It smells different here," Jefir said.

"The air of another country always smells better. At first," Shwarma replied. He took out his phone. "Get your things together."

Jefir got out of his seat and duck-walked into the back of the van. Rahim was sitting on a black backpack that was stuffed to cylindrical capacity. He slid off of it and the brothers knelt together in the darkness.

Rahim helped Jefir strap a twenty-liter plastic tank to his chest, then lifted the backpack to Jefir's shoulders. He leaned close to Jefir's ear.

"I want to come with you."

"No!" Shwarma snapped, putting down his phone and turning around. "No. We've discussed this many times, Rahim. Your duty to Jefir lies back in Taboor."

Jefir said, "I'm doing this to protect you, Rahim. To protect us."

Shwarma looked at his phone. "My contact has given the location. Block D, which is bordered by Rows five and six and Tracks two and three. Within the block, it's aisle two, slot eight, level five. Say it back, Jefir."

Jefir repeated, "Block D, between rows five and six and two and three. Aisle two, slot eight, level five."

"Good," Shwarma said. "I'm deleting the message now. For security." He tapped the phone. "My contact is a very valuable asset, Jefir. Protect him at all costs. Leave no traces. Good luck. It's time. Remember the signal, two shorts and a long."

Jefir nodded. Rahim embraced his bulky form. "I love you, Jef," he said. "Be careful."

"I love you, little brother. The hero melon flies, but the hero melon never hits the ground."

"Don't get caught," Shwarma said.

Jefir released Rahim and shuffled to the rear of the van. He quietly opened the door. He slipped out and pressed the van door shut, then stepped aside as Shwarma backed the van out into the deserted street.

Jefir edged to the mouth of the alley and peered out to watch as the van drove a few hundred meters and turned into the main entrance of the Logistics Hub Port. The entrance was blocked by a striped gate.

Almost immediately, a uniformed Quudi guard emerged from the gatehouse. His words were lost, but his waving arms clearly conveyed, *What the fuck?*

The fussy Quudis with their love of rules could not resist chastising the driver for being so woefully ill-prepared to enter the port. And at this hour? The port is closed for the day of rest! Come back tomorrow! The sea breeze carried the van's horn: *beeeeeeeeeeeep*. Jefir squinted to make out Shwarma's silhouette. He was waving his arms as well, probably going on about how some paperwork must be missing or some directions misgiven.

The guard continued to attempt to shoo Shwarma away from his gate and back to the unwashed hinterlands from whence he came as Shwarma countered each of his increasingly agitated waves with more droning horn: *beeeeeeeeeeeeeeeeeep*.

Now Rahim emerged from the rear of the van and walked to the gate, waving his arms as well. The Quudi guard raised a radio. Within seconds, a small security cart with a strobing red light rolled onto the scene from somewhere within the port.

Jefir watched as the guards, with increasing agitation, urged the unauthorized interlopers away. When a second security cart arrived, Jefir heard the signal. Two shorts and a long: *beepbeep beeeeeeeeeeeeeep*. He made his move.

He was out of the alley and across the quiet street in seconds, striding smoothly, despite the loads strapped to him front and back. He heaved himself up and over the wall as Rahim was being prodded back into the van. Shwarma gave one last parting shot of horn and chirped away from the gate.

Jefir landed inside the wall with a soft *thump* amidst a lush topiary feature. The satellite map photos of the port had proven accurate. Quudia's government had invested millions in aesthetic landscaping upgrades to the Logistics Hub in order to give what was formerly known as the Dock District better curb appeal. The close-studded shrubbery and palms provided excellent cover. Jefir cursed the Quudis for their ostentation, not to mention their stupid, stupid faces, but blessed them for their foppish arrogance.

Concealed in position behind a thick tuft of seagrass, Jefir surveyed the massive field of asphalt that was the shipping port. A few steps away, painted lines demarcated a two-lane road that ringed the entire facility. About twenty-five meters beyond the road, shipping containers of varied colors loomed like a mountain range, stretching hundreds of meters to Jefir's right and left. Massive two-legged gantry cranes, dark and inert in the moonlight, straddled the rows of containers. And somewhere beyond, the sea.

After a lifetime unknown to Jefir's Zazari eye, let alone the touch of his toe, the Gulf of Quudia introduced herself demurely, brinily, dieselily, to his nose.

Jefir exhaled and turned his attention to the stacks of containers. In rows that seemed to run on forever, piled six and seven high, the towering steel cuboids were taller than all but a few buildings Jefir had ever seen in person. The objective lay somewhere within.

WangleMap had shown that the containers awaiting shipment at the port were laid out in rectangular blocks, intersected with a gridded system of tracks and rows wide enough for trucks or forklifts. The layout of the containers reminded Jefir of the brightly familiar streets and avenues of Taboor City. And just like in Taboor, a certain kind of man could choose to wend himself through a tight sub-grid of narrow alleyways within the blocks themselves if that suited his purposes.

Railed tracks ran parallel to the water, supporting the huge rolling cranes. Spanning the width of an entire container block, the cranes looked very much like the ill-tempered robots Jefir had once seen on television. The viewing had been cut short when the guy who owned the TV yelled at Jefir and chased him away from the window before Jefir was able to see enough of the clip to determine if the man was watching a fictional movie or actual news footage of a building-sized robot snapping helicopters out of the sky using the cables that hung from its crotch like a whip. Upon hearing Jefir's recounting of the clip, Rahim and Tariq rendered the judgment that robots of that scale and temperament are "almost certainly" fictional. "For now," Tariq had added knowingly.

The rows led to the sea.

A flash of light. Jefir snapped his head to the left. The security carts, having dispatched that troublesome and grimy van from the gate, were returning to their appointed rounds within the port. One cart drove eastward, away from Jefir's position, but the other was heading toward him. He ducked lower behind his grassy cover. From between the sandpapery fronds, he got a very clear look at the blouse-booted security guard driving the cart and the automatic pistol on the man's hip. The cart rolled past, its electric motor a stealthy whisper. The guard hand-signaled and turned left, off the ring road toward the water. He drove down a row and disappeared between the containers.

The beeping distraction was fully spent.

Rahim was gone.

Jefir was truly on his own. Perhaps if he had made a run for the shadowy crevices between the shipping containers immediately after breaching the wall instead of hiding in the brush like a quivering bird, he could have been well hidden by now. His hesitation had cost him. Now he was forced into a game of cat-and-mouse against the roving guards within the maze of containers as he searched for the objective. And what if the guards had dogs? Whether he was the bird, the mouse or even the cat, he could be in a spot of trouble here. And he had to pee. He had been in the van for hours.

He shucked his backpack and moved behind a full-grown palm tree sprouting from an enormous ceramic pot. Just as the towering stacks of containers had given him pause, the scale of the pot took his notice. It looked as though it had been zapped with an enlarging ray.

He relieved himself in the giant palm pot. *Wait, what if the Quudis DID have guard dogs? Could the dogs sniff the urine? Is leaving a scent behind a tactical error?*

Of course, there's no problem that doesn't look a bit smaller when considered with an emptying bladder and Jefir took a deep, calming breath to assure himself that his plan was sound, his mind was sharp, his heart was pure, and his future stretched ahead of him like the glittering peestream he arced through the Quudian night.

With business done, he quickly threw a handful of gravel over the damp depression in the palm tree's sandy soil and kept moving. Duty, as well as common sense demanded it. If any pee-based errors were in fact made, it would be best for Jefir to distance himself from them as much as possible. He reshouldered his pack and made one last lookout for port security. He took a deep breath of that sea air and bolted from cover.

He tried to will himself invisible as he crossed the open stretch of road, making for the rows of containers. He slipped into a darkened space between two stacks, and not a second too soon, for just then another flash of red light reflected from the dull edges of the containers and chased him deeper within. Jefir ducked around the first corner he reached, a heartbeat before a security cart whirred past on the road he had crossed not five seconds before. Jefir held still and slowed his breathing. It was quiet amidst the containers and he waited until the sound of the cart receded into the ambience.

Jefir crept through the tight, dim warrens, moving toward the sea. He passed six containers until he came to the next track. It was deserted, but well lit. Three forklifts were parked in an orderly line to his left. Another cliff of containers rose ahead. Jefir hesitated and retreated back into the cover of the stacks. He shuffled to his left and squeezed the length of eight more containers to reach the nearest row to orient himself and maybe even get a glimpse of the water.

Jefir edged to the light that spilled in from the opening at the end of the block. Of course, the fastidious Quudis had stencil-painted directional reference numbers on the ground at every corner and Jefir saw that he stood at the intersection of Track 5 and Row 7. He scanned for security carts, then leaned out to see down the row. His first glimpse of the water was a narrow slice of depthless black. Infinite and without horizon.

Except wait, that wasn't the water. The flat black hull of a fantastically sized ship filled the space between containers. The *Star of Panama* rose at least thirty meters out of the water and must have been hundreds of meters long. The palm tree pot now seemed much less impressive.

From his concealed vantage, Jefir watched as a security cart, looking like a toy compared to the ship, puttered through an intersection two or three blocks away. Jefir gave one more glance at the enormous cargo ship, then stepped back within the containers to continue his search.

Keeping to the inky alleys, Jefir slowly and quietly slipped through the port, moving toward the water.

When he reached Track 4 and was working up the courage to cross the open space to the next block, he spotted not *the* objective, but something like it. Across the track, five levels up. A brick-red container. Four square windows and a rectangular front door, all shrink-wrapped in white plastic for shipping. A move-in ready, fully furnished, KozyHome Lucky Seven model seven-window tiny home (some assembly required), fresh from the Quudian factory in Darqaa and destined for some upwardly mobile infidel jackass in the West.

The issue of upward mobility also pressed down on Jefir at that moment. Like his objective, this KozyHome was stacked five levels up, ten meters in the air. He had no means by which to access it. Free-climbing the sheer, vertically grooved wall of containers was plainly impossible. How was he supposed to do this?

If he had any rope, he could probably grapple-hook the uppermost container and do whatever-the-opposite-of-rappelling is to climb up to the KozyHome's door level, but unfortunately, not only was this plan short of rope and the proper vocabulary, Jefir lacked a grappling hook. The plan was discarded quickly. Although Jefir thought he would be good at throwing the hook, guessing it would take two tries *at most* to grapple purchase on some convenient rail or grommet atop the container stack.

A security cart turned onto Track 4 and Jefir ducked back into the shadows. How many of these roving patrols were there? The longer he stayed out here, the more likely he was to be caught. He watched the cart drive away and weighed the age-old calculation of stroll-casually-and-be-exposed-for-longer-time or run-as-quickly-as-possible-and-hope-short-burst-of-motion-is-over-before-anyone-notices. The cart turned up Row 6. Jefir hauled ass across Track 4.

In the midst of the containers, it was almost completely dark. Only faint gasps of moonlight reached the ground. Jefir felt his way quietly through the narrow spaces. His front-and-back packs made the occasional ringing scrape through the tighter gaps as he passed container after container, seeking his purpose.

Jefir made one last heart-pounding dash to cross a track and conceal himself safe-ishly within the dim confines of Sector D. The objective was close.

Two aisles over. Eight slots in. Five levels up, and there it was. Just as Shwarma said. The objective. The KozyHome was stacked away in the shadows, less than a meter from any of its neighbors. Jefir moved directly under it. Looking up, he removed his water tank and backpack and set them on the narrow strip of asphalt. Within the backpack, describing its stiffly cylindrical shape, was his five-gallon bucket. Jefir stepped up onto the bucket and grabbed the lower rail of the second-level container. The surrounding stacks were close enough that he was able to also grab the rail of the opposite container and suspend himself by pressing his hands and sneakered feet into their sides. He inched upward, ninja-style, taking a moment's rest at the railed footholds of each level until he stood scissor-legged in the ten-meter breeze at his objective's plastic-sheathed front door.

Shwarma's contact at the port, The amateur poet and Assistant Export Deputy Hamid El-Qami, had proven his worth. El-Qami's tips on foreign travel, weak points and infiltration tactics had literally led Jefir to the doorstep of his goal without incident. Shwarma's faith in El-Qami was well-earned and Jefir was instructed *repeatedly* to protect the man by leaving as small a footprint as possible in the port and beyond.

Jefir clicked Zoey open and noiselessly incised a top-to-bottom slit in the door's filmy plastic shrinkwrap. He reached through and twisted the tiny home's doorknob. Locked. But a hollow realtor's padlock hung from the knob. Again, in consistency with what El-Qami, by way of

Shwarma, had told him to expect. Unfortunately, the lock's combination was not within El-Qami's purview.

Jefir pocketed Zoey. He gently pulled the plastic apart and bent to examine the lock, with its four spinning tumblers. Light glinted on the plastic's cut edge. A security cart strobed on Row 5, about thirty meters to his right. Jefir froze in the shadows as the cart flashed past. The seconds drew out. The security guard had surely spotted Jefir splayed out between containers and was now calling for backup, his weapon drawn and dog, crazed by the smell of interloper urine, straining at the leash.

But the cart's light faded, then winked out altogether.

By the thin light, with a pounding heart, Jefir pried the door's plastic sheath apart and examined the padlock. The tumblers were set to 0-0-0-0.

He withdrew Zoey again, and even under the tense circumstances, marveled once more at the utter preparedness of the Swiss Army. For a neutral country with no enemies, they were truly ready for any number of threats, from loose screws to unstripped electrical wires to ragged fingernails. He called Zoey's smallest blade into action.

By the method he had learned from Shwarma's training videos, he slipped the point of the knife into the narrow gap to the left of the first 0 and slowly drew the blade down, tracing the roundness of the tumbler's hidden axle.

No.

He clicked the tumbler to 1 and probed again. No.

2? The blade dropped where the axle flattened. Yes.

He quickly looked around for any sign of security, then moved on to the second tumbler.

0? No.

1? No.

2? No.

3? Drop. Yes.

A few seconds later, Jefir had cracked the third tumbler as another 2, and with increasing nervousness, finally coaxed a 5 to reveal itself as the fourth digit.

2-3-2-5. He tugged on the lock. It gave and the face flopped open. A set of keys slid out and dropped into darkness. They ricocheted off the side of his foot and clanged a few containers on the way down before landing on asphalt, making about the same amount of noise as an empty handle of gin tossed in the curbside recycling bin while the neighbor kids are outside waiting for the bus.

Jefir ninja-ed down in a panic. It took a moment, but he spotted the keys, which fortunately hadn't gone skidding beneath tons of steel, cargo and modern living space. He snatched them up and climbed back into position. He carefully keyed the door's lock and the bolt slid open smoothly. He hurriedly replaced the keys in the lockbox, reset the code to 0-0-0-0, and pushed the door open. He wedged his body through the plastic slit and stepped inside the tiny home.

Letitia Kozler didn't get where she was in the man's world of prefab housing by not delivering on a promise. And just as promised, the standard 8 x 40 x 8.5-foot container that Jefir now stood inside had an industry-leading seven windows, all neatly shrouded in white plastic that let in the barest light. A quick inspection of the very dark interior revealed little more than that it smelled like paint.

Jefir stepped back outside and climbed to the ground. He ferried his backpack and water tank up to the KozyHome and began unpacking. The white plastic bucket, foreshadowing its eventual utility, was extruded from his backpack with a few small, grunting efforts and set on the wall-to-wall carpet. As his eyes adjusted to the near darkness, Jefir inventoried his worldly possessions: Twenty liters of lukewarm Taboor City water, three changes of clothes, a Dopp kit, three dozen nut bars, four oranges, a flashlight, three US twenty-dollar bills, his journal, two pens, and of course, a distrust of any depraved Westerners he may meet in the course of his travels. All intact and ready to serve their purposes.

The excitement of his successful infiltration quickly wore off, and suddenly there was little to occupy his mind. The near-total darkness made journaling impossible and he thought he should husband the flashlight's batteries anyway. The journal's tenets, such as "Blend in," "Say yes a lot," "Go with the flow," and "Trust your instincts" were well committed to memory and required no review.

Jefir felt his way around the tiny home's layout. At one end, an unfurnished bedroom adjoined by a plastic-walled bathroom with shrink-wrapped fixtures. At the other, a sleeping loft built above the breakfast nook. The KozyHome's solar panels, furniture and custom decorations were packed in large cardboard boxes strapped along the back wall. Jefir had been repeatedly instructed to not disturb anything inside the container, but he quickly assured himself that no harm would come of slipping those boxes out of their restraints (taking careful note of their original order and position) and constructing a snug fort out of them in the middle of the carpeted floor.

As sometimes happened when he lay still in the quiet dark, with all relativity stripped away, Jefir envisioned himself as if seen through a telescope, at once large and tiny.

Were the stars just grains of sand or was each grain of sand a star? Was he sailing by the stars of fate, which are not so much fixed as slowly ever spinning over our heads, or was he charting his own course across an untracked desert of sand? The sole answer that came to him in the close, dark air, the single pole around which his personal heavens rotated, was that anything was possible; outside this fort, the world was an unfathomably large and intensely weird place. Jefir hoped only for a place to stand, in it or on it, to occupy that slim and rolling toehold between belief and faith.

Belief? Faith? Belief was past. Hard experience, paid in full. The ground covered, the trail of footprints behind. Jefir believed he would be thirsty by this time tomorrow, and hungry the day after that. He believed he was doing the right thing.

Faith. The unblazed plain, the luxury of the wanderer's choice. Jefir had faith in exactly twenty liters of lukewarm water, three changes of clothing, a Dopp kit, three dozen nut bars, four oranges, a flashlight, three US twenty-dollar bills, his journal and two pens.

And between? In a box within a box, crossing an ocean without destination. (Hamid, the ethically limber Quudia Port Authority Assistant Export Deputy was privy to only so much information, which did not include where the container would end up. "North America. Probably," he had solemnly promised). Surely fate or fortune could not have possibly anticipated this. On the other hand, the world is an unfathomably large and intensely weird place.

The container was clankily gripped by a crane. It lurched upward. Jefir felt swoops and drops in his stomach as he was swung through the air. His short flight punctuated with a bone-jarring clang as his container was set into place, somewhere on the vast deck of the *Star of Panama.*

Jefir peeked from his fort. Sunlight hazed through the seven plastic-shrouded windows. Over the next few minutes, containers boomed into place around and above him. The light was cut to a trickle.

Your typical cruise passenger is way too drunk to notice the moment when the ship's engines spin up and the vessel begins to ease out of port, but if you're lying on a carpeted floor, sober as a judge and silent as a stone, you can tell.

Before long, Jefir heard the bellow of the ship's horn, then felt the fury of nautical horsepower vibrating up through the ship's hull and 37,935 tonnes of consumer goods into his body to let him know he was on his way.

As the *Star of Panama* cut effortlessly through the Gulf, it was impossible for Jefir to say which direction she was sailing, relative to the orientation of his dim berth. Was the KozyHome's bedroom toward the front of the ship? Or was the breakfast nook? With no visual reference and a negligible sense of inertia, there were no clues. Like a train passenger looking out at another train on a parallel track, Jefir found he could convince himself he was traveling in any direction at all. Forward? Yes. Backward? Sure. Sideways? Why not?

The sun provided enough light for Jefir to journal and occasionally pace the KozyHome's length without bumping a hip on the kitchenette counter or a head on the sleeping loft. At night, the darkness crept in gradually until everything was black as a boot.

In the darkness that first night, Jefir felt his way to the KozyHome's door. Shipping containers will get a bit stuffy en route, and while Jefir, a native and lifelong resident of Zazaristan, was quite accustomed to warm weather, the deep hits of sea air he had taken the previous night on the Quudian coast had hooked him well and through. He carefully opened the front door and was greeted by the blank sheet of white plastic. The cut edges rippled steadily in the wind. The pleasant sound mixed with the low rumble of the ship's engines so strongly suggested an effortless, endless freedom that without thinking, Jefir stuck his hand out through the plastic to touch it. Unconsciously he reached further, and his hand bonked into the neighboring container.

Jefir pulled his hand back and popped his head out. As is almost always the case, the thin wedge of night allotted to Jefir was a trove of joys in direct proportion to its scarcity. The aforementioned fresh air of the open ocean, and a rip of wind so steady it could only be caused by the ship's momentum. The ship was sailing breakfast nookward, after all. Jefir looked up. The sky blazed with stars.

CHAPTER 3

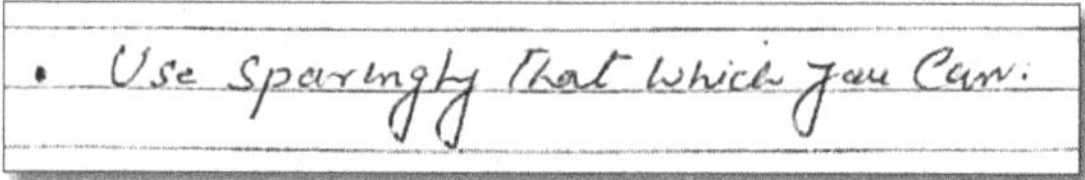

Jefir passed the next eight days reviewing his journal and jotting down the occasional thought by watery day and bathing in his slice of outside world by whistling night.

It was hot in the container and Jefir rode out most of the trip wearing just his undershorts.

After over a week on the high seas, some high seas indeed rolled in Jefir's bucket latrine. Since he realized he needed to carefully ration the bucket's capacity, he kept his eating and drinking to a minimum and warily eyed the rising level daily. Periodic dumping was impossible due to the limited opening afforded by the door's plastic shroud. Yes, the opening stretched a bit each night when Jefir stuck his head out, but he felt duty-bound to keep the plastic as intact as possible. In the same spirit, he could see that even the most careful attempt to empty the bucket would create some befouling backsplash and thus compromise the whole operation by alerting subsequent residents that their tiny home may have been previously used for some light human trafficking.

On the ninth morning, and less than five centimeters from critical bucket mass, the *Star of Panama* gave a long wail of horn and the engines dropped a pitch. Jefir had arrived. He celebrated by drinking the last of his plastic-y water and peeing luxuriantly into the bucket. He carefully snapped the bucket's lid shut for the final time. Not a drop spilled. He pulled on what would be his Day One (and Four and Seven and so on) clothing. White t-shirt. Blue jeans. Billed maroon cap with a "P" on it.

He then deconstructed his homey fort and replaced the boxes as he had found them while the cargo ship gingerly covered the last few feet of ocean and silently met land. Another link in the supply chain completed.

Within minutes, light flooded through the windows. The containers around him were being removed and winched away. Jefir's container was no longer boxed in. He could now have a look around. Surely no harm in that.

Jefir walked to the door, opened it and gingerly pushed his head through the slit plastic. Humid air hit him like the hot breath of a lover.

From thirty meters above the water, Jefir marveled at his view. The *Star of Panama* was docked at the edge of a small island about two kilometers wide and one kilometer across. To his left, beyond the rear of the ship, an unbroken stretch of jewel-blue water met the horizon. To his right, he saw a four-lane bridge linking the small island to the mainland. Trucks and cars busily crossed to and fro. The island was largely paved over, and just like the port back in Quudia, row upon row of shipping containers were stacked everywhere, although this place looked somewhat more jumbled and shabby compared to the gleaming Quudian operation. Across the industrial cargo port, the United States flag flew in front of a two-story building and beyond that, on the far side of the island, Jefir could see a swath of green grass and a small strip of sandy beach.

Massive cranes towered overhead, plucking containers off the ship, then slowly tracked them away to place them in rows on the ground. Jefir spotted a tiny person on the dock below, walking along the row of containers closest to the ship. The tiny person looked up, then stopped and pointed up at Jefir. Jefir pulled his head back and slammed the door shut.

CHAPTER 4

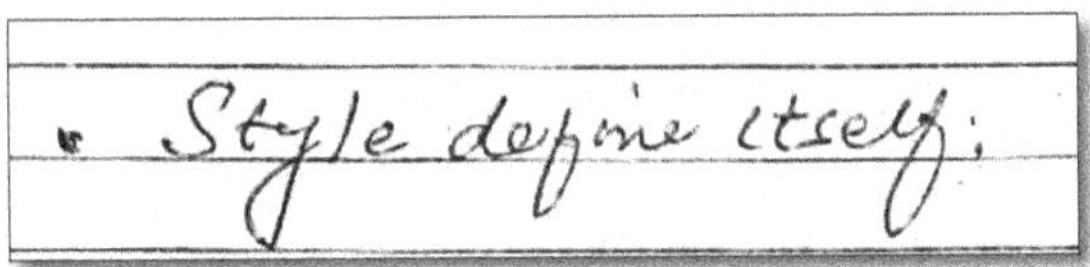

In Jefir's defense, the now-clear mistake of opening the door of his container to have a look around was, technically, a necessary matter of procedure. "Constantly orient yourself" was clearly written right there in the journal.

Loud, metallic clanks echoed from above as a crane clamped onto the container. A sudden jerk upward, and Jefir once more sensed he was flying through the air. He quickly put on his backpack and steadied himself in the Lucky Seven's foyer. The container made an abrupt turn and with a stomach-tickling jolt, began its descent.

Jefir risked opening the door again and dared another quick look outside. Directly below, he saw the same tiny man (now looking bigger). The man wore a security guard's uniform. He was looking directly up at Jefir.

Jefir slammed the door shut again. His heart raced. His bladder pulsed. A passage from page seven of the journal was summoned to his mind: "Improvise. Make do."

He opened Zoey's largest blade.

A triangular flap opened in the shrink-wrap that covered the tiny home's door. GossCo Sand Island Logistical NetPort Facility Security Guard Trent Calvin had time to utter only the briefest of what-the-fucks before a white bucket began to tumble menacingly toward him.

You know the joke about two people facing a hungry bear and one of the people notes that he needn't outrun the bear, only his companion? This was a similar situation except that Calvin was alone, and instead of a bear, there were 4.8 gallons of human waste in a five gallon container accelerating toward him at exactly 9.8 meters per second per second from sixty feet in the air and there's no punchline because nobody's outrunning that.

Calvin was less than ten feet from ground zero when the bucket impacted the pavement. Isaac Newton could tell you all about how equal and opposite reactions work, but simply put, when the bucket hit the ground, the lid ejected and the bucket torqued into a slight clockwise spin, creating a whirling and quite literal shitstorm which efficiently and thoroughly drenched a twenty-foot radius, including Calvin.

Not many people have ever really been soaked with excrement, so it's a strange fact that we all know just how to stand when it happens. A slightly inward-curving X, like you're hugging a giant ball. As Calvin stood in dripping disbelief, the shipping container thudded to earth, covering half of the wet, fetid puddle that now semi-circled the front of the KozyHome like the world's worst welcome mat.

Calvin staggered outside the foul perimeter and frantically peeled off his soaked shirt, then danced out of his pants to get down to his relatively uncontaminated underwear while keeping one eye on the KozyHome's door, watching for his attacker's next move.

He grabbed his radio. "Kalami!"

"What happened?" Danny Kalami said, peering down through the plexiglass floor of his cargo crane. "I couldn't see, you're right under my seat."

Heaving with rage and disgust, Calvin howled, "He dropped shit on me!"

"What kind of shit?" Kalami came back.

Calvin had an idea. "Kalami! Get this container back up in the air!"

"Copy," said Kalami. He pushed a lever and the container slowly rose from the ground.

"Now drop it in the fucking harbor!"

"No can, Trent. Sorry," Kalami said as he continued raising the container.

Seeing the dripping container gently swaying on the crane cables, Calvin had another idea. "Give him a hard landing, at least," he said into the radio. "Shake him up."

The container jerked to a stop.

"Copy," said Danny. This seemed like a reasonable compromise to Calvin's earlier request to drop the container in the fucking harbor. Containers took the occasional bump, sure, but putting one in the drink was pretty much unheard of. He released the brake and the KozyHome Lucky Seven crashed to the ground with a ringing boom. Glass shattered and two of the faux plastic shutters popped off. Kalami then hauled the KozyHome back in the air about thirty feet in order to keep the assailant from escaping and also to plausibly argue that the damage to the container was done *before* it touched GossCo's property.

Calvin switched his radio to the security channel. "This is Calvin! I need backup in Lot D."

The radio crackled, "This is Ed Sakamoto. What is going on out there?"

When GossCo's OHSA Compliance Officer "Easy" Ed Sakamoto heard the Lot D incident play out over the radio, he, as always, anticipated the worst.

"There's shit everywhere!" Calvin yelled.

"Officer Calvin, that language is inappropriate for the workplace," said Sakamoto.

"The container was damaged when I picked it off the ship, Easy," Kalami added.

"Everyone, stay where you are," Sakamoto radioed back. "If there's no imminent danger, don't do anything, don't touch anything. I'll be right there."

At his desk in the GossCo Sand Island Logistical NetPort Facility office building a half-mile away, Sakamoto noted the time of day, tucked a blank Form 301 Injury and Illness Incident (The Triple I) Report into a folder, liaised with the security office to have someone meet him in Lot

D, and rolled out there in the GossCo stretch golf cart reserved for his department's exclusive use.

Sakamoto had seen it many times. Slack controls in the small areas lead to breakdowns down the line and before you know it, half the dock is covered with action figures or golf balls or whatever shit happened to be in the broken container.

After a short drive of moderate speeds and complete stops at intersections, the smell hit him at the edge of Lot D, about a hundred feet downwind of where a tiny home hung in the air from a crane's cables. A triangular section of the door's protective plastic hung down like a pennant. Two plastic window shutters lay on the ground, in the middle of a dark, wet stain on the asphalt. Security Guard Trent Calvin sat on a concrete Jersey barrier wearing only underwear.

Sakamoto stopped his cart and began filling out the Triple I. Completed by: *Edmund Sakamoto*. Title: *OSHA Compliance Officer*. Date: *July 8*. Location: *GossCo Sand Island Logistical NetPort Facility, Lot D*. Information about the employee: *Trent Calvin, GossCo Security*.

Sakamoto looked up from the form. "Officer Calvin! Where are your clothes?"

Calvin pointed to a wet and crumpled pile on the ground at the edge of the large, slick puddle. "Covered with shit."

Sakamoto drove to the edge of the puddle for a closer look. "Why aren't you wearing a hazmat suit?" he asked.

Calvin said, "Fuck you, Easy."

Employee wearing inappropriate workplace attire.

Sakamoto put the Triple I down and removed a packaged hazmat suit from one of his cart's compartments. As he pulled the suit on, two security guards, Max Tibo and Phillipe St. Germaine, rolled up in another cart on the far side of the puddle. Seeing Easy donning a biohaz suit, they stopped short and scrambled to pull suits from their own cart's supply bin. Tibo then frisbeed a packaged suit to Calvin.

Fully suited, Sakamoto slid his pen to Box 15 of the Triple I, a finger-sized rectangle labeled "What Happened? Tell us how the injury occurred?"

Sakamoto said, "What happened, Officer Calvin? Tell me how the injury occurred."

"What is everyone waiting for?" Calvin yelled. "He's in there!" He waved his still-packed suit up toward the container that hung from the crane. "He's trapped."

"There's a person in there?" Sakamoto said. "Are you sure the person is alive?" The answer would greatly influence the short arc Sakamoto was building within the confines of Box 15. An unticketed passenger would require a whole different form, in fact. As well as a call into Customs and Border Protection, just to be safe.

"Yes, Easy! How do you think this happened?" Calvin said, as he pulled on his papery hazmat suit.

"What happened? Was there some sort of spill or leak?" Sakamoto asked.

"There's a guy in that container, Easy!" Calvin yelled. "I saw him stick his head out. He had a dark beard, I think. He dumped his pissbucket on me. I told Danny Kalami to keep the container up in the air to trap the asshole!" He shouted the last part up to the container.

Sakamoto looked up. One of the tiny home's windows had broken. "Aloha!" he shouted. "Unticketed passenger! You are trespassing on the private property of the GossCo corporation! Your container is unsealed! United States Customs and Border law authorizes GossCo security to open and enter your container and use reasonable force to apprehend!"

The container was silent.

Sakamoto opened his radio. "Kalami. Bring this container down. Gently."

The crane's motor whined to life and the tiny home slowly settled to earth.

Sakamoto waved Tibo and St. Germaine forward. "Open the container. Apprehend whoever is in there. I'm calling CBP."

Sakamoto tapped his phone as the white-suited guards approached the KozyHome's front door. Calvin moved to a vantage where he would be able to enjoy the sight of this asshole getting Tased. St. Germaine tugged the white plastic free of the doorframe and tossed it aside. He unholstered his Taser, gently twisted the doorknob, then flung the door open. The door swung easily despite its recent traumatic drop, testament to the KozyHome's fit and finish. St. Germaine burst inside, Tibo just behind. They were met by nothing more than a gently gusting, paint-smelling breeze.

"What the fuck?" Calvin said, pushing past the guards. "My cousin lives in one of these. His ain't got windows in the back."

Like the cut and flapping shroud that had faithfully protected window #7 during its long ocean journey, Jefir Zaqq was in the wind.

CHAPTER 5

• Say YES a lot.

"Don't get caught" was the cardinal rule. It was literally on page one of the journal.

After weaponizing his bucket, Jefir slammed the KozyHome's door shut and spun to the back wall. In seconds, he had the large window open, the bug screen out, and he'd used Zoey to slice the filmy plastic corner-to-corner. A quick peek outside revealed the *Star of Panama*'s hull, and on the ground, a row of containers running parallel to the waterfront.

When his container first boomed to earth, Jefir quickly shoved his backpack and empty water tank through the window then wiggled out behind them to drop a short distance to the pavement. He collected the pack, picked up the tank and looked up to see the underbelly of a grumbling gantry crane. His adrenaline was already redlining, but another splash hit him when he saw the shiny convex lens of a camera fixed to the crane's belly. Through the plexiglass floor of the crane's cab, Jefir could see the underside of the operator's seat. From his limited vantage, Jefir clocked the operator as a typical American: wide in the gut, inappropriate footwear.

Keeping his eyes locked upward, Jefir nimbly sidestepped along, keeping out of sight by staying directly beneath the operator's seat until he was behind the cab. He darted into the first shadow that would have him.

The sheer black cliff of the *Star of Panama* rose from the water about five meters away. No foot or vehicle traffic traveled this strip of asphalt between the containers and the ship, which was ribboned with the shiny steel rail of the crane's track.

A train-like line of recently offloaded containers stretched off to Jefir's left. His brief birds-eye view of the island had shown that a bridge, the island's single entry-exit point, lay in the same direction. He made the bridge Escape Plan A. He ran for it.

Jefir stuck to the morning's hard shadow as he bolted through the thick tropical air. Between the humidity and lack of cardio training over the past week-and-a-half, he was breathing hard by the time he had covered two hundred meters and reached the end of the row of containers. The edge of the small island was a sheer concrete wall that dropped four or five meters to a channel of blue-green water. More docks and industrial apparatus could be seen on the far side of the channel, half a kilometer away.

Swimming was out of the question, barely worth considering, even as a Plan B. Like most citizens of the arid and landlocked Zazaristan, Jefir was familiar with swimming in theory only. He knew enough to realize that leaping into deep water wearing a full backpack and then crossing an active shipping lane in broad daylight while being pursued by security forces would be considered an advanced skill. The calm water looked inviting, though. The stuff that kills you often does.

Jefir wiped sweat from his forehead. This humidity was insane. It was like holding your face over a boiling pot, but instead of soup, it smelled like BO. Jefir allowed that the smell had more to do with his spare washing-up habits over the past ten days than the humidity itself, but still, a bath was overdue.

He looked back. It seemed he had gotten out of his container just in time. The KozyHome now hung from the crane's cables ten meters above the dock, swinging slightly in the warm salty air. A scent more agreeable than whatever came out of that bucket, Jefir thought. Hopefully, that stunt had bought him some time. He last glimpsed the man on the dock scrambling for cover, little did the poor fellow know what was coming. Speaking of which, security/law enforcement would surely be alerted to Jefir's incursion by now. Staying on the island would be a trap. With the dual advantages of numbers and familiar territory, Jefir's pursuers would no doubt quickly secure the bridge, the only means of escape, then scour the small island at their leisure until Jefir was apprehended. Unless Jefir could get across first.

Jefir eyeballed the bridge and guessed he could run across the span in less than a minute. If he could get to it.

Beyond his protective cover of stacked shipping containers, a vast asphalt plain bustled with trucks and small vehicles going about their business. Jefir counted a handful of people on foot as well. Fifty meters away, a small knot of hardhatted workers confabbed, cell phones dueling.

A few men crossed here and there, toting this and that. Most of the workers were dressed similarly to Jefir in blue jeans and t-shirts. Nobody was wearing a backpack. Towering yellow light poles were planted in a wide grid pattern across the lot and although they were fairly distant, Jefir spotted bulbed cameras on these as well.

Huddled in a narrow crack between containers. Jefir felt sure that he was unobserved for the moment. He unzipped his backpack and quick-changed from his white shirt into his dark blue Day Two shirt in case anyone had gotten a glimpse of him earlier. After a brief contemplation, he decided his water tank had served its full duty and tossed it into the harbor.

Jefir had noticed that some of the dock workers had fashioned a sort of *shemagh* to drape over their hardhats in order to keep the sun off their necks, so he wrapped the white shirt around his hat to camouflage its softness and curtain off the back and sides of his head.

Now, the next time anyone might see him, he would appear not very different from the average dock worker and hopefully *very* different from whatever the man on the dock or the crane's camera may have noted.

Jefir stood in the shelter of shadow, then stepped into the sunlight. Trying to convey a law-abiding Westernness with his gait, he walked along the edge of the island and casually stepped out of sight behind a small pump house. And there! Another piece of make-do! He squatted and quickly unscrewed a green hose from its spigot. He hefted the coiled bulk to his shoulder so that it draped over his backpack.

Jefir figured no American would offer to help a stranger struggling under burden, so it was good that the hose was heavy because Jefir had no trouble affecting the manner of a man doing a difficult task. Keeping his proletarian camo in place, he moved away from the pump house and worked toward the bridge, while staying out of sight as much as possible by weaving behind small sheds and stacks of industrial whatnot, every second expecting to hear an alarm or see some flurried response to his messy arrival.

After minutes that seemed like hours, lungs burning, sweat pouring from his brow like any other dock employee, Jefir took cover in a quiet corner of the port between a large, tent-topped bunker and a giant spool of wrist-thick black cable. The foot of the bridge was now just ten meters away, on the other side of a chain link fence beyond an overgrown greenspace. To his right, at the corner of the port's waterfront boundary, a bent and rusted gate spanned a washed-out slope of sand.

Cars and trucks whooshed across the four-lane bridge. Across the roadway, Jefir spotted a yellow pictographic sign for pedestrians. Surely this was, well, a sign that fortune would be with him in the days ahead. The bridge had a sidewalk, literally inviting him to escape! He was relieved that a foot crossing was legal. If the training videos had taught him anything, it was that American law enforcement was, for the most part, swift and powerful, yet detail-oriented. Also curiously unwilling to smoothly bargain away the ripples of any minor misunderstandings. Perhaps due to their slavish dedication to surveillance technology, as the videos also depicted repeatedly.

And sure as the sun is hot, here they were again. The menacing bulbs of security cameras, like the shiny black eyes of a mouse, mounted under three of the five T-shaped light poles that ran down the middle of the bridge.

A bridge that shall be crossed now that it has been come to.

The steady flow of traffic leaving the island mocked Jefir. Should he have tried to beg, borrow or steal a ride on one of these trucks?

If there was a fault in the training videos, it was that they focused solely on the cross-the-sparking-wires part of vehicle theft and not the access-and-identify-the-proper-wires-to-spark aspect which Jefir, now more than ever, felt was a glaring oversight. He was an experienced stowaway of course, but getting into the back of one of those trucks unseen and without help—*I made it here, Rahim. Wherever this is, I made it*—in broad daylight would be nearly impossible. Also, getting *out* of one's stowaway conveyance cleanly was no easy feat either, quite apparently.

Crossing the bridge on foot would mean exposure to the cameras. The lesser of the risks. Jefir dropped the hose from his shoulder. He adjusted the T-shirt draped from his hat, pulling it around his face a little more.

He glanced around, then walked to the rusty gate, casually laid down on the ground and rolled underneath. He got to his feet on a small, debris-strewn spit of sand. Across the channel of calm water, Jefir saw a densely built industrial area on the far waterfront that gave way to green hills dotted with houses.

The bridge deck towered above him to the left. Gray football-sized rocks surrounded the bridge's footing and formed a jumbled slope into the water. Jefir realized that he could probably dodge a camera or two by crossing *under* the bridge, rather than climbing back up to the level of the road.

He ducked into the damp shade of the overpass and the traffic noise dulled to an echoing din. Small, quick-surging waves lapped slick-looking boulders at the water's edge as he picked his way under the bridge.

He steadied himself and looked across the water. The bridge presumably marked the small island's closest point to the mainland, but the sandy bank on the far side was still hundreds of meters away. Although the bridge itself would give excellent cover, it was neither the time, nor the place to learn to swim. A water crossing here would most likely only offer the benefit of drowning privately rather than publicly. Swimming would remain Plan B, at best.

The shimmering water's reflection dappled the underside of the bridge. The bright bursts brought to Jefir's mind the image of a thousand tiny flags snapping in the wind.

He bouldered up the rocky slope and sat on a flattish rock just below the deck of the bridge. Traffic thundered over his head. He removed his black sneakers and dug into his pack once more, this time for Day Three's clothing. Gray t-shirt. Plaid pants in the yellow and blue colors of one of the Houses of Quud, but cut in the fashion of several generations ago. After almost two weeks of reduced rations, the pants were looser in the waist than they were the last time he wore them. The white headshirt went back in the pack.

Jefir tied his shoes and continued to pick his way under the bridge to emerge on the far side, now sporting a third distinct look to confound any witness or camera. He crouched behind some bushy overgrowth. From there, he observed a small marina with a dozen or so boats of various sizes slotted neatly into their wooden stalls. Beyond that, a strip of beach and in another stroke of luck, a rack of banana-ish sea kayaks.

Kayaks! A new and very solid Plan A: Paddle to Freedom Across Narrow Stretch Of Security Camera-less Water. Drown/Get Eaten By Sharks could now be demoted to Plan C, and likewise, Walk Calmly To Bridge Itself, Then Relent To Voice In Head Screaming, *RUN* And Full Sprint To Other Side While Keeping Face Semi-obscured From Security Cameras By Funk Smelling T-shirt was bumped down to Plan B.

Only a handful of people were in sight, working on the boats in the marina, none of them seeming to pay Jefir any particular mind. He pushed through the bushes and stepped over a guardrail to the marina's parking area.

The entrance to the bridge's walkway was just steps away. Should he just walk away? There was no roadblock, no sign of law enforcement or security. But those black-eyed cameras. Jefir retreated from the sidewalk and slipped into the shade of a tree near the marina office building. The man he had avoided back on the dock—Ten minutes ago? Twenty?—had of course alerted the authorities by now. It would be foolish to assume he hadn't. A response was coming. Did Jefir handle that initial contact correctly? Should he have just stepped out of the container and said hello? The training videos provided many examples of Western social engineering, but the examples were always very situation-specific and there was little to no advisement on how the skill was to be developed. It was always just there. Jefir could only glean it was an ability borne of both natural predisposition and steady practice and since he recognized in himself a lack of experience in that particular skill as well as a lack of skill to attain that particular experience, he tried to assure himself that dumping his latrine out the door and running away was the savviest maneuver, given the circumstances.

Not that it got him any closer to those yellow kayaks.

Jefir skirted around the marina building. He made his way down toward the water and turned left toward the beach, following the concrete waterfront.

The boats in the marina were larger than he thought when he first saw them. Some even had a smaller boat attached, like a child holding the hand of a parent. Many of the large boats were gleaming white, while some were painted various colors. Some were fighting rust and their decks were littered with nets and coils of rope and plastic tubs. Without exception, all the vessels had nonsensical names scripted across their rear ends and the majority of these vessels further informed passersby that the boat's home port was Honolulu, HI. Jefir was in Hawaii!

A woman lugging a bin across the cluttered deck of a boat named *Monkey Fist* looked up and nodded a greeting to Jefir as he passed by. She wore a black t-shirt, khaki shorts, rubber sandals, gold-framed aviator sunglasses and a mesh-backed trucker cap with a ponytail pulled through the hole. Jefir offered her a small smile, in what he hoped was the American fashion, and kept walking.

The marina was quiet and Jefir made it through largely unnoticed. He stopped where the concrete ran out at the edge of the beach. There were no surfers, volleyball games, red-clad lifeguards or dogs catching frisbees. He counted six people relaxing on the sand. Three looked out at the water, two looked at their phones and one appeared to be sleeping, a paperback book tented over his chest. Sitting on sand as recreation was a strange notion to Jefir's Zazari sensibilities, but he had prepared himself for a certain amount of culture shock.

Two couples, chatting away, emerged from a short path that led up to the beach's parking area. Without so much as a glance toward Jefir, the foursome approached the kayak rack. They unlocked(!) a thin cable that tethered their boats to the steel rack. The boats were locked?

Jefir waited until the couples had dragged their kayaks into the water, then made his way over to the remaining boats. He dropped his pack in the sand and sat down facing the water, his back against the rack. Closer inspection confirmed that each and every boat was secured to the rack with a cable or chain. With a little time and Zoey's help, Jefir could easily defeat the locks, but doing it in broad daylight in front of witnesses was the rub here. Plan A was looking shaky.

One of the more interesting and empirical nuggets Jefir picked up from the training videos was that sharks never stop swimming. Survival is dependent upon constant movement. He got to his feet and picked up his backpack. He had noticed that the smaller boats back in the marina weren't locked, but merely tied with rope to their parent vessel and almost all of them had a set of crossed oars. Jefir could easily emancipate one of these rafts and execute Plan A(2): Row To Freedom.

He walked back to the marina, searching for a small boat that looked like it wouldn't be missed for a while.

He spotted an inflatable raft tied to a boat at the end of one of the long piers that jutted into the channel. The raft even had a small electric motor. Plan A(3): Cruise Effortlessly To Freedom, was now on the table.

Jefir once again passed the *Monkey Fist*, a dark blue boat about thirty meters long with large masts, no not masts, long antennae and a jointed crane arm, jutting from the center of the elongated rear deck. The woman Jefir saw earlier was emerging from the stairwell of the vessel's enclosed cabin, talking on the phone, a worn square of cardboard tucked under her arm. "—heard from Kino?... He didn't?... If you see him, tell him to call me… K. Laters."

She pocketed the phone just as Jefir turned onto the pier. "Hey!" she said.

Jefir stopped in his tracks. He glanced quickly at the raft, his erstwhile escape vessel bobbing at the end of the pier. He turned to the woman.

Jefir now saw that the snugly fitting T-shirt he had noticed earlier bore the written message, *Look on my works, ye fish, and despair.* In addition to the shirt, the woman now wore a question on her face. She held up the square of cardboard. In large handwritten letters, it read, *Mate Wanted.* Her black ponytail glistened in the sun.

The training videos briefly covered European culture, so Jefir was familiar with a few different definitions of the word "mate." 1: A seagoing assistant. 2: A close friend. 3: A sexual partner.

"Yes," Jefir said.

CHAPTER 6

• The World Imposite the man of action.

Six months earlier, when Jefir was still in the melon game, a gray shipping container was unloaded from the GossCo cargo ship *Centurion* onto Lot A of the GossCo Sand Island Logistical NetPort Facility. Two United States Customs and Border Protection officers opened the container for a random inspection and made the gruesome discovery of twenty lifeless, nameless stowaways sprawled across thousands of bricks of poorly sealed fentanyl. Like the unfortunate would-be immigrants, the CBP officers were quickly overcome and also succumbed to a lethal dose of the airborne powder.

In an internal memo, GossCo CEO Heinz Gossler categorized the event as both "governmental overreach" and "bumblings of the druggies."

When the memo leaked, the tragic story of death, narcotics, border security, and blood on the hands of a massive corporation became high-grade, uncut news bait and the media all piled on, from the creaky international bureaus to social media bots with nineteen followers.

At the time, GossCo's in-house VP of PR was a man named Chuck Morey, who people will now recognize from that GIF of him dabbing his shiny brow.

Morey gave a few press conferences attempting damage control but his sweaty stammers only managed to fan the flames. GossCo quietly, but strongly invited him to pursue other endeavors, but not before purchasing the licensing rights to that GIF.

The woman who was called in to squash the spiraling crisis (and negotiate the GIF deal) was named Margot Carlene.

Margot Carlene's business card read: Media Consultant/Influencer but it could have said "Magician," or "Illusionist," whatever is less offensive. Margot's true talent was in making things disappear, or at least smoothly and quietly sliding them offstage. Like the time that actress sailing on ████ █████'s catamaran in the Pailolo Channel was killed by a pod of whales. Never heard of it? You don't say.

In terms of business attire and leadership style, Margot Carlene was a lot like Darth Vader: Keep it monochromatic with a few shiny accessories and if some pinch-faced dickhead gives you any shit, choke his stupid ass with an invisible hand.

Calm down. Not literally, of course. Margot's invisible hand was pre-emptive press releases, media leaks, injunctions, lawsuits, structured settlements, paperwork, light blackmail, that kind of thing. And don't for a moment think she was dumb enough to brand her way of doing things "The Dark Side." Who would do that? Margot preferred the term "efficacious."

Margot took over for Morey as the public face of GossCo. Her press conferences were studies in spin. NDAs were signed, condolences expressed, blame shifted, investigations pledged, promises made, donations paid. At the literal low point of the months-long publicity/human rights crisis, GossCo stock (GOSC, NYSE) had lost over three billion dollars of market cap, but now, on the very morning that Jefir Zaqq arrived in America, GOSC had finally recovered to its previous high of $185 per share. Hitting the target price triggered a prepared press release to the financial media letting them know Margot Carlene would be available (live via satellite) to comment on the stock's recovery and GossCo's continuing commitment to sustainable growth, but not *under any circumstances* the topics of stowaways, fentanyl or whales. $185 a share also triggered a contractually obligated $500,000 in bonus compensation to Margot herself.

Margot Carlene wore a black Burberry asymmetric blazer, gold earrings, Gucci crocodile slingbacks and look of mild disgust as she walked across her Hawaii Magazine-featured living room on the 23rd floor of Uraku Tower in the Ala Moana neighborhood of Honolulu. She had just completed media hits for six of New York's top eight financial networks. Her video backdrop was a sculptural table lamp and a blown-glass vase of fresh-cut anthurium and wax ginger, each set exactly twelve inches from the live-edge of her koa wood credenza, and the Pacific Ocean. Why people sat in front of their boring bookshelves for these things was beyond her.

Margot's assistant Geoffrey switched off the camera uplink and handed her a Saffiano leather handbag. It was nine in the morning and Geoffrey had already been at work for four hours.

Margot took the bag and dug out her phone. Twenty-six emails. Thirty-five texts. 980 ZoopZap notifications. The messages and notifications were quickly ranked for urgency and importance. There was a clear number one in both categories. She said, "Call the car, Geoffrey."

Geoffrey took out his phone as he pivoted to follow his boss out of the apartment to the elevator.

Margot called Steve Doyle, the Sand Island facility's VP of Logistical Deattenuation. Doyle reminded Margot of the football players (the fat kind) she hung out with during junior year when she was hooking up with the kicker.

"Good morning, Margot."

"What fresh fuckery is this, Steve?" The elevator arrived and Margot got in. Geoffrey followed, texting Margot's driver.

Doyle said, "You… said I should let you know anytime we find a stowaway—"

"Unticketed person," Margot corrected, pushing the lobby button.

"Unticketed person," Doyle repeated. "Yes. Anyway, this morning, one of my guys, a security guard, was attacked by an unticketed person who jumped out of a shipping container."

"Attacked how?"

"The guy dumped some shit on him and took off."

"What kind of shit?"

"You know, the kind that… comes out of… a… person."

If Margot had known that her day was going to take her out to the Sand Island facility, she wouldn't have worn the Guccis. The elevator arrived.

"What happened to the guy?" she asked. "The unticketed. Where is he now?"

"I don't know, he ran off. He's gone."

"Gone-alive? Or gone-dead?"

"He's alive," Doyle said.

"Are you 100 percent sure?"

In his managerial duties, Doyle was used to quantifying things in increments of 110 percent, so the math threw him for a moment. "Yes," he said. "This all happened over an hour ago. Nobody's seen him since. He's got to be gone from the port by now. Probably just walked right over the bridge."

The last thing Margot wanted was another hi-def shot of a dead body being carted out of a GossCo facility. The alternative, a violent criminal on the loose in Honolulu who caught a free ride to America's shores thanks to the porous incompetence of the GossCo corporation, wasn't *ideal*, but what was? If life was an exercise in just sitting back and dumbly marveling at how swell things were going, those twenty people never would have set sandal in that container, Chuck Morey would still have a job, and that half mil never would have left Heinz Gossler's Brussels account.

"Who knows about this?" Margot asked.

Doyle said, “The guard, Trent Calvin. A crane operator. Two other security guards. My OSHA Compliance Officer Ed Sakamoto. He heard about it over the internal radio channel he keeps open in his office.”

“Anyone else?”

“Sakamoto made a report and sent a copy to Customs and Border.”

“What? Why?”

“That’s what he does. Calvin told him he was attacked and Sakamoto thought he should report it as a crime. There’s going to be a mandatory OSHA safety meeting in my future, I just know it.”

“Get your people under control, Steve,” Margot said. “But Sakamoto didn’t actually witness anything, did he? He just made the report, correct?”

“That’s right,” said Doyle. “Only Calvin actually saw the guy.”

“Here’s what’s going to happen,” Margot said, checking her watch. “Order pizza and chicken wings. Food you eat with your hands. Get everyone except Sakamoto into the conference room on the second floor. Do NOT give them napkins, understand?”

“Why?”

“To keep their greasy fingers off their phones until I get there. I’m trying to keep this *off* Friendbook, Steve. In the meantime, you get on that open radio channel and ask about the *accident.*”

“Ask who?” Doyle said.

“Doesn’t matter. Anybody in the port who’s listening. Just get the word out that this was only a routine accident.”

“What about the guys who were there?”

“Give them the pizza to eat! Order plenty of drinks, too.”

"I mean, those guys know it wasn't an accident. Calvin saw the unticketed guy."

"There was no unticketed guy, Steve. There are differing accounts as to exactly what happened, but we know that a minor incident caused a GossCo employee to be briefly exposed to some hazardous material, but he is fine and uninjured. He requests privacy at this time. GossCo takes workplace safety and human rights very seriously as we strive to connect the world."

The line was silent. "Steve?"

"I'm writing that down. What was the last part?"

"Never mind. Just get everyone in that conference room. Don't let them leave until I get there. I have to make a quick stop. I'll be there in thirty minutes."

The elevator opened and Margot clacked through the polished lobby. A GossCo SUV waited outside at the curb.

"Sand Island," she told the driver. "But first, the PacBank on Kapiolani."

She got in the car and posted her Zoop of the Day. (**Create something of value and you will become that thing.**) She then tagged and Zapped promos for her TV appearances and began to work down the rest of the morning's messages.

CHAPTER 7

• Find Immediate, preferably lucrative employment.

"What do you mean, 'yes'?" the woman said to Jefir. "You want a job as a fishing mate?" She put down her cardboard sign. "We're fitting out the boat this morning and I'm short one guy for my crew. You spent any time on boats?"

From the journal: "Find immediate, preferably lucrative employment." The lucrative part was admittedly yet to be seen, but Jefir was very pleased to have ticked this box so soon and was prepared to be very flexible if it came to negotiations. More importantly, the fringe benefits of this fishing mate job included access to a boat and therefore the means to escape the possible manhunt rising around him, not to mention what looked to be a box of muffins or perhaps small cakes sitting on a hatch cover in the rear of the *Monkey Fist* boat.

"Yes. A lot, recently," Jefir said.

"What do you know about fishing?" the woman asked.

Jefir glanced searchingly over the boat. Another line from the journal came to him: "Make simple, declarative statements."

He gestured broadly toward the open sea. "The fish are in there."

The woman took off her sunglasses. She smiled and dimples formed on her cheeks. "That is true," she said. She took one step closer to Jefir. "OK, let's see. Your eyes are clear. You've got big hands. *-sniff-* You don't mind missing a shower here and there." She glanced down at his plaid pants. "You make bold fashion choices. What's your name?"

Choosing the proper name can make all the difference, Mr. Shwarma had said. It was not a decision to be made lightly. One should select a name common, yet forgettable. Familiar, yet new. In the time-worn service of practical convention over daring style ("Steele Cuboid," for example, would have been vetoed), Jefir Zaqq had chosen to simply shear his first name of one syllable—"Jeff."—then tack two syllables onto his surname, to create a moniker so solidly American it was simultaneously a mutton-chopped president and a ten-year-old proto-hipster.

"Zachary. Jeff Zachary." The journal and training videos both advised saying your name twice.

"OK, Jeff Zachary," the woman said. "Now I know how to make out all the big paychecks." She chuckled. "I'm just kidding. I pay in cash. Hope you don't mind. I'm Tasha Hale." She jerked a thumb over her shoulder. "This is my boat. I'm captain of the *Monkey Fist.* Welcome aboard."

"Thank you, Captain. I can start right now?"

"Right now." Tasha pulled a Velcro wallet from her back pocket, ripped it open and fished out a ten dollar bill. "This is your first job: Take this money. Go up to the marina office. There's a vending machine just inside the door. Buy me a bag of barbeque potato chips. If they don't have barbeque, get sweet onion."

She reached up to hand the bill to Jeff, who plucked it from her fingers, then turned and ran, literally *ran*, up the pier. If Jeff Zachary was going to take off with her ten bucks, there was no way Tasha could even think of catching him. She watched him sprint across the parking lot and disappear into the marina building. Moments later, he burst out the door holding a small red bag. He ran back across the lot, thumped down the pier and *leapt* onto the boat to pantingly deliver the chips and eight dollars change.

"Don't jump onto the boat like that," Tasha said. "It's dangerous. But I respect the hustle." She smiled.

"Thank… you," Jeff breathed. His eyes lingered on the chips for a few seconds before being drawn again to the box of muffins.

Tasha said, "Have you had breakfast, Jeff?"

"I drank some water earlier."

"Follow me," she said. She strode toward the boat's pilothouse structure, which looked like a small house sprouting from the deck. Jeff liked how it raked slightly forward, as if gamely leaning into the wind.

The *Monkey Fist* had three levels. From the main deck where Jeff and Tasha stood, a ladder led up to the bridge. To the left of the ladder, a staircase descended below. Tasha pointed down the stairs. "Get yourself cleaned up, the head's on the right. There's coffee in the galley. Help yourself and come back up here for a muffin. Then we get this boat screwed and glued."

Another fringe benefit would seem to be access to Captain Tasha Hale herself. She struck Jeff in a way that suggested a casual competence, the invisible veil that covers the inveterate cool and the covert agent alike. A wariness of Westerners had been instilled in Jeff, but so had an engagement and trust in his instincts and if this woman was an evil imperialist infidel, perhaps the definition needed to be narrowed. Not that one can trust an evil imperialist. And speaking of definitions, head = washroom, galley = kitchen.

The training videos had done a fine job of burnishing Jeff's English, but there was bound to be some jargon left uncovered. Context, he reminded himself as he ducked his head to enter the tight stairway. Context is everything. For example, Jeff's peculiar Zazarish accent could pass for that of a resident of deepest Delaware County, Pennsylvania, especially if the listener was looking at Jeff's Phillies hat as he spoke.

Wedged into the boat's tiny washroo—head, Jeff stripped off his shirt, wet a towel in the small sink, and gave himself a long-overdue scrubbing. He looked in the mirror. The beard would have to go. It was too distinguishing a feature. The man on the dock had no doubt gotten a look at Jeff's face as he leaned out the container's door and who knew how many of those cameras had caught him. He dug through his backpack to find his Dopp kit with its disposable razor.

The symbolism of shaving his ten-day beard was not lost on Jeff. Out with the old, in with the new and all that, but in this case, practicality demanded it as well. Mr. Shwarma had informed him that in the West, beards were typically the mark of the very poor or the very easily influenced by trends of fashion and that one should make every effort to avoid becoming either. Mustaches, however, were tacitly endorsed by the training videos and Jeff decided that since a clean slate was called for in almost every other area of his new life, under his nose could be an exception.

After cleaning up, Jeff quickly investigated the bowels of the boat. The smell of coffee led him to a cramped galley with well-worn appliances shrunk to half-size, including a stacked clothes washer-dryer. The galley shared space with an eating area that had a table bolted to the floor, built-in benches and a flat television screen mounted on the wall. Further toward the front of the boat, a room with two sets of narrow bunk beds. Each of the four berths had a lipped cubby at the head. Three of the cubbies held the kinds of things a young man takes with him to sea: Trade paperback books, sports magazines, phone chargers, DVDs with sans serif title logos, pornography and personal grooming items.

The top left bunk's cubby was empty, its lip swung loose. Jeff tossed his backpack up onto the bed's thin, but cush mattress and returned to the galley. After rooting through a few cabinets to find a cup, he poured himself a steaming coffee and went back upstairs.

Tasha offered him a blueberry muffin wider than his fist. Jeff peeled off the muffin's paper pants and a fair bit of muffin residue came with them, so he folded up the paper and slipped it into his pocket for later.

Tasha had a snap-lidded metal mug of coffee and a yellow muffin. She set them down on a barrelhead and boosted herself up to sit. "You shaved," she said.

"Yes."

"Looks good. The beard was a little rough, TBH."

"TBH?" Jeff repeated.

"To be honest." Tasha sipped her coffee. "So, Jeff. What brings a scraggly-bearded dude to backpack around Sand Island at 8am on a Monday? What's your deal? Tell me your story."

Although Jeff hoped his story would be told at some point, he wasn't sure this was the time. He said, "Well, I was looking for work you see, and when I saw you here in the back of the boat—"

"JEFF, WHAT'S YOUR DEAL? TELL ME YOUR STORY!" Tasha shouted.

CHAPTER 8

• Position yourself accurately.

It was 9:47. Danny Kalami, Max Tibo and Phillipe St. Germain sat at one end of the twenty-seat conference room table in GossCo's Sand Island offices. Trent Calvin sat at the other end wearing a GossCo Walk for Equity T-shirt that Steve Doyle's secretary Suzy unboxed from the back of the supply closet. The formaldehyde-y new T-shirt smell mixed with the not *quite* completely hosed-off shit turned Margot's stomach as she circled the table passing out wet napkins, pens, blank OSHA Form 301 Injury and Illness Incident Reports and one-page Non-Disclosure Agreements to each man. The documents bore tiny yellow "SIGN HERE!" flags. She had the flags specially printed to include the exclamation point, which Margot found would usually help to hurry this sort of thing along. There was $40,000 in cash bundled at the bottom of the Saffiano.

"Who here knows who Achmed Sukarno is?" she asked. The men all looked up from their pizza with greasy, puzzled expressions.

Margot said, "Achmed Sukarno was President of Indonesia in the sixties. Indonesia was leaning communist at the time, but teetering, and the Soviets wanted to keep Sukarno in line, so they invited him to fly to Moscow for a meeting. As part of the Soviet's plan to influence him, the KGB had set up a honeypot sex-sting operation where attractive female agents posing as airline stewardesses would proposition Sukarno to join them for a post-flight orgy. I believe there were three of them."

The men at the table exchanged glances, but no one said anything and Margot went on. "Remember. The sixties," she explained. "So, as you might imagine, Sukarno agreed to join the stewardesses. When they all arrived in Moscow, the stewardess/agents took Sukarno to a pre-arranged hotel room, where the KGB secretly filmed the whole thing to use as a blackmail video. Afterward, they approached Sukarno and threatened to release it unless Sukarno supported some pro-communist policies back in Indonesia.

Unfortunately for the Soviets, Sukarno was delighted. He asked the KGB for as many copies of the film as they could make in order to show his friends and impress the people of Indonesia."

Margot paused to take in the grinning looks of the men around the table. "Why am I telling you this?" she said. "Because in this world, getting ahead means just that. Going a bit farther than the other guy. As Sukarno said, 'Let us not be bitter about the past, but let us keep our eyes firmly on the future.'"

"GossCo has a problem, gentlemen. And you know what they say: With every problem, there comes opportunity. But that's only what *they* say, isn't it? That's just for Presidents and guys who have four-way sex with Russia's hottest KGB agents. When was the last time that any of *you guys* came out of a problem on the opportunity end?"

Calvin and the rest silently agreed that it had been quite a while, notwithstanding the free lunch they had just enjoyed.

Margot went on, "Customs and Border Protection received a report that a crime took place on our dock this morning. And that would mean investigations, interrogations, slowdowns, problems, problems, and more problems."

"This says we get ten thousand dollars," Calvin said, holding up the NDA.

"That's right. And four weeks of vacation. Starting immediately," Margot said. This could have been done for five thousand and two weeks, but Margot was more interested in saving time than money these days.

The other men quickly scanned their personalized forms.

Margot said, "Mr. Kalami, Mr. Tibo and Mr. St. Germaine will be receiving five thousand. They didn't…" she wrinkled her nose, "suffer to the extent that you did, Mr. Calvin."

"And this is supposed to keep us quiet about it?" Calvin asked. He wiped his fingers and held up the paper.

"Just the opposite, actually," said Margot. She started circling the table again and reached into her bag. She dropped bank-banded packs of cash in front of each man. "You're all going to fill out detailed OSHA Form 301 reports and send them to Customs and Border Protection. Don't worry, I'll tell you what to write."

"Uh, Ma'am?" Calvin said, as a strap of fifties slapped onto the polished table in front of him.

"What is it, Mr. Calvin?"

"Who are you, again?"

"My name is Margot Carlene."

Margot barely broke stride as she circled the room two times more. Once to dictate a short Triple I report to each man, and once more to collect the signed forms. She walked out of the conference room at 9:52.

CHAPTER 9

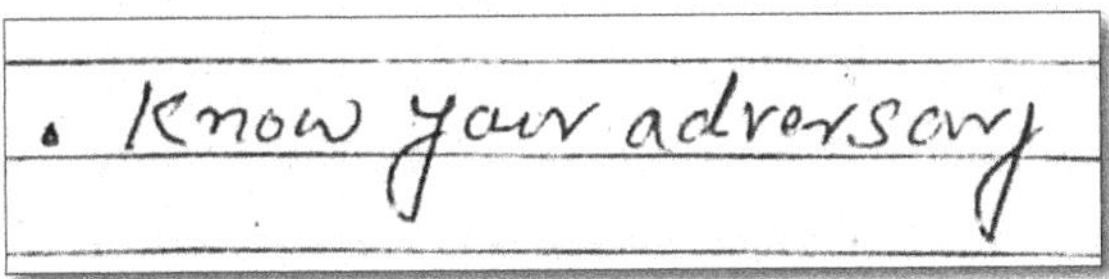

From the back of the line during the morning coffee machine rush at the Honolulu Office of Customs and Border Protection, Officer Matt Porter said, "Let's go. Let's go. Let's go. Let's go."

"There's always one more drop," Officer Sue Kazumi said, holding her cup under the drip dispenser.

"What you're saying is impossible, Kaz," Porter said. "At some point the drops run out. There is not an indefinite supply of coffee in that filter. In 5,000 years, the entire coffee machine will have decayed to dust. At that point, there won't be any more drops, will there?"

Kaz tapped the side of the coffee machine. One last ebony drop landed in her cup. She ceded her place in line to another navy blue-uniformed CBP officer and walked back to join Porter. "With any luck, we'll be long dead by then," she said.

The coffee machine scoffed in surprise (as if it were uncommon for it to be lightly beaten), but then gurgled into action for a fiftieth time that morning.

Kaz took a sip, then said, “The drops. It’s a metaphor, Porter. The wait is the weight.” She used an invisible pen to jot a note in the air.

Porter rolled his eyes and produced a small notepad with “Things the Wise and Powerful Susan W. Kazumi Teaches Me That I Better Fucking Believe Will Save My Ass Someday” written on it in blue ink. “The wait is the what?”

“Waiting…” said Kazumi. She took another sip. “can make you strong, like lifting weights.”

“And the coffee drops? Anything there?” Porter asked, his pen poised.

“This isn’t English class. Just the second part,” Kaz said. “Patience is strength.”

Porter nodded and noted. He added: “Not English Class.”

The coffee line advanced.

CBP Captain Pascal Benito approached, holding a manila file folder. “Get out to Sand Island,” he said to Kaz as he cut to the front of the coffee line. “I just got a call and email from the OSHA Safety Officer at the GossCo port. He sent a report about a stowaway, a damaged container and a spill of…” he referred to the file. “…human fecal matter.”

“Porter, you’re investigating that part,” said Kaz. Another sip of coffee.

Porter said, “When I was on patrol, homeless guys threw shit at us all the time.”

“Description of the stowaway?” Kaz asked Benito.

“The OSHA report says a security guard saw someone’s head sticking out of a container as it came off a ship.” He referred to the file again. “‘Possibly bearded.’ That’s it. Whatever we have, it’s all in here.” Benito handed the file to Kaz. It contained two pages: Sakamoto’s printed email and a copy of his OSHA Form 301 Injury and Illness Incident report.

“So what’s going on?” Porter asked.

Kaz said, “That’s what we’re going to find out. Let’s go.” She turned to leave.

Porter looked longingly at the coffee machine, then followed.

CHAPTER 10

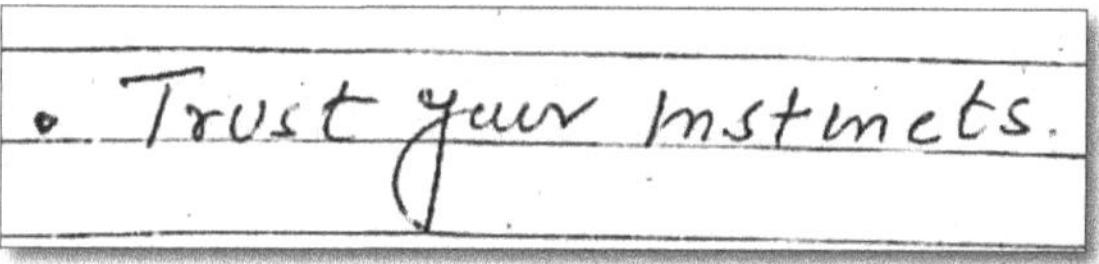

"I SAID, TELL ME YOUR STORY, JEFF! NOW!" Tasha shouted.

Jeff was stunned speechless. Tasha had been good-natured and easygoing until now. His mind flooded with questions: Did she suspect something? Had the dock workers somehow contacted her about him? Was she going to attempt to capture him? Should he flee?

All of his gear was inside, down in the bunk room. The training videos covered hand-to-hand combat extensively (but not against females, he just then realized). The videos also covered hostage situations, from both the captor and captive perspective, but Jeff was uncertain as to which one he would end up if it came down to a physical struggle with Tasha. She was small, but appeared to be in good physical shape, and a long, sharply hooked gaff rested arm's reach behind her. Jeff pictured it piercing his kidney.

Tasha calmly took another sip of coffee and pried off a chunk of her muffin.

Jeff managed to stammer, "Captain, I—"

She waved him off. "I don't really care. But you heard how I just said that? Stern, right? On a boat, we don't call it the 'back' Jeff, it's the stern. We're in the stern. I talked to you sternly. Now you'll never forget."

Jeff relaxed. Tasha went on. "As for your story, I'm not looking for Supreme Court Justices here, man. A lot of the guys I hire have… complicated lives. Musicians, night-club proprietors and fishing mates." She smirked and the shallow dimples flashed in and out. "Sometimes complicated is a good thing and sometimes it isn't, but simple's harder to find," she said, and popped the muffin in her mouth.

"Yes," Jeff agreed. "There is always another thing to consider."

Through some muffin, Tasha said, "Mm. Well said, Jeff. I knew we'd get along." She swallowed. "Work hard, listen to me and the other mates and we'll be good. At least until we're not."

A bargain more than fair, Jeff thought. He was now fairly drowning in success, almost all of which was directly related to meeting this fishing boat captain. He would follow her advice, at least until he didn't. Time to get to work.

"How many other mates are there?" he asked.

"Full crew's four. We were a man down until you showed up. I haven't heard from my fourth guy, Kino, in a few days and I'm considering him gone."

"Dead?" Jeff asked.

"No, not dead," Tasha said, regarding him strangely. "I don't think so. Well, maybe, who knows? Complicated lives."

"Yes," Jeff said again. And speaking of complicated, he knew that he would soon have to reveal the fact that his knowledge of commercial fishing extended only so far as the very generally abstract, and that his ignorance would be difficult to conceal if he was one of just four employees. "I'm not very familiar with this type of boat. What will my job be?"

Tasha pushed herself off the barrel and her flip-flopped feet slapped to the deck. "The *Fist* is a 99-foot longline tuna boat." She walked over to a giant spool of heavy monofilament fishing line that lay horizontal to the deck resting in a sort of motorized cradle. She placed her hand on it. "Twenty miles of line."

"That is long," Jeff said.

"Right. So, we cruise along and pay this mainline out the back of the boat. Every so often, you and the mates clip on a gangion line with a baited hook that hangs down into the water where, as you mentioned earlier, the fish are. Every ten hooks, you clip a buoy to the mainline to keep it all afloat." She pointed to a large pile of round, rubbery orange balls. "After the gear is set, we cut the line loose and circle back to find the beginning. That takes a few hours. Then we haul the line back in, it's always longer coming back, with a shitload of tuna hooked to it, hopefully." She knocked delicately with a single knuckle on the wooden handle of the gaff.

Jeff asked, "You, I mean, we, cut the line from the boat? It floats loose in the water? Do the tuna not try to swim away with it once they're hooked?"

"They try, the sneaky fucks," Tasha said. "They try. But some of the buoys have GPS, so we can track the line down. Every now and then, the line breaks or a beacon buoy dies out and some gear will get ghosted." She shrugged. "Cost of doing business."

She moved to a large white hatch that rose about a half meter from the center of the deck. She bent and swung it open. "After we catch a fish, we clean it, pack it in ice and stow it down here in the freezer."

Jeff leaned over and peered down into the hollow space below. Impossibly, absurdly cold air bloomed out. Crushed ice belched from a humming, unseen source into a sloping pile in a corner of the dark compartment.

Tasha kicked the hatch shut. "We usually stay out five to seven days, or until the freezer's full, whatever comes first. When we get back, we sell the tuna right off the boat to the sushi buyers and wholesalers at Honolulu Fish Market. One big, high-quality fish can bring fifteen thousand, cash. In Japan, a big bluefin can go for millions."

Jeff pictured a tin of tuna from the market.

"How large are these fish?" he asked.

"Bigeyes average about fifty pounds, yellowfins are a little bigger. Big ones get to three hundred." Tasha spread her arms as wide as they could go, as fisherman will do.

Jeff was under the impression that there was a steep drop-off in fish size after: 1. Whale, 2. Shark/Dolphin. He had no idea that man-sized fish were so common. What other mysterious wonders was the deep sea concealing?

"Where do you catch them? How far must we travel?" While his mind once again filled with questions, Jeff had grown fairly certain of a few things. This novel, this transient, this so-called "complicated" life, a good part of it spent crossing miles of open ocean as a member of the *Monkey Fist*'s small crew, would be an ideal opportunity to "Blend in," "Go with the flow," "Say yes a lot," as well as "Trust your instincts," not to mention "Keep your options open," all tenets of his journal.

Tasha said, "This time of year, we work the western Molokai Fracture Zone, north of O'ahu. We follow temperature breaks in the water, usually a couple hundred miles offshore. Come on, I'll show you around the boat."

For the next fifteen minutes Tasha led Jeff around and through the *Monkey Fist.* As they climbed the short ladder up to the bridge, Tasha said, "Jeff, when we're out to sea, do not do what I am doing right now, which is climb this ladder with a coffee in one hand. Not safe. For the kind of work we do, sometimes good enough is perfect. But when we're out there and the shit's hitting the fan, sometimes only perfect is good enough. Be skillful. Be careful. Care leads skill. Skill makes care. Understand? I had a guy on my crew once that slipped off this ladder and cracked his head on the deck. Knocked himself out cold. A huge wave came over the deck and almost washed this dude right overboard, still out like a light. Hemi had to gaff him in the leg. So here we have the bridge."

The elevated bridge had a lot of blinking electronics and an anachronistic spoked wooden wheel. The black leather captain's chair in the center of the small room appeared to be the only thing on the entire boat designed with comfort in mind rather than utility. In contrast, the captain's private berth was little more than a mattress-sized closet wedged into the rear of the bridge behind a thin folding door.

Down the ladder again, Tasha made a quick lap around the deck, spouting nautical vocabulary and gory anecdotes. She concluded the tour at the front of the boat. Just as she was straightening up from a theatrical bow, a pickup truck loaded with crates and boxes pulled up to the edge of the pier alongside the boat.

"That's my crew," Tasha said, pointing out the three men sitting abreast in the cab. "Go help them unload."

Jeff stepped off the boat onto the pier, as two men with bald heads, wearing shorts and t-shirts, slid out the passenger side of the truck. They could be nothing if not brothers.

"Hemi! Kai!" Tasha called to them. "That's Jeff. New guy. Show him what to do."

"'Sup, Jeff," Hemi and Kai said as one.

One brother, who Jeff guessed was the elder (slightly heavier, more lushly tattooed) climbed into the bed of the truck. The younger (he had occupied the middle seat) waved Jeff over to join him at the tailgate.

"Are you Kai?" Jeff asked him.

Kai nodded once and extended his arms from the elbow, palms up. Jeff was under the impression that 'slapping ten' was a bygone practice, but when in Hawaii, etc.

He slapped Kai's palms. "I'm Jeff."

Kai shared a glance and grin with his brother Hemi, who tossed a large, frosty box into his brother's waiting arms. The brothers had been unimposing at first glance, but up close, Jeff saw balls of muscle rolling through the men's bodies as they worked. They had to be immensely strong. As if to prove the point, a second box quickly landed atop the first in Kai's ropy arms and he carried them both onto the boat with apparent ease while motioning with his head for Jeff to take his place at the tailgate. Hemi was already reaching for the next box.

Jeff stepped forward and extended his arms. Not, as he now realized, to invite a probably antiquated physical greeting, but rather to arrest and carry two heavy boxes onto the boat. He set his feet and looked to Hemi, whose grin had settled into a smile. Hemi flung a box and it thudded into Jeff's chest, staggering him. The box was ice cold and twenty kilos if it was a gram.

Hemi already held a second box, but paused for a moment, unsure of whether Jeff was willing or able to handle it. Jeff glanced over at Kai, who had lightly stepped onto the boat and was now carrying his two boxes to the far side of the freezer hatch. Jeff was determined to blend in by working as hard as his new crewmates, which meant accepting and carrying a second box, but he was not at all confident that he could match Kai's physical feat. To decline would be to diminish himself in the eyes of his new mates and draw unwanted attention, but *dropping* two boxes and/or falling into the undulating crevasse between the pier and the boat wouldn't exactly be flying under the radar either.

Nevertheless, Jeff gritted his teeth and again looked to Hemi. The second box nearly clipped his chin as it landed atop the first. Jeff adjusted his grip and began waddling toward the boat when he felt a hand on his shoulder.

“What’s up, bro, I’m Tommy. Deck boss.”

Jeff craned his neck around. Tommy the deck boss wore a sun-faded, sweat-ringed Seattle Mariners cap. The royal blue retro version with the downward-facing yellow trident logo. Hattery fashion trends of the AL West were *not* covered in any of Jeff’s training materials and so he assumed that the forked spear represented the fishing trade while simultaneously (and rather snappily) honoring the *Monkey Fist*’s first initial.

I’m Jeff,” he grunted. He made a little hop and regripped the boxes. Tommy’s hand on his shoulder didn’t weigh all that much, but Jeff was acutely aware of every last bit of weight he bore at the moment. His brain and his arms synchronized their watches and began to negotiate *when*, not *if*, they would allow the boxes to drop.

Tommy mercifully lifted his hand in order to light a cigarette using a Zippo lighter inscribed with the phrase, *I’d rather be fucking*. He stepped in front of Jeff and blocked his path to the boat. “You have a fishing license, Jeff?” he asked.

“No,” Jeff strained.

The watches ticked.

Tommy stared at Jeff for two full seconds, then reached for his wallet.

Jeff was beginning to breathe harder. He could feel sweat rolling down his fresh-shaven cheeks.

From his wallet, Tommy pulled a thin stack of laminated cards. He fanned through them. “How old are you?” he asked Jeff.

“Nineteen.”

Tommy picked out a card and showed it to Jeff. It was a State of Hawaii Commercial Fishing License. "If anyone asks, you're Claude Ohanu." He tucked the card into Jeff's back pocket. "Nice pants," he said. "Now, Claude. What would you say are your biggest strengths and weaknesses? Where do you see yourself in five years?"

"Well…" Jeff puffed. "I'm—"

"Tommy! Shut the fuck up, and take one of those boxes!" Tasha said from the deck. "Jeff, he's messing with you. And we try to do just one thing at a time around here." She looked toward Kai, who had stacked his two boxes next to the freezer and was returning for another trip. "For example, no one will see Kai carrying two frozen boxes of bait at a time anymore, now that he's done showing off. Right, Kai?"

Kai smiled. The cigarette clamped between Tommy's lips flexed upward. He slid the top box out of Jeff's arms and soft-tossed it over the boat's gunwale to Kai.

The remaining box in Jeff's arms now seemed so light as to float in the air.

"Don't drop any of this shit in the water," Tommy said. "Anything that goes in, you go in after." He hopped down to the deck and fell into executive-level conversation with Tasha (Re: Jeff is using Claude's old license/What the fuck happened to Kino?) as they walked toward the pilothouse.

Kai put down the box Tommy had tossed and now stood waiting for Jeff's box, arms outstretched, fingers awiggle. Jeff pumped his knees and heaved the box to him. Kai caught it, and with neither sound nor wasted motion stacked it atop the others. Jeff realized the plan was to transfer the rapidly warming boxes onto the deck, human-chain-style, then re-form the chain to stow them in the freezer hold. It was also clear to him that he was quite literally the weakest link in this chain.

Jeff turned back to the truck where Hemi waited, already holding the next box. Aping Kai, he gave the wiggly *unburden yourself unto me* digital semaphore. With compact torque and a slight grunt, Hemi flicked the next box. Perhaps the box was lighter, or perhaps Hemi didn't throw it as hard, but whatever the case, it seemed to land more softly in Jeff's arms, and softer still the next and the next as he and the brothers fell into rhythm transferring the small mountain of boxes from truck to deck and deck to hold.

When the boxes (containing frozen mackerel) had been stacked at one end of the freezer hold, Tommy handed Jeff a shovel and tasked him with burying the boxes in the crushed ice that spat from the ice machine on the other end. It soon became clear why working in the freezer for any length of time fell to the lowest ranking crewmember. Dark, foul smelling, and with seemingly endless shoveling, it was exactly like Hell, except cold. Tommy had advised Jeff to "Get used to it," and disappeared elsewhere abovedecks.

Jeff took this first moment of solitude to examine the card Tommy had slipped him earlier.

The stiff plastic license named it's bearer as Claude Ohanu of 1060 Kamehameha Hwy, Pearl City, Hawaii, 96782. Claude was five years older than Jeff, but the card had no photo. In the space where Jeff would have expected one, the ID card noted that Claude holds the shellfish endorsement.

Jeff/Claude put the card away and got shoveling.

Like the echoing sound waves that droned from the ice-making machine and ship's idling engine in the adjacent belowdecks compartment, Jeff made countless and ever-weakening trips back and forth across the freezer hold that morning.

He was just a few shovelfuls from completing the job when Tommy returned to survey his handiwork and to formally declare that the *Monkey Fist* would sail "ASAP."

"Asap?" Jeff asked.

"As. Soon. As. Fucking. Possible," Tommy clarified.

Apparently, the water temperature, moon phase and a number of other factors that, to Jeff, seemed to dwell on the blurred line between the scientific and the superstitional, were ideal for fishing and Tasha was anxious to get to sea in pursuit of her sworn enemies, the yellowfin and bigeye tuna. The potential rewards outweighed the risks of venturing out with an untested, inexperienced crewman, it seemed. They would set sail that afternoon.

CHAPTER 11

- Every environment has a rhythm or pattern.

Porter's phone dinged for the fourth time in as many minutes.

"Captain Benito forwarded another one," he said to Kaz as they crossed the Sand Island bridge in their white, green-striped CBP SUV. "Another OSHA report sent from GossCo. This one is filled out by a… Danny Kalami. He states that he observed a 'spill' but no mention of a stowaway, bearded or not."

"So let me get this straight," Kaz said. "The OSHA guy, Sakamoto, says an 'unknown person' escaped from a container, but he didn't actually see the person."

"Right," Porter said. "Sakamoto told Benito in his email that a security guard, Trent Calvin, reported at the scene that he saw a bearded man poke his head out of a container and that the guy dumped shit out on him."

"But in Calvin's own OSHA report," Kaz said, "he said what?"

Porter scrolled back through his emails and zoomed into the PDF file. "Trent Calvin wrote, 'I thought I saw a head sticking out the door, but it could have been the torn plastic flapping in the wind. Nobody was inside.'"

"So where did the shit come from?" Kaz asked.

"The boxes on these forms are very small, Kaz," Porter said. "They don't allow for much detail. But one of the other guards, Phillipe St. Germain, wrote that when he arrived, there was… hold on." Porter tapped another file open and scrolled. "'An apparent sewage leak.' The third guard, Max Tibo wrote, 'It smelled like spoiled food.'"

"Keep your eyes open, Porter," Kaz said as the truck clanked off the bridge. "*Something* happened, but this could be anything. Some poor mule with an assful of oxy, a drunk stevedore, homeless guy. I suppose it could even be a sober stevedore, anything's possible. He could still be hiding on the island. He could've caught a ride out on a truck. He could have swam for it for all we know."

"Swum. He could have swum for it," Porter said.

"When I said, 'keep your eyes open' a second ago, that means mouth shut, too," Kaz said. She scribbled the air with a finger.

Porter wearily pulled the notebook from his pocket. He flipped to an empty page, noted date and time, and wrote: "Eyes open = mouth shut."

Kaz turned into the entrance of the GossCo Sand Island Logistical NetPort Facility. Customs and Border Protection officers came in and out of the port on a daily basis doing routine inspections and the GossCo security guard waved her through the gate without leaving his windowed hut. Kaz tossed him a return wave and drove on to the two-story GossCo office, where they had been told by Captain Benito that they were expected by a Steve Doyle.

Kaz and Porter were shown into Doyle's second-story office by his secretary. The office overlooked the port. Doyle wore a short-sleeved shirt and he used his laminated GossCo ID badge as a tie clip.

"Steve Doyle," he said, rising from his desk chair. "What can I do for you?"

"Officer Sue Kazumi," Kaz said, handing him her card. "This is Officer Matt Porter. We heard you had an incident this morning."

"I don't know if I'd call it an 'incident,'" Doyle said. "More like an accident. There was a spill, and a shipping container became unsealed upon delivery. My OSHA safety officer Ed Sakamoto took it upon himself to call your office. He's an i-dotter, that one."

"And what about the stowaway?" Kaz asked. "The report said there was someone *in* the container and that he assaulted a man on the dock."

"Again, I'm not sure we're talking about the same thing, Officer," said Doyle. "We didn't find any unticketed passengers in the container or around the port. There was no 'assault.' No one was hurt. One of my security guards was… soiled, but that's about it."

Kaz said, "You're referring to Trent Calvin. Where is Mr. Calvin now? I'd like to ask him a few questions."

"I gave him the rest of the day off." Doyle shrugged.

"Have you been to the scene of this accident yourself, Mr. Doyle?"

"I don't get down to the dock very often, Officer. They keep me pretty busy here in the office. Sakamoto made a thorough report and I'm sure everything you need to know is in there. Now, if you'll excuse me, I have several million tons of cargo to logist."

"Don't worry, Mr. Doyle, I'm sure the widgets will be fine for a few more minutes."

"Who the hell are the widgets?" Doyle said. He thought he knew most of the ethnic slurs.

Kaz waved a hand at the sprawl of containers outside. "All that is widgets. Now. If you'll excuse *me*, I am a federal agent here to investigate a threat against national security. The more cooperation I get, the faster we'll be on our way. Do you have a manifest from the ship?"

Doyle held up a thick file. "Here. The container came off the *Star of Panama*. Sailed out of Quudia nine days ago." He handed Kaz the file. "Lists all the uh, widgets and whatnot."

"Thank you," said Kaz. She flipped through the paperwork and saw the elegant loops of Quudia Port Authority Assistant Export Deputy Hamid S. El-Qami's signature, the compact and hard-bored mark of *Star of Panama* Captain Ricardo Garcia, and the linear slash of Steven Doyle above "Importing Port Authority." The manifest listed hundreds of containers as line items, each dutifully checked off at every completed stage of their journey. Except one. Container 5138008, originating from Jufarrq Manufacturing of Quudia, DBA KozyHome Homeworks and destined for Pearl City Tiny Homes in Honolulu. Container 5138008 was designated "Damaged in Transit."

"What happened here?" Kaz asked, tapping the line.

Doyle was quick. "Damaged in shipping."

Kaz said, "Where is this container now?"

"Taking up space on my dock until our insurance company decides what to do."

"Mr. Doyle, would you show Officer Porter to the scene of the, what did we decide to call it? The accident? In the meantime, I'll need to see your security tapes and speak to the OSHA rep who wrote this report."

"Security's in the basement. Sakamoto's office is downstairs," said Doyle. "First floor, end of the hall." He swiveled in his chair and raised his arm like a periscope to point out directions through the window. "Officer Porter, Lot D. Go down there, through the gate, make a right toward the water, make a left before you fall in."

Doyle's desk phone rang and he looked at the caller ID: GossCo Security office. "Excuse me, officers. I have to take this," he said. "Shut the door behind you, please."

Kaz nodded that they should go and Porter followed her out.

Doyle picked up his desk phone as the door clicked shut. "Yeah?"

"Good work, Steve," said Margot. "You handled that well. I forgot you're not an idiot. The scene is cleaned up. I have everything. I'm leaving the security office now."

Doyle's cell phone lay face down on his desk. He flipped it over and ended the speakerphone connection to Margot's cell that had allowed her to listen in to his meeting with the CBP officers.

"Did you get everything you needed?" he asked her.

"I always do."

In the elevator, Kaz said to Porter, "Get down to the dock and check out the container. See if you can pick up any trail of the suspect."

"On it, Kaz," Porter said.

The elevator stopped and the doors opened to the first floor. GossCo's breakroom was directly across the hall. Kaz said, "I'm going to talk to Ed Sakamoto and then check out the security office to see what they have on video. You—"

Porter's attention wandered into the breakroom, following the aroma of coffee.

"Porter!" Kaz said. "You get out to that container. Hurry up. Take the truck. Stay on the radio."

Porter managed to ignore the scent of what smelled to be fairly high-end, private sector communal coffee and exited the GossCo building. He stepped outside into the warming morning. The *Star of Panama* on the near horizon was so ludicrously large, it was hard to judge how far away the ship was with any degree of certainty.

Following Doyle's directions, it took Porter about two minutes to drive to Lot D. He parked at the end of a row of containers and approached a neon-shirted, rubber-booted worker pulling a collapsible WET FLOOR sign from the bed of a tiny maintenance truck.

"Good morning!" Porter said. "Officer Matt Porter, CBP. Did you see what happened here this morning?"

"No, brah. I wasn't here. I cleaned it up, though. Shit everywhere. Had to hose down half the dock."

"So much for evidence," Porter mumbled.

"Sorry," the worker said, "She said to clean it up. I wasn't about to argue. Hazard pay." He paused to make a small, clenched-fist *ka-ching* motion. "Exposure to bio-waste," he explained. The worker pointed toward a drain at the edge of the dock. "There may be a little turd left over there, if you want to grab it," he said.

"Never mind," said Porter, in truth grateful for this turn of events that would send any further scatological concerns quite literally down the drain.

He walked with careful, tip-toeing steps over the wet asphalt, trying to keep any bio-waste residue off his shoes as he approached the tiny home container. It appeared to have sustained some damage. The front door had been popped ajar and it was missing two of its faux shutters.

Porter pushed the door open with his pen to avoid contaminating the scene, although he saw that someone had already tossed a large wad of white plastic sheeting and the two broken-off shutters into the home's foyer. He stepped over the wet mess.

The interior of the tiny home was not unlike the one his old college roommate Bonghit Bob lived in, although Porter didn't recall Bonghit's place having a large window in the back wall, as this one did. The window stood open, its protective plastic shroud cut in a large X. Porter walked to the window, bent and poked his head through. The hull of the cargo ship loomed a few yards in front of him. To his left, a long, unbroken row of containers created a shadowed warren along the edge of the dock, bending out of sight several hundred yards away with the natural contour of Sand Island. To the right, a shorter train of containers stretched along the waterfront, growing by the minute as the cargo cranes continued to unload the ship.

Porter pulled his head back inside and keyed his radio. "Kaz. Porter. Not much evidence at the scene. I'm going to try to pick up the suspect's trail. It looks like he jumped out the back of the container and my guess is he headed west, to try get to the bridge."

"Copy," came Kaz's voice.

CHAPTER 12

• Embrace the mindset of continuous improvement.

A fishing mate is expected to perform a seemingly limitless cycle of small tasks and each of these tasks at first confounded Jeff to some degree. In his brief time with Tasha, he had received more of a big-picture, high-concept fishing mate tutorial. Teaching the finer points fell to her second-in-command, Tommy. As the crew began to prep the boat for imminent departure, the deck boss rapidly described the dozens of duties Jeff would be expected to perform. Most of these lessons began with, "Watch how I do this," followed by a practical demonstration of the task illustrated with a colorful example about some poor guy being maimed because he mishandled it. The lessons would then conclude with either "He fucked around and found out," or "Poor fucker never saw it coming," and then it was on to the next thing.

The most frightening thing about these cautionary tales was the sheer number of them. Among the crushed fingers, cracked bones and fish hook-snagged body parts, Tommy also told the story of "Dave Gets Knocked Out And Then Gaffed by Hemi," although Tommy attributed

Dave's mishap *not* to a lapse in ladder safety procedure, but to being "fucked up."

As the boat was getting fit to depart, Tommy was often summoned by Tasha to tend to something or another. Almost without exception, these interruptions would come immediately after Tommy would point out, for example, a paintball gun in a bulkhead storage cabinet and say something like, "This is the walrus gun. Don't use it unless you have to." Then he'd walk away and disappear into some nook or compartment of the boat without taking follow-up questions.

In Tommy's absence, Jeff's practical, hands-on deck mate training was delegated to Hemi and Kai. As the brothers showed Jeff the ropes (which on a ship are called "lines"), it was abundantly clear that they had a rookie mate on their hands. The fact wasn't lost on Jeff, either. Once again, he was the weakest link in a chain, but now a link dangling from the end, easily clipped away if he couldn't hang on. He vowed to earn his keep by doing as Tommy said, and as the brothers did, including an assimilation of their strict verbal economy. A steady stream of orders, directions, rebukes, jokes and gratuitous profanity had gushed forth out of Tommy, but "Heres," "Theres," "Like thises," and "Nos" dripped sparingly from the mouths of the brothers. Thankfully, patient demonstration ran off their broad backs.

CHAPTER 13

• Make simple, declarative statements.

Porter flashed the lights, squawked the siren, slowed the SUV and pulled onto the median at the foot of the Sand Island bridge. An eighteen-wheeler loaded with boxes of latex marital aids that were manufactured in a Chinese factory by three shifts of baffled, just completely baffled workers whizzed past in the outbound lane.

Porter had followed what he reasoned to be the stowaway suspect's trail from the container to the bridge, assuming that any fugitive would naturally make for the only route off the island, but he'd found no trace of his quarry. As he slowly drove across the vast GossCo port, he had flagged down three dockworkers and a forklift driver, hoping to find eyewitnesses, but nobody could recall seeing anyone unusual scurrying away from the cargo docks that morning.

By this point, a lot of time had passed since the incident, leaving Porter's suspect ample time and opportunity to escape. The port was fenced, but with hundreds of people and vehicles coming and going all day long, it wasn't completely secure. Fortunately, the bridge had security cameras. If the suspect had crossed the bridge on foot, there would be video. With any luck, Kaz was, at that moment, capturing a usable image of their man.

As Porter watched the traffic flow steadily past, it also seemed very possible, indeed likely, that his suspect had caught a ride, either by arrangement or opportunity, and had slipped away concealed in a vehicle.

There was even a chance, as Kaz had suggested, that the guy had made a swim for it. From this point on Sand Island, the channel of the Kapālama Basin was only a couple hundred yards wide. A strong swimmer could have easily crossed by sea and made a dripping escape into the city.

There was even a fourth scenario, Porter now realized. The suspect could have left the island by boat. Stowing away by sea was clearly not beyond his capability and there was a marina across the road, west of the bridge.

Porter waited for a break in the traffic, made a U-turn and headed down to the marina.

Topside on the *Monkey Fist*, Tasha had put away her well-worn "Mate Wanted" sign and was enjoying her second cup of coffee when she saw a lanky, bespectacled man wearing the uniform of US Customs and Border Protection walking toward her from the marina parking lot. He caught Tasha's eye and gave a short wave.

The man stopped at the edge of the pier. "Good morning. Matt Porter, CBP. Can I ask you a few questions?"

"Sure," said Tasha.

"What's your name?" asked Porter.

"Is that one of the questions?"

"It's just *a* question. I don't really need to know, but to be honest, I couldn't decide whether to call you 'Ma'am' or 'Miss.' I could see myself going wrong either way."

"You can call me Captain, Officer Porter. Captain Natasha Hale. What can I do for you?"

"I'm looking for a stowaway. Jumped out of a container over in the port," Porter answered.

"What does he look like?" asked Tasha.

"It's unknown at this time."

"It's unknown? How do I know *you're* not the guy," Tasha asked, reasonably.

"I'm not."

"Yes, but how do I know,"—here she made air quotes—'Matt Porter, CBP?'"

"If I was the stowaway, where would I have gotten this uniform?" Porter asked, tapping the badge on his chest.

"Maybe you knocked Officer Porter out and stole his uniform, like Indiana Jones or whatever."

Porter showed Tasha his CBP photo ID. "Have you seen anything strange this morning, Captain? Someone who looked out of place?"

Tasha would hesitate to call Jeff's appearance strange. A lot of guys trolled the docks looking for work. And more importantly, he was an able-bodied fishing mate, currently fucking around in the galley with the other guys, but who, for the most part, pulled his weight all morning as the *Fist* got fit to go out for what should be a monster trip.

"Besides you?" Tasha said. "No, nothing unusual. We've been busy fitting out the boat this morning. Give me your card. I'll be sure to call you if I see anything." Tasha moved to the edge of the boat and reached over the gunwale.

Porter dug for a card as he said, "Who's 'we'?"

Tasha said, "Me and my crew."

"Bring them out here, if you don't mind, Captain," Porter said.

When the CBP officer had first appeared in the marina parking lot, Jeff didn't even notice. He was bent over, rooting through a storage locker looking for a roll of duct tape. When he found it and straightened up, Tommy, Hemi and Kai had quietly stopped working and were filing downstairs into the galley. Jeff put the tape down and followed without question. Apparently it was time for a midmorning break and maybe another muffin.

In the cramped galley, Tommy and Hemi slid into the table's bench seat. Despite the hours of hard work, Jeff felt the energized thrill of his escape and wasn't very tired. He remained standing and drifted toward Kai, who was wheeling coffee from a pot and dealing insulated mugs.

"Jeff," said Tommy. "You know the code of the sea?" He lit a cigarette.

Jeff said, "The codewords? Yes. Captain Tasha told me some." He waved his hand around. "This is the galley, for example."

"No, fuck that," Tommy said, blowing out blue smoke. "Not the fucking codewords. The fucking code of the sea is to watch each other's fucking backs."

Jeff nodded. "Yes."

"What's CBP doing here?" Tommy said.

"CBP?" Jeff asked.

"Customs and Border Patrol. The fucking cops. Why did they show up the same morning you did? You holding anything Jeff? You got warrants? If these guys ask for your license, remember you're Claude Ohanu. Don't fuck this up, Claude. We're trying to get out fishing today, Claude. If you get picked up by CBP, none of us will get paid this week, Claude." Tommy looked to Hemi and Kai, who were eyeing Jeff curiously. "Jeff's Claude," he said.

The brothers shrugged their OK.

Tasha's voice bounced down the stairs. "Guys! Get topside. CBP wants to talk to you."

The crewmates glared at Jeff. "The fuck's this about, Jeff?" Tommy hissed.

Jeff could only manage a small shrug of his own. Kai's heavy hand slapped down on his shoulder. He steered Jeff toward the stairs. "You go up first."

Jeff turned, eyes wide. "So you can watch my back?"

"Right. We got you, brah," Kai said.

"Yeah, whatever," said Tommy.

Jeff emerged from the galley first, clean-shaven, holding a cup of coffee. The energized thrill he felt a few moments earlier froze solid in his belly when he saw the uniformed officer.

Tasha said, “Guys, come over here.” She locked eyes with Jeff and gave him the slightest of nods. Jeff and his crewmates slowly made their way to where she stood. “This man wants to ask you a few questions.”

Porter stepped forward. “I’m Officer Matt Porter, CBP. You guys have some ID on you?”

Tommy produced a Washington State driver’s license and the brothers handed over their Hawaiian licenses. Jeff/Claude gave Porter his fishing license.

Porter took the crew’s IDs and sorted quickly through them, comparing the faces. Tommy had light blond stubble and both brothers' heads were shaved entirely clean.

“He found Jeff’s eyes. “You don’t have a driver’s license, Claude?”

“No.”

“Passport? Something with a photo.”

“Officer,” Tasha said. “We’re not sailing to Japan. These guys don’t keep passports on the boat.”

Porter said, “How old are you, Claude?”

“Twenty-four,” Jeff said.

“Clean fucking living,” Tommy said. He blew out some smoke.

Tasha said, “Officer Porter?” She raised her voice slightly. “These guys all need to get back to work.”

Porter held out the IDs. As Jeff stepped forward, Porter studied his face. “You shave this morning, Claude?”

"Yes," said Jeff, stroking his chin.

"Are you the beard police?" said Tasha. "I thought Customs and Borders was more about checking out dates on imported fruit and stuff."

Porter straightened up. He reached into his hip pocket and withdrew his notebook and a few blaze-orange, postcard-sized stickers. He showed Tasha one of them. The CBP seal and the word "Quarantine" leapt out.

"Why?" he said. "Do you have any illegal fruit on board? Because if you did, I could slap this sticker on your vessel and you won't be sailing anywhere. If I wanted, I could spend all week inspecting every inch of this ship."

"This isn't a ship, Officer Porter," Tasha said. "It's a boat."

"A ship can carry a boat, but a boat can't carry a ship," said Kai.

Porter paused, at some mental stop sign. He withdrew his notebook and jotted down: "Ship carries boat/boat cannot carry ship."

"There's nothing illegal on my boat, Officer Porter," Tasha said. Porter looked up and put his notebook away. "But I do *not* give you permission to come aboard. Not that I have anything to hide, of course, but we have a lot of work to do, and you know, the Constitution and everything. Good luck with your search. I will call you immediately if I see any stowaways. In the meantime, would you like a muffin before you go? Claude, get this man a muffin."

"Yes, Captain," Jeff said. He quickly spun away.

Porter watched him go. He said, "I assure you that the safety and protection of everyone is our goal at CBP, Captain. I should also mention that the person I'm looking for attacked a man as he got away. He's dangerous. Watch your back."

Tasha resisted the urge to follow Porter's gaze at Jeff, who was indeed about half-past her six at the moment. Could Jeff be a dangerous stowaway? Assuming there was such a thing? She had hired guys right off the dock before, and almost to the man, they worked hard. Until they didn't. And violent? Tasha had noticed Jeff's hands earlier. There were no cuts or scrapes that suggested a violent attack. His face was unmarked as well, except for a faded scar on the side of his forehead and this new trim mustache that made him look like a cool jazz drummer from the fifties or something. And those pants. Anyway, there was nothing to worry about. The guys were all here. Code of the sea.

Porter's radio beeped. "Porter. Kaz. I'm in GossCo's security office. Strangely, all their cameras run on a 24-hour loop that deletes itself at 9:45 every morning. There's no video from the dock this morning or anywhere in the GossCo port facility."

"Copy," said Porter.

"I also called Hawaii DOT to check their bridge cameras. Nothing to see there, either. Our guy probably got a ride out on a truck. What's your twenty?"

Porter responded, "Just west of the bridge. The marina."

"Any sign of the suspect?"

Porter looked up as Jeff approached and silently offered the muffin box.

Porter bent down close to the young fisherman. Those plaid pants were a real rich man/poor man situation. Porter drew in a long breath. Strong tones of fishing boat. There was salt in the air and cinnamon on the muffins.

"Negative, Kaz," Porter said into the radio. "No sign of suspect."

"You want a coffee to go with that?" Tasha asked him.

"Come pick me up, Porter," Kaz crackled.

Porter paused for a moment, then regretfully shook his head at Tasha. He reached down to take a muffin. "I'll be there in five, Kaz. Porter out."

"Where's *my* muffin, Porter?" Kaz said as she settled into the driver's seat and set a file folder on the center console, next to a crumb-crowned coffee cake muffin with a chunk missing.

Porter swung into the passenger's seat. He said, "A fisherman gave me this, Kaz. I only have the one."

"Did this fisherman give you any coffee, like a civilized person?"

"She offered, but I didn't have time. I came when you called."

"And how about suspects? Did you get around to discussing national security breaches or did you just join this fisherman for brunch?" She put the SUV in gear and drove toward the docks.

"I talked to a few guys working at the port and the crew of the fishing boat. No sign of anything strange or suspicious." Porter plucked the muffin from the cup holder. He moved to split it. "You want half of this?"

"Only a small piece. Two-fifths."

Porter began to gingerly engineer a fault line in the muffin that avoided the larger nuggets of crumby topping. "Two-fifths of the whole thing, or two-fifths of what's left?"

"Just give me one corner."

"It's a circle, Kaz."

"Use your judgment, Porter."

"Do you think he got off the island?" Porter asked. He handed Kaz a piece of muffin.

"Thank you," said Kaz. "Not on foot. The traffic camera at the end of the bridge didn't show anyone walk across, but trucks have been going out the whole time. If he caught a ride somehow, we wouldn't know it. He could've been gone by the time we even got the call."

"Where are we going?" Porter asked. "Back to the container? It's one of those tiny homes."

Kaz said, "KozyHome model Lucky Seven. Purchased by Pearl City Tiny Homes. Manufactured in Quudia, shipped out here nonstop on June 29th. All here in the manifest and OSHA report." She tapped the file.

Porter mentally counted back the dates. "He was in that container for nine days? There must be fingerprints everywhere." He took a bite of muffin.

"Probably," Kaz answered. "But Captain Benito won't authorize the forensics team."

"Why not? Someone assaulted a man and destroyed that container," Porter said.

Kaz said, "No, that was the very well-documented 'accident.'" She tapped the file again. "No criminal charges, no malicious property damage, no identifiable suspect. Benito told me to get back to the office and close the report."

"So why are we going back to the container?" Porter asked.

"Because a few minutes ago, before you picked me up, I saw Steve Doyle get in a golf cart and head toward the docks, a place he said he almost never goes. I think there's more to this. I want to ask him a few more questions." Kaz pulled the SUV up to the edge of Lot D. "And there he is."

Doyle stood with his back to them, speaking into a radio handset and looking up, watching a gantry crane slowly clank toward the KozyHome, which was sitting exactly where it had crashed down several hours earlier.

Porter gently set his muffin on the dashboard and got out of the SUV.

"Mr. Doyle," Kaz said as she and Porter approached. "You're a long way from your busy office. What are you doing down here?"

Doyle turned. "Oh, Officer Kazumi. Good news. Our insurance company has expedited the accident claim and we are returning the cargo back to the sender. All our problems will be solved." He glanced back up and spoke into his radio as the crane slid into position above the KozyHome. "Put this container back on the ship. Top level, outer edge."

Kaz said "What's the rush? CBP hasn't had the opportunity to investigate that container yet. There's evidence in there."

"Evidence of what?" replied Doyle. "Nothing happened. I believe that was explained to a Captain Benito in your office. It was just an accident and one that's already been cleaned up."

The crane's clamp began to lower.

"We don't know *evidence of what*, Mr. Doyle. That's the point," said Kaz. "Why not just leave the container on the dock until we can investigate."

"Until we can investigate!" Doyle mocked. "Officer, here in the real world, we have to get things done, not waste taxpayer money running in circles. This container's going back on the ship. I'm sure there's more serious problems you could be investigating." He raised his radio. "Take it."

The clamp thundered into place and locked onto the container. The slack in the crane's cables was slowly taken up and the container was tugged from the ground.

Porter reached into his hip pocket and took off running toward the container. A pen appeared in his right hand, a square of paper in his left. Without slowing, he scribbled a furious glyph. He dropped the pen and it skittered along the asphalt. A curling slip of paper fluttered behind him.

The rising container was almost ten feet off the ground when Porter leapt and slapped a blaze orange sticker onto it, affixing the sticker about six inches from the bottom of the front door. The crane continued hauling the container upward.

Porter turned back to Doyle and Kaz, puffing and grinning.

"What was that sticker?" Doyle shouted to him.

Kaz snatched the radio from Doyle. "This is Officer Sue Kazumi, United States Customs and Border Protection. You are committing a federal crime by removing and transporting cargo that has been tagged for inspection quarantine by the CBP."

The crane jerked to a stop.

Kaz opened the radio again. "Put the tiny home down."

Doyle tried to grab the radio back. Kaz pulled it out of his reach and said, "I'm going to put you back on with Mr. Doyle. Have him tell you where to set that container where it won't disrupt his day. He's very busy, you know, he doesn't need to be charged with a federal crime either." She handed the radio back to Doyle.

Doyle glared at Kaz, but took the radio. "Put it on a truck. I'll have it driven out and dropped in Lot X."

Doyle watched as the crane began to creep away toward the loading depot, swinging the KozyHome. He turned without a word and drove off in his golf cart.

Porter walked up next to Kaz, who said, "Watch that container. Make sure it gets on a truck. I'll meet you at the loading depot." She began walking back to the SUV.

"Where are you going?" Porter asked.

"To get you some coffee."

Kaz returned to the depot just as a flatbed truck carrying the KozyHome chugged off across the port. Porter got in the SUV and Kaz handed him a ceramic mug before falling in behind the truck to follow it.

"Whose mug is this?" Porter asked.

"I found it in the GossCo breakroom," answered Kaz.

"Don't you think it belongs to somebody?"

The mug read:

Like a
BOSS

"It belongs to the GossCo corporation," Kaz said. "Porter, small-minded bureaucrats like you and I don't understand these things of course, but having a crime scene and a law enforcement investigation in the middle of GossCo's dock was going to be a huge headache for them, so they made it go away. If there's no container, there's no problem. It was marked as damaged and GossCo never officially took possession of it. They were probably going to roll the thing into the ocean during return shipping, document it "lost" and reimburse KozyHome. Done."

"What do you mean, 'done'? What about the guy who was attacked?" Porter asked.

"When I talked to Sakamoto the OSHA guy, he told me everyone who was at the scene this morning is currently on a four-week vacation after meeting with some GossCo corporate type. He said everyone looked pretty happy when they left. Those guys probably signed some NDA's, signed away their rights, and saved GossCo who-knows-how-much in liability and bad press, in exchange for a few weeks off and probably a gift card or something."

Porter said, "Doesn't anyone care what really happened?"

"Don't worry, Porter. Everything's insured."

"Is that your way of telling me that this mug you stole is insured by GossCo?"

"That's right," said Kaz. "Also, fuck those guys," she added. "The container's not going anywhere for thirty days, thanks to your vertical leap."

Lot X was in the most remote corner of the GossCo facility, near the fence separating the port from the Sand Island Coast Guard Base. The KozyHome was rolled off the flatbed trailer with the aid of a forklift and placed next to a pile of sun-grayed wooden pallets. The quarantine sticker was shin-level and askew, but could not be missed. The CBP officers got out of their SUV as the truck and forklift drove away.

"Do you know what box you checked on the sticker?" Kaz said to Porter as they approached.

"Not really," Porter admitted. The sticker had four choices of quarantine designation for the impounding officer to choose from: Fruit, Tropical Fruit, Seafood, and Biohazard. "I barely had time to sign my name before I slapped it on."

Kaz bent to see Porter's scrawled mark that ran across the lower corner of the quarantine sticker, under a slashing check mark that neatly bisected the box marked "Biohazard."

Porter said, "So what do we do now?"

Kaz straightened up. "Now we get to wait."

CHAPTER 14

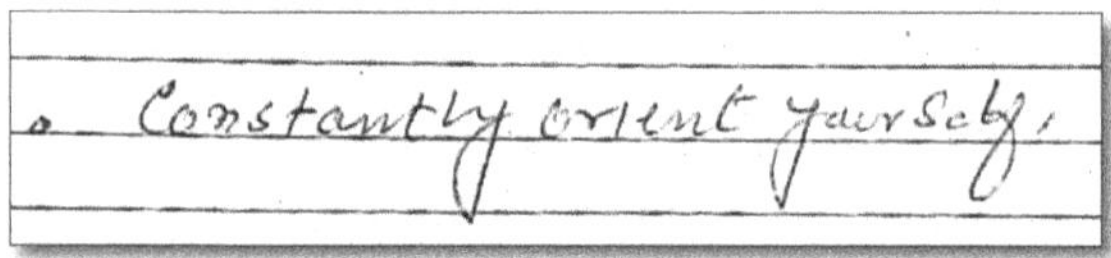

By late afternoon, items without number aboard the *Monkey Fist* had been stowed, tied, tested, lashed, dumped, pumped, washed, coiled, painted, and scrubbed. The boat was fit for sea.

Tasha blasted a farewell from the air horn, Tommy lit a cigarette, Hemi and Kai cast off the lines, and Jeff cast his lot. The *Fist* motored out of the Sand Island Marina.

After the events of his morning, to say that Jeff was "escaping" the island would be to overstate the word's implication of covert daring. And speed. The boat was much slower than Jeff would have guessed. Nevertheless, he had made it away.

As it is with all things, proximity barred judgment. As Jeff's distance from Honolulu grew, so did his understanding of its geographical layout. The industrial jumble of the cargo port gave way to the gleaming towers of downtown, which in turn gave way to jagged green peaks crowned with mist. Although not as imposing as the rocky and bare Pir range back in Zazaristan, these mountains were verdantly stubbled with trees. Or maybe they were small bushes. Distance also barred judgment, as it is with all things.

Clear of the harbor, Tasha headed east and opened up the engine. (Now this was more like it!) The *Monkey Fist* reared up to face the open sea, putting the sun, a four-knot wind and more than a few cares behind.

Music began to beat from the boat's speakers. Cool ocean wind whipped over Jeff's newly bare chin and the t-shirt rippling over his back felt like the pats of a hundred tiny hands.

Hemi rolled out a wheeled bin full of coiled segments of monofilament line that looked like a giant bowl of translucent rice noodles. Jeff followed his crewmates as they gathered around it. Tommy pulled out the end of one line and said to Jeff, "Make a gangion knot. Loop, pinch, bend, flip it over, under and through."

Sunlight rainbowed through the fishing line and a tidy loop blossomed at the end of it as if charmed by a wizard's spell. Tommy slipped the looped gangion onto a rack that spanned the cart.

Jeff blinked and picked out an end of line, but held it dumbly, unsure how to proceed.

Tommy grabbed a second piece. "Loop, pinch, bend, flip it over, under and through."

Jeff tentatively made a loop, which promptly unspun itself into a limp curve that was unfit to capture even the most simpleminded and docile creature of the sea, let alone the crafty and powerful tuna.

Tommy picked up a third piece. "Fucking loop. Pinch. Bend. Flip it over. Under. Through."

Jeff said, "How are you bending—"

"Watch Hemi," Tommy suggested, his tutorial limits reached.

Hemi was already on his fifth knot. His knots were conjured with silent rote ease, in half the time and with half the motion of Tommy's. *How—*

Kai nudged Jeff. He held an end of line. "You go out. You come back home." Loop. "You lie down in bed." Bend. "Under the blanket." Flip. "Pahulu flies in and looks under the bed." Under. "Then she flies away out your window." And through.

Jeff tugged his gangion knot snug.

Again and again, it was by this general method that over the next few hours, Jeff continued to learn the ways of the mate. Tommy's telling, Hemi's showing and Kai's patience were all the instruction that one could need. And the music was good.

Cellular service can only reach about ten miles out to sea and the crew all seemed to know just when this invisible barrier was about to be reached. Everyone but Jeff took a moment to make one last call, text or ZoopZap.

Then the crew stowed their phones, so clearly it was the captain who had ultimate dominion over the playlist, but Jeff noticed a very wide variety of songs throughout the afternoon, obviously meant as a concession to the diverse tastes of the crew. Tommy, for example, favored a guitar/yelp-based sound ("Van fucking Halen") almost to the exclusion of all other forms. ("I fucking hate Interpol. How can you listen to this shit, Hemi?") Kai seemed to enliven a bit when Travis Scott or J. Cole pumped from the speaker mounted above the cabin doorway, and the rest, from The Beatles to Billie Eilish must have been curated by Tasha herself.

Jeff enjoyed most of the unfamiliar music and he was grateful that its generous volume, along with the whipping wind, droning engine and rush of bowsplit water, discouraged small decktalk. Tommy kept up a near-constant monologue that covered not just music criticism, but many far-ranging topics, and Jeff soon realized that he was the type of man who asked very few questions, which very much suited Jeff for the time being.

The music cut off. Tasha's voice crackled from the ship's PA system. "We're coming up on the beds. Stow the gear."

"You heard her," Tommy said to the crew, "Stow this shit. Let's call it a day." He fished out his cigarettes. Kai disappeared belowdecks.

Jeff was perplexed. The crew had been steadily working their way through a large bin of gore-flecked fish hooks, cleaning and sharpening them, but they were nowhere near done. Why was the crew retiring? Was "coming up on the beds" sea-speak for "preparing for sleep?"

Hemi rolled the bin away and slipped a fitted tarp over it.

"I'm not very tired," said Jeff, still eager to prove his fitness for the job.

"Cool story, bro," said Tommy, as he sat on the freezer hatch. "You can run laps around the fucking deck if you want, but personally, I'm going to get off my feet while I can."

Jeff said, "I mean, I could continue working."

Tommy reached into a chest cooler for three water bottles. "We're about to leave the US EEZ." He tossed a bottle to Hemi, who set it aside and lay down on the sun-warmed freezer hatch to grimacingly stretch his back.

"The US EEZ?" Jeff asked, catching his bottle.

Tommy opened his water and took a gulp. "United States Exclusive Economic Zone. Only American companies can work here, fishing or mining or whatever. Once we get past the EEZ, it's like international waters, 'cept it ain't international because it's all owned by separate countries. They got it gridded out with their own mining claims." Tommy waved widely. "Around here, there's beds of minerals all over the bottom. Fucking… cobalt and shit. Manganese. Anyway, it's illegal for us to fish there. We can't even have our gear out on deck. These countries take that shit serious, the claim is like their home soil. We're only a few hours out of Hawaii, but we're about to split right between Nicaragua and China." He took another swig. "The fucking Chinese buzzed us with a helicopter once. Cocksuckers blew my favorite fucking hat in the water." Tommy squinted and pointed. "That's one of their platforms, right there."

Jeff followed Tommy's finger to a blurry gray square of indeterminate scale on the horizon. He stared for a moment, then turned to scan the rest of the ocean. With a shock, he saw that at some point while he was busily working, the green leviathan of O'ahu and every other speck of land on Earth had somehow receded from his sight. There were no usable bearings whatsoever! Jeff lighthoused the featureless seascape again. A vast blue plane stretched like liquid desert to a razor-edged horizon, unbroken but for the Chinese mining platform. Based on its size, Jeff estimated it to be somewhere between one and fifty kilometers away. Cloudless blue sky domed to a tropical sun that hovered above. Three seabirds that had been tailing them for hours glided behind the stern.

"Constantly orient yourself." Jeff had read that in his journal a hundred times, and yet, here he was, nowhere.

Now, from a certain perspective, losing sight of land could be reasonably excused because in a later section, Jeff's journal also advised: "Never look over your shoulder (someone/thing is always watching)." His busy afternoon certainly left him no time for leisurely contemplations over the stern rail and the land had simply slipped away without his notice as he tended to more pressing matters. In fairness, the context of the no-looking-over-shoulder advice would suggest that it is not meant to be taken literally when orienteering and that it's more of a counter-surveillance tactic, but at the same time, the underlying message is that one should avoid dwelling on mistakes of the past and focus on what lies ahead.

"How far away is that platform?" Jeff asked.

Kai had returned with a handful of C4 Proteinsanity™ energy bars. He handed out the snacks and sat down next to his brother. Tommy handed Kai a bottle of water.

Tommy unwrapped his Proteinsanity™ bar. "Five, six miles maybe. They probably got their robot miners crawling underneath us right now."

Robot miners! Jeff was finding the talkative Tommy to be a great source of intel.

Jeff's stiff, waxy Proteinsanity™ bar looked as if it had been extruded from a machine. He wondered if the energy bar extrusion machine worked nonstop, producing a single, yet infinite bar that subsequently gets cut into 1.94 oz (per the wrapper) segments. If that was the case, would that mean that the bar he was eating on a boat somewhere in the Pacific Ocean was, technically, the very same bar being squeezed out at the C4 factory (in Gig Harbor, WA, also per wrapper) at that very moment?

It tasted like it probably was. He asked, "Do we have any fishing robots?"

Tommy regarded Jeff for a moment. He said, "No, we don't have any fucking robots. You should be happy about that, because you'd be the first to go if we got one."

Jeff pictured what a shoveling robot would look like. Probably bulldozerish. He said, "If we can't fish in these zones, why don't the fish just stay here for protection?"

Tommy said, "A lot of this job depends on being smarter than the fish, kid. Tasha's looking at a nice temperature break about a couple hundred miles out from here, so we got a ways to go. We'll steam overnight to get there and start setting when the sun goes down tomorrow night." He tore a bite of his Proteinsanity™ bar.

"We set in the dark?" Jeff asked.

"Got to."

"Why?"

"Make a guess," said Tommy.

"Is that when the fish like to eat?"

"Nope. Guess again."

Jeff thought. "Because of those cocksuckers-the-fucking-Chinese?"

"The fuck? No," Tommy said. "Aku birds." He pointed out the three seagulls that had been gliding behind the boat.

"Aku birds? I thought those were seagulls," Jeff said.

"An aku bird wants something for nothing," Kai explained. He twisted off a pinch of Proteinsanity™ bar and casually tossed it in the air. The three gulls shot toward the morsel and collided. The prize blooped into the ocean and the birds dove after it. After a brief splashing, squawking melee, one bird flew away victorious, his gullet pumping. The other two gave half-hearted pursuit, but quickly saw that this was one of those zero-sum situations and veered up to reform their original positions in the airy draft of the boat. The third gull joined them, with no hard feelings to be seen.

"They'll leave at night," Tommy said. "If we try to set when they're around, they go after the bait and get caught in the line. Fucking aku birds." He stood up, drained his water and tossed the bottle at the birds. One of them made an abbreviated dive for it before realizing it wasn't food, then tried to play it off as if he was just stretching his wings.

Tasha swung the pilothouse door open and shouted down, "Hey! How about *not* throwing shit in the water, Tommy!"

"We're not in Hawaiian waters anymore," Tommy rebutted. "Don't worry, Cap, nobody's going to hit us with a fine out here."

"Not worried about the fine," Tasha said. "You're setting a bad example for the new guy." She pointed to Jeff.

The bottle disappeared into the boat's foamy wake and the *Monkey Fist* sailed on.

The crew finished their snacks and Jeff followed as they headed down the stairs into the cabin. Kai, the boat's cook, slid a foil-topped lasagna made by his wife June into the galley oven. Tommy lifted the seat of the bench to reveal the *Fist*'s library of books and DVDs. Hemi selected a copy of David Shafer's *Whiskey Tango Foxtrot* that had been dropped in water at least once and Tommy chose the film *Kill Zone 3.* Jeff was unfamiliar with both of these works, but since he hadn't seen *Kill Zone*s *1* or *2,* he decided against joining Tommy and Kai to watch. He had done enough catching up for one day.

Hemi punched and kneaded his pillow and seabag to transform his bunk into a makeshift zero-g recliner and gingerly settled himself in with a small sigh.

Jeff climbed up to the opposite bunk and dug his journal and pen from his backpack. He took the folded muffin paper out of his pocket and enjoyed the cakey residue as he opened the journal. He snuck a look down at Hemi. The journal was a private matter of course, but its mere existence was no secret. And even if it was to fall out of Jeff's possession, the journal was written in English and designed to appear as no more than an aphoristic aide-mémoire, a Jimmy Gatz-esque list of General Resolves.

Jeff flipped to page nine, asterisked "Always Suspect All People," and annotated, "*aka: As Soon As F Possible."

Jeff's English was stitched together from a few years of schooling, joking practice with Rahim, and in the weeks before he left Zazaristan, some intense cramming to absorb what he could from the training videos. He was aware that, despite what Americans may think, English is not a default of the world's population. A thought struck him.

Jeff tucked the journal under his pillow and turned again to observe Hemi, who seemed engrossed in his tale of drink and dance, the book rested on his broad chest. Hemi flipped a page, taking no notice of Jeff. Perhaps the big man's laconic nature may not be a choice, but a limitation. Perhaps *he* didn't possess much English. Now obviously, Hemi was reading an English language novel. But that could be misdirection. Jeff was doing it too, after all.

Thirty minutes later, the obstinate odor of dirty socks was vanquished from the bunkroom by the smell of lasagna. Kai called dinner. Hemi marked his page and rolled from his bunk. Jeff jumped down to follow.

In the galley, Kai cut a steaming square of lasagna. He opened an upper cabinet. A small avalanche of Tupperware containers teetered forth. Kai quickly fought it back and plucked from the jumble an abraded, orange-tinted 6x6 square model. He put the lasagna into it.

"For the Cap," he said, impaling the food with a fork and handing it to Jeff.

The crew served themselves and settled around the table as Jeff took Tasha's dinner up to the bridge.

Tasha's voice had come through the ship's PA regularly throughout the day, but Jeff had not seen much of her since they left the marina, hours ago. He found her in the captain's chair, hands behind her head, feet on the console.

"Your dinner, Captain," Jeff said.

"Thanks Jeff. Did you eat?"

"Not yet."

Tasha sat up to take the food. "I love Junie's lasagna. This is the best meal you're going to get on this trip. Better get back downstairs before it's gone."

"Won't you join us?" Jeff asked. He pointed to the unmanned wheel, making jittering corrections as the boat plunged through the waves. "The ship can steer itself, can't it?"

"The ship can steer *her*self, yes," Tasha said. "But just to get from place to place. Someone always has to be on watch. I'll stay on until ten. Tommy 'til midnight. Kai 'til two, Hemi 'til four." She forked a chunk of lasagna, blew on it, and pointed at Jeff. "Four am to six."

"What are we watching for?" Jeff asked, looking through the front windshield at the glittering water.

"Other ships, buoys, trash, ghost gear, whales, rogue waves, you name it. Any kind of trouble."

"And then what? If I see trouble?"

"When you see trouble, grab the fucking wheel and steer around it."

"Yes," Jeff said.

CHAPTER 15

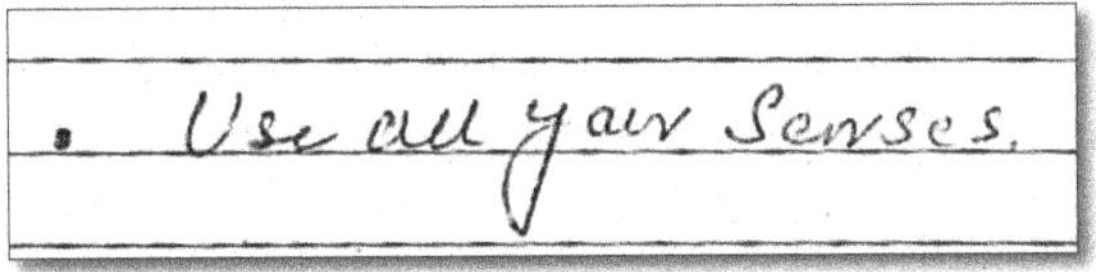

The lasagna, the first hot meal Jeff had eaten in weeks, was a savory delight. *Kill Zone 3,* however, was incomprehensible and riddled with plot holes.

After he ate, Jeff excused himself and returned upstairs. He sat on the port foredeck and watched the sun set the clouds aflame.

Transfixed by the Hawaiian sunset, Jeff didn't hear Tommy approach, but he smelled the smoke of a cigarette.

Tommy smoked in uncharacteristic silence and expertly paced his cigarette so that the butt and the sun were extinguished by the sea at the same moment. "Get used to it," he said, and was gone without another word.

Jeff enjoyed the fresh air and afterglow for a few minutes, then cut himself a few short lengths of fishing line for knot practice, imagining that even the most zealous Chinese Mining Security helicopter could not object to a meter-long, hookless segment of line being out in the open. On the infinite ocean, time was free. Free and infinite.

He didn't notice when the three seagulls peeled off and flew away as one. At some point, an ancient spark had fired in their pea-sized brains signaling, "If I want to live, I better turn back now and get the fuck out of here." And so they left.

In an hour that passed like a minute, the milk-colored moon coaxed her friends the stars out for the night.

Jeff retired to a bunk that was four inches too short. Hard against the hull of the boat, he absorbed the thrumming vibrations of a diesel engine and the rolling Pacific. He fell immediately into a dreamless sleep.

CHAPTER 16

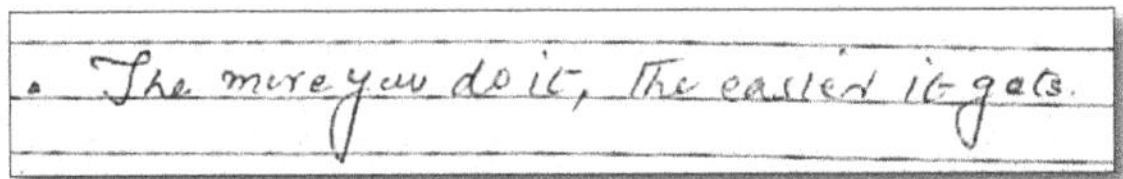

Whether his exhausted brain rolled blank tape as he slumbered, or simply deleted the files when his watch beeped at 0345 to relieve Hemi, Jeff couldn't know.

He killed the alarm and lowered himself to the floor like a draft of cold air. A dozen or so digital clocks and power lights illuminated the cabin. Mostly cool blues and greens. A few reds and yellows, one orange.

Outside, visibility around the *Monkey Fist* was limited to the small dome of light she carried with her. But from what Jeff could see and feel, the waves were higher than they had been earlier.

With Tasha asleep just a thin door away in the bridge, the changing of the watch was done in silence. Jeff took up his post in the Hemi-warm chair.

The spotlit swath of ocean that could be observed from the bridge of the *Fist* didn't reveal any ships, nor ghosts, nor rogues, although any of them could very well have passed within meters of the boat, such was the narrow scope of her light and the weight of the dark curtain just beyond.

Gradually, the eastern sky brightened and the sun greeted its audience of one with a one of one show.

At exactly six am, Jeff heard an alarm ring in Tasha's berth. Thirty seconds later, she appeared wearing the same clothes as the day before. She surveyed the morning seas and checked the boat's position on her instruments. She pulled her empty mug from a dash-mounted cup holder.

"Get me a coffee," she said. "And tell those guys, on deck by six-thirty. The horn waits for no man."

Down in the galley, Kai had already started the coffee. Jeff refilled Tasha's mug, snapped the travel lid shut and clambered back up the stairs to the main deck. Tasha was waiting at the railing of the pilothouse. "Toss it," she said. She gave a short clap and opened her palms.

Jeff lobbed the mug up to her with perfect arc. It hovered at her chest level for what seemed like a full second and she simply plucked it from the air.

Tasha blasted the ship's horn at 6:30 on the dot and the morning's playlist started up a moment later with some Sudden Rush.

Hemi rolled out a tackle cart and the crew gathered around it, wearing sweatshirts and jeans in the cool, damp morning. There was little talk, even from Tommy, as the crew continued prepping the gear. Gangions still needed to be tied and assembled. Hooks the size of crooked fingers were looped onto one end of the gangions, swivel clips to the other.

When all the new gangions were made, Jeff continued to do as the deck boss said and as the brothers did for another long day in preparation for the first set that night. By late afternoon, the sweatshirts and jeans had been shed in favor of t-shirts and shorts. Hooks were sharpened, floats attached, batteries charged, ice shoveled, everything set, checked, clipped, turned and lashed until there was nothing left to do except watch the sun set.

"Jeff! You looking for someone to make out with or something?" Tommy said. "Grab six cases of bait, put 'em out on the deck to thaw. Then, get downstairs to rack out while you can. We'll set in about two hours."

Jeff looked around to see that Hemi and Kai had already disappeared into the cabin and Tommy's sunset smoke was getting short. "Yes," he said.

He climbed down into the freezer hold and excavated the frozen boxes. One-by-one, he pressed them overhead, up and over the lip of the hatch and then carried them to the stern.

By the time he slid into his bunk, his three crewmates were already gently snoring.

Jeff dreamed of knots.

The *Fist*'s engines cut to an idle and the boat sloshingly pitched forward. The horn blasted and Tasha's voice rang from the boat's speaker. "Let's get that line wet, boys."

Working the last bite of a meat pie down his gullet like a seagull, Jeff climbed the stairs and moved aft through the blue gloam, past the giant spool of mainline, poised to pay out. Hemi lay on the freezer hatch and twisted at the waist, loosening his back.

Tommy emerged from the cabin in a cloud of Merit smoke. He walked past Jeff and leaned on the gunwale rail. "Ninety percent of the people on earth live less than fifty miles from the ocean," he said.

Out of habit, Jeff didn't place himself into this category. But then he realized he was currently living less than two meters from the ocean. "Yes," he replied.

"I'll bet it killed five billion people," Tommy said. "This shit," he gestured to the black and heaving water, "gets out of control quick. Code of the sea, Jeff. Watch each other's fucking backs." He pinched the stub of his cigarette and pinwheeled it overboard.

Kai walked over to where Hemi was stretching. He lightly pressed Hemi's leg down and two soft cracks slipped from his brother's spine. Hemi sighed with relief, then accepted Kai's hand to pull himself to his feet.

Kai swung the mainline spool to starboard. Hemi grabbed the loose end of the line, threaded it through a pulley screwed to the gunwale and then pulled it aft, where he fed it through the line shooter, the humming contraption clamped to the stern of the boat that fed the line into the water. Jeff was relieved that Hemi didn't even attempt to instruct him on the complex routing of the line as he serpentined it through the shooter's labyrinth of rollers and tensioners.

Tommy set an orange GPS beacon on the cart next to the shooter. The beacon looked like a one-year-old's birthday cake with a whip antenna instead of a candle. Tommy switched the beacon on and looked up to the bridge.

Tasha's voice came from the PA, "Good signal on beacon one." Tommy gave a thumbs-up and clipped the beacon to a buoy, stenciled with the *Fist*'s logo.

Kai pushed a lever on the mainline hauler controls. An electric motor whined to life and the big spool gave up some slack.

Hemi still held the end of the mainline. He made a figure eight knot and Tommy clipped the GPS buoy into the loop. Hemi gripped the beacon by the antenna and lifted it over the rail. He said a few low words that were carried away by the wind.

"Hemi! Wait!" Tasha's voice called. "Let Jeff do it."

Jeff was opening a case of bait. He stood at the sound of his name. The door to the bridge swung open. Tasha shouted down, "Jeff, throw the line in. Get us started off right. It's your lucky week, after all."

A wave of unease rolled through Jeff. Was Tasha referring to his escape from the port? Did she suspect something?

"You met us, didn't you?" Tasha said, grinning. She extended her fist to the crew. "*Monkey Fist* on three!" Jeff joined his three crewmates as they pressed their fists in, spokes in a wheel. "1-2-3 MONKEYFIST!"

Hemi still held the beacon and he offered it to Jeff.

It was much heavier than it looked.

Jeff stepped to the rail and hefted the beacon over the side, but didn't let it go. He almost couldn't believe the thing would float. "Just drop it in?" he asked.

"I heard that's where the fish are!" Tasha shouted.

Jeff let the beacon drop and watched it get swallowed by the night.

The actual work of setting the line was simple. After the floating beacon, clip a 5kg weight onto the mainline. Toss in the water. Clip one end of a gangion onto the mainline. Hook a dead, marble-eyed mackerel to the other end. Toss it in the water. After every ten hooks, clip on a fist-stenciled buoy. Toss it in the water. Repeat like the chorus of a song.

The nature of repetitive work will cause conversations to wander as far and wide as the open sea. At one point, Tommy insisted that if one encounters a dried earthworm on the sidewalk, pouring a bit of warm coffee on the creature will revive it. Kai disagreed, arguing that coffee would kill the worm. Hemi said that since a worm is seventy-five percent water and has nervous system very similar to that of a human, caffeinated coffee would not only revive a (not completely desiccated) worm, but the worm's burrowing rate would increase "significantly" in the short term. Jeff felt unqualified to offer an opinion.

After a couple hours of setting, with smooth seas and no major snags, snarls or snafus on deck, the mainline parted from the boat. As soon as the final buoy splashed, Tasha turned the boat hard to port and began to track down and recover the first GPS beacon, now twenty miles to the southeast.

The crew relaxed visibly, seemingly pleased with their evening's work. To Jeff's relief, it seemed a respite was at hand. The training videos often suggested a high-five in such circumstances, so Jeff turned to Tommy, holding his palm aloft. Tommy obliged him, then shook out a cigarette.

"We set a lot of hooks," Jeff said. "Is the freezer big enough? How will we fit all the fish?"

“We don’t catch a fish on every hook,” Tommy chuckled.

“Ah. Yes,” Jeff said. “So the fishing, it’s a matter of value over sheer numbers, then?”

Tommy nodded and said, “Yeah, I guess it’s like everything else. ‘Cept when it ain’t.”

This was not the kind of thing one high-fives over, Jeff felt fairly certain.

CHAPTER 17

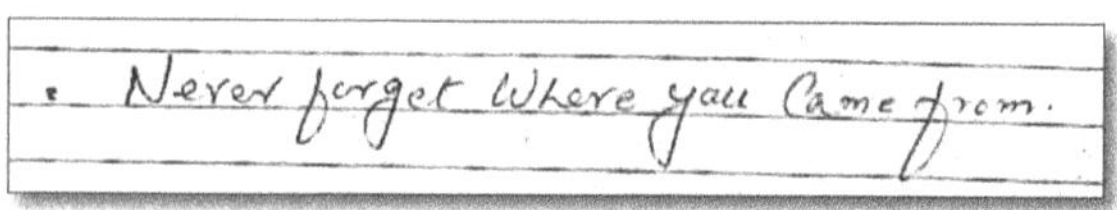

"Find some boots, bro. There's going to be blood everywhere." Tommy pointed to the oil gear bin.

Jeff quickly pried off his sneakers, tied them together with a sheet bend and tossed them in the bin. He booted up in knee-high yellow galoshes and clomped to the starboard rail, where Tommy, Hemi and Kai were leaned over as if waiting for a horse to race past. Tommy held a grappling hook tied to a coil of line at his feet.

Tasha came out of the bridge and stepped to the auxiliary helm on the small platform outside the pilothouse.

"The first thing we have to catch is the beacon!" Tasha called down to Jeff. "See it?" She pointed off the bow and slowed the engine.

Jeff joined the crew at the rail and looked ahead. A blinking light bobbed in the darkness. Hemi hit it with the spotlight and held it with focus.

Tommy said, "Stand the fuck back a little." He prepared to throw the hook.

Kai and Jeff shuffled a few steps away. Everyone seemed tense as the orange beacon floated into sight. Everyone but Jeff, who had never seen an instance of a grappling hook failing.

"What happens if he doesn't grapple it?" Jeff asked Kai.

"If he misses? No prob. The line's long. You get plenty of shots. But it's easier to haul in when we catch it close to the end and Tasha doesn't like if the line gets past us and starts drifting near the prop."

Tasha eased the *Fist* to a near-stop. The beacon was about twenty feet off the starboard bow and rolling closer. "Get it," she called. "Let's go fucking fishing!"

Tommy checked the line at his feet, then reared back and flung the hook. It splashed well beyond the buoy and he immediately started drawing it back. The hook grabbed the line (of course) and Jeff and Kai helped pull it back aboard through the gated door in the waist-high starboard rail.

Jeff said, "Tasha said the line is always longer coming back."

"Monofilament stretches out a little," Kai explained.

Hemi stripped the gear from the line and threaded the end of it through a zigzagging route of pulleys and back onto the mainline spool.

Tasha cracked the engine and turned the boat. The mainline drew out of the water at a flat angle that disappeared into the darkness. It caught a glint of light and Jeff spotted where it broke the surface about five meters off the starboard stern. Tommy took Kai's place at the line hauler controls. He feathered the winch speed to match the pace Tasha set and the line began slowly winding back up. The first gangion emerged from the water, its hook unbaited and impotent. Hemi unclipped it and slid it onto a rack with one gloved hand while keeping the other hand rested lightly on the mainline as it passed—"FISH ON CHEEEEEHOOOOOO!" he screamed.

Hemi leaned over the rail and snatched the spasming gangion line. It disappeared into the black water, slashing quick wounds in the surface that closed as quickly as they opened. Tommy slowed the hauler to a crawl and hand-signaled with a downward finger for Tasha to throttle the boat down as well.

"Grab the line, brah!" Hemi yelled at Jeff, pulling him close with his free hand. Hemi grabbed the cuff of Jeff's glove and guided his hand to the taut gangion.

The hot wind that blows through Taboor City used to sort of sphincter down as it slipped between some of the taller buildings that ringed the southern end of Taboor Square Park to focus a near-constant gust on the ancient Taboor City Obelisk. For reasons lost to history, and whether by ingenious design or happy accident, the stone pillar had a hole bored near the top which whistled a warbling and doleful note as the miles of wind passed through.

A few years back, those tall buildings were made considerably shorter. Readers will please excuse the use of the passive voice in this case, but if getting reduced to rubble by a series of cruise missiles and mortar shells while just standing there minding your own business isn't passive, one must wonder what is.

The Obelisk survived, but for only about a thousand days more, until it was showily removed one afternoon after the junta *du jour* decreed whistling illegal. But before all that, the park was a bustling oasis of kites, footballs, friendly insults and the hopes of strolling lovers, all flying about to one degree or another.

On this particular day, a honking border of vehicles inches around the park on all sides. Jefir and Rahim dart through the traffic, giving thought and deference in the following order (from the top): Goat, truck, bus, car, motorcycle rickshaw, motorcycle with sidecar, bicycle rickshaw, regular motorcycle, moped/scooter, dog, bicycle, man, woman, child, bird.

Jefir stiff-arms a final lumbering truck, then skips behind his brother onto the wide sidewalk at the mouth of the park. As he passes through the gate, Jefir leaps to try to touch the overhead span of wrought-iron, and comes up about a meter short, as is his custom.

Rahim invites himself to join a rolling football match being played by about forty other kids and is immediately subsumed in a swarm of knees and elbows.

Jefir has come to watch the kites. Dozens of them ripple in the air. The diamond-shaped fighters do their dances over here, the aerodynamically puzzling box kites over there. Lording over them all is a massive red dragon, long as a city bus, a monster eating wind and shitting anti-gravity. The dragon flies high enough as to render the business end of its string invisible, but Jefir's young eyes pick up the gently curving line as it comes to earth. The string is tied to a wooden stake, the stake driven into the ground at the feet of a reclining man.

Can the man not hold the string by hand for fear of being carried away by the kite? Is he indulging in the fantastical conceit that he owns a domesticated red dragon that, by law, he must keep leashed in the park, but calls to earth at the end of the afternoon to ride home astride? Jefir cannot say. All possibilities seem reasonable enough. He resolves to stay at the park as long as it takes to witness the manner in which the red dragon leaves. Most likely bundled up and carried by the man, but Jefir wants to be sure and the answer will cost him nothing but time, which is free of course, not to mention in infinite supply when you are nine years old.

Jefir takes a seat on the Obelisk's plinth. A stiff wind is coming from the south-south-east, which means the whistling is in E flat. Jefir leans back, resting his shoulders against stone roughened and warmed by a million sunrises.

Jefir counts twenty-nine kites. He handicaps and ranks the fighters by design, skill of operator, then a combination of both.

He imagines the various skills and personality traits of a group of passing schoolgirls, each one prettier than the last. She can make anyone laugh. She is gifted artist. She can name any flower.

Jefir smells meat grilling and cake frying. He gets a drink from the water fountain and returns to his spot.

He imagines a scenario where the huge dragon's stake pulls free from the ground and the dragon is only seconds away from escaping over the city. If/when this happened, Jefir would spring to his feet and sprint into action. He'd hurdle a park bench to make a desperate dive for the stake, grabbing for it as it tumbled and lurched across the grass. A fistful of string would zing hotly through his fist before the wooden stake snapped surely into his grip. But he is too small! The powerful dragon would drag him along for a few meters and then begin lifting him off the ground! In desperation, Jefir would have to grab the water fountain or something with his free hand to anchor himself to earth as the dragon jerked him aloft. Arms fully extended, feet dangling, Jefir would strain like a superhero, refusing to be the weakest link in the chain that restrains the roaring dragon. Finally, the kite's inattentive and slow-footed owner would come puffing to Jefir's aid. He and perhaps two other grown men would struggle to relieve Jefir and restake the bucking dragon to the ground. Then, with solemn gratitude and respect, and in full view of a gathering of goggle-eyed park goers, the owner would insist that Jefir take possession of the kite as a reward for his quick thinking and bravery, and Jefir would say something smooth and clever like, "Think nothing of it, my good fellow, I only—"

"Hey, shitstain!"

Jefir sits up. An older boy steering a red fighter is calling over his shoulder as he backs toward Jefir. The kite snaps in the wind.

Jefir looks around. "Me?" he says.

"Yeah, you. Shitstain. Hold my kite."

All Jefir hears is 'hold my kite.' He hops off the plinth, trots up to the older boy and holds out his hands. At last.

"I'm going over there," the older boy says, nodding to an ice cream truck that has pulled up just outside the park gate, announcing itself by that strange music with its ever-slowing tempo. "If you let go of this kite, or let it hit the ground, I'll shove my popsicle stick up your ass."

A smooth and clever retort is called for in this instance as well, but Jefir can't manage it just now. He hopes the boy wasn't planning to buy one of those push-up pops with the disc-shaped base at the end of the stick.

The boy presses the kite's twin reels into Jefir's hands and glares a final warning.

The kite string, quick and pulsing, feels like a recurring dream he hasn't yet had. Resisting and dancing, on the edge of control, it is unmistakably alive.

The yellowfin breached and the line went slack in Jeff's hand. Kai and Hemi quickly hooked it *chunkchunk* with their gaffs and 1-2-3 heaved it out of the water and onto the deck. The gleaming fish was a two-meter-long spearhead with scythe-like crescent fins. Toothy, triangular spikes ran along its spine like it was some kind of dragon from the depths. A moment ago, in its natural element, the fish fought with outsized strength, but now that the poor creature was out of the water, it was hopelessly inept, its torquing thrusts reduced to gasping twitches.

Hemi removed the hook and stowed the gangion. Kai knelt and set upon the fish. He ran his hand down the tuna's broad, yellow-striped side.

He tapped Jeff's leg. "Watch how I do this." Kai produced from his belt what looked like a screwdriver, its metal end sharpened to a point.

"Spike the brain." He jammed the spike between the eyes of the tuna. The fish thrashed and then went still. "Make it quick. Better for the fish."

He swapped his spike for a curved knife. "Bleed it. This guy fought hard and his blood's hot, full of acid. Bad for the meat." With delicate precision, Kai pierced the tuna behind its pectoral fin. Blood spurted and gushed to the deck. The knife was silent, but the scarlet so loud Jeff thought he could hear it.

Kai continued to edify as he unmade the tuna, his words as quick as his blade. “Gill it. Cut the fins off. Toss ‘em. Cut here. Run the knife all the way through. Pull the guts out. Toss. Slide it over to Tommy. He rinses it with the hose and then you pack it in the hold.” He looked back at Jeff. “Got it?”

It seemed simple enough. “Yes,” said Jeff.

The presence of the fish brought a new energy to the boat, and to Jeff, understandably so. Catching the fish was as exhilarating as baiting the hooks was tedious. It’s not called ‘baiting,’ for a reason.

He left Kai and climbed down into the freezer to await the steaming carcass in the belly of the *Monkey Fist* as she motored on through the Pacific darkness.

Tommy dropped the smooth, cleaned fish into Jeff’s arms. Its rich flesh was the same color as the center of a ripe rainbow melon. Jeff had no sooner buried it under a few shovelfuls of ice than he heard Hemi scream above the echoing din of the hold, “FISH ON CHEEEEEHOOOOOO!”

CHAPTER 18

• Everybody thinks they work hard.

Tasha had set the mainline along a twisting ribbon of fifty-six degree water and the crew hauled it back in with tuna dangling from it like charms from a stripper's bracelet.

Over the course of the night, Tommy had frequently remarked that the fish were coming in at a fucking unbelievable rate, and even more often reminded the crew that their fucking pockets grew fatter with every fucking pound of bigeye and yellowfin they hauled onto the fucking deck.

As the sun broke the horizon and the final buoy was pulled from the water, Tasha's logbook marked sixty bigeye tuna and twenty-one yellowfin hauled aboard along with bycatch including albacore, skipjack, mahi mahi, wahoo, opah (at some point Jeff suspected that Tommy was just making up the names), a fearsome eight-foot tiger shark and a huge knot of snarled ghost gear.

Even though the ship's deck-mounted hydraulic crane had been employed to land a few of the heaviest fish, Jeff had felt every ounce of the 22,460 pounds that came through the gate. He had never been more tired. His second wind came with a two-hundred pound yellowfin around midnight, his third hit at about 2:30 and he caught his fourth wind after gobbling down some potato salad on deck at 4. After that he lost count of how many winds he'd burned through. The time seemed infinite, indeed. He had expected the Americans to be more slothful. His body, running on that strange devil's bargain of auxiliary power one gets after staying up all night, felt hollow but heavy.

At the aux helm, Tasha cut the *Monkey Fist*'s engine to a low mumble. The boat slowed and rocked forward. Tasha slid down the ladder to the main deck. Jeff had not seen much of her all night, but her voice had rained down a steady stream of baffling navigational updates, direct orders, whoops of encouragement and personal insults like so much salty spray.

Tommy sat on the freezer hatch. His Circadian rhythm was nicotine-and-work-based, rather than solar, so despite the very recent sunrise, he considered the cigarette he lit to be the day's final, not the first.

Tasha gave Tommy a silent fist bump and shook off his offer of a smoke. She jumped up on the freezer hatch and beckoned Hemi as he headed toward the galley. He walked over and turned his back to her. Standing on the hatch over him, Tasha leaned into massaging his shoulders.

As she worked out the knots, she looked over her shoulder at Kai. "Good fight, Kai. Nice job," she said.

She turned over her other shoulder to Jeff, who may have been asleep sitting up, and nudged him with her boot. "Jeff, long night, no? You sure you want to hang with us? Jeff?"

Exactly forty-six hours earlier, the *Star of Panama* had docked in Honolulu Harbor. Jeff had come a long way.

He opened his eyes and leaned backward to see Tasha. "Yes," he said.

"Good," said Tasha. "It's a long swim home." She finished Hemi's massage and released him with a friendly pat. "Kai's going to make breakfast. Get something to eat and grab some rack. We've got a lot of gear to fix and then we set again tonight."

CHAPTER 19

The second full day of the *Monkey Fist*'s voyage was much the same as the first. Shovel, tie, hose, scrub, carry, get used to.

"Don't get used to it," Tasha said as she climbed down from the bridge, where she had spent the morning consulting the colorful charts on her screens.

"This energy bar?" Jeff asked, looking at his midday snack. "I don't think I will." The crew sat on the freezer hatch. The boat was autopiloting northwest.

"No, the catch last night," she said as she stepped to the deck. "We don't rake like that very often."

"Fuckin' raked," Tommy agreed. "On the first set, though. It's bad luck, like catching a fish on the first cast."

"Is that true? Bad luck?" Jeff asked. He didn't expect Tommy, or any of the Americans for that matter, to be superstitious. But it was telling that they considered good luck to be bad.

"Worse luck than having a woman on board?" Tasha asked. She took a water from the cooler and sat down. "I've heard that one, too. You want to know about bad luck, Jeff? Ask these eighty-one frozen motherfuckers." She rapped the freezer hatch. "And tonight, you can ask their friends."

"Yes," said Jeff.

That night, Jeff was far too busy to ask any of the seventy-eight tuna that thrashed through the gate to explain just how they came to be in this fix. But had he had the time (and interpretive skills to understand the fish), he would have heard seventy-eight distinct stories that all started with the promise of a free meal and ended with a spike through the brain.

Around three in the morning, as Jeff wrestled yet another fat bigeye aboard, Tommy posited that the beginner's luck emanating from the new guy could perhaps be trumping any bad juju associated with their first-cast success.

A fisherman is always looking for signs. There is meaning in all of it for those who care to look for such things. The fish. The flutter of fortune. A gust of wind, a tint of sky, the look in a soaring seabird's beady eye. Of course, a fisherman is also always looking for an argument. Interpretation of the signs is rarely agreed upon.

Following the third set in as many nights, the freezer hold was packed to capacity. It was time to head homeward. "*Mauka*," as Tasha had said.

Once the fishing was done and the lethal mainline had been retired for the trip, the *Monkey Fist* took on a more relaxed, almost leisurely atmosphere. For the first time in days, Jeff enjoyed a full eight hours of sleep, although his dreams remained almost exclusively in the knot-tying/shoveling genre.

But working a fishing boat isn't one of those jobs where you can say, "I'm just going to relax and let my subconscious work on this for a while." The pace had slowed considerably, but the *Monkey Fist* still required constant attention.

"That's why they call boats 'she,'" Tommy said, as he and Jeff re-made broken gangions together in the shade of the pilothouse. "Also, she takes half our money."

The unprecedented success of the trip had prompted a lot of scuttlebutt about a potentially unprecedented payday, but hard figures had not been discussed, at least not within Jeff's earshot. To do so was possibly bad luck and Jeff was hesitant to broach the subject.

"First, expenses get paid off the top," Tommy said. "Fuel, food, bait, tackle. What's left, half goes to the boat, half to the crew. Tasha gets a captain share, I get a deck boss share, Hemi and Kai get full mate shares. Kai gets extra to cook. You get a googan share."

"Googan?" Jeff asked.

"FNG."

"FNG?"

"Fucking new guy."

Jeff was going to point out that the pay scale seemed to violate the spirit, if not the letter of the code of the sea, but you don't catch a fish on every hook. Some things are bound to pass you by.

The boat's air horn blasted. Jeff looked up. The green mass of O'ahu rose in the distance.

CHAPTER 20

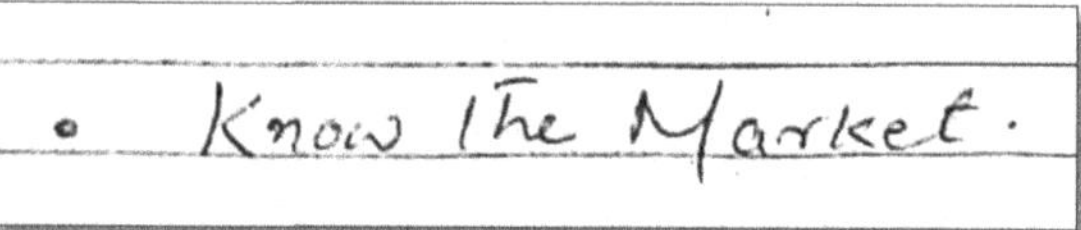

The *Monkey Fist* cruised under the Sand Island bridge into the Kapālama Basin and headed for the waterfront on the western outskirts of Honolulu. As Tasha guided the boat across the channel toward the city, Jeff noted that the *Star of Panama* had departed the GossCo cargo port and sailed on to wherever the next may be.

The *Fist* docked at a wide, paved pier near a windowless blue building with "Honolulu Fish Market" painted in meter-high letters in English as well as what Jeff assumed was the Japanese translation.

Now that the money was close, the pace of work picked up once again. After days at sea, the freshness and therefore value of the tuna in the hold was measured in minutes. Tasha had radioed ahead to announce their arrival and three forklifts stood waiting on the pier in a short queue. Tasha docked the boat, disembarked and disappeared into the market to do some pre-negotiating. Tommy climbed up to the pier and stood by the forklifts. Hemi manned the boat's crane. Kai and Jeff opened the freezer hold and hooked the tails of their frozen catch, a half-dozen at a time, to the crane cable. Hemi hoisted the fish up and out onto the forklift's pallets where Tommy tagged them with an identifying sticker and sent them on into the market. Jeff couldn't help but notice how much the giant fish dangling from the cable resembled the tiny bait that had lured them into this mess in the first place.

When the last of the fish were unloaded, Kai climbed the ladder out of the hold. Before Jeff could follow, Kai turned and said, "Now we clean out the ice."

He disappeared and left Jeff in the hold, staring up into a square of Hawaiian sky. A moment later, a large plastic barrel rattled through the opening and landed with a crunch on the slushy ice at the bottom of the hold. There was a single shovel in the barrel. By 'we,' Kai meant Jeff would shovel two feet of gray ice into the barrel, Hemi would hoist the barrel out of the hold by crane and Kai would tip the barrel out into the harbor. While pondering this division of labor, it occurred to Jeff that Tommy had failed to mention a 'shoveler share' when breaking down the pay scale earlier.

Shovel by shovel and barrel by barrel, the ice was cleaned out. When Jeff deposited the last scoop, he tossed the shovel in after it. The barrel rose from the hold and just as Jeff reached for the ladder to climb out, a hose dropped through the hatch. The hose (as any kid working at a car wash fundraiser will tell you) represented a promotion. Kai peered down and said, "Wash it out, and you're done."

Minutes later, Jeff was chasing the last of the trip's oily, scaly flotsam down the hold's drain when Tasha's head appeared above him, framed in the sky blue square.

"Nice job," she said, her voice echoing in the empty space as she inspected the spotless hold.

Jeff turned off the hose and looked up. A centimeter-thick envelope dropped into the hold and landed in his palm.

CHAPTER 21

• Act like the natives.

They say that prostitution is the oldest profession, but as they often are, they're wrong. Think about it. In order for anything to be called a profession, the professional would have to accept payment; money would have to change hands. Who, pray tell, was paying these prostitutes, and furthermore, with *what*? If prostitution is the old*est* profession, then by definition we must accept that in this alleged (and horny) economic prehistory there were no other professions in existence. Therefore, there would be no circulation of disposable income to stimulate supply, and thus, market demand for even the greatest mousetrap man has ever known could not exist. All of which is to say that it's fisherman. Fisherman is the oldest profession. (Although prostitution is a very close second.) Jeff had been paid $3,060.

The fisherman has a millennia-long and strange relationship with money. Constantly in need of it, yet can't seem to get rid of it fast enough.

"*Pau hana*," Tasha announced. The *Fist* was tied up at the Sand Island marina once again and the crew was gathered on deck. The sun was about to sink behind the mountains to the west, throwing the ridgeline into dark, jagged relief as though the lower half of the sky had been torn away to reveal the unlit backstage of the universe.

"Can't," said Tommy. "I've got a date."

Tasha said, "Yeah? Spill the tea, Thomas. With who? Your laptop?"

Tommy smiled and lit up a cig. "No. But like porn, I'll know her when I see her."

"Come to the IC with us. Have a drink."

Tommy shook his head. "That spot's been fished out."

Tasha shrugged. "Don't fall in love and run away. We're going back out in a few days." She turned to the brothers. "Hemi? Kai? Coming with? Call your wives to meet us there."

Kai said, "I called from the market after we got paid. Junie's getting something ready back at the house. Come with us. There's plenty." He looked at Jeff. "You come, too."

Tasha shook her head. "Next time. I've got to get into the city. Say hi to Junie and Mal for me." She turned to Jeff. "Jeff? Looks like you're the belle of the ball. You want to go with these guys for a homecooked meal and wholesome family fun or come watch your captain get drunk at a dive bar?"

Cash, women, porn, liquor, plentiful food, options. Now this was the America Jeff had been told to expect. "Thank you for the invitation, Kai," he said. "But I think I will join the captain."

That small dimple flashed in and out as Tasha said, "OK." She extended a fist. "Nice trip, boys. Bring it in." Her fist was met by four others.

"1-2-3 MONKEYFIST!"

Tasha climbed up the ladder to the bridge and disappeared. Jeff waited on deck as Tommy, Hemi and Kai all went below and came back with their seabags shouldered. They tossed Jeff quick waves and disembarked the boat, heading to Tommy's truck in the marina parking lot.

Tasha's seabag landed on the deck with a soft thud. She slid down the ladder and hefted it to her shoulder over the strap of a scarred and water-stained leather satchel that hung at her opposite hip.

"Where's your stuff, Jeff?" she asked.

Jeff's stuff was down in the bunkroom, all of it sorely in need of a turn in that washer-dryer. A realization had begun to dawn on him with Kai's mention of 'the house.' A realization that rose further as he watched the crew carry their belongings away. Tasha's question now bathed his ignorance in a blinding light. "Captain, I thought that we… do… we not… live on the boat?"

Tasha dropped her bag and took a deep breath. "No. Nobody lives on the boat, man."

"Ah," said Jeff. "I'm sorry. I didn't understand. It's just that the beds, the kitchen—er, galley…"

"Do you need a place to live?" Tasha asked. Complicated lives.

"Well. Yes. Again, I thought it was included in the mate job."

"A hundred bucks a week. Up front." She held out her hand.

"In the bow?" Jeff asked. The front of the boat was a cramped triangular compartment. "Couldn't I stay in the bunk room?"

"*Pay me* up front, dummy." Tasha's hand remained out.

Jeff pulled his pay envelope from his pocket, carefully pinched out five twenties (the largest sum of money he had ever parted with) and handed them over.

Tasha slipped the cash in her back pocket. "No wahine on my boat, Jeff."

Jeff nodded and reminded himself to ask Kai what "wahine" is later. In the meantime, it seemed best to just keep any further questions to himself.

Tasha said, "And you're buying the first round." She kicked her bag toward him. "And you're doing my laundry tomorrow. Now let's go, I'm hungry. Also, wash everybody's nasty bedsheets."

Tasha's blue Toyota Tacoma pickup had a bumper sticker that read:

FUCK THE PATRIARCHY

That's it, baby. Fuck it real good.
Oh yeah, just like that.

A lime-sized monkey's fist knot of yellow paracord swung at the end of Tasha's keychain as she cranked the engine, and a few minutes later, at last, Jeff Zachary crossed the bridge from Sand Island and infiltrated Honolulu proper.

From the open windows, warm tropical air washed over him like Hawaiian 105 KINE, the Hawaiian music station. Tasha clearly enjoyed the music. "Wahine" was definitely not music.

Across the bridge, the waterfront was unmarked boat yards, giant round oil tanks and warehouses. Some of the buildings stretched to fill an entire block, with truck-sized bays beyond counting. Jeff recognized the public-facing side of the blue fish market building on his right as they drove past.

Tasha turned left, away from the water and they entered a different sort of commercial area, brighter and more colorful than the flat-painted, industrial vibe of the seagoing trades.

Glass. A lot of plate glass. Jeff waved to his reflection as it rippled across the storefronts. He rode the warm wave of wind with his palm.

"Life's like that," Tasha said, seeing Jeff's arm dip and rise. "It'll drive you up or drive you down. All depends on your attitude."

"Yes," Jeff said.

They stopped at a red light next to an orange, three-wheeled motorcycle-car, disorientingly futuristic. Before he could stop himself, Jeff thought, *What year is it here?*

Across the street, in front of a car dealer, a tubular inflatable man popped and locked to beckon the general public to come within. Even if they had bad credit or no credit whatsoever. That was notable.

The light turned green. The next block was a single strip mall building where one could: Obtain a cell phone, eat tacos, eat pizza, eat noodles (all of which sounded good to Jeff), get a massage (also intriguing), purchase fine wines and liquors, consult an attorney, buy a pet, and about a dozen other things. Jeff tried, but it was impossible to take in the details of every last sign and grease-painted window. He was unable to find any mention of "wahine" among them, despite an extra-close look at the fine wine and liquors place as they trucked past.

Another few blocks and Tasha turned into the parking lot of a one-story building with decorative brown tiles running along an overhanging roof. The meter-square tiles, the visual signature of the United States Post Office Kapālama Station, Honolulu Hawaii 96817, looked costly, but upon closer scrutiny, each tile was drably identical and Jeff concluded that there was no message or artistic meaning behind them other than the obvious "Welcome to a government building."

"I have to grab my mail, I'll just be minute," Tasha said. She parked the pickup truck and hopped out. The yellow monkey's fist still swung from the ignition.

In the slack hours of their trip homeward from the fishing grounds, Kai had taught Jeff how to tie their boat's namesake knot, but all of Jeff's efforts thus far looked like loose spaghetti around a fork, not these tight orbs everyone else was getting.

The engine was still idling. Had the captain forgotten to turn off the engine? Using fuel like this, just sitting in a lot was grossly wasteful. ("Use sparingly that which you can.") Unless the truck was left running for some specific reason? Would Tasha be upset if Jeff was to reach over and twist the key off? Or would she thank him for his thoughtful and thrifty alertness? On the boat, Tasha had been very strict about certain rules and pretty loose with some others and Jeff was still struggling to sort out her system. It would require more study. But if he had to guess Tasha's intent about the running engine? Jeff certainly heard a lot of talk about the high price of fuel while they were on the boat, so Tasha would definitely want the engine shut off. He reached for the keys.

On the other hand, the boat's engine was never shut off at any point during the trip. And Tasha had never demonstrated absent-mindedness, let alone to the degree that would cause one to walk away from one's running vehicle, so therefore Tasha intended to leave the truck running and Jeff should not shut it down. His hand drew back.

On a third hand—

Tasha snatched the door open and swung into the driver's seat. She tossed a rubber-banded clutch of mail onto the dashboard.

"You thirsty, Jeff?"

"Yes. Did you mean to leave the truck running while you went inside?"

"Yes," Tasha replied. "Oh, I love this song." She turned up the radio and music flooded the cab.

Rahim entered Jeff's thoughts. He would enjoy this truck's sound system, which was far, far, superior to that of the rattling van they rode out of Zazaristan two weeks ago.

Tasha pulled out of the Post Office's lot and turned east.

A few blocks later, a squat brick building informed passersby in neon letters, "WE BUY GOLD!" *Of course*, thought Jeff. Gold is valuable. Who wouldn't want to buy some? Presumably the car dealer, the taco restaurant, the pet shop, and possibly even the Post Office (Jeff wasn't sure how integrated the various American governmental bureaus were. The Post Office and the Federal Reserve, for example.) would all buy gold if the price was right. The unseemly outright declaration of this strange building had a whiff of desperation that surely put them in a weakened position when it came time to bargain? The Tacoma drove on.

Unlike its neighbors with their garish commercial bleatings, The Intercontinental Lounge favored a small, poorly lit sign. The building sat on the corner of Kukui Street and Nu'uanu Avenue, but faced neither street. It shared a lot on Kukui with two truckdoored warehouses and all three buildings faced inward toward their shared parking area, as if none could afford to take their eyes off the comings and goings of their clientele (or each other) for a second.

Tasha pulled her truck into the lot, backed it into a spot and dropped the keys on the floor. Jeff got out and paused to take in the skyscrapers that loomed a few blocks to the east. They made the stacked shipping containers back in Quudia look like a child's blocks.

According to the sticker-lettered sign on the smoked glass door, the Intercontinental offered "Liquor in the front, Poke in the rear" as well as "Karaoke 7 days." Jeff had no idea what "Poke" meant, but the rest of it was made clear enough when he followed Tasha inside and was greeted by a cocktail bar and an amateurish version of Taylor Swift's "Getaway Car."

At first, it seemed the busy room was segregated by sex: Women at the round tables in the center of the room and the men seated at the U-shaped bar on the right, but Jeff soon saw a few exceptions. In fact, Tasha was one of them. She had waved off the hostess stationed near the door and began weaving through the tables to claim one of two open seats at the far end of the U, near a Golden Tee golf video game.

Behind the bar, scores of liquor bottles glittered like jewels in the grass-green light of a baseball match played mutely on a TV hanging from the ceiling.

A brief moment of elucidation. When it comes to alcohol, Zazaristan is, by and large, a temperate nation. Dry as the desert sands that blow across her plains. However. Among certain elements of her more discreet citizenry, in select circumstances and locations, a gentleman may find the opportunity to slake his thirst.

A bartender came over and dealt out two cocktail napkins.

"The usual?" he asked Tasha.

"Yeah. Thanks, Brad. Start a tab." She flicked her head toward Jeff to indicate where the tab should land. She turned to watch the singer do the chorus.

Brad the bartender turned his attention to Jeff. "How 'bout you, my dude?"

From the journal, page three: "Act like the natives." "I will have the usual, too. Thank you."

Brad squinted. "Do I know you, man?"

Tasha said, "This is Jeff, my new guy. Jeff, Brad. Brad, Jeff."

"Good to meet you," said Brad. "What's your usual, Jeff?"

Jeff leaned toward Brad. In a low voice, he said, "Wahine./?"

Brad shot a look at Tasha, whose attention was back on the singer. He leaned close to Jeff and grinned. "Me too, bro."

Jeff nodded knowingly for a few seconds.

"What do you want to drink?" Brad finally said.

"Yes," said Jeff. "I will have wa—whatever the captain is having, please."

Brad shot another glance at Tasha. "Aye-aye. Two Fid Street gee and tees, splash of pineapple, coming up." Brad stepped away and began fixing the drinks. "Tasha! You just get back in?" he half-shouted over the music. "How'd you do?"

Tasha turned. "Fucking raked," she said. "They were practically jumping in the boat."

"Nice," said Brad, as he cut a massive lime into wedges. He impaled the wedges on tiny plastic swords and slipped them into the drinks.

Tasha glanced around. "Is he here?"

Brad set the two drinks on the bar and checked his watch. "He should be, soon."

"Thanks," said Tasha. She adjusted the leather satchel still crossed over her shoulder as Brad turned to tend to another customer. She raised her glass to Jeff, who was trying to make sense of the baseball game. "Health to man, death to fish. Thanks to the sea, that paid for this," she said.

"Yes," Jeff agreed. He met Tasha's glass. He took a close sniff of the drink and a measured sip. He guiltily noted that this stuff was liquid Hawaii, fragrant and sweet, wet, hot.

Tasha reached over the bar to grab a pair of laminated menus. "What do you feel like eating, Jeff?"

"Food?" Jeff answered, and then ate his lime wedge, peel and all.

Tasha put the menus down. She waved to get Brad's attention.

"Two spicy poke bowls," she told him. She pronounced it "pokay."

Brad tapped the order into a touchscreen. The opening drumbeats of "Love Shack" tumbled from the karaoke speakers.

Tasha took a long, ice-shifting drink. "So. What's your deal, Jeff?"

Before Jeff could answer, the door opened, and golden twilight spilled into the Intercontinental, at least as much as could fit around the figure that filled the doorway. He wasn't so much *wearing* a straw fedora as it just sat atop his exceptionally round head. His crisp, untucked, short-sleeved shirt had three wide vertical stripes, struggling mightily to provide a slimming effect. The man wasn't exactly obese, but if he were to step out of his flip-flops, Jeff expected that the rubbery soles would swell up to at least twice their thickness with a sigh of relief.

Tasha looked up when the door opened and the man locked eyes with her. He gave a chin-up greeting and started making his way over to the bar, waving greetings to a few diners and waitstaff on his way. Half the bar-sitters made an effort to make eye contact with this fellow and the other half suddenly became fascinated with their cocktail napkins as he walked past, slapping backs and squeezing shoulders (some harder than others).

Brad hurriedly poured an *okolehao* over ice in a tall glass, added a wedge of lime and the drink arrived at Tasha's elbow exactly one second before the man did.

The man slid between Tasha and Jeff. His girthy back brushed against Jeff and Jeff slid his stool away a few inches. The man took off his hat and set it on the bar. Jeff estimated his bald head took up no more than twenty percent of the hat's volume.

"What's the haps, Cap?" the man said to Tasha, with a grin.

Tasha replied, "Jonny." She drained her drink and set her glass down. Jonny picked it up and rattled the ice in the bartender's direction. "Brad! Another for Captain Hale! She drinks on me tonight!"

Tasha made a small nod of thanks.

Jonny reached into the pocket of his shorts and came out with a phone. The gold nugget rings on his wide fingers reflected the grassy light of the television. Jeff only caught a glimpse of the phone, but it seemed oddly large, much too thick.

Jonny said to Tasha, "Check this out." He put the contraption to his lips and took a long, chest-swelling drag.

Jeff saw that Jonny had somehow strapped or taped his phone back-to-back with a black vaping box.

Tasha's second drink arrived and she turned her attention to it. Jonny nudged her as he exhaled a cumulus cloud of pungent cannabis smoke. He rotated the box, which Jeff could now see consisted of a *third* component: a short black tube, like a mini flashlight. Jonny pressed a button. The letters "JK" projected from the tube onto the smoke in dancing green laser light.

"JK? Just kidding?" Tasha said, sipping her drink.

Jonny clicked the laser projector off and repocketed it. The smoke cloud slowly dissipated into the black and dusty ceiling ducts. "My initials." Tasha seemed unimpressed. "Branding. Good for business," Jonny clarified. "Speaking of, you have something for me?" He glanced at Tasha's satchel.

Tasha swung the satchel onto her lap, pulled out a file and handed it to Jonny. "Fuel, bait, gear, parts, repair. Seventeen thousand pounds of bigeye, eleven thousand yellowfin, twelve hundred mahi. Average price, five-ten."

Jonny flipped through the papers. "It was five-twenty-five on Wednesday," he said.

Tasha shrugged. "On Wednesday, we were three hundred miles from the market." She reached back into the satchel and placed a brick of hundred-dollar bills on the bar.

When the stack of money came out, Jeff's eyes popped, but then he quickly glanced away. He scrambled to assume an air of nonchalance, glugging his drink and turning toward the TV in order to study a baseball player adjusting his crotch as if it were the most gripping drama.

Jonny stuffed the money in his pockets and nodded his assent to the logistical realities that bent the market this way and that. "I know. I've got satellite GPS on my phone. I had an eye on you. Great trip, Tash. When are you going out next?"

"We're off tomorrow. The engine's getting oil and filters changed. But we'll turn her around and get out to catch the backside of the moon Monday."

"Expecting another good trip?" Jonny asked.

"Should be," Tasha said.

"Promise?"

"You don't pay me for promises."

"For Natasha Hale, I make an exception."

"In that case, it will be the greatest trip of all time. Six, seven hundred million fish, at least."

Jonny grinned and flipped the file closed. "Enough business. Tasha. Go Your Own Way," he said. "Come up with me." He jerked his head toward the karaoke stage.

Tasha shook her head. "I don't think so."

"Come on," said Jonny.

"I don't sing backup."

Jonny said, "Stevie Nicks is no backup."

"I've been yelling at the crew for five days," Tasha said. "My voice isn't up to it."

Jonny looked disappointed. "Fine," he said. "I'll guess I'll just have to do "So Lonely.""

"Good luck with that falsetto, Sting," Tasha said.

Three women finished "Love Shack" and tottered off the stage.

Tasha called out to the bartender as the trio of singers reseated themselves at a nearby table. "Brad! Send these badass wahine a round on me!"

The wahine (Women! Of course. That made a lot of sense now.) whooped their gratitude.

Jonny saw his opening and made a beeline for the stage. Before the hostess could call up the next singer, Jonny was standing next to her. After a whispered, giggling conference, he took the mic from her and fiddled with the karaoke machine.

He took center stage and said, "Welcome to the Intercontinental. Everything on the lunch menu is under fifteen dollars," then proceeded to croon out a melodious, if slightly straining version of "So Lonely."

Jonny eschewed the final high note, opting to close the show by blowing another laser-branded cloud of pot smoke out over the audience, which obviously caused them to cheer wildly.

He handed the mic back to the hostess, bowed and stepped from the stage. Once again, Brad had an *okolehao* on the rocks ready when Jonny arrived back at the corner of the bar.

"You were right about the falsetto, Natasha," he said. "You sure you don't want to go up? Stage is open."

"Nobody follows the killer."

As he took a sip of his drink, Jonny looked at his gold watch. "Mm! That reminds me, I've gotta be somewhere." He put his glass down. "Brad! Put this in a to-go cup."

Brad sloshed the Hawaiian moonshine into a plastic cup and added a straw. Jonny grabbed the drink and bid Tasha good luck on the next trip. He reversed his glad-handing entrance through the bar, and was gone.

"Captain," Jeff said, as their spicy poke bowls arrived. "Who was that?"

"The Police," she said, snapping her chopsticks apart.

"That man, Jonny, was the police?" Jeff was now relieved that Tasha had not introduced them.

"No. That was the name of the band." She looked up at the TV. "Who's winning?"

"CHW has zero, OAK has four," Jeff said, pronouncing "CHW" as "chwuh." He copied Tasha's chopstick action.

"Big fan, are you?" Tasha plucked a shiny pink cube of tuna from her bowl and popped it in her mouth.

Jeff studied the two skewer-like sticks and made a few experimental pinches. "Who was that man, I meant. Jonny," Jeff asked.

"Jonny Kalawai'a. Everyone calls him Jonny K. He owns this place," she said.

"What was all that money for? How much do these poke bowls cost?"

Tasha put down her chopsticks. "Booze makes you curious, doesn't it?" she said sharply.

Jeff felt blood rush to his face. "I'm sorry. It isn't my business." He looked down and chased some tuna.

Tasha said, "No, it's OK. It kind of is your business. Jonny K also owns the *Fist*." She ate another cube.

"You told me *you* owned the *Monkey Fist*," Jeff said. Ah. The trick was to anchor one stick against the base of the thumb and pivot the other stick like so.

"I said she's my boat," Tasha replied. "Which she is. I'm the captain. But I don't own her."

Jeff managed to capture a cube of tuna. When he tasted it, all the work on the boat was explained.

Tasha said, "It's a long story that I don't feel like going over right now. Let's just enjoy the fruits of our labor." She tweezed another chunk of fish.

They ate their bowls to a crowd-pleasing rendition of George Michael's "Freedom '90," which earned another drink from Tasha.

There was a short break from the singing and the karaoke hostess took the mic to tell everyone about the weeknight happy hour specials.

Tasha said again, "So Jeff. What's your deal? What brings you to Hawaii?"

The clear liquor, and possibly the second-hand Maui Wowie vapor, had clouded Jeff's judgment a bit. A full accounting of his backstory was probably inadvisable, but Tasha was no dimwit. Outright lies would likely raise more suspicions than they would allay. Lies. The barbs in life's hook, aren't they? Slipping right in, great pain to get out. And so, like many a young man sitting next to an attractive woman at a bar, he draped himself in a loosely woven garment of truth and hoped that when viewed from a certain angle, if the light hit him just right, he could pull off the look.

"Money," Jeff answered.

Tasha offered a silent toast. She finished her drink and set the glass down slightly harder than necessary in order to summon Brad for a refill.

Brad swept away the glass. A man at the karaoke mic began growling out "Pennyroyal Tea."

Tasha asked Jeff, "You know this song?"

Jeff shook his head.

"Nirvana," Tasha explained.

"It does sound nice," Jeff agreed.

"The lead singer shot himself in the head."

Jeff read the lyrics from the screen. Of course.

A man from the far end of the bar wandered over and, like Jonny had done, inserted himself between Jeff and Tasha. The man and Tasha seemed to know each other, and from what Jeff could hear over the man's shoulder, they mainly discussed the price of tuna and diesel fuel, but more than once, the man mentioned that he and Mandy were broken up for good this time.

The evening went on and a succession of men, smelling of fish and desperation, stopped by Tasha's corner of the bar to engage her in conversation. Between these listing visitors, Brad the bartender also began paying Tasha what Jeff felt was excessive attention.

OAK went on to win the baseball game five to one. They declined to even take their turn to bat in the ninth inning which Jeff could not determine was meant as a show of gentlemanly sportsmanship or a casual humiliation of their hapless opponent, Chwuh.

At 1:45 Tasha dispatched Brad for a water. She turned to Jeff. "How drunk'r you?" she asked.

Again, there was nothing to be gained by lying. "Just enough, I think," Jeff replied.

Tasha puffed out a short laugh. Brad appeared with the water. Tasha took a long drink and without a word, got up and crossed the room to the karaoke stage. She waved away a question from the hostess and took the microphone. The screen remained blank as Tasha stepped to the edge of the stage, took a deep breath, closed her eyes, and gripped the mic with two hands. She mouthed a few silent words and then, swaying ever so slightly, she sang, a capella, a song in Hawaiian. Jeff couldn't understand a word, only that the song must have been about loss.

Toward the end, a tear found the dimple on Tasha's left cheek as her voice poured over the Intercontinental like glowing liquid rock.

When the hostess took the mic back, she immediately began coiling the cord to pack it away for the night. Nobody follows the killer.

Tasha wiped her face and stepped down, barely acknowledging the claps and cheers of the late night crowd as she returned to her seat next to Jeff.

"Captain," he said. "You sang beautifully."

"Thanks," she said, and gulped the rest of her water, feeling the eyes of the room upon her. "You ready to get outta here?"

"Yes. But are you… fit to drive?"

"Fuuuuuuuck no. You?"

"I don't think so."

"Brad!" Tasha called out. "Drive us home!"

"Sure thing!" Brad said. "Give me a few minutes. I'm just closing out."

"We'll meet you outside," Tasha declared, getting up from her stool and heading for the restroom at the rear of the lounge.

"We?" Brad said, and glared at Jeff. He had, perhaps with willful optimism, misinterpreted the 'us' in Tasha's request. He mashed a few buttons on the register, snatched a printed slip from it and slapped it on the bar in front of Jeff.

$385.50. Suggested tip: $96.38. Almost five hundred dollars.

"Can this be correct?" Jeff asked.

"It can and it is."

"But… Jonny said he would pay the bill," Jeff protested.

"He said he would pay Tasha's bill. Not your bill. Not the bill for all those drinks she bought for everybody who got up to sing." Brad tapped the slip of paper on the bar. "Do I need to ask Tasha for the money?" he asked, a little too loudly. Some of the customers who had yet to filter out looked over. "Can you pay your tab or not?"

"Yes," said Jeff. "Yes. I can pay." He carefully counted out cash from his envelope under the level of the bar top and slowly handed it over. The remaining customers went back to draining the last watery drops of their drinks, all that they would have to sustain them over the long journey home. Except for those of them who kept a nip flask under the seats of their trucks.

"Let's go!" Tasha said in her captain voice as she strode past the bar. "Brad! Meet us outside!"

Brad slid some of Jeff's cash into the register and the rest into his pocket.

Jeff fell in behind Tasha and followed her out to the parking lot. After a few hours in the air-conditioned Intercontinental, the wee-hour air felt like a warm bath.

Tasha went to her truck and bent to retrieve her keys from under the seat. Jeff then followed her to a white Tacoma with a cap over the bed. She leaned against the tailgate. "This is Brad's truck. He'll drop me off and bring you back to the marina. He lives out past the airport."

Jeff felt relieved that Brad the bartender would not be accompanying Tasha alone for any part of their trip, but it was a little concerning that Tasha was familiar with this character's vehicle, let alone where he lived.

"Jeff," Tasha went on, "Don't fuck up my boat. I'm trusting you to take care of the *Fist.* I'm not supposed to let anyone live on board. I can trust you, right?"

"Yes," Jeff said.

"I have your word?" Tasha asked.

"Yes," Jeff said.

"Your word or Claude Ohanu's?" She grinned. The drunk dimples were even better.

"Mine. Jeff Zachary."

The half-truths were like those poke cubes. One passes the lips and you're already reaching for the next. Jeff said, "You can trust me, Captain."

"It sounds weird when you say 'Captain.' Call me Tasha."

"Tasha," said Jeff.

The jingle of Brad's keys pulled their attention and Brad popped the truck's locks open. "Where can we drop you, Jeff?" he said.

Tasha gestured for Jeff to climb into the cab ahead of her. "Drop me first, I'm just up Nu'uanu." Jeff climbed in, and Tasha followed, "Jeff lives on Sand Island. Just drop him at the bridge later." She gave Jeff's leg a secret squeeze in the dark as a reminder that his living arrangement was meant to remain privileged information. Jeff couldn't decide what he enjoyed more, the squeeze or the secret.

"I live out past there," Brad said. "I'll just drop Jeff off first, then swing back here and—"

"Brad, I'm getting out at the first place you stop, whether it's Jeff's place or my place."

Brad realized it was not happening that night, but he took solace in knowing that Jeff would be returning home alone as well. He put the truck in gear, pulled out of the lot and made a right on Nu'uanu. "Turn left on Wyllie," Tasha said.

Jeff, for his part, was pleased that Tasha would be returning home safely by herself. He felt a duty to his captain. The code of the sea said to watch each other's fucking backs, certainly not the other way around.

Jeff was also relieved to see that Brad was unfamiliar with the route to Tasha's apartment building, and required turn-by-turn directions.

As they pulled up to Tasha's apartment complex on Liliha Street, she said, "Jeff. The mechanic is coming tomorrow. I'll come by in the afternoon. We're going out again Monday." As Brad put the truck in park, she said, "Don't forget my laundry. Thanks for the lift, Brad."

Tasha took out her keys, slipped out of the truck and disappeared into the dark breezeway between two apartment building units.

Brad backed out into the street. After a few moments of priapic silence, he said, "Sand Island?"

"Yes," Jeff said. At first, he had assumed that his agreement with Tasha to keep his lodging on the *Monkey Fist* discreet was to prevent the appearance of favored treatment amongst the crewmates, but after learning that Jonny K was the boat's true owner, Jeff realized that perhaps the boat was not Tasha's to rent and it was the jovial bar owner that was out of the loop. And Brad worked for Jonny.

"Where on Sand Island?" Brad asked. "I didn't know there were apartments out there. You rent a room at the marina or something?"

"Yes," said Jeff. "Oh, I love this song!" He turned up the knob on KDDP 102.7 Da Bomb All The Hits Now and they listened to a trance remix of "I Wanna Sex You Up" for twenty minutes until Brad pulled to the curb short of the Sand Island bridge.

"This is fine! Right here!" Jeff shouted above the radio.

"I'm not about to drive across that bridge, bro!"

Jeff got out. Brad quickly U-turned and drove away.

As Jeff walked across the deserted bridge, angling his face away from the cameras, the reflections of the bridge's lights on the glassy water looked like pearls on a string.

CHAPTER 22

• That which cannot be taught must be learned.

On Saturday morning, Jeff rose from his bunk as the sole (and now ranking!) crew member aboard the *Monkey Fist.* He did seven loads of laundry: Two of his, two of Tasha's, one mixed and two rounds of sheets. While Jeff waited for the clothes, he fixed himself breakfast and ate on the sunny deck, sharing a few crumbs with a friendly seagull he named Steele Cuboid.

When the galley was tidied and all the clothes neatly folded, Jeff left the marina and made for the morning's destination, his belly full, his underwear refreshed.

When you're wanted by the authorities, it's a constant cycle between being perfectly clean and cool, sailing namelessly through international waters with a crew of incurious fishermen, for example, and then there are other times when the heat gets turned up, such as when you're walking through a foreign city in broad daylight as a wanted fugitive who escaped apprehension using Claude Ohanu's abandoned fishing license.

And these cycles never stop coming. It was much like the laundry, now that Jeff thought about it.

Invisibility is like greatness; some are born into it, some achieve it and some have it thrust upon them. Growing up as he did on the streets of Taboor City, Jeff had gotten plenty of practice in all three ways. As he crossed the Sand Island bridge, he affected the pace, gait and demeanor of a ball-capped weekend stroller, someone whose attention would just happen to be drawn to this or that in the harbor, causing him to casually turn his face away from the overhead cameras as he made his way across.

On the far side, Jeff made his way past white oil tanks that looked like giant frosted cakes on the left and rows of warehouses on the right. The streets were busy with traffic and as Jeff crossed an intersection, he saw a blue city bus ease to a stop a half block ahead. The bus sank to the ground as if all four tires spontaneously went flat. Two people stepped aboard and the bus drew itself again to its full height and chugged away.

Jeff had a pocketful of money, more than he had ever had in his life in fact, even after the unexpected and quite outrageous bar tab he had to settle at the Intercontinental the night before. Even so, he didn't want to indulge in any transportation for hire. For one, he was unfamiliar with the customs of payment and would draw unwanted attention as he stumbled through a transaction with the driver. Also, he had no idea of the routes. Not that he didn't know where he was going. Retracing the route Tasha had driven the prior evening meant making a right at the gas station with the green logo, going past the post office, then left at the car dealer with a yellow truck parked on a giant rock out front. Just before the final left turn toward the IC was Jeff's destination. The "WE BUY GOLD" place. Pawn1^2.

In addition to their thirst for gold, Pawn1^2 advertised electronics for sale, and their front window sported the logo for Botcoin that always reminded Jeff of a pair of breasts. Jeff assumed they knew what they were doing with that.

Botcoin had been a mystery to Jeff until recently. As Shwarma had explained it, Botcoin was an untraceable digital currency that derived its value from work done on the blockchain. The "blockchain" part was left undefined. It was also unclear as to whether the work being done on this chain was to build it or break it, but eventually Jeff understood that it was not an actual chain, which made sense. No value there, after all. The chain was digital. Possibly metaphorical.

The man behind the counter of Pawn1^2, with his do-rag and tattoos, looked like a pirate/celebrity chef. He looked up from a laptop when Jeff entered. "What's up, man?" he said.

"I don't have any gold to sell you, if that's what you're asking," Jeff answered.

"That's cool," said the man. But Pawn1^2 day manager Ike Kekoa Jr. knew that already. This young man wasn't a seller, rushing right to the counter, carrying his cordless drill and shame. No. This fellow lingered in the doorway a moment to take a look around. A buyer.

Ike Kekoa Sr. raised no fools. Sell the customer his own time, he would say. Also, don't carry inventory on the floor for more than ninety days. Ike closed his laptop and busied himself at the counter while Jeff wandered past a bin of impulse-buy DVDs toward Aisle 3, Electronics.

Aisle 3 of Pawn1[2] had cliffs of coiled cables on either side. Adaptors, chargers, connectors. Batteries. A lot of batteries. Computers of every vintage. One section of the aisle was a locked glass case containing video game consoles. Jeff found the lock ironic. It was his understanding that everything in these American pawn stores had already been stolen at least twice.

Jeff examined the video games through the glass for a few moments, as one would a museum exhibit, before continuing to his goal.

Jeff needed a phone. Communications. There was much to report. The bulge in his front pocket wasn't because of the Botcoin logo. Jeff carried $2,200. $240 more was stuffed deep in his backpack in the bunkroom of the *Fist*. Another $100 was folded into the pages of his journal, which was tucked deep under the sheets of his bunk, where it would be safe enough. One of his crewmates spontaneously washing the ship's bedding was a remote, remote possibility. And $460 had disappeared into Brad's cash register and pocket the last Jeff saw of it.

Pawn1[2] had a wide phone selection. Some were obviously used, the previous owner's data wiped. Except that which gets scattered like dust across the internet. There were also prepaid phones, in plastic blister packs that hung in queues four and five deep on long metal pegs. There were cheap flip phones and some were late model smart phones that came with a Kgig data card.

Jeff selected a smartphone, including data plan, for $49. The phone's rigid package gave a shrill and tiny shriek as it scraped off its peg. And now, the big purchase.

Jeff carried the phone to the front of the store. Another customer had come in and was standing at the counter. The man took a gold necklace from his pocket and laid it before Ike.

Ike tweezed the necklace onto a digital scale and read the weight. "I can give you three hundred if it's fourteen carat and nine hundred if it's twenty-four," he said.

"It's definitely twenty-four carat," the man said.

Ike was already zapping the necklace with a pistol-like scanner. He said, "The XRF analyzer says…" The analyzer beeped. "twenty-four carat. Nine hundred it is." He put his scanner down. "ID?"

The man handed Ike a driver's license. Ike fed it through a scanning device, then handed it back along with nine bills from his cash drawer. He dropped the necklace into a slotted metal box. The man pocketed his cash and exited quickly. Jeff stepped up to the counter.

"Find what you need, friend?" Ike said.

"Yes," Jeff said. He placed the phone on the counter. "I also would like two thousand dollars on a debit card, please."

Ike started pecking away at his register. "Paying cash?" he asked, as if Jeff was about to whip out his Amex Black card.

"Yes."

A minute later, Jeff sat in the cool shadow of the Pawn1^{2} building. The demure nibbles of Zoey's scissors, probably the weakest of her many tools if they had to be ranked, were not up to the task of piercing the thick plastic bubble that packaged his new phone. Extricating it was a job for the 60mm knife blade. It gutted the plastic shell like a tuna, quick and clean.

Jeff booted the phone. He had not spoken to Rahim in weeks and was anxious to hear his brother's voice. He dialed the number they shared back in Zazaristan. Voicemail. Jeff ended the call and sent him a text:

> This is Jefir. I arrived safely in Honolulu Hawaii, USA. Working on fishing boat, making $$$. Stay safe. Call me.

Jeff sent the message and spent a few minutes getting Jeff Zachary up and on the grid with an email account. He returned inside the store and made straight for the Botcoin terminal.

Jeff created a new user account as JeffZachary262@wmail.com and after a furtive glance over his shoulder at Ike, he entered his password: 0be1isk! He tapped out a few instructions, and a 300 character-capped message:

> Have arrived in Honolulu HI. Is Rahim OK? Give him my #525-749-9688. Travel was good. Quudi contact was correct about all. I am working as a fisherman as Jeff Zachary. Phone does not work while I am at sea. There was a minor incident exiting container. I had to dump latrine bucket on a guy to escape

Jeff debated whether a period or exclamation point was called for at the end, but he had run out of characters anyway.

He assured the Botcoin machine that yes, he was sure he wanted to send 1989.771 botcoins to mohammad.mohammad54321@zmail.zaz, and hit SEND.

CHAPTER 23

• Absence of Connections will raise questions.

In the intelligence community, there's only one thing worse than when Mossad has a dossier on you: When they don't.

Eventually, Mossad will build a thin jacket on Wahiri M. Shwarma, including his adoption of the alias Mohammad Mohammad, but for now, Mohammad's identity and duties were limited to stealth emailing and trafficking in Botcoin. Shwarma liked to think of his alter-ego Mohammad Mohammad as a globe-trotting superagent who also did quite well with the ladies, but again, none of this will be documented in any verifiable way for quite some time.

What Mossad will ultimately have on Shwarma will go back only so far as when he was either twenty-three or twenty-seven years old and enrolled in the MFA program at King Abbas College in Al Quwar, Quudia, which, according to the Mossad report, is "ranked second best in the Quudian University System."

The dossier will contain some brief reports of his time in the program. One of Shwarma's old professors, for example, recalled him as "A bit much, but also lacking." Late in his first semester, the school's Office of Admissions discovered that Shwarma had completely fabricated the scholastic records on his application and he was asked to leave. He was given a stern warning about fraud by the Quudi authorities and a bus ticket to Taboor City, Zazaristan, the least expensive "extra-border" destination available. Mossad will also note that Shwarma neglected to return some university property including "library materials" when he left campus.

Shwarma himself would dispute many of these claims. For example, he would explain that he was granted a "gap year" by the school, and it was because of "bureaucratic incompetence" that his student visa was revoked, and that he had in fact, left Quudia of his own volition, but whatever the case, the part about Taboor City is true.

On the day Hamid dropped him off at the marble curb in front of Quudia Grand Station, Shwarma had never been to Taboor before.

He'd heard the tales, of course. Taboor City, Zazaristan was an almost mythic place in the minds of his classmates. And not without cause, it must be said. Hamid's roommate's older brother drove his BMW to Taboor City one spring break and he returned five days later riding a moped with mismatched wheels and wearing a shirt celebrating the champion of American football, Buffalo.

Going back even further in its long history, Zazaristan was once known as the Rock of Central Asia. Steady and strong, it was the solid point around which its neighbors flowed like a river as they churned with war and strife. Zazaristan was an oasis of culture, a mighty beacon of learning, prosperity and goodwill. But. After a hundred generations of the old people saying, "The youth today! Their slothful ways will surely be the ruin of us all," it actually happened.

Historians debate the exact point or cause of Zazaristan's collapse, but since most historians are old, they universally agree on the fact that it was bound to have happened at some point and the only surprise is that it didn't happen sooner.

Since then, Zazaristan has dabbled in a few different systems of government during their centuries-long struggle to reseat themselves. Centrally Planned Market Oligarchy, Proletarian Empire, Traditional Monarchy, Mixed Fascism, Second Wave Monarchy, Plutocratic Democracy, Full-on Anarchy, Uruguayan-Style Co-Participation, Social Republic, etc. All of them flawed to a certain extent, but to be fair, it must be said that each had their supporters as well. Zazaris are nothing if not adaptable. So, early in the new millennium, when the young and charismatic Zapar Ghachii promised that *when* the citizens of Zazaristan made him their next President (Zazaristan was at the time coming out of a Constitutional Fascism phase), he would provide every man, woman and child, every last Zazari citizen, with a nylon drawstring backpack (sunny yellow, featuring Ghachii's silk-screened portrait), and on that citizen's birthday, he or she shall be free, shall be *encouraged,* to fill his or her so-called Birthday Sack with any item or items that are being offered for sale anywhere in the country, free of charge. Ghachii's hope was that this Birthday Sack idea would stimulate the economy (and garner popular support). Zazaris generally thought the idea was sound, at least compared to what the last few governments had trotted out, and Ghachii won the Presidency handily.

The eyes of the world's economists then fell upon the Zazaris as they instituted this bold and unconventional system. To the surprise of most, all of that birthday-sack-exchange-of-goods created, like heat from friction, an external benefit. Every legitimate business* saw leaps and gains in prosperity. But even the most optimistic economic forecasts could not have predicted the exponential growth of the Zazari party supply industry.

In retrospect, the reason is plain. When a person's birthday becomes such a wild and potentially lucrative bonanza, that person wants to party. Balloons, decorations, costumes, tents, nylon drawstring backpacks, tables, chairs, all of it, came to be in major demand. Zazari party stores seemed to spring from the sandy ground overnight. Not only was the party store business booming, party store inventory was virtually impervious to the growing threat of so-called "Birthday Sack Retail Shrinkage." Look, obviously nobody's running into a party store to load up with cheap rubber balloons. And good luck getting a twenty-meter tent into a Birthday Sack.

With such a growing market, the only problem most Zazari party supply stores had during this period was maintaining market share, so when a young Wahiri Shwarma stepped off that bus in Taboor City, utterly alone and with the pong of fresh defeat blowing off him, there were a lot of expanding party store operations that were looking to hire

*Yes, even the jewelers, they have birthdays, too.

advertising copywriters.

Soon, on the strength of his interview, Shwarma was hired by Party Party Party Event Supply. It was while working there that he came up with the slogan "Party Party Party Party." Party Party Party liked it so much, they hired Shwarma as a full-time in-house copywriter, but he was let go after just two months for using one of the Party Party Party delivery vans for personal business.

After Party Party Party, Shwarma worked briefly as a stringer for a few Taboor City alt-weeklies, but the still-booming party economy never fully left his mind.

Mossad believes that it was around this time that Shwarma formed Shwarmco Security and Party Supply, where he was able to create and popularize the idea of "Party Security" and sell it as an upcharge to status-minded party hosts.

Among the influencers in Zazari party circles, it became fashionable to hire an armed Party Security guard detail to protect their parties while simultaneously impressing their guests. And never was it more impressive than when the guards from Taboor City's #1 Party Security firm, Shwarmco Security and Party Supply, would run off a truckload of goons at some point during the evening with a festive pop of warning shots. (But not too many. Bullets were a major expense, even the cheap, reloaded blanks Shwarma bought. Two of the guns in Shwarmco's arsenal were actually theater props. He usually assigned those to the goon crew.)

All during the Ghachii years, business was great. Shwarma had a loose passel of about twenty men on his payroll, a van, a technical, two motorcycles and a rotation of a dozen flags emblazoned with the names and symbols of non-existent extremist groups that were designed to flap menacingly from the vehicles as they buzzed outside the gates of a client's party. On busy nights, Shwarma would juggle five or six parties and several hundred guests would go home impressed with the thrilling exclusivity of the event they had just attended, not to mention the calm efficacy of Shwarmco.

Eventually, President Ghachii was deposed. His successor was a Party Man, but not that kind of party, and his first act was to ban Birthday Sacks. Soon thereafter, the Zazari party industry bubble burst, and almost every party store went out of business. Parties were becoming few and far between and the ones that still happened were smaller of scale and had no budget for security. Business dried up and Shwarma was forced to lay off most of the staff, sell the technical and one of the motorcycles. He gave most of the flags away as souvenir gifts as a last-ditch effort to retain his rapidly dwindling client list.

Forced to downsize, Shwarma pivoted from Party Security into *Business* Security and found it to be surprisingly profitable. Costs were much lower, for one thing. Instead of hiring a whole truckload of goons, it only took one strange character loitering near, say, a hotel to convince the hotel to sign a security contract for protection from threats foreign, domestic and sometimes hyperlocal. Business Security took a leap forward the day Shwarma found that posting an armed guard at Business A and instructing him to stink-eye Business B across the street would make it a simple matter to approach Business B and convince them that the world was a dangerous place. ("Look no further than your own neighborhood, sir. Armed guards are becoming commonplace.") After closing the sale, Shwarma would always add a final precaution against talking too much with Business A in the future, ("I find them to be elitist, don't you, sir?")

Business was OK, but making payroll killed Shwarma every two weeks. Thousands upon thousands of zazars out the door to these guards and goons, goons and guards, dullards all, paid to simply stand and glare at each other when it was Shwarma who had done *and was doing* all the work. They should be paying *him*!

It was this line of thought that was running through Shwarma's mind one hot Sunday evening when the minor-keyed tune of the Ice Cream Whenever Truck came tinkling through his apartment window.

What if he told the goons—some, not all—that they were being promoted. Recruited for a special mission. In the West. Where glorious opportunity awaited. Or where all problems took their root. Whatever. That could be decided on a goon-to-goon basis.

He put down his pen and went downstairs.

The goons... he thought. *No, the men... no, the agents. The agents would no longer spend a long life trudging toward some mirage here in the desert. It is their unseen foes from overseas, beyond our borders that are the unruly zealots, not they. Here at Shwarmco, we are building something today, so that tomorrow will be yours, my young friend.*

The ice cream truck chugged past just as Shwarma stepped out onto his stoop. The truck stopped down the block, near the corner.

But how, you ask? And why? The answer is quite simple, quite evident.

At least three or four people would already be in line at the truck by the time Shwarma got there, two of them dumb-looking kids who would take forever to decide what they wanted.

Very simple. Very evident. The answer is very, very simple, indeed. Well, I would ask YOU a question. Would you say you're the type of person who enjoys a challenge, stealth adventure, that sort of thing? And honestly, are things really going that great for you here in Taboor? What are you leaving behind, anyway?

Shwarma joined the ice cream line.

Yes, he thought, with a private nod. *That's the key. A push in one direction AND a pull from the other. Both. This calls for a Grügel Frøj bar. Vanilla and that thick chocolate shell with the satisfying crack.*

The first kid stepped up to the Ice Cream Whenever truck's window and was quick in her decision, but like an idiot she asked for a sno-cone.

Is there profit in this? Obviously, it all depended on the goo—the agent's ability to find employment in the West. Plenty of Zazaris have moved to America, but has an American ever moved here? It's safe to assume that a man can make a decent living over there.

The second kid couldn't decide.

Agents should speak some English. And get to know a few Western customs in order to blend in. This training represents costs, of course. Time, materials. Transportation. Transportation would be the biggest one, for certain. But that's where the value lies, you see. It's not like the government is just handing out visas, passports and airline tickets in a Birthday Sack, is it? Shwarmco will provide all that is needed in the form of training, supplies and logistical support.

Cartoon character with gumball eyeballs. Big surprise there.

Hamid. Hamid is going to have to be involved in this. He published that book of poetry that has eight reviews on Wanglebooks, (Seven 5-star and one 1-star.) His LinkedUp page says he still works at the port in Quudia.

A young couple stepped up to the window. The man asked for spanachocokopita and the woman wanted strawberry shortcake.

I'll just call, no, text, no call Hamid up and offer him a book sale and five-star review (which I will have to write) in the name of every goon he helps to smuggle out of Quudia, plus ten—no, make it five thousand z.

It was Shwarma's turn. "Vanilla Grügel Frøj."

The training program. Again, just like with a client, the agent has to perceive some value here. English, customs, security protocols. All included in one flat price.

The ice cream guy handed Shwarma his chocolate-coated bar and took his money.

The price, the price. Would depend on a few factors. How much Hamid wants, the desperation of the agent. The price should be high, unexpectedly high even, to imply value. At least... a half-million zazars. Five thousand US dollars. Fifty botcoins. Yes, whatever the amount, it must be in secure Botcoin, the funds being repaid from the agent's exorbitant, overgenerous Western salary. And there you have it. The program pays for itself!

He bit into the Grügel Frøj. *-crack-*

That's when he heard the gunshots.

CHAPTER 24

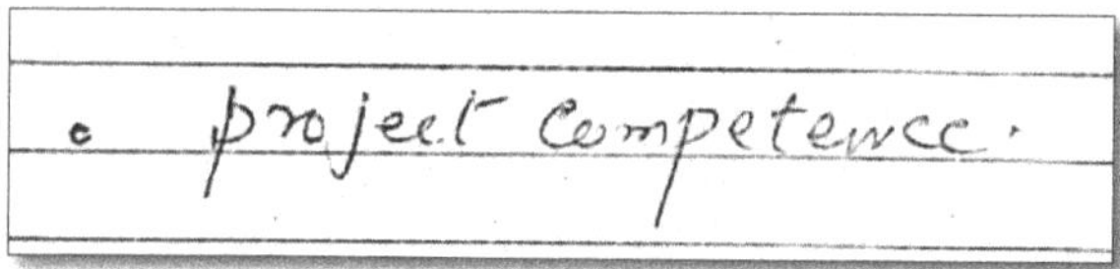

Jeff jogged back from the pawnshop to find Tasha and a marine diesel mechanic, who she introduced as her cousin Eddie, clanging around in the belly of the *Monkey Fist*. Despite the dimness of the engine room, Tasha wore her sunglasses. Jeff offered his assistance, which Tasha accepted in the form of "Anything quiet." Jeff spent the next thirty minutes standing in the corner. At one point he mutely held a trash bag open as Eddie disposed of a blackened oil filter.

When Eddie finished and was packing his tools, Jeff followed Tasha up to the sunny main deck.

"We're off today, Jeff," Tasha said. "I'm out. I have to do the drive of shame with Eddie back to the IC to get my truck. See you tomorrow. We're going out again Monday and we start turning the boat around at six. It would be nice if the coffee was going when I get here." Tasha turned to leave.

Jeff waved.

She turned back. "And thanks for doing the laundry. By the way, you don't have to fold my underwear next time."

"Yes," said Jeff. He lowered his voice. "Captain, please don't think I—"

"It's not that," Tasha said. "Life's too short to fold underwear. Look Jeff, a lot of this business is knowing when good enough is better than perfect. In a perfect world I'd know a guy who gets turned on by doing the dishes and ab workouts, but I don't. And don't fold the other clothes either. Roll 'em up. Less wrinkles."

"Yes," said Jeff. So it was core work. The training videos had been correct about that.

"Ready, cuz?" Eddie said as he walked past Tasha.

"Yeah," she said. "Laters, Jeff."

Jeff spent the rest of the afternoon on deck sharpening Zoey with his favorite of her many accessories: the removable whetstone. How clever Jeff found it, that stone. How neat-as-a-knot. The means to hone itself with something hidden within.

Jeff slid the stone away and checked his phone once again. Still no response to the text he sent Rahim. Some quick Wangling told him that Taboor City was half a day ahead of Honolulu and it was the wee hours of Sunday morning there. Maybe Rahim was asleep.

The "Your Botcoin has been accepted!" email had landed in Jeff's inbox only minutes after he sent it. Transfer of supposedly secure and untraceable Botcoin was to be his sole form of communication with Wahiri Shwarma. The $2,000 he sent the man represented almost half of the $5,000/50 botcoins Jeff had agreed to pay for the service of secreting him out of Taboor City and also for housing and protection in the five weeks that it took to arrange the trip. The money was also supposed to subsidize and protect Rahim, who Shwarma insisted must stay behind in Taboor City to serve as both a "Security Associate" at Shwarmco and also as a security *deposit* on Jeff's outstanding balance. If and when Jeff fulfilled his agreement, Shwarma implied that Rahim could, at some point, follow and rejoin his brother.

Jeff checked his phone again.

CHAPTER 25

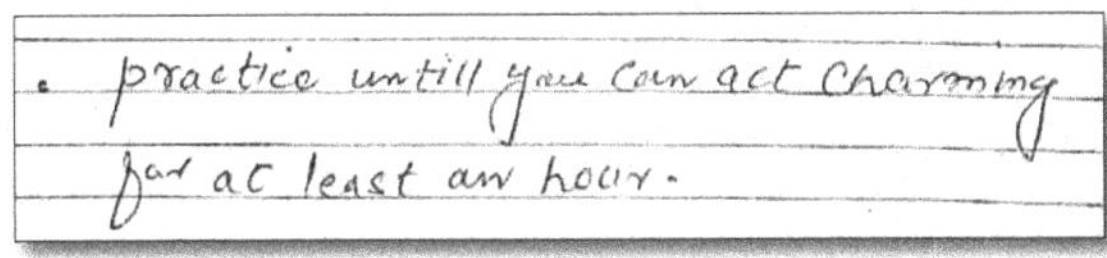

On Monday morning, Shwarmco Security and Party Rental held their weekly staff meeting, which is to say that Wahiri Shwarma and Rahim met outside the café on the corner across from the front gate of the park.

"Have you heard from Jefir, yet?" asked Rahim, from over a tiny espresso cup filled with regular coffee.

"Yes," Shwarma replied. "He transferred a nice amount of Botcoin yesterday."

"He did?" Rahim exclaimed. "How is he? *Where* is he?"

"Your brother is doing very well for himself in Honolulu, Hawaii, USA."

"Hawaii? The island state! But not Rhode Island, which is not an island at all," Rahim said.

"He is going by the name Jeff Zachary," said Shwarma. "And Jeff Zachary has apparently become a successful fisherman."

"Anything else? Is he OK?"

"That was it. He seems fine."

"Can I read the message?" Rahim asked.

"Sorry, I delete all my messages. Security," Shwarma explained. "Has Jeff not contacted you?"

"How would he?" Rahim snapped.

"Right," Shwarma said. "Right. But that's for the best, Rahim."

"And why is that, again?"

"Security," said Shwarma. "Perhaps you've heard of it from five seconds ago? It's in the name of the company you work for. It's the reason you are still alive, out here enjoying this fine morning, and not hiding in some dark hole from vengeance-minded zealots. Your brother seemed to understand the concept when he accepted my protection and I hope that's enough for you, Rahim." Shwarma picked up his cup. "Now. A toast to Jeff Zachary. Your brother has become a huge success. He sent two thousand US dollars back to our common cause! Much more than I was expecting so soon."

"I knew he would succeed," Rahim said with pride. "Does Jefir have a phone?"

"Who?"

"Jefir. My brother."

"I'm sorry, *who*?"

"Jeff," Rahim sighed. "Jeff Zachary."

"No, he does not," Shwarma lied. "Phones are difficult to acquire in the US without extensive documentation. They're worse than Quudis when it comes to that."

"How did he send the message? Email? What's his address?" asked Rahim.

"Do *not* try to contact him, Rahim!" Shwarma said. He leaned in. "Last month, when I called my old mate Hamid to propose my plan to spirit Jeff out of danger, which your brother agreed to, may I remind you, Hamid warned me that Quudi and American technology is very advanced when it comes to digital surveillance. 'You must assume every non-encrypted message is being read,' he said. He was very afraid of being caught and implicated in Jeff's illicit transport. He took a great risk to help Jeff. I promised him that we would keep our circle of communication very tight. And that we'd buy those three copies of his book. Thank you again for writing that review, Rahim."

"*Garden of Delights* was the shit, actually," said Rahim.

"Yes, but regardless, Hamid is right," Shwarma said. "We cannot risk contacting Jeff by phone, text or unsecured email. And there's something else. I didn't want to tell you this, but Jeff had to… fight his way out of the entry port in Hawaii."

Rahim set his cup down. "What? How? With Zoey?"

"I don't know all the details," said Shwarma. "But don't worry. As I said, Jeff's safe for now. But American security forces are no doubt aware of his presence. We cannot risk exposing him. All messages must be encrypted through the Botcoin system. Jeff is maintaining his cover and we shall honor his sacrifice by not exposing him with unnecessary communication."

Rahim nodded.

Shwarma pushed his chair back and stood up.

"Where are you going?" asked Rahim.

"The future, Rahim," said Shwarma. "The future."

"After the future, can we go phone shopping? You said you'd replace mine when Jefir sent his first payment."

"Of course. And again, sincere apologies for dropping it."

The slogan of Jama Tycaani Real Estate was, "Looking Ahead to the Future." It was on bus benches all over Taboor City, next to Tycanni's smiling face and razor-edged beard. And for the most part, Tycanni did just that. Sometimes a bit too far, however, as in the case of that two-year old listing for the three-story, mixed-use listing in South Taboor City, which had proven to be something of an unsellable albatross.

In his tastefully decorated office, Tycanni slid not a flimsy sheet of common paper, but a richly bound booklet, embossed with the Jama Tycanni Real Estate logo, across his tidy desk. "Do you enjoy park views, Mr. Shwarma?" he asked. "I've had a lot of interest in this location. The price is very reasonable."

Shwarma opened the creamy folder. It was all glossy pages of sunbeams slanting artfully across polished marble floors, close-ups of millwork and kinetic adjectives. The monthly price, broken out over the last two pages, was almost physically painful to contemplate. Shwarma shielded that part from Rahim, who sat next to him. "Perhaps something less, Mr. Tycanni," he said as he closed the folder and slid it away.

Tycanni carefully replaced the folder in his desk and pulled the albatross. "Expansive," he said as he presented the round-cornered file to Shwarma. "but not *expensive*." He chuckled at his own joke, if you could call it that.

Shwarma opened the file. “It has no windows,” he said, pointing out the exterior photo.

“What is your business, again, Mr. Shwarma?” asked Tycanni.

“Security.”

“What could be more secure than a building without windows?”

“What did the previous occupant do?”

“I’m sure I don’t know, Mr. Shwarma,” said Tycanni. “Such was the security of the building.”

“Look,” Shwarma said. “Clearly I don’t have to tell you that image counts for a great deal in business. I’m looking for something with greater… aesthetic.” Although the price was very reasonable.

“Of course, of course,” Tycanni said. “But between you and I, there is some flexibility in that price.”

Shwarma sat up a bit straighter. “My business is expanding, Mr. Tycanni. As we speak, things are falling into place that will allow me to deal in a slightly higher price range.” He slid the folder back to Tycanni with a single finger as if it was somehow tainted with low-rent germs.

“Say no more, Mr. Shwarma. I have just the thing for you.” Tycanni pulled another file from his desk. “Prime location.”

Shwarma flipped the listing open. 505 H Street. West Taboor. Three stories of filigreed cerulean with orange trim and arched windows. The interior looked cool and dark. Behind one of the windows there was a snug garret office and even Tycanni’s skillful photographer couldn’t hide the fact that the room was mostly desk, but the desk itself was a magnificent piece. 505 H featured a spacious reception area and common workspace, which could be purposed as a conference room. Shwarmco employees worked remotely at their various guard assignments around the city and Shwarma quite liked it this way, because at the moment, Shwarmco headquarters was his apartment, but he had hopes of growing his administrative staff beyond just Rahim and 505 H would be the perfect location to expand Shwarmco now that the Overseas Agent Program was flourishing thanks to Shwarma's bold vision (and Jefir's somewhat inexplicable success).

Shwarma tipped the folder toward Rahim to show him the photos. "Do you know the West Side, Rahim?"

"Not very well," Rahim said, studying the pictures.

Shwarma flipped to the final page and the office's monthly cost. Surely, this was just a beginning point to negotiations. He composed himself and flipped the booklet closed. If this well-coiffed realtor would be more reasonable, the days of Wahiri Shwarma taking his morning coffee on a public street corner under the blazing sun like some common laborer would soon be a distant, odorous memory.

"That price is an affront," he declared. But manageable. IF Jefir doesn't get twisted over there.

"I'm afraid I cannot let it go for much less," Tycanni said. "That address is very much in demand."

"I'm interested," said Shwarma. "As I said, I have a very large deal in the works right now." If Jefir proved to be a consistent earner, Shwarma could actually swing this. "If things go the way I expect, I will come back next week to make an offer."

Tycanni gave the obligatory warning that properties like 505 H don't come along every day, then shook hands with Shwarma. "I shall look forward to hearing from you, Mr. Shwarma," he said. "Do you have any other questions?"

"Yes. Where do you get your beard done?"

CHAPTER 26

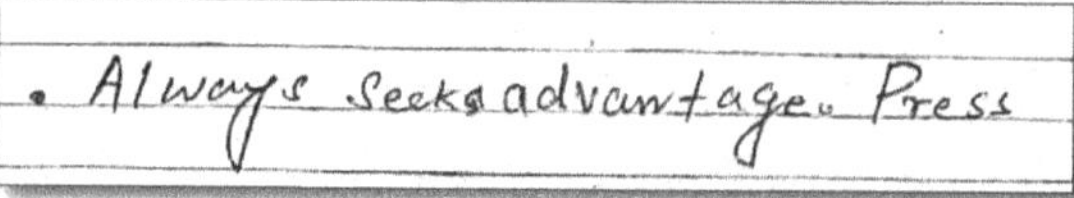

The Dapper Man's Grooming, Barbering and Social Club, commonly known as the Dapper, was the ground floor tenant of a pink, three-story building a few blocks north of Taboor Square Park. Built during the heady, economically booming days of the Birthday Sack Bubble by a Quudi developer, using Zazari craftsmen, the building was inspired by Creole Style architecture, such as one would find on Bourbon Street in New Orleans. White iron railings, ornately wrought to look like vines, belted the second and third-floor balconies.

In that National Geographic article, the written form of the Zazarish language was described as "ornately wrought." So it was perhaps no surprise that Zazarish jokes, most of them quite literally made at the expense of the Quudis (with America catching a few strays), twisted with surreptitious elegance through the iron vines of the railings, belying the generally lowbrow nature of the humor itself.

The humor went literally over Shwarma's head as he approached the Dapper that morning with Rahim in tow. He noted the "By Appointment

Only" sign on the door and below that, the stickered Botcoin logo, which was becoming more and more common around the city. There was a terminal, for example, in Jazzy Cuts, which Shwarma occasionally used as an ATM when he stopped in for his semimonthly beard shape-up.

If there was anything Shwarma liked more than the feeling of walking around with a sharp beard, it was having a plump roll of cash in his pocket. He stacked his zazars in descending denominations so that the various portraits of kings, emirs and presidents all faced the same direction, then did the same with whatever collection of US dollars he had at the time. He would then put the two stacks back-to-back, fold them in half zazar-side-out, and secure them with a wide rubber band. Recent expenditures, however, had thinned his roll to a Z100,000 note, two 10,000s, a 500, four US singles, two twenties and a lone hundred. Sadly, its center could not hold against the rubber band and Shwarma had to truss up the sorry-looking operation with a splint made from his debit card and various laminated IDs. But not for long! This sudden and unexpected windfall from Jefir would fatten his pocket with cash quite nicely, and the fact that the gains were drained from the United States economy made it all the better.

And what better way to drain it than with Botcoin? Dealing in the cryptocurrency required nothing more than an email address and provided the ability to move money anywhere on Earth instantly and anonymously. Not only that, but botcoins were an appreciating asset! The reasons behind this upward trend were difficult to predict or explain, but it was perfectly clear that the green arrow on Shwarma's Botcoin app zigzagged steadily up by the day, practically by the hour.

As much as he enjoyed seeing his small fortune grow, Shwarma had a business to run and that required cash. He paid his small staff in zazars (guards got 500 per day, goons 350) and payday always loomed. The van payment. Not to mention the pending real estate deal. All these hands and seemingly a hundred more tried to breach his pockets during the course of a typical day, each seeming to know when they were fullest, just as they somehow knew to ignore and avoid him when his pockets were empty.

Zebar Talmahani stood up as Shwarma and Rahim entered the Dapper. As one should think, the shop's doorman had a superbly groomed beard. "Do you have an appointment?" he asked.

"No," answered Shwarma, as the door swung shut.

The Dapper had two stations. An old man sporting a white barber's smock and an impeccably razored silver beard was reclined in the closest chair, watching sport on the television mounted high in the near corner. A cricket player named Lotfi was taking his position to bat.

A large man sat in Chair #2. His face was wrapped in a hot towel, but his bushy beard protruded below and it was being intensely tended by a young barber wearing earbuds. Another young man stood a pace or two away, as if observing or assisting in some way. He wore a green vest and looked vaguely familiar to Shwarma.

Three customers sat among eight chairs in the waiting area, all of them working cell phones. In the far corner, Shwarma spotted the Botcoin terminal, right next to a video arcade game with a trackball controller. It was Golden Golf Tee. Too bad the game wasn't SuperMegaBikes, the game where you actually sit astride a life-sized plastic motorcycle and control it with gentle tos and fros. It had been a few years since he had last played, but Shwarma still considered himself an expert at SuperMegaBikes. At one time, he held four of the top ten high scores on the machine in the King Abbas student center game room, which was the kind with four bikes lined up for head-to-head racing.

"This is a private club, sir," said Zebar, eyeing the state and style of Shwarma's beard and pausing ever so slightly between "club" and "sir" in the way doormen will.

Shwarma had to squash this attitude. He needed to spin things back in his favor, tilt the doorman off balance by subverting his assumptions.

"Yes, I'm well aware of that. I'm simply here to use the Botcoin terminal."

"I assumed you were here for a beard treatment," Zebar said, his eye again roving Shwarma's beard. It had been almost two weeks since Shwarma's last visit to Jazzy Cuts.

"The machine is right there," Shwarma deflected, pointing. "I just need to use it for a minute." He started for it.

Zebar quickly stood up and stepped in front of Shwarma. "The machine is for members only. Sir."

Zebar's sudden move drew some eyes in the shop.

Shwarma glanced around. There may be potential clients in this room. Fortunately, no former ones. The toweled customer sitting in Chair #2 had also turned slightly Shwarma's way. The large man's striking beard looked like it had been roughly hewn from granite. It dawned on Shwarma that maintaining this unkempt style actually required a careful tonsorial skill and he vowed then and there to never set foot in JazzyCuts again.

"Then I shall become a member," he said. "My name is Wahiri Shwarma. Wahiri. Shwarma."

Zebar stepped back. "The initiation fee is two hundred thousand zazars, Mr. Shwarma. Which includes a free Gentleman's Choice."

It never failed. As soon as his little dune of money piled up, some wind whipped up to wear it back down.

"See here, my friend," Shwarma said, a touch too loudly. "Obviously, the cost is not an issue. I run a successful security business that offers its customers the utmost value at a competitive price. And what kind of security expert would I be, I ask you, if I walked around with such a large amount of cash?"

"I would think the idea is to simply keep the cash secure," said the bushy-bearded man in Chair #2 with a chuckle. The man's barber remained stoic, but the young man posted near the chair made a mirthful puff, and Shwarma now saw this idiot to be some kind of lackey or executive assistant. Shwarma was glad he had brought Rahim along.

"Do I know you, sir?" said Shwarma. "I'll thank you to mind your own affairs."

The man made a tiny gesture and his barber smoothly removed the towel from his face. "Bashir Hallazallah," he said.

That's where he knew that younger guy from. He was one of Hallazallah's flunkies, Toasted Almond Bar. Shwarma met him and his partner, Bomb Pop, on the street that night they were looking for Jefir. The night that Jefir killed Hallazallah's son with a corkscrew.

Hallazallah said, "And I'm sure that we haven't met, Mr.... Shwarma, was it?"

"Yes. Shwarma. Wahiri Shwarma. Shwarmco Security."

Shwarma glanced back at Rahim, who had gone white at the recognition of the man who had a blood vendetta for his brother.

Hallazallah's ward was the neighborhoods of Northeast Taboor. He had been combing those streets for weeks, looking for Jefir Zaqq to avenge his son. It was the whole reason Rahim couldn't be seen in the market anymore and had to begin working for Shwarma on the south side of the city.

Shwarma caught his eye. "And this is my assistant Rahim. Rahim Lotfi."

"Rahim," Hallazallah said without looking at him.

"Sheik Hallazallah," Rahim said in a small voice.

Shwarma turned his attention back to Zebar. "Two hundred thousand z, you say? Again, the cost is not an issue. But I wasn't expecting to make such a large... commitment today. The next time I come in—"

"You'll want to get a deposit from him, Zebar," Hallazallah said. "You know, for security."

"Security," Shwarma said. "Yes, security is *precisely* the idea. That's why I keep most of my money as Botcoin. But since they've been invented since 1990, old sport, you wouldn't grasp the idea. If you will now excuse me, I'll continue with my conversation." Hallazallah stared for a second, then rotated his head away and allowed his barber to continue working his magic.

The old barber in Chair #1 was Samir Talmahani, the owner of the Dapper. He looked down from the cricket match on the screen to render his judgement. "Half today," he said. "Half next week." His eyes flashed over Shwarma's beard. "And I'll get you in the chair right now."

Shwarma could use a trim, it was true. And he felt he had pushed back enough, withheld enough. He'd forced The Dapper Man's Grooming, Barbering and Social Club to wait for the second half of his initiation fee, thereby proving the cash in his pocket more valuable than some barber's time. And "next week" was his preferred method of paying for most things anyway.

Shielding his thinnish bankroll from view with a demure turn, Shwarma peeled off his last Z100,000 note, then handed it to Zebar, who then passed it into his father's knotted and slightly quaking hand.

"Fill this out," Zebar said, producing a pentethered clipboard that pinched a sheaf of photocopied application forms.

"Zebi?" The elder Talmahani said, his eyes still on SportsNet Asia. "Manners."

"Excuse me. Fill this out, *please,*" Zebar said to Shwarma.

"Rahim!" Shwarma barked. "Fill that out!"

Zebar handed Rahim the clipboard, breaking Rahim's dazed stare at Hallazallah. Rahim corralled the pen and started to work on the form.

"And now," said Shwarma, "I will be using the Botcoin machine." He sassily added, "If that's OK with Mr. Hallazallah."

Hallazallah said, "Yes! Please, by all means! And take as long as you need, Shwarma. I feel better already knowing that a security expert like yourself is here keeping the barbershop safe. What if, God forbid it, some American SEAL team or something were to suddenly attack? Do please protect us, Shwarma."

Toasted Almond Bar smirked. Shwarma glared at him and made a few strides toward Chair #2. The lackey stiffened and his hand slipped under his vest.

"I'll have you know, Hallazallah," Shwarma hissed, "I have covert agents positioned in America as we speak. One of my men executed an attack… a biological attack, in a major American port just a week ago."

"Is that so?" asked Hallazallah. "What city was this? I'm surprised I haven't heard about it. I try to keep up with current events. A deadly attack on Americans will usually make the news, don't you think, Rizwan?"

"Yes, sir," Toasted Almond Bar agreed.

"Typically. Typically, yes," said Shwarma, glancing around. Rahim had taken a seat in the corner of the waiting area to fill out the application form. Shwarma went on, "In this case, however, the nature of the attack was more… congruent with clandestiny."

Rizwan said, almost to himself, "What the fuck?"

Shwarma continued, "Was my agent's bold attack deadly? Did it kill any Americans? No. Not *yet*. But a… bacterial… mmm… pathogen was released. It takes a certain amount of time to… incubate. I am not a scientist, Hallazallah. I've said too much already. What I just told you is classified information."

"This asks for the name of your sponsoring member," Rahim called out, tapping the application form with his pen.

Rizwan stepped closer to Hallazallah and said, “I know Mr. Shwarma, sir. Saeed and I met him on the street last month. The night that… we lost Bash. He actually tried to help us.”

“I thought I recognized you,” Shwarma said to Rizwan. “Toasted almond bar, right?”

“Put my name down, young fellow!” Hallazallah shouted to Rahim. He offered his hand to Shwarma “It seems we share an enemy, Mr. Shwarma.”

“Luckily, I have many,” Shwarma said. “Did you ever find that man you were looking for?”

“No,” Hallazallah said softly. “Although we shall never stop looking. Jefir Zaqq cannot hide forever. He killed my son, Shwarma. Do you have children?”

“I do not.”

Hallazallah said, “If it was my father that was killed, I’d be an orphan. If it were one of my wives, I’d be a widower. But when your son is killed, it is a grief so powerful, we dare not speak its name. Bash died once that night and again when I put his body in the ground. But he will not be gone until his name is spoken for the final time. Vengeance will be mine, Mr. Shwarma. This I say freely.”

Rahim, who had been chatting with Zebar at the front of the shop, filled in a final line of the membership application and edged over to hand the clipboard to Shwarma.

“Did I introduce my assistant, Rahim Lotfi?” Shwarma asked. “Rahim Lotfi, Bashir Hallazallah. And his friend Rizwan.”

The three exchanged small nods as Shwarma quickly scanned the application form, then grandly signed it and handed it back.

Hallazallah said, "I get my beard done every Monday around this time, Shwarma. Why don't you come back next week? Perhaps Mr. Talmahani would have an opening."

Only then did Shwarma put it together that Mr. Talmahani hadn't been working the entire time, despite having customers waiting. Also, Shwarma now noticed that the beard of Hallazallah's barber was slightly jacked up, whereas Mr. Talmahani and his son Zebar had beards that were immaculately groomed. A simple deduction. The Dapper's #1 man worked Chair #2.

"Thank you," Shwarma said, stroking his beard. "Thank you, but no. I can't—"

"Don't insult the man in his own shop, Shwarma," Hallazallah said.

"See you next week, Shwarma. 9:45," Mr. Talmahani said, without bothering to look down from the cricket match or make any sort of note.

"Fine," Shwarma said. "Rahim! Put that in my calendar."

"I don't have my phone, but I will make a note, sir," Rahim said. He bummed a blank application from Zebar and wrote: "Dapper w/ Talmahani Sr. Monday 22 July. 0945."

Hallazallah's barber put the finishing touch on and whipped off the cape. Hallazallah stood and paid the young man from an impressive wad of cash. "Excellent work as always, Taj," he said. He turned to Mr. Talmahani and accepted from him the Dapper's customary new member referral fee, which he then passed along to Taj as a tip. "See you again on Friday."

Hallazallah made for the door and Rizwan fell in behind. “Until next week, Shwarma,” he said. “Unfortunately, business now calls.”

Shwarma said, “And what business is that?”

“Security.”

Hallazallah strode out of the Dapper. Rizwan handed a nervous Rahim one of his boss’s cards and followed him out. They got into a truck and drove off.

Mr. Talmahani snapped his barber’s cape like a bullfighter. “You’re next, Mr. Shwarma.”

Later, outside the Dapper, Shwarma was examining Mr. Talmahani’s asymmetrical handiwork in the side mirror of his motorcycle.

Rahim asked, “Did you know Bashir Hallazallah was going to be in there?”

The Dapper was on Hallazallah’s side of the city, but there was no way Shwarma could have known Jeff’s vengeful pursuer would be there. He looked up from the mirror, hoping he might be able to even things out a little bit with scissors at home later. “No. No, I didn’t. But aren’t you thankful that I gave you a new name? If I spoke ‘Zaqq’ in there, you may not have walked out. Security, Rahim. Security at all times.”

“Yes, thank you,” Rahim said. “He didn’t recognize me.”

“How would he?” Shwarma asked. “He may have heard Jefir Zaqq worked at the market with his brother Rahim, but there’s no reason he would connect you.”

“How did you come up with the name Lotfi?”

"I thought of it weeks ago, Rahim," Shwarma answered quickly, shifting from self-grooming mode to executive-level jargonist. "As a delta-level contingency, the Lotfi alias was something I never imagined we would be using—well, obviously I *imagined* it, otherwise I wouldn't have been prepared back there in the shop, but nevertheless, it worked. And may I say that this chance meeting with Bashir Hallazallah was actually a stroke of good fortune? It proved that he is still actively seeking Jeff, but is no closer to finding him. Or you. Stick with me, Rahim Lotfi."

Shwarma swung a leg over his motorcycle and Rahim mounted his moped. "Although to be safe, you still need to stay out of your old neighborhood," Shwarma said. "Speaking of which, follow me."

Shwarma and Rahim rode downtown and over to the West Side. They parked on the sidewalk of H Street and Shwarma dispatched Rahim to canvass the neighborhood. "Ask the kebab places for the best coffee and the coffee places for the best kebab," he instructed.

With a task to occupy his mind, Rahim wandered off and Shwarma took a self-guided tour of 505 H Street, the blue building that Tycanni had showed them. In person, it was even more impressive than the realtor's brochure. In addition to the arched front door, there were not one, but *two* additional exits, located side and back. The ground floor was split into mirrored units. A bookstore on the left and Shinni's Café on the right. Upstairs, the vacant third-floor office space was locked.

Shwarma walked down into the bookstore. It had no signage whatsoever. The shelves were of random size and haphazardly arranged. In the front of the shop, if that's what it was, a young woman slouched sideways in a stuffed chair, reading in the morning light of the shop's front window. Her book had an embossed sword on the cover and was an absolute brick. A dainty round table stood on one side of the chair. On the other side, displayed in the window, a battered and loose-jointed etagere stuffed with books parallelogrammed slightly to the left.

The woman was the only person in the shop and she ignored Shwarma exquisitely. Shwarma sidestepped her chair and bent to examine the lower section of the etagere. He pulled the spine of a book he hadn't heard of. The woman put the brick down and craned her head around. "Do you mind?" she asked Shwarma peevishly.

Shwarma looked up. "Don't mind me."

"You've disturbed my reading," the woman said.

Shwarma narrowed his eyes. "I've done you a favor," he said, arching an eyebrow at the woman's book.

"Do we know each other?" the woman said.

"My name's Wahiri Shwarma. I'm thinking of moving my office to this neighborhood. Right upstairs, in fact." He began flipping through the dated, but still crisp paperback.

"Bina," said the woman. "Now, if you don't mind, I'd like to return to my book."

Shwarma pointed at the brick. "The king's advisor is the source of the dark whatever," he said, and walked out with a grin. Shwarma was liking 505 H more and more.

Rahim had reported, citing multiple opinions, that the best coffee AND the best kebabs on the West Side would be found, not surprisingly, at

Shinni's Café. Shinni's had two exits, a chrome coffee machine that was either two weeks or two hundred years old, six rectangular tables and two round tables, all with solid looking chairs and not so much as a single floating leg among them. Shinni's coffee was top-drawer. The lamb kebab equaled Tariq's and the chicken was *almost* as good, but even that was saying something.

As they sat at a round table in the back corner, finishing a plate of mini-donuts (also exceptional), Shwarma said to Rahim, "If your brother continues as he has been, we'll be enjoying this much more often."

CHAPTER 27

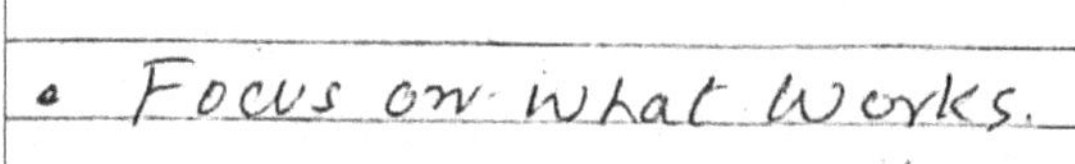

The bunk of a fishing boat and the king size bed in the Penthouse Suite of the Surfrider Hotel overlooking Waikīkī beach feel exactly the same to the person who has been up sixty-two of the last seventy-four hours fighting 30,240 pounds of tuna through the gate. Not that any such person has ever stayed in the Surfrider Penthouse. (The hotel commanded the price of, according to Tommy, "a fuckton a night.") Jeff would be no exception. But in this life, what more does a person need than a bunk and a purpose? And at the moment, as the *Monkey Fist* cruised past the Surfrider on her way into Honolulu Harbor, Jeff was rich in both.

And money. He was very rich in money, too. It turned out that fishing for (handsome) profit was not all that difficult. Obviously, Tasha's modern equipment (one of the devices on the bridge was literally called a "fish-finder") and her skillful captaining were the keys to making it so, but whatever the reason, the *Monkey Fist* was once again returning to the fish market with a packed freezer hold and Jeff was told that he could expect a second four-figure paycheck in as many weeks. Although, as one of Kai's songs warned, mo' money, mo' problems. It was concerning to Jeff that Rahim had not yet replied to any of his texts.

When the *Fist* had returned to island cell phone range, Jeff checked his messages. Still nothing from Rahim. Jeff thought back to Shwarma's many warnings about "operational security" and the dangers of unencrypted, which was to say non-Botcoin-platformed messaging. Was Rahim not responding under orders from Shwarma? Or worse, maybe Shwarma was right and Jeff was somehow broadcasting his identity and location to any government agency with access to cell phone transmissions, which was probably all of them. Only Botcoin messaging was secure. He would stop texting Rahim for now. There was a lot at stake.

Over the past few days, as fish after fish stacked up in the freezer, Jeff had started to imagine a near future where Rahim would join him in Honolulu and they would work side-by-side on the *Monkey Fist.* Back in Taboor City, Jeff had considered Shwarma's $5,000 fee to be wildly exorbitant, but now, after a mere two weeks of employment, $5,000 seemed a perfectly reasonable amount to transport a visa-less person across the globe, especially if that person would be armed with practical knowledge of how to evade Quudi and US security and also have a job waiting for them. The person on the *Monkey Fist* crew whose place Rahim might take was a problem that required mo' time to consider for the time being.

The next morning, while the poolboys at the Surfrider were laying out fluffy towels in the cabanas, Jeff jogged through the streets of western Honolulu.

His pay for the second trip was $3,210, minus $100 to Tasha for another week's berthing on the *Fist*, leaving him more than enough to fully settle his outstanding $3,000 with Shwarma *and* leave over $500 in savings, to boot. The best part was, there was plenty more money where that came from, just like the fish in the wide, deep ocean.

At Pawn1[2], Jeff sent $3,000 and the max 300 characters to Shwarma back in Zazaristan.

> If it is safe, please have Rahim text me: 525-749-9688. Now that my $5,000 debt has been paid, I'd like to arrange for Rahim to join me in Honolulu ASAP. I would be willing to pay some $ in advance for your promise to send him. Normally I do not pay for promises, but for you I will make an exception.

CHAPTER 28

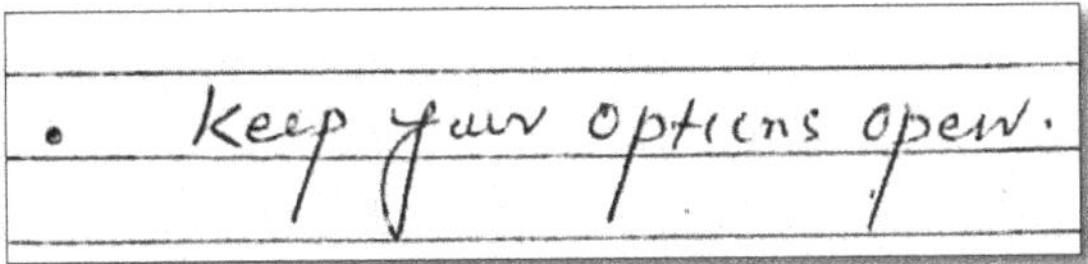

Mr. Talmahani, Shwarma's new barber, kept one eye on his work and one eye on the cricket and that was more than enough attention for each. The owner of the Dapper was at an age where there was very little in life he hadn't seen before, whether it was growing out of a man's head or on the cricket grounds. So he wasn't very surprised when a few months ago, his hands started to shake at the blade, just like his old man's had.

"Just a trim," Shwarma said warily.

"Who do you like in this match, Shwarma?" Bashir Hallazallah said from Chair #2, where his barber Taj had been stoically working since Shwarma had come in. Rizwan stood at his post, scrolling through his phone. Rahim had asked to be excused from accompanying Shwarma to the Dapper that Monday morning, still nervous about being around Hallazallah.

The TV was playing a cricket match. If there was anything Shwarma liked less than walking around with a shaggy beard, it was watching sport. He felt it was for children and the elderly. But he was in an expansive mood after confirming receipt of 30.06 botcoins from Jeff.

"Who's playing?" Shwarma asked.

"Bulacan vs. AFC 1," said Hallazallah, his face barely twitching as Taj's clipper glided over his bushy beard like a tiny, chrome-plated chariot sailing through the clouds.

"I vote for AFC 1," said Shwarma.

"I am a Bulacan man, myself," Hallazallah said. "As an AFC supporter, you must be a big fan of Singh."

"Mm. I feel he is a bit overrated," Shwarma said, thinking it a safe assumption/assertion. An assassurtion. His knowledge of athletics was something of a blind spot. He had stumbled pantingly through a small, but impactful sampling of matches in his youth. He knew a few of the footballers. Mohammad, for example. And the racecar driver, that British fellow.

"True," Hallazallah said. "Ah, here he comes to bat."

On the screen, AFC 1's #1 batsman strode toward the wicket. He took his stance, made a whistling practice stroke and glared at the bowler as if the man had just stolen his girlfriend.

"I suppose you believe Singh will fail in this spot?" Hallazallah asked.

"Mm. Yes. Probably," Shwarma replied, trying to move his chin as little as possible as Mr. Talmahani made his passes.

"Care to make it interesting?"

The only thing that would make this interesting to Shwarma would be changing the channel. “I don’t…” he said, and then with a quiet distaste, “gamble.”

“Gambling?” Taj’s hands hovered in perfect synchronicity above Hallazallah’s face as he spoke. “The mere making of decisions. I daresay rising each morning to go about your activities is a decision, and thus a gamble. Are you not gambling right now, Shwarma, by sitting in Sami’s chair.”

“I heard that, Bashir,” Mr. Talmahani said.

“I mean no disrespect, old friend,” Hallazallah said. “Merely a comment on the uncertainty of these trying times.”

“Zebi!” Mr. Talmahani called out to his son, stationed near the front door. “Schedule my old friend Bashir Hallazallah for a Number Three in my chair, next Monday at nine.”

“He’s Taj’s client, Baba,” Zebar said.

Taj continued working, his head bobbing with whatever was coming out of his earbuds.

Mr. Talmahani said, “Do as I say. I gave him a gift card for a free Number Three ten years ago that he never used.”

“Surely that has expired by now,” Hallazallah said, without much conviction.

“Dapper gift cards never expire!” Talmahani snapped. “See you next Monday. Nine.”

This is where your better lieutenants will pipe up with some important-sounding schedule conflict, but Rizwan just stood there like a dumb statue.

"Very well," Hallazallah grunted, staring at Riz. "But you take my point, Shwarma?"

Shwarma did not. But it was good to know about the gift cards. "I'm afraid I don't."

"This 'gamble' as you called it. You haven't even heard what I would offer yet. Please tell me Shwarma, that it isn't beyond your sensitive tolerance for risk to sit in a barber's chair while an opportunity for profit settles upon you like the gentlest mountain snowfall."

"I take your point," Shwarma said. "But God willing, life is a long season—"

"For the passive, yes," Hallazallah agreed loudly. "Look here, Shwarma." He pointed up to the television, where Singh deflected the ball with a short swing. "I choose to believe in this poor fellow. Unworthy of your esteem as he may be. A hundred thousand z says he hits a six." He rummaged under his barber cape and produced a thick wad of banknotes, drawing eyes from around the shop.

"A six?" Shwarma repeated. "Over the boundary?"

"That's what a six is, yes, Shwarma. Outside the rope. Anything else, and you win. A hundred thousand. What do you say?"

Singh took a massive slash at the bowler's next offering but hit it almost straight into the ground. The bouncing ball was easily stopped by one of the fielders for two points. Shwarma knew that much because two points equaled his amateur cricket career total.

Shwarma tried to work through the odds. He knew the thrower—the hurler? The bowler. The bowler was trying to hit the three-legged post, the wicket. He also knew, only too well from those times he joined in to play on Hamid's team, that, aside from humiliation, there was no penalty for the batsman when he missed the ball entirely. In truth, it happened all the time. But batting for six points in a single swing? Judging from the team's reaction when Hamid hit a six that time, the feat was rare. But a hundred thousand? Right now? It was a lot. Surely though, some of Hallazallah's blustery bet was simply an opportunity to wave around a big knot of cash in front of his lieutenant and Taj and all these other men in here, most of whose pockets were considerably thinner, and then have a good laugh when Shwarma failed to meet the challenge.

Shwarma held up a hand and said, "Stop for a moment, Mr. Talmahani." He reached into his pocket and pulled forth his own bankroll, freshly plumped from the Botcoin machine that morning. "Agreed. Anything less than six, I win a hundred thousand?"

No sooner did he say it, than the bowler fired a ball that skipped wickedly past Singh and knocked the wicket.

"Win!" Shwarma said. "I win!"

"Hold on. Were you asking me or telling me just then?" asked Hallazallah. "It sounded like you weren't sure about the terms and were still dithering."

"I said *agreed*," Shwarma quickly countered. He shot a glance around for witnesses. "Come now, Mr. Hallazallah. I won fairly. Don't give the impression to our fellow club members that you are not one to pay your debts." Indeed, every eye in the shop was following the action between Chairs #1 and #2.

"Of course. Well judged, Shwarma," Hallazallah said. He handed a pinch of cash to Taj, who removed one bill for himself and passed the rest to Rizwan, who *also* took a bill before handing the rest Mr. Talmahani, who took two bills and handed the remains to Shwarma.

Shwarma tucked away his winnings. He made a plan to go to Shinni's for lunch and maybe check out that weird bookstore again.

"Now this fellow," Hallazallah said, pointing to the screen. "Krishnan. He will hit a six for certain. What say you, Shwarma? Double or nothing? A six and I win, anything else, you win."

Krishnan corkscrewed to the dirt, such was his bewilderment by the bowler's first offer.

"Agreed," said Shwarma. Why not? His risk was almost zero at this point. Even *if* the cricketer, by some miracle, hits a six, the worst case would be that Shwarma would simply pay Hallazallah back with his own money. The small transaction fees taken by Taj, Rizwan and Mr. Talmahani could be written off as the cost of being seen by his new barbershop mates as a man not afraid to bet big and win. And besides, he was going to win.

Krishnan took a second anemic wave. If Shwarma won this bet, nearly Z200,000(!) would be added to the bonanza that was Jeff the fisherman's tribute. It would advance Shwarma's plans significantly. It would be more than enough to take on the payment for 505 H Street. Shwarma made silent plans to meet Tycanni the realtor later in the day to put a deposit down on the tony West Side, soon-to-be headquarters of Shwarmco.

The bowler lunged and flung the ball. It popped off Krishnan's bat, arced high, out of the television frame for a second, then dropped from the sky and splatted into the wet turf beyond the fence.

"Krishnan!" Hallazallah bellowed.

Of course. Shwarma's beard quivered. He forced his hand to move and slowly pulled out his money. Wordlessly, he counted out a hundred k, each note feeling like air driven from his lungs. He handed the cash to Mr. Talmahani. Instead of taking his commission, Talmahani just held the money in his hand, as if waiting.

"Go ahead and take your piece, Mr. Talmahani. I am well aware of how the world works," Shwarma said.

"I'm sure you are Shwarma," said Hallazallah. "I'm sure you are." He looked at Mr. Talmahani.

Mr. Talmahani said in a low voice, "Dapper members are expected to pay their debts in full, Mr. Shwarma."

"Yes," said Shwarma. "You are holding a hundred thousand."

"The bet was double or nothing, Shwarma," said Hallazallah, a little too loudly.

"Right," said Shwarma. "The bet is a hundred thousand. If I win, I get double, another hundred thousand. If I lose I get nothing because I only pay you back your money from the first bet."

"No," said Hallazallah, "Double or nothing means the bet doubles the second time. Two hundred thousand."

"Why would I make that bet?" Shwarma yelped.

"You didn't have to. What do you think the 'nothing' part means? You could have chosen to do nothing and not accepted the bet."

Shwarma said, "That's not—"

"That's not what, Shwarma? Not how they do it in Quudia?"

Shwarma was speechless.

Hallazallah said, "Sami, explain to Mr. Shwarma how things work."

Mr. Talmahani said, "Mr. Hallazallah is correct. I'm afraid you owe another hundred thousand, Mr. Shwarma. Do you have it?"

Zebar stood from his chair and repeated, "Do you have it?"

"Quiet, Zebi," Mr. Talmahani admonished.

"Of course I have it," Shwarma said, his face reddened. He snapped another 100,000 off his bankroll and thrust it toward Mr. Talmahani.

Hallazallah grinned. He lay his head back to let Taj work. He closed his eyes and opened his palm.

Shwarma looked in the mirror. "Fix this part," he groused at Mr. Talmahani, pointing to the right side of his beard.

When his beard was as good as it was going to get, Shwarma slid angrily from under Mr. Talmahani's cape and slinked to the Botcoin terminal where he sold another hundred thousand zazars worth of Botcoin and accepted the cash that the machine stuck out like a tongue.

Before closing out his Botcoin session, Shwarma went back to his previous transactions and read Jeff's last message again, the one with that sassy line at the end about paying for promises which Shwarma did not care for one little bit. Jeff wanted Rahim to join him in Hawaii.

No problem. Mo' money.

Shwarma searched the Botcoin machine's interface for a few minutes looking for a way to respond to a message without sending some Botcoin. Unfortunately, but not surprisingly, it can't be done. He sent .0001 botcoins to jeffzachary262@wmail.com along with the following:

> Transport to a specific destination requires a premium cost. Rahim's arrangements will require $10,000 US, all in advance. When, AND ONLY WHEN I receive $10k/100 bot, I will put Rahim's exfil plan to Honolulu into action. Or should I just send him and accept your "promise?"

Shwarma logged off the terminal and walked back to the front of the shop.

Hallazallah was still reclining in Taj's chair when Shwarma approached. The big man may have been sleeping. How much time did he spend in this chair? Up close, his beard looked even better, though. Like a fat purse.

"Hallazallah, that is not what double or nothing means, but I am a man who honors his commitments."

Hallazallah made no move, nor sound. Rizwan said, "Thank you, Mr. Shwarma. Have a pleasant day,"

"Yes," said Shwarma loudly, while giving Hallazallah's chair a subtle bump with his knee, hoping to knock Taj's hand off course. "I have many things to attend to. My American agent will be checking in at any time now."

Zebar held the door as Shwarma strode out and forth into Monday morning, already a hundred thousand light on the day.

A broader mind or some simple research would have revealed what sharper readers will have no doubt by now realized: AFC 1 and Bulacan play in the Philippine Cricket League. PCL matches are held on Sunday afternoons, when they coincide with Talmahani the elder's nap. Thus, he forces the shop to watch the Monday morning rebroadcasts on SportsNet Asia 2.

CHAPTER 29

• Your body is the only equipment you always carry. Run and plank regularly.

Can a person drown in rain?

It was coming down so hard Jeff estimated that at least half the air, the air which he hoped to keep breathing, consisted of fat bullets of water. The rainy season in his native Zazaristanian lowlands was usually one day long and unpredictable, so when the first drops spattered the deck of the *Monkey Fist* and Jeff's quickly upturned face, he felt a wave of thrilling nostalgia, like you would if someone walked up to you today and handed you your favorite toy from when you were four years old. Unlike say, a rubber salamander you named Larry, who now rests for eternity somewhere in your neighbor's bushes, this rain got old fast.

Tiny explosions of water fizzed every surface of the boat and her rubber-slickered crew. Shimmering halos bloomed around the boat's work lights. Droplets clung to the underside of the four millimeter mainline itself, merrily ziplining down the underside of its slope until, every ten seconds or so, the *Fist* would smash into the face of another wave and the drops would bail into the foaming ocean, which to them must have seemed safer.

The line snapped tight and the droplets shot up as if startled.

"Fish!" Hemi called for the first time in an hour. He grabbed the line. "Big. Tommy, crane!" he shouted over the wind. "Jeff, Grab the line."

Hemi let go of the line and inched down the rolling deck to unhook two gaffs from the bulkhead. Jeff gripped the rail and leaned out to get a hand on the line. Tommy took up position at the crane, but didn't let any cable out. One time, Dave let the cable get loose during a storm that was way calmer than this shit and the wind swung the hooked block right back into his fucking head.

The rough weather had come on sooner than any of Tasha's reports had forecast. The barometric pressure had been dropping slowly, which is good for catching tuna because the fish sense the need to eat before a coming storm, but when the pressure bottoms out and the storm actually hits, most of them get gone.

The boat pitched forward into a trough and the mainline hauler winch whined in protest at the strain. The line, which typically vibrated pleasingly with a fish on, was a knife edge. Kai was operating the hauler. He slowed it to a stalemate.

From the aux control on the top deck, Tasha called through the wind, "Kai, I've gotta keep us under power. If I slow down any more, we might get spun beam-to and rolled. Easy does it, don't let the line snap."

Tasha made the announcement that their empty-holded, top-heavy vessel was *this close* to going belly-up in a tone that one might use when they were running ten minutes late for dinner, but Jeff knew that getting the boat tossed sideways by wind or wave in high seas would be bad news. The boat had a pointy end for a reason. Expose the beam, the broad side of the boat, to oncoming waves and she could roll right over.

Normally, in smooth seas, Tasha would put the engine in neutral, or even reverse to help land a fish, but now, it would be up to Kai to haul the fish alongside the boat using a light touch on the—

"Holy fuck!" Tommy shouted. A dorsal fin broke the churning surface. The massive fish bucked against the line, exposing an ink blue flank "That's the biggest fucking bluefin I've ever fucking seen in my fucking life!"

If the crew landed this monster, it would make the whole trip, the whole month. Tommy let some slack go out of the crane's cable.

The boat cut into a black wave. Jeff was showered with cold water. Kai took advantage of the slowed momentum to capture a few feet of line and hoped the gangion would hold as the bluefin fought for her life. "Easy does it, Kai," Tasha shouted.

Hemi had rejoined Jeff at the rail and handed him a gaff. The tuna's tail was even with the stern of the boat.

Another wave cycled. The fish thrashed, but was carried closer. When its huge head was below the gated door in the rail, Hemi would call for the crane cable from Tommy, Jeff would gaff the fish to relieve the strain on the line, Hemi would hook the tuna through the gills, and Tommy would haul it onto the deck with the crane.

After two more wave cycles of slack and tight, slack and tight, the bluefin was right below the gate, exhausted and seemingly resigned to its fate. Hemi waved for the crane hook.

"Rogue wave from port! Hang on!" Tasha yelled, in just the tone one would expect. A rushing mountain of water rolled the *Monkey Fist*, pushing her starboard gunwale almost to the waterline. Jeff braced himself against the rail and looked into the tuna's cricket ball-sized eye. A second later, a wall of water crashed over the deck, knocking Jeff and Hemi off their feet. Jeff's right leg slipped through the gate and dipped into the ocean for a second before the ship bobbed back to right herself, shedding tons of seawater. As the crew scrambled to their feet, soaked with adrenaline, the crane's hook completed a looping arc through the dark and smashed into Hemi's spine, knocking him flat without slowing.

Kai skidded across the deck to aid his brother, leaving the hauler slowly turning.

"Gaff that fucking fish, Jeff!" Tommy yelled.

Jeff swung his eight-foot gaff and hooked the tuna behind the gill. He pulled, but it was like trying to lift a car. The tuna was a thousand pounds if it was an ounce. It wasn't getting on the deck without the hydraulic crane's hook. Speaking of which, Jeff looked over his shoulder to locate the block and saw it whistling toward his face.

Something flashed above his head and the hook swerved away. Tasha stood there, holding Hemi's gaff, the crane cable hooked into the bend.

"Who's driving the boat?" Jeff asked.

"You mean, who is *captaining* the boat? I am," Tasha shouted through the rain. She corralled the crane's cable in her hand, stumbling as another wave rolled under them. She yelled, "Kai! Is Hemi OK?"

Hemi was slouched against the bulkhead, wheezing, grimacing in pain. Kai knelt over him. "I think so! I don't know!" he yelled back.

The mainline was drawing tighter. The tuna's head was being dragged up and out of the water. The hauler motor hummed with protest.

"We need slack in the line!" Tasha shouted, "It's going to—"

SNAP! The line parted with a zoinging report. The tuna dropped back into the water. Still stunned and tired, the half-ton fish didn't realize it was now only held captive by a young man who weighed maybe 155 pounds soaking wet, holding a sharp stick.

"Fuck," said Tasha. "Tommy! Come hook this fish!" She hooked the cable's block onto the rail and slid in front of Jeff to grab onto the gaff. "Get low!" she ordered him. They dropped ass-to-deck with their legs splayed out as if they were riding a toboggan together. Tommy scrambled away from the crane controls and pulled himself hand-over-hand across the rolling deck of the boat.

The tuna was regaining its wits and strength. Jeff could maintain his grip on the gaff, but not his leverage. The tuna was trying to dive. The gaff handle angled up, and up some more, until Jeff and Tasha had to rise to a crouch, then a backward lean, then an upright stance.

Tommy arrived to hook the tuna with the crane cable, but it's head was already submerged.

Behind Tasha, Jeff's upright stance became a forward lean, then a forward lean on tiptoes, then a teetering slip toward the wet gunwale's edge. A few more degrees and they'd be pulled into the ocean. Jeff took one hand off the gaff and wrapped it around Tasha's rainslick waist.

The tuna thrashed its tail and was gone, wrenching the gaff away and taking it down into the depths along with quite a story to tell its friends, although some of them, of course, will just take the opportunity to point out that *they* were smart enough to eat *before* the storm and by the way, what were you doing so far east?

Hours later, after the crew had finally recovered and hauled the parted gear, with a single thirty-pound bigeye to show for their efforts, Tommy was so tired, he had only enough energy to lay in his bunk and either smoke a cigarette or continue to berate Jeff for letting go of the gaff like a fucking pussy, but not both. He lit up and remained quiet.

Hemi rolled and winced in his bunk. The purple bruise on his back had spilled into the negative space of his tattoos.

The cigarette gave Tommy back a small burst of energy. "Hemi, you're off from watch duty tonight, bro. Jeff, you take Hemi's watch," he said.

Hemi nodded his appreciation. Jeff nodded his acceptance. He closed his eyes and thought of the warm, dry sands of home.

Being woken from the depths of REM sleep can be disorienting. Sometimes a person will even forget where they are for a moment. But when you're in the belly of a smallish boat that's rolling through stormy seas, you don't forget for a second. When his watch beeped him awake, Jeff knew exactly where he was.

Tasha did not allow smoking on the bridge, so Tommy was extra cranky when Jeff relieved him. Cranky, but silent, because Tasha also didn't allow talking on the bridge while she was sleeping.

The boat's windshield wipers could barely keep up with the rain. The *Monkey Fist*'s 50,000 lumen spotlight, which could bore a wide tunnel of light hundreds of meters through a calm night, could only prod weakly at the gray and swirling tempest.

Much like the giant tuna itself, Tasha hadn't said anything to Jeff after wiggling out of his grasp earlier that night. She checked on Hemi, who had struggled to a hard-breathing crouch at that point, and then climbed back up to the bridge to manage the difficult maneuver of turning the boat around in a storm to track and recover the miles of lost gear.

Jeff had been certain that she would have been pulled overboard had he not grabbed her. He would have gone in too, he had no doubt. Momentum. Leverage. That's what this was about. Give a man a lever long enough and a place to stand and he can lift the world and all that.

Jeff thought he had found his place to stand, but it turned out he was just a part of the world like everybody else, feeling that lever dig under his ass to dislodge him. From where though? And who was pushing down the other end?

CHAPTER 30

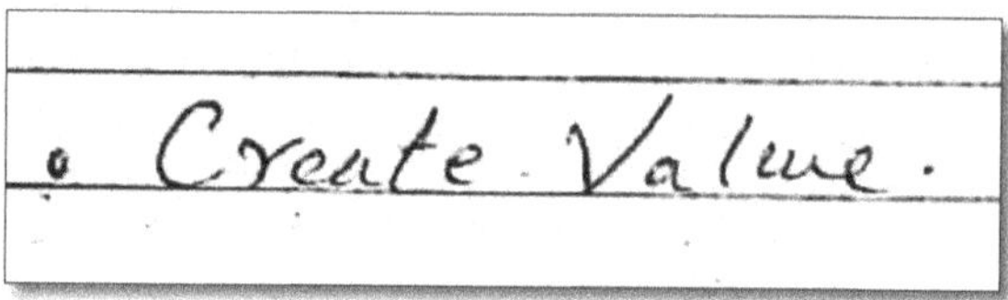

The *Monkey Fist*'s engine, which had been rumbling steady for fifty hours, gave a blood-chilling shriek and died. The boat dipped forward and a wave broke over the prow. Jeff pitched forward and fell out the captain's chair.

Tasha's berth door banged open. "What the fuck, Jeff?" She ran past him as he got to his feet. She checked gauges, switches. She popped the throttle into neutral and toggled the ignition. The engine growled back to life.

"Did we hit something? Did you run over a buoy or a net or anything?" She looked up and squinted into the night. "I told you to steer around shit, didn't I?"

She nudged the throttle into reverse.

"Yes," said Jeff, rubbing his eyes. "But no, I don't think I..."

The engine whined and choked. Tasha put it back in neutral and it recovered to a low idle.

"What the fuck?" Tommy appeared at the pilothouse door, rain dripping from his slicker's hood.

"Engine stalled. Something's tangled in the prop," Tasha said. "Some ghost gear probably got stirred up to the surface. I can't reverse out."

"You didn't fucking see it?" Tommy yelled at Jeff.

"Do *you* see it?" Tasha yelled back. "No, you don't, because its tangled in my fucking prop right now! Get down there with a gaff and pull it out!" Kai appeared behind Tommy in the doorway.

"Why did the engine stop?" he said.

"Prop snagged something," said Tasha. "Where's Hemi?"

Kai shook his head. "He can't straighten up."

"OK," Tasha said. "You and Jeff get down there and help Tommy. The engine's in neutral so the screw should turn. Whatever's snagged on it should just unwind off." She flipped the intercom on.

Kai and Jeff scrambled down the ladder. They staggered through the downpour across the listing deck as Tasha's voice cut through the wind. "Hurry it up! We're getting pushed around already."

In the misty cone of the stern worklight, Tommy was already leaning over the rail, jabbing a gaff into the water. He hooked something and heaved a knot of slimy, rotten net above the surface. "Fucking trawling net!" he said. "Help me, it's fucking heavy!"

Kai and Jeff grabbed gaffs and stood on either side of Tommy. They staggered in unison as the boat rolled to port.

"Let's go!" Tasha yelled.

The men gained their footing and all three rehooked the net. "Pull!" Tommy yelled. "Fucking pull!"

Pull as they fucking could, the net was not coming loose. They could get one corner of it a few feet above the water, but no more.

"It's caught on something! Someone's gotta get down there and cut it loose," Tommy said.

Jeff had been through the engine compartment several times by now, but he had not noticed where or how one would access the propeller.

"I'll do it," Jeff said. "I was on the watch. It's my fault we're tangled."

"You a strong swimmer, Jeff?" Tommy asked.

"What?" said Jeff. He had to have misheard that.

Kai unhooked his gaff from the net and, keeping one hand on the rail, moved toward the pilothouse. He stowed his gaff and began rummaging through a large storage bin attached to the bulkhead. The boat rolled wildly to port.

Tommy let go of his gaff with one hand and grabbed the rail. "Jeff, you're gonna get under the fucking boat to cut us loose."

"I can't—" Jeff began.

"Shut the fuck up! You don't really have to fucking swim! Kai's giving you gear so you can see and breathe and we're going to hold onto you by a line that's hooked to the crane. Just grab onto the net and pull yourself down there, find where it's snagged and cut it the fuck loose."

Tasha's voice rang from the boat speaker. "Why is this not happening, guys? Tommy, get up here and tell me what you're seeing."

Tommy staggered across the tilting deck past Kai, who was gripping the edge of the storage bin to keep his feet. Kai beckoned Jeff over to him. He handed Jeff a black vest with reflective patches sewn onto wide straps. "Put this on."

As Jeff shrugged the vest on and clipped the plastic buckles in front, Kai produced a diver's mask and a waterproof headlamp. "These, too."

As Kai dug into the bin again, Jeff lowered the rubbery mask over his eyes and nose, then slid the lamp's thick band down onto his forehead. Kai came up with a white canister about the size of Tasha's coffee mug.

"This is your air," Kai said. He tapped a knob near the canister's rubber mouthpiece. "Don't open the valve until you're in the water. This holds ten minutes." He shook it and handed it to Jeff. He pulled a second canister from the bin. "We've got two. Work fast, brah."

Jeff wiped rain from his mask. "I can't see!"

Tasha, from the speaker: "I'm calling mayday to the Coast Guard right now! But let's get this done, Jeff!"

The boat listed hard to port and Kai staggered into Jeff. He regained his footing and said, "You'll see fine once you're underwater." He shoved two plastic-sheathed knives into either side of Jeff's harness, making Jeff resemble a gunfighter who was bringing knives to the fight. Using his own knife, Kai slashed an arm's length of yellow nylon line from a coil hanging on the bulkhead and then steered Jeff toward the deck crane.

Tommy came back down the ladder from the bridge and made his way across the deck to the crane's controls. He payed out a few feet of the cable, and snagged the hook out of the wind with one hand. Kai looped the nylon line through the eye of the hook, quickly threaded it through the fat metal loop sewn into the back of Jeff's safety vest and tied it secure. "We won't let you go, brah," Kai said, tugging hard on the loop. They staggered again as a wave rolled the deck. Without forward power, the *Fist* was being turned beam-to the seas, taking the well-worn path of least resistance toward doom.

Tommy let enough cable out so that Kai could edge Jeff back to the stern rail. Jeff grabbed the rail with both hands in the gusting wind and looked over. A wave lifted and dropped the *Fist.* The boat's worklight penetrated a few feet of the surging green water and a dark netted mass could be seen waving under the surface.

Tommy tugged at the cable running from Jeff's back. "Don't get this tangled in anything! Happened to Dave once and he died for eighteen minutes."

"I can't swim," Jeff finally answered.

"Don't have to. Just hang on with one hand and cut with the other," Kai said. "Tug three times if you need to come up," He tugged a rapid 1-2-3 on the line. The already-soaked vest squelched against Jeff's chest, matching his racing heart.

Jeff took an unsteady step up onto the stern rail. Another wave hit and the rail was suddenly snatched from his grip. He flopped over the side, jerked to an immediate and painful stop and dangled above the angry water. As Kai strained to control the cable, Jeff spun at the end of it and swung backwards toward the boat. His body smashed into the steel hull with a ringing *clunk* and the air canister made a sharp *clink* as it was knocked from his grip. The canister splashed in the water and bobbed for exactly one second before it was erased by a wave. Jeff steadied himself with a hand against the hull.

Kai leaned over the rail instantly, holding the second canister. “All the air we got!” he shouted over the wind. “Ten minutes! Gotta hurry now.” He pressed the canister into Jeff’s hand, then turned away to signal Tommy with a quick thumbs-down to release the cable. Tommy jammed the crane lever forward.

Jeff was in the water. The line tugged sharply at his back as he was lifted and dropped by a wave.

Through the wind and rain, he could barely hear Tommy’s voice. “Hurry the fuck up!”

Jeff spat salty seawater and struggled to fit the air tank’s respirator into his mouth. He thrashed his arms and legs, fighting the water to stay upright.

Tasha’s voice on the deck speaker cut through the roar of water, “Coast Guard’s ninety minutes a—” then muted as a wave dunked Jeff under.

Something was wrong with Jeff’s air tank. It was choking him. As he reached to rip the tank from his face, he remembered the valve. He twisted it open and air hissed into his mouth. But now it seemed very buoyant, as if he couldn’t pull his own face under. Another wave swallowed him and he realized his mistake. It wasn’t .5 liters of compressed air that was keeping his head above water, it was just several million years of survival instinct. His head popped to the surface. He glimpsed Kai, with a hand on Jeff’s lifeline.

Tasha's voice: "—gonna go down—"

Another wave swept over Jeff, pushing him under again. For the first time in days, the rain quieted. Jeff's panicked inhalation roared in his ears as he desperately sucked on his respirator, and his rushed exhalation became a curtain of bubbles rising before his eyes.

He could see! Liquid-sharp vision through the diver's mask compensated for his dull underwater hearing. His headlamp illuminated a black cloud of mossy and ragged net trailing up from the boat's red fin-like rudder. The boat lurched in the storm. Jeff's vest dug under his rib cage, then slackened as he felt Kai give some cable back. A large tendril of net waved upward. Looking down, Jeff trapped it between his feet like he was climbing a rope.

At some point, the non-swimming would have to be addressed. But not today. Jeff crunched his body down and grabbed a fistful of the slimy net.

The weeks of training in Taboor City, limited by the constraints of Shwarma's small apartment, did not include as much running as Jeff would have liked, but the core/yoga-based physical program now served him well as he pulled himself first inverted and then down.

A large wave rocked the boat. Jeff maintained his grip, but his body whipped at the end of the net, the feeling reminding him of that game where a bigger kid grabs your arms, or sometimes one arm and one leg, then spins you around and around before flinging you into the sand.

The wave passed. Jeff regripped the net and continued pulling himself down. And down again until he could grab the upper pivot of the rudder with one hand, while clinging to the loose ends of tattered net with the other. He could see the tips of the ship's clover-shaped propeller in front of the rudder, but the center of it was choked in a swirled nest of weedy black netting.

Another invisible wave tossed the *Monkey Fist* sideways and Jeff was carried with it. The respirator was almost torqued from his mouth and he had to clamp his teeth to save it. The boat was now almost completely beam-to the seas. She rocked wildly, but with a semi-steady rhythm that allowed Jeff four-to-five second intervals wherein his life felt merely jeopardized, not in imminent, terrorizing danger.

Part of the net was looped around the lower rudder and it stretched across the ten centimeter gap to the prop like a spider's web. Jeff let go of the rudder and reached to grab the short section of driveshaft between the prop and the hull of the boat, noting it was about the same diameter as the air canister that was ripped from his grip a few seconds (a minute?) ago. He could feel the vibration of the idling engine through the metal.

With his free hand, he reached for one of the two… the two… there were definitely two knives in his vest when he went in the water. Now there was just one. Ah. Yes. Of course. The other knife slipped out as Jeff was ragdolled upside down and was now on its way to the bottom of the ocean.

He squeezed the remaining knife's handle and pulled it free. Working upward, he sawed through the barnacle-encrusted net that spanned the gap between rudder and prop. He tugged, but the net didn't come loose. It had somehow become wound around the rudder's grease-blackened upper pivot that hid another few loops. Jeff went back to the knife and worked the blade's tip under the remaining strands of net and jabbed up through them. The frayed ends floated free. Jeff tugged. One last loop held the net. Jeff tugged again. Unbreakable. One final dig of the knife parted it. Jeff kicked at the large section of net and it was dragged off into the murk.

Jeff turned his attention and blade to the fouled propeller. He was able to unwind a few laps of the freshly cut net from around the prop, but each time he pulled it free, the loose end grew longer, and it became tedious to feed it through the gap between the prop and rudder. At some point, it would become faster to cut than to unwind. He tugged the loose end of the net. Suddenly it didn't yield. Jeff pushed the prop by hand and it stopped at a quarter turn. The net had somehow wound around itself and was essentially tied in place. Several centimeters of tight nylon encased the prop. Cutting through it would take some time. The boat lurched again, dragging Jeff with it.

Jeff's arms strained to maintain grip, then he pulled himself closer to shine his headlamp on the twisted knot that strangled their boat. Something brushed across his leg! The net. A snarl of it, bigger than Jeff himself, trailed into the darkness below the boat.

Jeff pinched the net between his feet to anchor himself. Even as the boat was swaying more and more with every wave, he found that he could now dare to use both hands to work at the tangle. He sawed and pulled, sawed and pulled. Every few swipes with the knife, he pinched the loose ends he had cut and tugged them away. Some came loose, some did not. The closer he got to the core of the knot, the tighter it was wound around the prop and it became difficult to work the knife's blade under the slimy strands. Jeff had to push the point of the blade into—a massive wave rocked the boat, dragging Jeff to the surface by his ankle that was tangled in the loose end of the net. In the brief second his head was above water, he thought he heard screaming. The hull rolled and stopped a few degrees short of no return, then rushed back to upright. Jeff was dragged underwater again and the edge of the rudder smashed his knuckles. The knife fluttered away like a scared fish.

Jeff panicked and gulped air from his regulator. Now what? Should he tug on the cable three times to get pulled to the surface for (yet) another knife? Was there time? Or should he try to untie the last few strands of net with his hands? And was that last breath of air somewhat... less?

He clamped his feet together around the net and grabbed the rudder to steady himself. No, wait. He had Zoey. He burrowed into his pants pocket and pulled his knife out. Underwater, the knife somehow seemed *heavier,* and its shiny chrome grip felt as slippery as a bar of soap. Pinching the big blade tightly, like a person pulling a stack of bills from the ATM, Jeff levered it open. Heaving for air, he jammed the blade into the mass of sinewy nylon around the propeller and drew it back. Again. Again. Again.

The exertion was getting to him. He felt as if he'd run all night. His heart pounded in his ears. He couldn't catch his breath. The harder he drew on his regulator, the less oxygen he was getting. How many breaths had he taken? How many more did he have left?

Three, as it turned out. Suddenly the regulator was dead and Jeff might as well have tried sucking the metal end of the canister for all the oxygen it gave. There were still untold loops of net around the prop. Jeff held his breath and continued to hack away. His once-clear underwater vision got a little blurry and it became hard to see if he was still cutting anything, but it felt like maybe he was. But then, he swiped at empty water, which was strange because

Black-on-black fireworks.

Jeff coughed and felt warm seawater splatter from his mouth. He lay on the deck of the *Monkey Fist.* Rain poured down on his face. The metal loop of his harness dug painfully into his spine. Kai knelt over him.

"You were down there twelve minutes," Kai said. "We had to haul you up. You know, one way or the other. You good?"

"Bro, you were dead for four minutes," Tommy said.

"What?" Jeff coughed again.

"Is he *alright*?" Tasha's voice came over the speaker. The boat's engine was screaming at full throttle. The radar showed calmer weather to the south and Tasha was pushing to the edge of the storm. She had raised the Coast Guard again to call them off.

Kai gave a thumbs-up. "He's good!"

"Did I… is the…?" Jeff rasped.

"Yeah, you did, brah," said Kai. He pointed to a huge tangle of mossy, weedy net that lay at Jeff's feet, one end of it still wrapped around his right ankle.

Tommy kicked at it. "Bottom-dragger trawling net. Shit's been illegal for years. This thing's been out there for a while."

Jeff sat up and Kai cut him free of the cable.

"I'm getting a smoke," Tommy said. He staggered away across the listing deck toward the cabin.

"You good, Jeff?" Kai asked again.

"Yes. Yes, thank you, Kai." Jeff coughed. "I lost your knives."

Kai grinned. "All good. Come on." He pulled Jeff up by the elbow, but Jeff's head swam and he retched up more water.

There was thick pain in Jeff's chest. "I think I want to sit for a minute more," he said as he slumped back to the deck.

"You want some water?" Kai asked.

Jeff nodded and coughed again.

Kai went down into the cabin.

Jeff tried to remember what it was like being dead, but the last memory he had was cutting away at the net with Zoey. His knife! Where was it? He checked his pockets. No. He looked around the wet deck. No. He struggled to his knees and lifted a corner of the piled net to look under it. Yes! There, a glint of chrome. He shook the net and nothing clattered out but a couple rotted seashells. He wended his fingers through the dirty tangles and grasped metal. But it wasn't the familiar shape and feel of his knife. Rougher in texture and irregular in size. Whatever it was, Jeff wiggled it loose and drew it free.

He held in his hand a silvery shard, about the size of a Proteinsanity™ bar, shaped sort of like Kyrgyzstan, a dull point at one end and forked at the other.

The shard was in Jeff's pocket when Kai returned with the water.

The mysterious metallic shard found no company in Jeff's pocket after the *Monkey Fist* limped back into Honolulu the following night.

Tasha briefly docked to drop Hemi off at the marina, where his wife Mal was waiting. Hemi, his back purple and his face like gray stone, gingerly eased into their truck and was driven off into the rainy night as the *Fist* crossed the harbor to the fish market.

Unloading the catch was cruelly, embarrassingly, quick and easy.

Tasha returned to the boat while Jeff was still cleaning the freezer hold, but there were no pay envelopes to distribute. Jeff had been told, many times, mostly by Tommy as the boat sailed home, to expect a zero-pay week. They had failed to catch anything near the amount of fish needed to cover the costs of the trip. Get paid? With what?

A 1/32 share of nothing is still nothing, and the meager contents of the *Monkey Fist*'s hold didn't bring enough money to cover the expenses of fuel, food, tackle and supplies that the boat spent in vain pursuit. It was a quiet relief for Jeff when it became clear that it wasn't customary for the crewmembers to pitch in to cover the financial losses of the boat.

There must be a colorful nautical name for such an occurrence, when a commercial fishing trip *costs* you money, but if the captain knew what it was, she seemed in no mood to give vocab lessons. She grimly piloted the *Fist* back to the marina, went about her post-trip tasks quickly and drove away with barely a word.

The boat was quiet. The rain had stopped. Plumes of steam rose from every outdoor surface. Even the air was wet on this forsaken island.

It was Thursday evening in Honolulu. Sending a Wmail that would arrive instantly, yet on Friday morning in Taboor City was like using a portal to the near future. Which Jeff would have been more than willing to step through if it meant he could elude the present, which, as Tommy would say, fucking sucks right now.

Jeff sat in the captain's chair, warm and dry, as the crew's laundry tumbled belowdecks. How he wished he could be with Rahim again. He missed the closeness. Riding the moped together, sharing that narrow mat on Shwarma's floor in those last few weeks.

To bring his brother to join him in Honolulu would cost $10,000. The amount would have seemed ludicrous just a few weeks ago, but then, so did $5,000 when Shwarma quoted him the original cost of exfil from Zazaristan. Thousands of US dollars? But what choice did Jeff have?

During those weeks when he was hiding out in Shwarma's apartment, a technical would roll through Shwarma's neighborhood (and presumably the East Station Market and the rest of the city) almost daily, droning, "Jefir Zaqq… Reward for Jefir Zaqq… Jefir Zaqq."

By the time Shwarma had "completed negotiations" with Hamid at the Quudian port and Jefir was finally slinked out of Taboor City in the back of the van, Hallazallah's reward for the head of Jefir Zaqq had grown to fifty thousand zazars.

Every time Shwarma left the apartment, Jeff had expected to see the door fly back open and Green Vest's friends to burst in, guns blazing. He kept Zoey close.

But Shwarma never sold him out. And Jeff had seen why after his first few weeks in Honolulu. As Shwarma promised, the wages in the

West were fantastically high (and much more than some small-time blood money from a local warlord).

But not this week. A wageless trip wasn't something Jeff had anticipated. The ocean had seemed to be a bottomless repository of profit, but that was not the case, quite obviously. Jeff had hoped to make a start toward the $10,000 it would take for Rahim to join him, but he had less than $500 in his pocket. What would have seemed like a fortune a few months ago represented less than a month's survival today.

The following afternoon, Jeff jogged to Pawn1^2.

CHAPTER 31

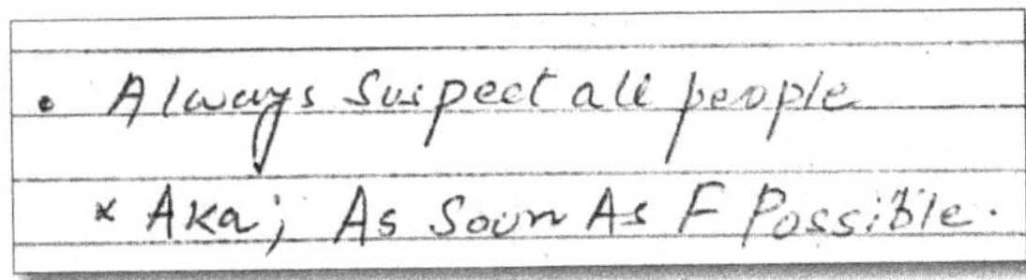

Jeff didn't mind following. Following beat falling behind. At least when following you can see what's in front of you, reach out and put a hand on the trusty shoulder of the man ahead. When you fall behind and that man disappears into the dust or over the horizon and you're left alone, therein lies the problem.

Also, not knowing *if* you're alone or not is problematic. Being unsure of who can be trusted is exhausting beyond any fishing trip. At least if you *know for sure* that you're alone, that's a conviction and you can take comfort in your convictions. Even if you have just the one.

The training videos mentioned death and taxes as the inevitable in life, but Jeff knew plenty of people who never paid taxes and after seventeen days in service he was still alive, wasn't he?

He hoped to stay that way, anyway. And he was still fairly cash-wealthy. He had about five hundred US dollars, his savings from the previous trips, the success of which Jeff now realized may have been exception rather than rule, but nevertheless, five hundred US dollars. He had paid his weekly rent on the boat to Tasha in advance. The galley was still abundantly stocked due to the shortened trip. He planned no more liquor-lacquered trips to the Intercontinental. His expenses were few. Well, there was that one.

There was only one way to work out of this jam with Taboor City. Which is to say there were many, many ways to work out of it, but what all these ways had in common is that they all pay you with money.

There's money won, money earned, money found, money given, money stolen, money swindled, money bamboozled, etc. The list is always growing. Money robot-scraped off the ocean floor in the form of precious minerals is one of the newer ones, for example.

Jeff had spent the morning Wangling on his phone to learn what he could about the mysterious metallic object he had found in the snagged net. The minerals that Tommy had mentioned were found in the ocean, manganese and cobalt, both had a silvery appearance, like the shard in his pocket. However, their values were widely different. Manganese was only worth about five US dollars *per ton.* If Jeff had a chunk of manganese, it was worthless. Cobalt on the other hand, was about eighty dollars per *kilogram.* If what he had was a chunk of cobalt, it was about sixty dollars' worth. In the name of thoroughness (and a certain curiosity) Jeff also had looked up the price of silver. Tommy hadn't mentioned silver as something mined in the ocean north of Hawai'i, but the nugget sure *looked* like silver. Silver sold for $700 a kilogram! The shard was becoming more and more (potentially) valuable. But again, how to know for sure?

The man at Pawn1^2 shot unknown metals with his X-Ray Fluorescent gun. (Which Jeff had also Wangled.) XRF: The ability to beam invisible rays at an object to determine its very essence and value. Wouldn't it be nice if humans came with this option?

Jeff entered Pawn1^2.

"What's up, man?" Ike said, from behind the counter.

"What's up," Jeff repeated, having noted by now that Americans do not care what, in fact, is up. "I have some metal to sell."

"Let's see what you got." Ike reached for his XRF gun.

Jeff opened his hand to display the shard. "I think it may be silver?" he said.

Ike's eyebrows pressed together, then raised. "Looks more like platinum. I'd say about ten grand worth. Put it on my scale."

Jeff hadn't even thought of platinum! And ten thousand would be enough to bring Rahim to the US where they would work on the *Fist* together. He quickly placed the shard on the round pedestal of Ike's countertop digital scale. Ike trained his XRF gun on it. The gun beeped.

Ike checked the scale. "25.23 ounces. But it's not platinum. It's not worth ten thousand."

"What is it? Manganese?" Jeff asked.

Ike said, "It's rhodium." He punched a few numbers into the scale's keypad. "It's worth $89,566.50."

"Rhodium?" Jeff gasped. "Yes, I would like to sell it."

"I'll bet you would," Ike said. "Can I see some ID, please?"

"What for?"

"You need to show ID for any transaction."

Jeff pulled out Claude Ohanu's fishing license.

Ike barely looked at the card. "Not that. Driver's license, military ID, something with a photo."

"I am here," Jeff pointed out. "With the rhodium. What more ID or proof is needed?"

"I need to know you didn't steal this, cuz."

"I didn't. I found it."

"K, stop right there," Ike said. "Don't say another word. I don't want to know." He nudged the rhodium away toward Jeff, as if afraid to touch it. "Take this back." Jeff took it.

Ike said, "You know how it's illegal to take sand from the beach, right? The state of Hawaii can hit you with a $100,000 fine if they want. The state of Hawaii. A hundred Gs. For sand." Ike raised a finger. "If, and I'm not saying this is where you found it, but *if,* you 'found' that nodule of rhodium someplace where you don't own the mineral rights? The owners tend to frown on that. They'll come after you hard. And anyone who dealt with you. So, no thanks."

"No one is looking for this rhodium, I promise you," Jeff said.

"I don't make the rules, cuz," said Ike. "Any pawnshop or jeweler would tell you the same thing. You could sell it privately to anyone who wanted to pay cash, I guess."

"How would I do that?" Jeff asked.

"Not my problem. I'm not about to have some cop or worse come back here asking about you. You asked, I said no. That's where this has to end. Sorry." He pointed to the rhodium. "Take care of that thing in the meantime."

Jeff slipped the rhodium into his pocket. "Yes," he said.

"Anything else?" Ike asked.

"Yes," Jeff said. "A debit card."

"How much?"

Jeff had ninety-thousand dollars in his pocket, but only about five hundred of it was negotiable. It's not like you can jam a hunk of metal into the Botcoin machine.

He said, "Two hundred and fifty."

CHAPTER 32

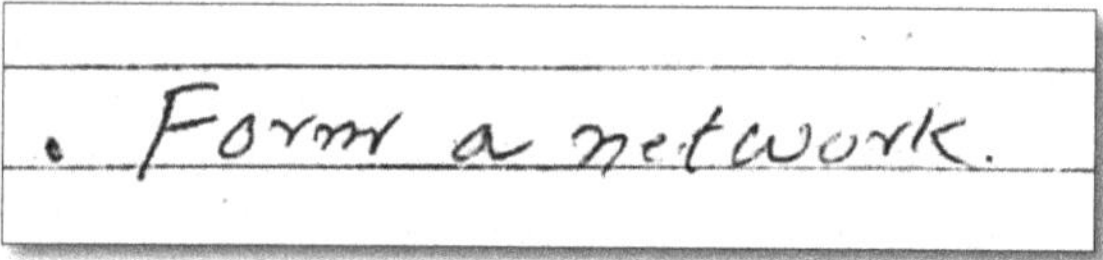

Shwarma's apartment building faced west and he liked to sit on the stoop in the morning's cool shadow and watch the neighborhood.

He was expecting to receive from Jefir Zaqq, his new star Overseas Stealth Agent, yet another large payment. The young fellow who introduced himself by running bloodily past this very spot had seemingly, and by unfathomable means, become successful in Hawaii. Perhaps more Overseas Stealth Agents *should* be deployed to Hawaii. Fishing was apparently wildly profitable.

And yes, "*Star* Overseas Stealth Agent" had a nice ring to it. He would have to add "Star" as one more coded rank in the byzantinely random branches of Shwarmco's budding organizational hierarchy that served to confuse and confound his employees, dimwits that, to a man, they were.

Shwarma's phone bleeped the email alert.

To: mohammad.mohammad54321@zmail.zaz

From: service@botcoin.bot

Subject: You've got Bot!

Jeffzachary262 sent you .245 botcoins!

Message from jeffzachary262:

I sent you some bot. There was a problem on the fishing boat this week (I actually died briefly). I did not get paid and I will not be paid next week either. But, I have found another (very large) source of income. It may take time to convert into $ but I will send the 9750 asap. Prepare to send Rahim

Less than a quarter botcoin? That's it? A small burst of air escaped Shwarma's nose. And what was this "very large source of income?" Yes, Jeff, thank you for letting us know that converting something into money is the tricky part. This weak attempt to stall for time had to be a tactic. Young Jefir was apparently feeling his oats, trying to make Shwarma blink in their negotiations to send Rahim to the US and reduce the price. Maybe they really did corrupt a person over there. But couldn't Jeff see that the advantage here was all Shwarma's? Yes, the loss of Z100,000 from that ill-advised, BS, double or nothing cricket gamble still rang clear and yes, a property like 505 H Street will not be on the market forever, but as long as Rahim was in Taboor City, Shwarma still held the cards. No, not the cards, no more gambling. Something less chance-based.

Shwarma shook his head. He looked up to see Rahim crossing the street toward him holding two cups of coffee.

"Your brother is getting some strange ideas about what it means to be part of a movement, Rahim," Shwarma said, putting his phone down.

"What do you mean?" said Rahim. "Did you hear from him again? What does he say?"

"Here's what Jeff said: 'Sorry, sorry, sorry! I can't pay this week! I'm keeping money for myself because I have no loyalty to my brother, friends or country!"

"That doesn't sound like Jefir," said Rahim.

"Here's a direct quote," Shwarma said. "I did not get paid and I will not be paid next week either."

"Let me see the message," Rahim said, reaching for the phone.

Shwarma covered it with his hand. "Deleted. Security."

"How do I know you're even in contact with him?" Rahim demanded. "I would like the security of knowing my brother is safe."

Shwarma tucked his phone into his jacket pocket and grinned. "I'm sure you've been working on that tiny speech a long time, Rahim." He stood up. "It would be a shame to waste it. You want to know if Jeff's OK? Let's go send him a message together."

CHAPTER 33

- Know which rules can be bent.

Ike the pawnshop guy didn't even have to touch the rhodium to ascertain what it was. $89,566.50 worth of it and small enough to fit in Jeff's pocket. Was it hot? It felt a little hot.

Jeff was sure that everyone he passed on the sidewalk outside Pawn1^2 could somehow see the chunk of metal in his pocket, glowing like a coal.

What is the effective range of one of those XRF scanners? How close would a person have to be to use one? Jeff passed a woman at the bus stop reading a novel with a very muscular man on the cover. Her large handbag could easily be concealing a rhodium-detecting ray gun.

There were dogs. He passed a man walking two of them, one large, one small. Could light wisps of sniffable rhodium odor be wafting from his pocket? The animals took no interest. Still, Jeff couldn't shake the feeling that he was being observed. There were conspicuous cameras in Pawn1^2 and on half the street corners. He looked around. Could someone have followed him from the pawnshop? Someone sent by Ike? Maybe just some dark-natured rando drawn to pawn-adjacent desperation like a sailor to siren song?

The woman at the bus stop remained engrossed in her book. Light traffic crossed the intersection. Jeff slowed his gait, then hopped quickly over a guardrail and sprinted across a gas station parking lot. He danced through piles of pallets and barrels behind the building, vaulted over a short fence and scrambled down a shaded embankment to find himself at the mouth of a long, narrow alley running between two cinder block warehouses.

The far end of the alley was partially blocked by a greasy brown trash dumpster. As he got close to it, Jeff was hit with an unholy stink the likes of which he had never smelled, bearing in mind he had spent over a week in a stifling shipping container with a bucket of his own waste and he currently worked on a fishing boat.

Holding his breath, he pushed aside the dumpster and slipped past it. He heard music.

He was at the Intercontinental Lounge! It looked invitingly cool and non-smelly inside. He had enjoyed his ginny times there with Tasha.

Jeff let out the breath he was holding. A moment later, he was in the dark entrance of the IC. A man was working out a solo version of "Go Your Own Way" on the karaoke stage. Jeff squinted and recognized the man as the lounge's owner, Jonny K himself.

Jeff took a seat at the end of the bar to watch.

A not-Brad bartender dealt him a napkin. "What can I get you?" he asked.

"Water, please," said Jeff.

Jonathan Kalawai'a, a.k.a. Jonny K. The owner of the *Monkey Fist.* Tasha's boss, and technically Jeff's as well. Two weeks ago, Jeff had seen a thick stack of US dollars swept into the man's pocket. And it was hard to miss the shine of Jonny's nugget-ringed fingers as he gripped the karaoke mic.

The bartender brought an ice-filled glass of water. Jeff took a long drink.

Jonny capped his performance with the now-customary billowing lungful of smoke with the initials "JK" green-lasered through it. He acknowledged the happy hour crowd with a short bow and wave, then left the stage and Jeff watched him walk down the back hallway toward his office.

The man at the pawnshop said to sell the rhodium to a private individual, someone with cash. A very large nightclub owner who literally projects his name into the sky is not ideally private, but he probably had the cash, at least.

Jeff put down his water, crossed the room and knocked on Jonny K's office door.

"Come on!"

Jeff opened the door and stubbed it on the end of a leather couch wedged into the corner. Across the room, two dark and busy rugs away, a sliding glass door was wedged secure with an aluminum baseball bat. The bat's worn painted logo could have once said Smasher, Basher, or Masher, maybe even Dasher or Flasher. Whatever it was, the bat had done a lot of it.

A high shelf ran along three walls. One corner supported a clutch of books including a few of the yellow-and-black ones for dummies. The rest of the shelf space held two semi-painted footballs encased in transparent cuboids, a scale model of a gold Chevrolet El Camino, and assorted framed photos of Jonny K posed grinningly with sun-and-booze-reddened friends. Jonny sat at a cluttered desk in the center of the room.

"Whattup," he said.

"Hello, sir. My name is Jeff Zachary. I work on the *Monkey Fist*."

"Shut the door. Sit down. How much you need?"

Jeff closed the door and settled carefully onto the couch. "How much what, sir?"

"Money. Jeff, you're not the first fishing mate to come into my office after a few dry weeks on the boat looking for a little something to get by until the fish start biting again. The deal is every hundred I give you today, I get one-twenty back the next time you bring fish to market. So, how much?"

Jeff pulled the rhodium from his pocket. "I've been told it's worth $89,566.50."

Jonny stared at the metal for a moment, then got up from his desk. "Do me a favor and lock that door," he said. As Jeff reached over and twisted the bolt, Jonny walked around his desk. He held out his hand. "Let me see that."

Jeff handed the dense chunk of metal over. He said, "It's rhodium. Would you like to buy it? Privately? In cash?"

Jonny K grinned as he hefted the metal. "No." He handed it back.

Jeff took it and said, “Why? Is $89,566.50 too much? That’s what I was told, but I would consider taking less.”

Jonny K returned to his desk chair. “I can give you… five thousand and free drinks at the bar.”

Jeff said, “That seems a little—”

Jonny K grinned again. “Say no, Jeff.”

“What?”

“I ain’t being serious,” Jonny K said. He quickly dug out his phone/vape/projector, took a small puff and projected “JK” into the room. “Get it? Just kidding!”

He put away the projector, still smiling. “Jeff. Serious, what makes you think I’ve got ninety grand laying around?”

“You own the *Monkey Fist*.” Jeff had also seen Tasha give Jonny K a stack of American cash that would choke a goat, but he kept this part to himself.

Jonny grinned again. “Owning something valuable isn’t the same thing as having cash. Right?” He pointed to the metal in Jeff’s hand. “Right?”

“Yes,” Jeff said.

Jonny said, “I don’t have that kind of kālā on hand. Why not go to a pawnshop? Or a jeweler? They’ll give you a good price.”

“Yes, so I was told,” said Jeff. “I also know they would ask for… information I don’t have.”

“Oh yeah, they’ll do that for sure. For sure, for sure. Jeff, I’m not going to ask where you got that rhodium. I’m not going to ask anything except this: Would you like me to help you sell it?”

"Yes," Jeff said. He hadn't considered this. But of course, Jonny K was a business owner, an upstanding citizen with a legitimate ID. He could go back to Pawn1² acting as Jeff's agent to sell the rhodium and simply hand the money over to Jeff. "Can you come with me now to the pawnshop?"

"No, bruddah, not like that," Jonny said. "Transactions over $10,000 get paid by check and reported to the IRS and I'm not trying to get my name in any of that. I meant that if a pawnshop offered you eighty-nine k, I can probably hook you up to walk away with *at least* sixty. Cash. Tax free, no ID. Sound good?"

"Sixty thousand seems… like a lot less than eighty-nine," Jeff said.

"The government will hit you with about twenty-five grand in taxes on that eighty-nine, bruddah. And that's *if* you had the ID you need. Any way you cut this, you're getting out with about the same number. Sixty."

"Yes," said Jeff.

"I know a few people who might be interested," Jonny K said. "I'll ask around over the weekend and set something up. Any cash sale over sixty thousand, I'll take five percent. Fair?"

"Yes," said Jeff.

"Can I get a picture of it? To show the buyers?"

Jeff laid the shard of rhodium on Jonny's desk. Jonny placed a pen next to it for scale. He shot a few angles of the rhodium with his phone. He picked it up to examine once again before handing it back. "Want a drink?" he asked.

"No, thank you," said Jeff. "I just had one."

"K-den," said Jonny. "So. Tasha told me Hemi's back is messed up and the boat's not going out anytime soon. What are you doing next week?"

"I was going to work on the *Monkey Fist* while she's in the marina," said Jeff, pocketing the metal. "During the day," he added, remembering not to advertise his sleeping arrangement.

"What about at night?" Jonny K said. "Look, Jeff, I dig your vibe, bruddah. I don't know how long it will take to find a buyer for your rhodium and it's probably going to be a few weeks at least before your next fishing payday. You want a job? Just until you go out again on the boat? Piecework."

"Peacework?"

"Yeah, piecework. And flexible hours. You in?"

"Yes."

"Come with me." Jonny K removed the —asher bat securing the sliding door that led to the side alley and his 1970 El Camino Super Sport in Champagne Gold.

"Get in," he said. Jeff opened the vehicle's heavy door and settled into the slick tan seat.

"You like Fleetwood Mac?" Jonny gently clicked an 8-track tape into the radio console.

"What is that, sir? Food? Yes."

"You're thinking of a Big Mac. And you can call me Jonny. Where'd you say you were from, again?"

"I don't think I did say," Jeff said.

"Right. That's right, you didn't," said Jonny. He put the car in reverse. "Fleetwood Mac is a band from the seventies. The dude singer's name is Lindsay and the wahine's is Stevie. Fleetwood Mac made one of the best-selling albums of all time, and that album, *Rumours*, was the last album ever to be released as an 8-track tape. And this," Jonny pointed to the tape, "is the very last of those. The last 8-track tape ever made." He slowed at the end of the alley and reversed left onto Nu'uanu Street. "Second Hand News" jangled from the El Camino's speakers.

Jonny's car's sound wasn't as clear as the stereo in Tasha's truck, but considering the vintage of the equipment, it wasn't too bad. "Where did you get it?" Jeff asked.

"Same place you got that rhodium," Jonny said. He grinned. "Actually, I'll tell you. It's a good story. A guy gave me this tape to settle a debt. It's not a big chunk of rhodium, but it's worth a lot. I bought this El Cam just so I'd have a cool place to listen to it."

"Was the guy a fisherman?" Jeff asked.

"He used to be a musician, but now? Restaurant business," Jonny replied. He stopped at the traffic light and took a giant hit from his vape rig. A pickup truck rolled up behind and stopped nose-to-nose with the El Camino.

Jonny exhaled a billow and lit the laser. He gave an American what's up with his chin and a small wave to the man in the pickup truck. The man didn't move to return the gesture.

Jonny yelled, "Hey bruddah, I wave, you wave back! Problem?"

Here come the guns, thought Jeff. His hand found the door handle. He looked around the intersection. He would run south.

The man in the truck made the thumb-pinky hang loose sign. Jonny K returned it.

A month in America and still no gunfights.

The light turned green. "How many businesses do you do?" Jeff asked.

Jonny looked over his shoulder and drove backwards through the intersection onto Kukui Street. "I have the IC. The *Fist.* I have a home furnishings business. I buy and sell distressed property. I loan money of course, and I'm into recycling. You know the secret to it all?"

"What is it?" Jeff asked.

"Don't stop thinking about tomorrow."

From Kukui, Jonny made a perfect backwards left into the parking lot in front of the IC, and backed up into the far corner near a wide roll-up door. The car was about a hundred yards from where it began.

Jonny cut the engine. "What do you know about home furnishings?"

Pateena, Jonny K's line of home furnishings, was a web-based business that sold reconditioned appliances, bathroom fixtures, kitchen gadgets, that sort of thing. The website design and upkeep were expensive, but the furnishings themselves were cheap, purchased by the truckload for between 88 and 97 cents a ton from the State of Hawaii's recycling program. Obviously, there was a fair amount of bycatch among this material, but the good stuff, the stuff deemed Pateena-worthy merchandise, was kept and hosed down with diluted acid solution, sandblasted, etched with wire brushes, painted, bashed with a ball peen hammer, buffed, epoxyed, or otherwise distressed to achieve that certain unique style that transformed a busted blender into a $2,000 "statement of modern ferocity," to quote the website. There weren't a *lot* of interior decorators with sufficiently large budgets and the requisite eye for Pateena's "bold and unique style," but there were *some* and that was the whole point, of course.

"I like marble countertops," Jeff answered.

They entered a small office and passed through to the workshop. It was a large open space. Two rows of segmented, cubic work stalls ran down the middle of the room below low-hanging vents and lights. Jumbled appliances and consumer goods were piled in one corner, their black cords looking like giant pubic hairs sprinkled throughout.

Pateena workers selected a piece from the pile, then brought it back to their workspace to grind a little here, crimp a little there, basically torture the doorknob or panini press or whatever it was. When the desired effect was reached, the worker affixed a Pateena brand badge to the item and brought it to a photo studio in the next room, where the piece was artfully staged and photographed in a sleek, anodyne home setting, the ideal of the modern, discerning, sage individualist.

The workers had begun to notice that Jonny K was in the shop. They put down their tools and made their way over.

"What's up Rafe?" Jonny said. "Tim, Nora, Chuck, B, Mikey, Nep2n, Finer. How's everybody? Yo, Mikey, that coffee urn you're working on looks fucking dooooooopppppe."

Everybody returned a grin and greeting to Jonny, Mikey especially.

Jonny laid a hand on Jeff's shoulder. "This is Jeff, he's going to start working here. Everybody help him out."

All the Pateeners stepped forward at once, thrusting hands and words of welcome at Jeff. They seemed like a fun bunch and/or members of a cult. After they had all introduced themselves, they returned to their work. Power tools whined back to life.

Jonny turned to Jeff. "So those are the guys. Here's the deal, bruddah. You grab something from the pile, fuck it up a little, but nice, you know? Put your thing on it and if it sells, you get half."

"You mean I give you half my pay?" Jeff asked.

"No, Jeff." Jonny pointed to the nearest work cube. "See that coffee urn Mikey's working on?"

Mikey was going at a silver urn with an angle-grinder, etching quarter-sized whorls on every surface.

Jonny continued. "That will sell for five grand, easy. Mikey gets twenty-five hundred by check. Twenty percent off for cash. Two grand. Some of these guys make ten Gs a week."

"That's a lot," Jeff said. "Why so much?"

"I know you're not from around here, Jeff. I'll explain like this: Respect is like heat, it only goes up. I think of these guys doing the work as my bosses, not my employees. So I show them respect. Respect that allows them to believe in themselves. A belief that allows them to create retail value for the customer."

Jeff said, "So the customers get the respect of the workers?" Pateena's hierarchy was confusing.

"Not workers," Jonny corrected. "At Pateena, we call them 'Craftsmiths.' Branding, bruddah. But no, the customer's at the bottom. It goes: Customer, Jonny K, Craftsmith."

"But the uh, Craftsmiths respect you." They practically fell over themselves greeting him.

"It only looks that way because I pay them so much, to answer your question from before," Jonny said. "My business is built on relationships. If you keep people happy, the money comes after. Are you in?"

"Yes," said Jeff. "Until the *Monkey Fist* goes out again."

"Great." Jonny K pumped Jeff's hand and hit his vape rig. "What are you doing right now?"

"I was going to go back to the boat."

"Tasha has you working today?" Jonny asked.

"Yes," Jeff said. "I have to work. There's always work to do on the boat."

"I didn't say you wouldn't be working." Jonny pointed to a strew of metal and plastic surrounding a roll-up door across the workshop. "That's last week's material. We have to make room for new stuff getting dropped off this afternoon. Put all of that shit into barrels and then roll the barrels into the bed of my El Camino. Welcome to Pateena. Use that shovel over there."

An hour later, once five barrels of irredeemable home goods had filled the back of Jonny's car-truck, Jonny had insisted that Jeff join him for a ride *makai*, toward the ocean. They drove to a small house with a long dock extending into a calm bay. At the end of the dock was a ski boat named *Monkey Fist Too*. Jonny directed Jeff to roll the barrels from the back of the El Camino into the *Too* and before Jeff knew it, he found himself a few miles offshore, bobbing with the waves and listening to "The Chain" cranking out across the dark water via Bluetooth.

"Now we drop the barrels in the water, bruddah!" Jonny shouted.

"What?" Jeff shouted back.

Jonny K took out his phone, hit the vape rig for the fourth time of their journey, then lowered the volume of the stereo.

"This all goes in the water," Jonny said, pointing to the barrels. "Help me lift them over the transom."

"Is that… allowed?" Jeff asked.

Jonny put his phone away. "Don't stop thinking about tomorrow. If I paid two hundred bones to bring this to the city transfer station, that would be two hundred I wouldn't have in my pocket tomorrow. I never pay more than I have to."

Jeff looked around. Only the slim moon looked back.

Jonny said, "If anyone asks, just say we were building an artificial reef for the turtles or some shit. I get a lot of mileage out of that one with the wahine, bruddah. Now help me lift."

CHAPTER 34

• Seek all advice, but do not take all of it.

The Dapper was Fridaybusy when Shwarma and Rahim arrived just before 10am. Rahim was a little nervous about returning to the shop and running into Bashir Hallazallah again, but Shwarma's promise of contact with Jefir overrode his fears.

Mr. Talmahani and Taj were both up on their feet working, Taj on his third appointment of the morning and Mr. Talmahani through a steady stream of walk-ins. Hallazallah was nowhere to be seen.

While waiting with Rahim for the Botcoin terminal to be free, Shwarma recalled Jeff's last message and the insulting .245 botcoins that came with it. All it took was less than a month's time for Jeff to lose his grip. But all things considered, Shwarmco's fledgling Overseas Agent Program had actually worked, and amazingly well. The $5,000 Shwarma had expected to wait months to recoup came back from America in just two weeks! There was definitely a future in this, it just needed a bit of fine-tuning. But this was what management was, wasn't it? Constantly correcting the meandering ways of subordinates, with no end in sight. Another job, infinitely.

When instinct works, we call it a plan. Shwarma's plan to keep the Zaqq brothers apart, including the destruction of Rahim's old phone, had been working just fine up until now, but that line about 'security' he kept repeating was only going to work for so long. Now, the time felt right to offer a bit more, to show what a reasonable and benevolent leader he was. A quick 300 characters from Rahim might just remind Jeff where to find his wallet. And if not, there was always the other thing. The other reason that Shwarma had brought them to the Dapper that morning.

A man stepped away from the Botcoin terminal and Shwarma took his place. He shielded the screen from Rahim's view as he tapped out his username and password.

The screen showed three lines of transactions. Shwarma jabbed Rahim's shoulder. "See, Rahim? Your brother is clearly alive and well. A transfer of twenty botcoins and change on 13 July. Another 30.06 on the 20th. And another today, although as you can see—"

"Is that his email address?" Rahim asked, a finger squashed on the screen. Jeffzachary262@wmail.com? I need to contact him!"

"Go right ahead. That's why I brought you here. This machine provides secure communication. But never, *never* use that address through your phone or any unsecured means." Shwarma stepped aside.

Rahim tapped open Jeff's previous messages and began reading. "He wants me to come to Honolulu?" he said.

"Not badly enough to pay for it, but apparently yes. So he says," Shwarma answered.

Rahim read more. "This says he died briefly!" he exclaimed. "You didn't tell me that, Mr. Shwarma!"

"That sounded a bit dramatic, don't you think? Clearly he is alive enough to send a message. Send him something back. Tell him how you look forward to seeing him. To send the message will cost you a little Botcoin, but I'll take it out of your pay this week."

Shwarma set the machine up to transfer some Botcoin and Rahim typed the following:

> Hi Jefir, This is Rahim. I'm so happy to hear you are doing well in Hawaii and I hope I will be able to come there soon. I have not been back to the market or seen Mrs. Khan, but I am doing well working for Mr. Shwarma. Please be careful. I love you, brother.

Rahim stepped back from the machine. Shwarma read the message. "Very nice," he said. He tapped SEND.

"Next!" Mr. Talmahani called.

Some of the men who had been waiting had formed a foursome around the arcade game to begin a round of Golden Golf Tee when they saw Mr. Talmahani putting the final shaky touches on his previous customer's now slightly crooked beard. A few other men had congregated in the back hall, looking deep in conversation. Nobody made a move for Talmahani's chair.

"You." Mr. Talmahani pointed his clippers at Shwarma.

"I have Botcoin business, sir!" Shwarma called, patting the console of the machine.

Mr. Talmahani looked at Rahim. He said, "You, young man. A trim for the weekend? Surely there is some young lady who would appreciate it."

Rahim blushed, knowing that a Dapper trim would nearly bust him for the week.

Shwarma checked his watch. "Go ahead, Rahim," he said. "Tell Mr. Talmahani that I will cover the cost."

Rahim grinned and got in Chair #1.

Shwarma turned back to the Botcoin terminal and arranged to transfer .0001 botcoins, the minimum amount allowed, along with the following message:

> Jeff, this is Shwarma. Rahim is depending on you. If you are serious about bringing him to Hawaii, provide me some details/proof of your "very large source of income" and dates you expect to get it and I will begin arrangements.

He sent the message, closed the Botcoin session and wandered into the waiting area where he sat alone with both of his thoughts. The thought of losing Z100,000 to Hallazallah the other day and the thought of how to get it back. He kept an eye on the door.

Mr. Talmahani finished up Rahim and dusted him off. Rahim thanked him and slipped out of the chair. He drifted to the door to chat with Zebar. Mr. Talmahani said to Shwarma, "You're next."

"Thank you, but no," Shwarma said. "I'm here to meet someone."

"This is a barbershop, not one of your discotheques."

"A business meeting," Shwarma said.

"And you're going to it looking like that?" Mr. Talmahani asked, eyeing Shwarma's beard. "Let me sharpen you up a bit."

"Fine," Shwarma said, unable to resist test-stroking his beard. He got to his feet. "Just one moment." He interrupted Rahim and Zebar's discussion about football or some such nonsense and dispatched Rahim to Shinni's with instructions to secure "one of the round tables" for lunch at noon. Rahim left and Shwarma took a seat in Chair #1.

"Do you expect to see Bashir Hallazallah today?" he asked Mr. Talmahani casually.

"That'll be two thousand," Mr. Talmahani said.

"For the answer? Do be serious, old man."

"For the kid's trim, Shwarma," Mr. Talmahani said.

"Oh. Yes, of course." Shwarma reached into his pocket and handed Mr. Talmahani the pink card entitling its bearer to a free Gentleman's Choice that Shwarma had received with his Dapper membership package. No tip. "And do you expect Mr. Hallazallah to come in today?"

Mr. Talmahani shrugged in the Zazari style.

Shwarma said, "Just a light trim for me."

Shwarma winced through Mr. Talmahani's wobbly work while glancing at the door every few minutes. When it was over, Shwarma paid and rather than leaving, hung around the shop, killing time.

He was six shots over par on the fourteenth hole when Hallazallah entered the Dapper with his lieutenant Rizwan. Hallazallah heartily greeted Zebar and then Mr. Talmahani discreetly beckoned him close. The older men spoke quietly, both glancing toward Shwarma, who was watching the whole thing.

Hallazallah made a quick comment to Taj and then continued toward the rear of the shop, catching Shwarma's eye.

Shwarma abandoned his round to join Hallazallah in the quiet and dim back hallway.

Hallazallah said, "Mr. Talmahani informs me that we have a business meeting scheduled today. Strange that I don't remember."

"It was not in your calendar, sir," said Rizwan, from over Shwarma's shoulder.

Shwarma ignored Lieutenant Toasted Almond Bar and leaned closer to Hallazallah. "As a fellow member of the club, I was hoping you could offer me some advice."

"Taj. Always go with Taj. Chair #2."

"Not about that," Shwarma said, stroking his beard again. "I told you about my agent embedded in America the other day?"

"I remember," Hallazallah said.

"I understand you have some experience in this area. How would you suggest, you know, activating him?" Shwarma asked.

"I thought you already did. The biological attack, was it?"

"Yes, there was that," Shwarma said. "But I want to achieve a more… maximal effect. What would you suggest?"

"Depends on your budget," Hallazallah hemmed.

"The budget's a little tight at the moment," Shwarma admitted.

"I remember that as well," said Hallazallah, smirking. "Here's my free advice: There's very little Westerners fear more than the unknown. Give them what and who, but not when or how—and never why. Save the why for your own men. Belief in purpose is key."

"Thank you," Shwarma said. "Very helpful."

Rizwan interrupted. "Excuse me, sir. Taj is waiting. And we need to be going by noon."

Shwarma looked at his watch. It was 10:30. "It takes ninety minutes to do that?" he asked Hallazallah, casting an eye over Hallazallah's beard. "Twice a week?"

"These things take time. Taj is an artist. You know how they are. Good luck with your man, Shwarma. Let me know how it goes."

"Agreed," said Shwarma.

CHAPTER 35

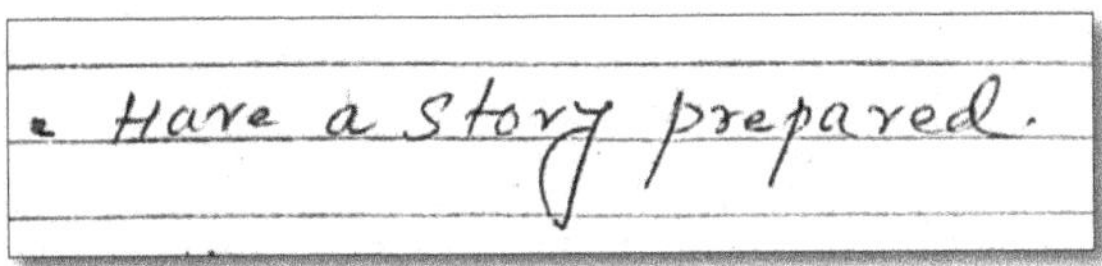

"Friday night on the boat" means different things to different people. For example, if someone from, say, the Florida Panhandle offers you a "Friday night on the boat," do it, do it, *do it.* But if someone from Newfoundland says, "Hey, Friday night on the boat?" start walking in the other direction immediately.

Jeff had no way of knowing any of this, of course. In his case, Friday night on the boat meant corn tortillas, beans, and knot practice on the deck until the sun set and then slightly beyond. It meant waiting.

Pawn1^{2} opened at 11am on Saturday.

Saturday morning brought light fog, corn tortillas, beans and knot practice. At 10:30 Jeff snugged his new belt, fashioned from yellow paracord and secured with a tight, round monkey's fist, and leapt from the boat onto the pier. He was over the bridge in under a minute.

He ran medium through the industrial fringe around Honolulu Harbor. His steps were light and Jeff increased his pace as he thought of the message from Rahim. His brother was safe. He was sorry to hear that he hadn't seen Mrs. Khan, but Rahim wasn't going to sell melons forever. He was destined for greater things. They both were, apparently. He sped up a little more.

There was more cinder block than glass in this neighborhood. The business signs did not break-dance pneumatically. They warned trespassers, solicitors, and loiterers to keep it moving. Most of the concrete sidewalk squares were tilted a few degrees leeward, windward and all the other directions, whatever they were called.

Saturday seemed to be as busy as every other day. Trucks chuffed from every warehouse and depot, sometimes stopping on giant scales at the gates. Some of the drivers got out, some didn't. Jeff saw one case where the truck driver invited the guy working the scale to step aboard as well. Reliable proof of anything is hard to come by in this world. Proof. The thin, yet unbreakable string tied to your fate. Sometimes just a light tug on it is enough. You know, just to be sure something's really there at the other end. Other times, people feel like they have to haul it all the way in to see it with their own eyes.

In his last message, Shwarma said he wanted proof that the rhodium was… well, that it was. Just like Ike at Pawn1^2 wanted "legal ID." Everyone wanted proof of something. Fortunately, it was Ike's suspicious nature that would be Jeff's ally this morning.

It turned out that Ike didn't work Saturdays. A kid about Jefir's age rode up to Pawn1^2 on a black electric bike at 10:57. The kid's name was Hito Nakamura. Hito locked up his bike, and when he unlocked the pawnshop door, Jeff went to follow him in, but Hito told him to wait outside while he "turned everything on." He went in and locked the door behind him. Sure enough, after a few moments, lights flickered on, and a light hum of A/C kicked in.

Hito returned to the door and from inside, turned his jangling keys to let Jeff in. "Sorry to keep you waiting," he said. "Usually we don't get our first customer 'til around noon on Saturday." He stepped behind the counter. "What can I do for you?"

Jeff reached into his right pocket and pulled out the gleaming rhodium. "I have some… metal I'd like to sell."

"What is that? Silver?" Hito asked. "Throw it up on the scale." He reached under the counter to grab the orange XRF gun. He fiddled with its switches.

Jeff continued to hold the rhodium in his hand, and with the other, dug out his phone. "Is it OK if I record video on my phone while you… measure it?"

Jeff had an elaborate fiction prepared in case he was asked *why* he wanted to document the XRF scan. The story had to do with the last wishes of a dying man, the bond between brothers and the outrageous price of diesel fuel.

"Sure, bro," Hito said. "TikTok? ZoopZap?"

Elaborate fiction not needed. Perhaps merely preparing was enough. "Yes," said Jeff. He started to record video and turned the phone's lens on himself. He spoke into the video image of his own tiny and slightly delayed face. "Hello Rahim! It's me. I'm doing well…" Jeff remembered Shwarma's warning about non-Botcoin encrypted messages. He had to assume that this message may not be entirely secure. "...here, in the place where I am. I'm sorry I can't see you in person, but I hope to see you soon, brother. Mr. Shwarma, I hope this is enough proof for you." He turned his camera on the rhodium in his outstretched palm. Still recording, he stepped forward to place it on the scale.

Hito didn't know who Rahim and Mr. Shwarma were, but as the lead singer of the punk/ska band Waveslayer, he knew what to do when the camera was on.

"YOWHATSUPTHISYOURBOYHITO! My man here brought something to sell at the Pawn-One-Baby-Deuce and we're going to see what's what!" He aimed the XRF gun at the rhodium. "Check out my band Waveslayer, playing Thursday night at—OH SHIT! This is almost pure rhodium! Twenty-five point two-three ounces!" He jumped back and banged out a few numbers on an adding machine. "My man's nug is worth eighty-nine Geeeeeeeeees!"

Hito was jumping around a lot and it was difficult for Jeff to keep him in frame. Shwarma would not be satisfied with anything but a single, unbroken shot that included the XRF gun's readout.

Jeff said, "Could you—"

"Rhodium BAYBEEEE! Waveslayer! Thursday! Nine o'clock. The District! Hito out!"

"Hito? Hito. Could you turn that readout so I can see it in the camera?" Jeff asked.

"Sure, bro!" Hito twisted the XRF gun around and Jeff stepped close enough for his phone's camera to pick up the LED readout:

WEIGHT:	25.2307 oz
COMPOSITION:	
97.76%	Rh (RHODIUM)
00.97%	Co (COBALT)
00.56%	Mn (MANGANESE)
00.32%	Ni (NICKEL)

Jeff held the phone steady for a few seconds, then cut the video. "Thank you, Hito."

"Yeah dude, no worries. But I can't pay you that much right now. Anything over 10,000 my boss has to sign the check. Sorry. Come back Monday."

"Yes, I understand," Jeff said. He had what he needed. "Thank you, Hito. Have a good day."

"All good, bro. Be cool. Tag me in that video. At waveslayer808."

CHAPTER 36

• Steer things toward a conclusion.

When Jeff had sent $5,000 in just two weeks, and seemed positively anxious to follow it up with another 10, Shwarma made the call to Tycanni's real estate office to schedule a tour of 505 H Street's 3rd floor office space. But that was two days ago. Now, after the gush of Botcoin had suddenly become a trickle, the office had cruelly retreated from Shwarma's budgetary grasp. But he still wanted to see the inside.

505 H was actually more spacious in person than the photos in the brochure had led Shwarma to believe. The office was bright and airy and Tycanni said he could probably arrange for the massive desk to be included in the deal if the full asking price was met. When the arched window and both office doors were open, a cool zephyr flowed through the office like a dream through the mind.

After the tour, Tycanni once again reflexively mentioned that properties like 505 H don't come along every day. He shook hands with Shwarma while confiding that he had a loose Quudi buyer coming through town in a few days and he'd be surprised if the listing was still available at this time next week. He encouraged Shwarma to make a quick decision, then bid him a good day and walked off down the block.

Shwarma squatted in the shade of a palm tree near the stoop. The office was out of reach. First, last and security would pretty much clean him out. Especially if he was losing Jeff. For now, 505 H was more than he could safely afford. For now.

His phone buzzed. A Wmail to the Mohammad Mohammad account. A video file from Jeff Zachary. Subject line: Proof.

The first half of the video was Jeff blabbering into the camera. Then he held a silvery chunk of metal in his hand. Then he put it on a scale in front of a young man in some kind of shop, Then—

Shwarma hurried to bang out a reply: "Good work, sell ASAP. When?" Send.

He jumped up. "Mr. Tycanni! Wait!"

CHAPTER 37

• Consider both side of a things, no matter
• how stupid, weak or offensive.

Selling the rhodium ASAP was exactly what Jeff intended to do. He decided to wait before responding to Shwarma, hoping that Jonny K would contact him with a buyer over the weekend, but by Monday morning, he thought he should send an update. In a short Wmail, Jeff explained to Shwarma that he couldn't provide specific dates at the moment, but that he had engaged a well-connected partner and repeated that the sale was happening ASAP.

In the meantime, Jeff had the day to himself aboard the *Monkey Fist* as she bobbed in her berth. He made himself breakfast of corn tortillas and beans. (Page 3: "Adopt the customs.") After he ate, he washed his dishes. (Page 2: "Cover your tracks.") He then organized the Tupperware so it would not spill out whenever Kai opened the cabinet. (Code of the Sea.) He was in the middle of wiping off the counter when he heard someone coming down the stairs.

"Jeff? Are you here?" Tasha asked.

"Yes."

"Everything all right?" She stepped into the galley "I'm just stopping by to check the boat." She stepped to the coffeemaker and topped off her travel mug.

"Everything is fine, Captain," said Jeff.

"I told you it's weird when you call me that, Jeff. Tasha."

"Tasha," Jeff repeated. "When will we go fishing next?"

"I talked to Hemi this morning. He needs another week at least." She screwed the lid back onto her mug. "Do you know anyone who can take his spot for one trip?"

"To work with us on the boat?" Jeff's first thought was Rahim of course, but even in the best case, it would be weeks before his brother could arrive in the US. "What about Jonny K? He lives nearby. And it's his boat, after all."

"First off," Tasha said, "I told you it's *my* boat. Jonny just owns it. Second, as the owner, he controls what we call the means of production, which means that he doesn't have to handle fish guts if he doesn't want to. Third, what makes you think I'd have him on my crew?"

Jeff shrugged. "I just thought it would be better for everyone if the boat was out catching fish."

"You would think," Tasha agreed. "It's alright. The moon's not great for fishing right now, anyway. We could take a few days off. You don't have any plans, do you?"

"Why would I have plans? I mean, what kind of plans?" Jeff suavely asked.

In fact, he did have plans. That very afternoon, he was to begin his first day of work as a Craftsmith at Pateena, Jonny K's defurbished home goods factory, creating "artisanal decoria," as the company's sleek and enticing website referred to them.

As with the fisherman, the Craftsmith only receives pay upon production, and to put a point on it even finer than that of the gaff or jagged wine glass, they only receive pay when someone actually pays them negotiable currency for that which has been produced. At Pateena, Jeff would be working on commission. At first, Jeff wasn't sure why it was called a "co-mission," when it seemed that he would be doing almost all the work by himself, but Jonny K explained that high costs of shipping, to name one example, needed to be met, not to mention the ongoing maintenance of the company's internet presence. Speaking of which, even if one of Jeff's statements spoke sweetly or firmly enough to a high-end online home furnishings buyer, Jeff would not receive his due pay until after Pateena's stated thirty-day free return period. So Jeff was prepared to wait for at least a month before his first payday. Until that happened, until he had Botcoin firmly in hand, he had decided to keep the news of his new job from Shwarma, in the style of the college student who switches his major from Pre-med to Puppetry and puts off telling his parents for a few semesters, hoping it will somehow all work out. Tasha, however, was more like the college student's roommate. You can't be bringing marionettes back to the room every night without expecting a few questions.

"What are you doing this week?" she asked.

Jeff said, "Until we can go out fishing again, Jonny K gave me a job at Pateena. His factory."

"I know what it is," Tasha said. She rapped a knuckle on the boat's microwave. "That's where this came from."

Now that she mentioned it, Jeff thought he recognized the style of the battered appliance.

"I also know that they don't start work over there until 3pm Hawaiian," Tasha continued. "Who starts work at 3pm? It's both too late AND too early. Has Jonny paid you yet?"

"A little. I did some shoveling the other day. But today is my first full day."

Tasha said, "Jeff, what you do on your own time is your business, but you still work on the *Monkey Fist*. This job isn't just landing fat fish and counting your money. Taking care of the boat is part of the job. Finish up here in the galley. Mop the floors down here. Clean up the head. Laundry. There's bait in the hold that's going no-can. Get rid of it today. Then you can head over to Pateena. Got it?"

"Yes," said Jeff.

"And remember you're not on the *Fist* over there. Nobody's going to be watching out for you at that place. Especially Jonny. You gotta watch your own back. That's all I'm going to say."

"Yes, thank you."

"There is also the matter of a hundred dollars for this week's rent," Tasha said.

"Yes, of course!" said Jeff. "Just a minute." He went into the bunkroom and pulled five twenties from the crinkled envelope that, securely zipped into his backpack's inner pocket, served as his personal safe. His cash balance was now $184.

"Thanks," Tasha said as he handed it over. "Laters." She turned and disappeared up the stairs. "Have a good day at work. Remember what I said."

Jeff busied himself cleaning up belowdecks. He then lugged a case-and-a-half of overripe mackerel from the hold to the stern rail, where he tossed them one-by-one to some seagulls who registered no complaints, even when all the bait was gone. He washed up and changed into what he now considered his lucky plaid pants, fastened the monkey's fist that served as his belt buckle and did a few small deck jobs in the shade of the pilothouse. At 2:15, he put aside the snarl of line he had been working to respool, hopped from the deck and lightly jogged the 3.7 miles to Pateena.

Unlike the *Monkey Fist*, Pateena's workplace ethos was pretty light on things like practical advice and power tool safety, but rather leaned more on the ineffable.

According to Rafe, the trick to upcycling the slightly-less-than-durable home goods into commercially viable, avant-garde statement pieces was mostly in selecting the proper item from the jumbled workpile in the corner of the loading dock. "It's all about the vibe," he explained to Jeff.

According to B, the trick was to spray-paint the items a certain shade of metallic blue-green, but it was made very clear to Jeff that this particular shade was for B's exclusive use and was strictly off-limits for Jeff and everyone else working in the "Studio Space."

Tim advised Jeff, "Don't learn the tricks of the trade. Learn the trade."

Nora offered, "This whole damn trade is a trick."

The others, Chuck, Mikey, Nep2n and Finer all presumably had their own thoughts and methods, but they seemed very engaged in their respective projects and they didn't offer them and Jeff didn't ask.

With Rafe's help, he selected his first workpiece, a chrome four-slice toaster, because of its "strong energy."

Jeff brought the toaster to his work station. He considered. Tried to see the toaster's "inner spirit." He plugged it in and depressed the lever. Perhaps the inner spirit would be revealed through the glowing orange heating coils. Or perhaps not. The coils remained cold and dark.

"Does it matter if it doesn't work?" he asked Rafe, who was working at the station to Jeff's right.

Rafe took his earbud out. Faint beats of music could be heard through the zizz and clang of the studio. "What?"

"What if it doesn't work?" Jeff said, peering into the toaster's slots.

"Doesn't work as what? A toaster?"

"Yes," Jeff said.

"You just gotta feel that, Jeff."

"Yes, but—"

Earbud back in.

Jeff picked up the toaster and lightly shook it. "Should I clean out all the crumbs, at least?"

Rafe was concentrating on finding just the right angle that a brass lighting sconce could be affixed to a small inkjet printer/scanner.

"Rafe?"

Rafe took out an earbud. "What?"

Jeff repeated, "Should I clean out all the crumbs?"

"Yeah, whatever, man. Probably. But it's not about what you take out, it's about what you put in. Look, I'm trying to get in the zone over here. Just trust your flow. Do your own thing." Earbud back in.

This must have been what Tasha had warned him about. The Pateena employees were more a band of individuals, each working on their disparate jobs, than they were a crew united in common cause.

Jeff considered the toaster again in the context of his personal flow. He shook the toaster upside down and banged a shower of crumbs into the trash can that he and Rafe shared. He set the toaster back on his bench. He stretched the communal air hose that curlicued from the ceiling and meticulously cleaned the toaster with compressed air. Wiped it off with a damp rag. Considered it some more.

Hours later, Rafe had the brass sconce and a semi-circle of sparkplugs firmly superglued to the printer. The effect of light and shadow playing through the glass scanning bed was simply stunning. Rafe signed a chrome-and-teak Pateena badge and affixed it to his piece. He stood back, clearly pleased with it. Jeff noted that while the light was functional, the printer/scanner was quite clearly not.

Jeff's toaster was completely clean inside and out. He estimated there had been at least a full bread slice's worth of crumbs caked on the machine's innards when he unscrewed and popped the shiny chrome casing off in search of inspiration. The good news was that the crumb build-up on the electrical contacts was the cause of the toaster's failure to fire and now the toaster worked like a charm. The bad news was that hot, orange heating elements alone were probably not considered Pateena-level aesthetic.

The hot glow reminded Jeff of the feeling that the rhodium gave him when he left the pawnshop on Friday after learning its value. Since then, the shard had not left his pocket. Even the deepest depths of his backpack, under the blanket in the *Monkey Fist*'s bunkroom did not seem secure enough for his fortune, so Jeff had been carrying it with him wherever he went, squeezing and checking it a few times every hour. Staring now at his toaster, his fingers unconsciously pressed the hard outline of the rhodium. The flow, the vibe, the whatever, hit him. Why didn't he think of this sooner?

"Rafe," Jeff said. "Rafe!"

Earbud out. "What?"

"Your… lamp looks great."

"Thanks, Jeff. It's not a lamp, it's a Luminscape."

"Yes. Luminscape. How much do you think it will sell for?"

Rafe said, "Four, five thousand. Luminscapes have been selling great in California lately."

"I see," Jeff said. "What if you had, for example, a gold… watch, that was worth, say, ninety thousand dollars. Wouldn't it be smart to somehow attach the watch to the Luminscape? Then it would be worth ninety-five thousand."

Rafe said, "Ninety thousand? That's a very nice watch."

"Yes," said Jeff.

"If I had a watch like that," Rafe said, "I would just keep it. Once you add it to a piece, you'd be giving up half. Remember, we split everything we make." He looked at Jeff's toaster. "How's that coming?"

"I'm still working on it," said Jeff, putting down the superglue.

A voice cut through the buzz of the shop. "What is that? A new Luminscape? Rafe, that is the shit!" Jonny K said, as he clapped Rafe on the shoulder. "Bruddah, we're not even putting this on the site! We'll offer it to Malibu Interiors exclusive. They'll buy this for five grand all day, guaranz ballbearanz! Let's get the photos shot and box this thing up."

Rafe grinned and Jeff watched as he proudly carried his creation to the photo studio in the next room, accepting the nods and laurels of his co-workers along the way.

"Jeff!" Jonny K said, stepping into Jeff's work area. "How'd your first day go? Nice toaster."

"Yes. Thank you, Jonny. My first day was good. I enjoyed the work."

"Good," Jonny said, sidling closer. "Good. Hey, you remember what we talked about in my office the other day? The sale of that thing you showed me?"

"Yes," said Jeff.

"Jeff, you know how money works, right?" Jonny K paused and took a draw from his vape. It made the tiniest of buzzing sounds. He flashed the JK laser show quickly, as if projecting one's initials through a swirling haze of pot smoke via green laser light was the most burdensome of formalities. Despite the brevity, the Pateena employees let out small cheers of appreciation.

Meanwhile, yes, Jeff knew that money was exchanged for goods and services. A sort of rope that tethered the world together. And the rope was invisible. At least it was to Jeff. He made a small shrug, hoping the dissipating smoke would cloud his uncertainty.

Jonny said, “Money doesn’t grow like a seed, Jeff, all alone buried in the ground. Money’s made like people. It needs to get out in the world and start fucking around.”

Jeff waited. There had to be more to it than that.

Jonny continued, “I’m just letting you know that *I know* you wanted to keep this thing downlow. But it’s out there. Things are tight around here, so I had to ask around a little. But I keep it a hunnie with you, bruddah.”

“Yes.”

“The first few guys I called didn’t want to touch it.”

Jeff recalled the man at the pawnshop who had literally avoided touching the rhodium.

Jonny said, “But one of those guys knew a guy, who knew a guy. He’s FBI.”

“What?” Jeff gasped.

“From the Big Island. Maui. He's one of these guys doesn’t trust the banks. Keeps all his money in metal. I heard he walks around with one of those… you know… like a cloth purse… a Crown Royal bag… a satchel! Fucking satchel full of gold flakes. That’s how he pays for shit. Gives the waiter a pinch of gold, traded a brick for a car.”

Jeff was relieved to know that Jonny K was not calling federal investigators, but he was afraid there was still a misunderstanding, perhaps due to Jonny K's game of underworld telephone. "I don't want gold. I want money," he said.

"I know, bruddah. That's where I come in to help," Jonny said. "The FBI guy's going to pay you in gold, two ounces for every one ounce of your rhodium. Then I'll pay you for the gold in cash. It's about fourteen hundred an ounce these days, but I'll give you fifteen hundred. Everybody gets what they want. He gets rhodium, I get a little gold," he wiggled his rings, "And you'll walk out with about sixty thousand dollars. Cash."

"Before, I thought you said you didn't have the cash."

"I said I didn't have ninety-thousand. I can swing sixty if it means helping you out. Sixty thousand, Jeff. Sound good?"

"Yes."

"Good," Jonny said.

"When?" Jeff asked.

"Tomorrow. Noon. The IC." Jonny's eyes roamed to Jeff's workspace. He pointed to the toaster. "Does that work?"

"Yes," said Jeff, depressing the lever.

Jonny said, "I'll take it. Congrats, bruddah. You made your first sale." He counted out and handed Jeff ten one-hundred dollar bills. "See you tomorrow." He unplugged the toaster, picked it up by the cord and carried it out the way a taxidermist carries a cat after the customer leaves the shop.

Jeff looked at the bills in his hand. Franklin stared back at him with what looked to be purse-lipped disappointment. Jeff ignored him and folded the bills. He slipped them into his pocket, trying to imagine what six hundred more might feel like.

CHAPTER 38

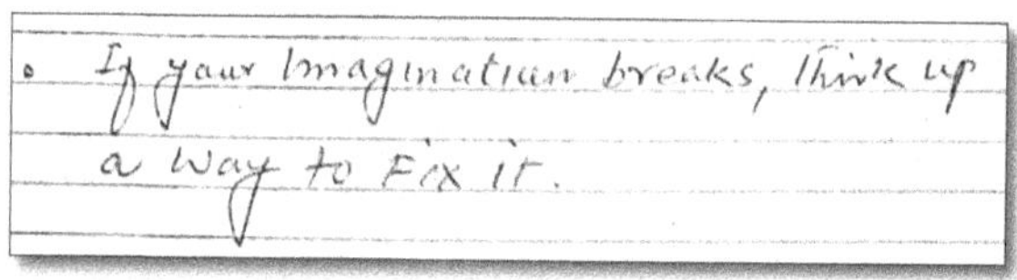

Jeff declined a ride home in the El Camino, choosing to trot home to the marina through the syrupy Hawaiian night. Thoughts rattled in his brain like the rhodium in his pocket.

Rhodium that, in about twelve hours time, would become sixty thousand US dollars. What would the cash look like? Would it be presented in an envelope, like his pay from Tasha? Maybe in a briefcase? If so, would Jeff be allowed to keep the case?

Whatever the… well, case, the larger issue was what his windfall meant. Freedom and Rahim's full passage to Hawaii in just a few short weeks. Not to mention the mind-boggling sum of fifty thousand remaining dollars to start their new lives together. At some point, Jeff thought that he should mention to Tasha that his whip-smart and able-bodied brother would be moving to Honolulu and could use a job, but not until things were actually in motion, not until definite plans had been made.

Jeff glided over the Sand Island bridge, composing the email to Shwarma in his head. Shwarma's request for proof and his response to the video told Jeff that using unencrypted Wmail was an acceptable risk. Jeff was glad for that, as it meant he didn't have to run halfway across town to the Pawn1[2] Botcoin machine every time he had something to report.

Nevertheless, Jeff thought he should go easy on the details in his message. No sense blaring it out to the internet that he routinely walked around carrying a fortune in his pocket. Keep things brief. Sale tomorrow. Full payment in twenty-four hours. Send Rahim.

He cut across the quiet marina parking lot, down the pier, and skipped aboard the darkened *Monkey Fist*.

Down in the stuffy bunkroom, he dug his phone out of his backpack, anxious to report his imminent triumph.

But first, a text notification! The tiny red dot on his phone blazed with a "1." From Rahim? Jeff tapped. From Tasha. After the second trip, Jeff had suggested they trade phone numbers. When Jeff was alone on the boat, he had adopted the habit of reporting to Tasha a nightly all's-well. Most nights, she replied with a photo of her left hand giving the thumbs-up. Tonight, her message read:

Tommy found a guy. We sail Wednesday PM. B ready. 

Jeff replied with the short, declarative statement of a photo of his fist.

Thankfully, the boat wouldn't be going out to sea tomorrow. Jeff didn't know what he would do if he would be needed to outfit and prep the boat while Jonny K also expected him at the Intercontinental for a multi-thousand-dollar meeting at noon. What would have been an impossible scheduling dilemma had formed an orderly line such that Jeff could still attend to both without conflict, solidifying his sense that success and life were meshing together like the cogged spindle gears of the *Monkey Fist*'s engine room.

With a pronoid smile, Jeff opened Wmail.

To: mohammad.mohammad54321@zmail.zaz

From: jeffzachary262@wmail.com

Subject: Re: Proof

I will be selling the material tomorrow. (Tuesday). In 24 hours I will settle our debt in full. Begin making arrangements for Rahim's trip.

CHAPTER 39

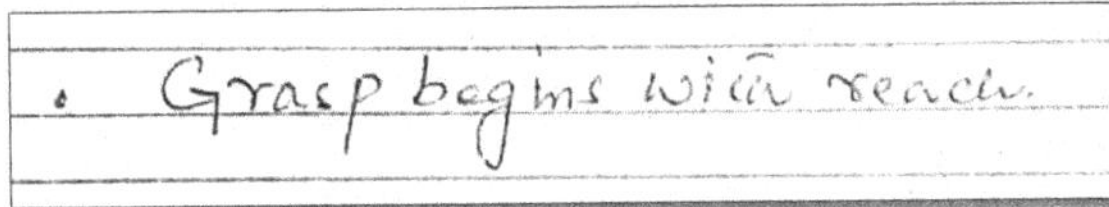

Jama Tycanni made a point of presenting himself as a forward-looking sort of fellow and he told Shwarma that he would have "no problem whatsoever" accepting first, last and security on 505 H Street in the form of Botcoin. "I have been known to utilize the terminal at the Dapper from time to time," he said on the phone. "In fact, I am seeing Taj in an hour. Why don't you meet me there, Wahiri? We can arrange payment and sign the papers."

At the appointed hour, while Tycanni gossiped with some other Dapperians in the waiting area, Shwarma logged onto his Botcoin account and took a moment to admire the upwardly jagging digital slope that marked the pleasing profile of what he liked to think of as Botcoin Mountain.

He took a deep breath and began the transfer to Tycanni's account, shearing Botcoin Mountain to a near-vertical cliff.

CHAPTER 40

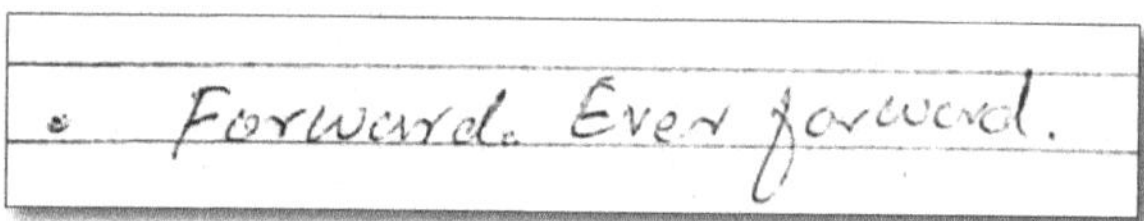

Karaoke is like shooting off fireworks. Nothing's really stopping you from doing it during the day, but you don't get the full effect until it's dark and you have a few drinks in you.

The stage at the Intercontinental was quiet when Jeff walked in at 11:50am, but a light lunch crowd was scattered through the tables and a few dedicated day drinkers dotted the bar.

Through the house speakers, George Benson assured everybody that nothing was gonna change his love for them.

The hostess offered Jeff a table, but he explained to her that he was there for a meeting with Jonny K, his hand unconsciously groping the metallic lump in his pocket.

"He's in his office," she said. "Go on back."

Jeff thanked her and made his way across the room. Brad the bartender was working, but Jeff avoided his eye as he passed.

Jonny K's door was open ninety degrees, as far as the couch arm would allow. Jeff poked his head in and knocked lightly on the doorframe. Jonny looked up, finished a few taps on his phone/vape/laser combo and laid it on his desk next to a slushy drink in a highball glass. He sprang to his feet, his nimble movement belying his ample carriage.

"Jeff!" he said, coming around his desk to shake Jeff's sweaty hand. "You're early. I like that. Sit down, sit down." He gestured to the couch and Jeff took a seat.

Jonny shut the office door and sat back down. "K-den. So here's the haps." He looked at his gold watch. "I had to call around a little. Not everyone rolls high enough to buy that much rhodium. But I hooked up with a dude from the Big Island, we'll call him Mr. A. He's gonna check out your rhodium. You got it, right?"

Jeff pulled the body-warm nugget from his pocket.

Jonny smiled. "Put it here," he said, nudging a flat, square device on a corner of his desk that Jeff recognized as a digital scale.

As Jeff stood, Jonny said, "The guy's probably gonna bring his own scale, but you never know, sometimes the other guy's scale goes a little light. I don't want you to get shorted."

Jeff placed the rhodium on Jonny's scale. The digital readout flickered to report 25.23 ounces.

"K-den," Jonny said again. "So after Mr. A weighs it, he's gonna test it with his scanner to make sure it's really rhodium, then you get paid. Sound good?"

Jeff said, "Yes."

Jonny picked up his phone. "Mr. A agreed to two-to-one gold-to-rhodium." He tapped a few more times. "He'll give up fifty point four-six ounces of gold. He's shorting you a little on the two-to-one swap, but

I got you, bruddah. Gold is selling for about fourteen hundred an ounce right now, but I'll give you fifteen hundred." He tapped a few more keys. "Making your end… 75,690. All cash. No tax man, no ID, no nothing. You slip me… thirty-seven hundred for setting up the meet and that leaves you… just under 72 Gs, and we're even steven. Everyone goes home happy. Cool?"

"Yes," said Jeff. "Thank you for helping me."

"No prob," Jonny said. "What you gonna do with all that kālā?"

"Kālā?" asked Jeff.

"Cash money. Dollar bills, bruddah."

"Yes. Well—"

A knock on the door interrupted him.

"Come on," Jonny called out.

The door swung open, stopping at the arm of the couch, and a short, silver-haired man entered the office. He wore a summer weight suit and too much cologne. A black leather satchel hung over his shoulder.

Jonny stood up. "There he is! Mr. A!"

Mr. A closed the door and stepped into the office to shake Jonny's hand. "Nice to meet you," he said.

Jonny pumped Mr. A's hand. "Thanks for coming." He then gestured to Jeff, who was rising from the couch. "Mr. A, meet my friend… Mr. J. Mr. J has something I think you'll be interested in."

"Yes, so I've heard," said Mr. A. He set his satchel down on the couch and shook hands with Jeff. "A pleasure to meet you." His hands were very soft.

"A pleasure to meet you," Jeff said.

Mr. A smiled, a smile softer than his hands. "I understand you have quite a specimen of rhodium." His eyes found the scale on Jonny's desk. "Is that it?"

"Yes," Jeff said.

Mr. A bent to examine the glittering shard, murmuring, "Hm. Quite something."

He went to his satchel and removed a small digital scale. "If you'll indulge me?"

Jonny cleared a space on his desk and Mr. A placed his scale down, switched it on and made a show of zeroing it out. He gingerly moved the rhodium onto his scale's plate, then dug once more in his satchel for an XRF scanner gun much like the one Jeff had seen used at the pawnshop.

Mr. A bent to see the scale's readout. "Twenty-five point two-three ounces of…" He fiddled with the scanner and aimed it at the nugget. "... rhodium. Ninety-seven point seven-six percent pure." He grinned and looked at Jeff. "I'll take it."

"Boom kanani!" Jonny yelped. "Now we gonna celebrate! I'll text Brad to bring us some champagne." He tapped out a short message on his phone.

Mr. A had put the rhodium in a velvet drawstring bag and tucked it carefully into his jacket pocket. He was now working his phone as well, doing calculations. "Twenty-five point two-three… times two—"

The door banged open, but it wasn't Brad with the champagne, it was a hard-eyed Asian man wearing a navy windbreaker with a red and yellow insignia on the chest. "Nobody move!" he commanded.

"Who the hell are you?" Jonny K said, getting to his feet.

The man flashed a badge. "Inspector Han Li. People's Republic of China Ministry of Security. Sit down, Mr. Kalawai'a."

Jeff caught a glimpse of a black handgun on Inspector Li's hip. Mr. A had shrunk to a corner of the office and had his hands raised.

Jonny K's eyes found the weapon as well and he slowly sat back down. "What do you want?" he said. "This is my place. You got no business here."

"Your thief had no business in the sovereign mineral beds of China, Mr. Kalawai'a. But here we are." He turned to Jeff. "Is this him?" He drew his pistol and aimed it at Jeff's chest. "You thought you could steal from my people?"

Jeff stammered, "I didn't steal anything! I found it—"

"Hold up, hold up," Jonny K said to Li. "What are you even talking about?"

Still glaring at Jeff, Li drew a folded piece of paper from his jacket and flicked it onto Jonny's desk. "This. A twenty-five point two-three ounce nugget of ninety-seven point seven-six percent pure rhodium that went missing from the Yang Shi mineral platform in the Molokai Fracture Zone."

Jonny unfolded the paper and stared at it for a few moments. He turned the paper to Mr. A, then showed it to Jeff.

It was some kind of official-looking document printed in Chinese. In the lower right corner, there was a photo of Jeff's unmistakably Kyrgyzstan-shaped piece of rhodium lying like a scientific specimen on a centimeter-gridded surface.

How could this be? Could the rhodium have been accidentally dropped or lost from this Yang Shi platform before being recovered by Jeff in the storm that night? It seemed unlikely, unthinkable, impossible. Yet Jeff recognized something all too familiar about this, something inevitable. The feeling of something being pulled from his grasp.

"But I didn't steal any—"

"Do not lie!" Li snapped. "The first thing a thief steals is the truth. Since the theft, the Ministry of Security has been investigating known black market mineral traffickers like this criminal." He flicked his gun toward Mr. A. "I followed him from Maui last night after he received an unencrypted text with a photo of our rhodium next to a pen printed with the logo of the Intercontinental Cocktail Lounge. Should I go on? I'm talking about receiving stolen property, Mr. Kalawai'a. I'm talking about tax evasion, money laundering. I'm talking about everyone in this room going to prison if I decide to make a phone call to your FBI. Unless one of you thieving criminals puts China's rhodium on this desk in the next ten seconds."

Jeff looked at Jonny K. Jonny K looked at Mr. A. Mr. A looked at Li's pistol. "I don't want any trouble," he said. He slowly reached a trembling hand into his jacket and withdrew the velvet sack.

"Take it out," Li ordered. He jerked his head toward the scale on Jonny's desk. "Put it on that scale."

Mr. A shook the rhodium into his hand and edged to the desk. He placed the rhodium on the scale.

Li's eyes flicked to the readout. "Twenty-five point two-three. What a surprise." He snatched up the rhodium and dropped it into his jacket pocket. "Exactly the same weight as the stolen rhodium." He raised his pistol. "My superiors made it clear to me that the recovery of our property, rather than… punishment, was the priority of my mission." Li waved his pistol across the room as he backed toward the door. "Consider yourselves fortunate."

In one quick motion, Li swung the door open and slipped through. In a blink, the door slammed behind him and he was gone.

A few seconds of stunned silence passed in the office, then Jonny jumped up and ran to the door. Jeff got to his feet to follow, and as Jonny yanked the door open, he heard the rear exit of the IC bang open and a moment later, a car screeched away.

Jonny closed the door. With a deep breath, he walked back to his desk.

"Are you crazy?" Mr. A shouted at Jeff. "Stealing from the Chinese? You could have gotten us killed." He looked a little shaky. He sat down on the couch and put his head in his hands.

Jeff said, "I didn't steal that rhodium. I found it."

"Found it on a Chinese mineral platform! Are you out of your mind? I'm almost curious how you did it. Do you deliver supplies out there, do repairs, something like that?" Mr. A said.

"I don't—"

"Shut up," Jonny said. "Get out." He picked up the —asher bat.

Jeff reached for the door.

"Hold up," said Jonny. "Where you going, J? You're good, bruddah. I'm talking to this man." He pointed the bat at Mr. A. "The man who led a Chinese agent right into my house."

"Me? You blame me for this?" Mr. A said. He pointed at Jeff. "He could've gotten us killed!"

Jeff was frozen with his hand on the doorknob.

Mr. A stood up as Jonny walked around the desk, still carrying the bat.

Jonny smacked the arm of the couch with the bat. "Blame you for what? You came with your gold, you leave with your gold. Nothing happened to you, Mr. A. And we can keep it that way if you want. This is my island and I want you off it. You get back to the Big Island today and you never come back. I see you again, I'll cut you into bait, cuz. Right, J?"

In Jeff's mind, he answered Jonny's question: *Blame for losing my rhodium! And the blame is shared almost equally between Mr. A, who may have led a hostile foreign agent to the Intercontinental, and you, Jonny K, who admitted making multiple inquiries about the rhodium and didn't the Inspector say something about an unencrypted text? But since you're the one holding the baseball bat, I will overlook these problems and just say,* "Yes."

Jeff stepped aside as Mr. A was prodded out the door. Jonny closed it behind him with the head of the bat and then turned to Jeff. "You really fucked us, bruddah. I know you got joosed, but now I got the Chinese on me?" He walked back to his desk and sat down heavily.

Jeff stood in front of the desk. "I'm sorry, Mr. K. But I didn't steal the rhodium. I don't know how the Chinese knew about it."

"Jeff, when you asked me to help with this sale, I didn't ask questions. I trusted you, right?" Jonny set the bat on his desk, its prickled plastic endcap pointing directly at Jeff's groin.

"Yes," Jeff admitted.

"Serious. How'd you get that rhodium?"

"I found it. In the ocean."

Jonny K shook his head. "You seem like a good dude, Jeff, but if you don't wanna trust me with the truth, then we can't do this." He picked up the bat. "Look, bruddah, I can't have the Chinese all in my business. They're going to be watching us both for a while. Can't have them seeing us together anywhere. You can't be hanging around here no more. You're banned from the IC."

"But—"

"But what? You can still work on the *Fist*, you can still work at Pateena. Don't act like you're the only one who lost out. I got shorted on this deal, too! I was counting on my cut. And my rep, my brand is going to take a hit if word gets out that some Chinaman jacked me in my own place." He placed the end of the bat onto Jeff's kneecap. Leaned on it. "You keep this between us, you hear me? We cool?"

Jeff's knee blazed with pain. "Yes," he said.

CHAPTER 41

> • Choose first, but do not choose the first choice

As Jeff trudged back over the Sand Island bridge, still in the habit of averting his face from the center-lane cameras, he looked down to the marina and noticed two pickup trucks slant-parked on the pier alongside the *Monkey Fist.* Tasha and Tommy were there. He trotted the rest of the way to the boat.

As Jeff hopped to the deck, Tasha and Tommy were emerging from the engine room hatch, followed by a sunworn man in his thirties, forties or fifties wearing paint-spattered jeans.

"Jeff!" Tasha called.

Tommy lit a cigarette in greeting.

"What are you doing here?" Jeff said. "I thought we were prepping the boat in the morning."

Tasha said, "I wanted to meet the new guy. Tommy brought him."

Tommy said, "Izzo, meet Jeff. Jeff, Izzo. Our new googan for the week."

"How's it hanging, Jeff?" Izzo said.

"How's it hanging, Izzo."

Tasha said, "We're getting fit all day tomorrow. Tommy, get the bait when they open and be here by eight. See you guys in the morning."

Dismissed, Tommy and Izzo headed for Tommy's truck. Tasha turned to Jeff. "Meet me here at six." She looked at him in a certain way that muted him. "Right now, I need you to help me chase down a short."

Jeff didn't know what chasing down a short meant, but Tasha's look was still working on him. Wordlessly, he followed her toward the stern.

"I'm a very fast runner," he said when Tasha stopped near the line shooter.

"Cool, man," Tasha said. "I just—Wait, do you think 'chase down a short' involves running?"

"Yes," said Jeff slowly. He shook his head. "But now, no. Not anymore."

Tasha smiled. The dimples were asynchronous. The left one appeared a microsecond before the right and sometimes, for the briefest of moments, the left one was dispatched alone. "Chasing a short is finding a short circuit in the electrical system. It sucks. Hope you never have to do it." She watched Tommy and Izzo drive away. "I just didn't want Tommy knowing you were staying on the boat."

Jeff nodded.

Tasha looked at him closely. "You seem a little… off. You good?" she asked.

I just had a life-threatening run-in with the Chinese Ministry of Security, who took my only means to reunite with my brother.

"Yes," Jeff said. "Yes. I'm just ready to get back to work on the boat again."

"Good. I'm going to need you to help Izzo. This will be his first trip."

"He's never fished before?"

"Can you even imagine?" Tasha said. "I get the feeling he's probably a mountain person, not an ocean person."

"What does that mean?" Jeff asked.

"There're two types of people: Mountain and ocean."

"What does that mean?" Jeff repeated. "Does he live in the mountains?"

"I don't know where he lives. Mountain people like being on top of something," Tasha said, "Ocean people would rather be in the middle of something."

"You're an ocean person?" Jeff asked rhetorically. "What am I?"

"I don't know, Jeff. What are you?" Tasha rhetoricalled back. "But you better try to be both tomorrow. You need to help get Izzo up to speed. See you at six."

"Yes," Jeff said. "See you then."

Tasha waved as she walked away. She got in her truck and drove off.

Jeff went belowdecks and pulled out his phone. He must be an ocean person. There wasn't much that he was feeling on top of at the moment.

To: mohammad.mohammad54321@zmail.zaz

From: jeffzachary262@wmail.com

Subject: Sorry

Dear Sir,

There was a problem (not my fault). The rhodium was lost and I was not able to get paid for it.

Please be patient. I am going out to sea tomorrow and I will be out of contact for about a week. (I was promoted in rank on the fishing crew.)

Please tell Rahim I am very sorry. Assure him that I will do everything I can.

CHAPTER 42

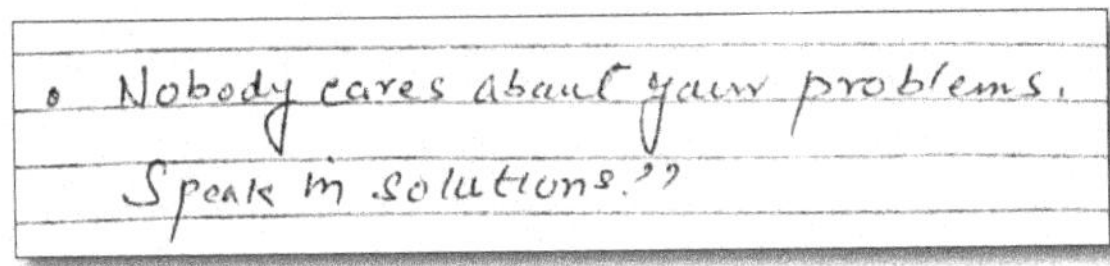

Night had settled over West Taboor.

In the sparsely furnished new headquarters of Shwarmco Security and Party Supply on the 3rd floor of 505 H Street, Shwarma sat behind his maybe-too-big desk in his maybe-too-small office, thinking about Jeff.

How very clever Zaqq must think himself. How proud. The first payment, made weeks ago, was a brief tease to whet Shwarma's appetite, to make him pliable. Then, when the second payment came sooner and larger, Shwarma was hooked. A fisherman indeed, Zaqq was. And now, apparently, it was time for the fight. Who would pull the other, gasping and struggling, into submission?

Business, whether it be timing the commercial real estate market or remote-managing a cipher agent on the run from a homicidal zealot, comes down to relationships. And as in any relationship, it obviously goes without saying that the person who gets the most is the person who wants it the least.

Leasing the expensive office space before having the rhodium proceeds in hand was, in hindsight, possibly a mistake. But a bigger mistake was made when Jeff decided to go rogue and leave Shwarma twisting in the warm evening's breeze that so pleasantly flowed through 505 H. Did Jeff think Shwarma would be dazzled by the sight of that hunk of metal? That Jeff could now dictate the terms of Rahim's transport? How quickly the melon-hawker forgot the reason he had to flee in the first place. While on the subject of unsettled accounts, did Jeff not think that Bashir Hallazallah would gladly square his personal blood ledger with Rahim if Jeff wasn't around? Come to think of it, there's no word for when you're left with a dead brother, either.

All Shwarma would have to do is call Hallazallah and simply point a finger at Rahim. How far would Jeff go to test the limits of his new Western freedom? Surely not so far as to endanger his brother's life. Jeff's absurd game of brinksmanship had gone far enough. Shwarma was confident that Jeff would quickly find the "lost" rhodium if he thought it meant protecting Rahim's life. The advantage remained with Shwarma.

But was Shwarma missing something here? Could Rahim be planning to run? Could he and Jeff have hatched some plan for Rahim to leave Zazaristan and get to Honolulu without Shwarma's knowledge (and Hamid's help)? Doubtful. How could they communicate to make plans? Shwarma had tossed Rahim's old phone out the window of the van. Jeff cannot reach that number and doesn't know the number of Rahim's new burner. Shwarma told the brothers that the only "secure" comms are through the Botcoin terminal. It was possible, of course, that Rahim was secretly using the email address he spotted on Jeff's Botcoin account and the Zaqq brothers have been talking unbeknownst to Shwarma, but by doing so, they would have to believe it would mean exposing Jeff to risk of capture by the Americans, which in itself may be useful.

Could Rahim make it to Hawaii on his own? Without Hamid's assistance? Rahim was proving to be a capable and resourceful assistant. Just yesterday, in fact, without being asked, he collected a half-dozen round stones from the riverbed to serve as much-needed paperweights in the office. But no. Picking up rocks is one thing, solo-navigating halfway around the globe, *to a specific island*, without legal documentation and only a few zazars in his pocket is quite another. There's only so much those videos can teach a person.

What was once a simple, mutually beneficial agreement between two people has leaned, listed and lurched to the brink of collapse. What a fool Jeff was. Another job interrupted.

His betrayal could not go unanswered. Let it be known: Break a promise to Wahiri Shwarma and pay the price. Shwarma had been hoping to simply shear Jeff repeatedly, but the time had come to skin him.

Shwarma heard the outer office door open. Boots on the floor. He stood and scooched through the narrow gap between his desk and the arched wall to greet his visitor. "Welcome to Shwarmco, Bashir."

Hallazallah crowded into the office. "Nice desk," he commented. "How did you get it in here?"

"I don't know," said Shwarma, shimmying back around it. "I'm afraid there are some of life's questions that will go unanswered. But I don't let that stop me from using it." He sat down.

Hallazallah took the visitor's chair. "What do you make of this Sayem business?"

Shwarma had studied the sporting pages of the newspaper that afternoon in preparation for this meeting. He regurgitated a columnist's opinion on Jahanana Sayem. After a few minutes of oblique cricket talk, Hallazallah glanced at his watch and said, "Why did you ask me here, Shwarma?"

"Bashir, we are colleagues, fellow club members at the Dapper, and I consider us to be friends," Shwarma said. "I feel comfortable confiding in you a bit more than I did the other day. As you know, I have an agent embedded in America. He has already attacked once. He is trained and ready to execute again. This time, at your command."

Hallazallah said, "At *my* command? And why would he do that?"

"He will be loyal to any commander I name."

"And why would you name me as this man's commander?"

"Don't misunderstand me, Bashir. I don't want to let this man go. But I'm expanding my operation here in Taboor City," he waved around the office. "Put simply, I need some capital. A million zazars. This is an opportunity for you. This man is my most trusted operative. Agent One. He has a solid cover as a fisherman. He will pay for himself in a few months if you choose. You can activate him at any time."

"And what about this so-called attack?" Hallazallah asked. "I still haven't seen any news reports about it. Why didn't you claim it?"

"I told you," Shwarma said. "It was meant to be a quiet operation."

"In that case, you succeeded grandly," said Hallazallah. "But I am not in the 'quiet' business. I'm not paying a million z, or anything, unless I see some proof this 'Agent One' of yours exists. Show me something that confirms your man is real and has real abilities and maybe then we'll talk. I'll be at the Dapper on Monday."

He stood up and opened the office door. Rizwan was standing in the outer office. "Riz, put Mr. Shwarma in the calendar for Monday morning."

Rizwan flipped open a date book. "You are seeing Taj this coming Monday, five August, at nine. I will add Mr. Shwarma at 10:30."

CHAPTER 43

- Stern = back of boat.

The call to the American authorities was definitely, *definitely* crossing a Rubicon. Wide, deep and rushing. Shwarma had been wandering along the bank for a while now, but if he ever wanted to see the other side, the time had finally come to strap a metaphorical inner tube to his ass in the form of the Shadow Holy War And Radical Militia Cooperative and leap into the roaring river to ride it as long as he could.

The morning after his meeting with Hallazallah, Shwarma dispatched Rahim to the guy on the corner for the cheapest new phone that could be had in West Taboor. He wouldn't be going near this job with his personal phone. In fact, he shut it off just to be safe. Shwarma had to assume that the US government had the ability to trace not only a call to the CIA, but any phone in Zazaristan (or anywhere else, for that matter) that so much as Wangles the CIA's phone number. And how else to get it? It's not like there's a fat book of phone numbers dangling on every street corner.

Shwarma could almost feel the long lenses of some geosynchronous satellite camera zooming in on the roof of 505 H Street, marking it as a target. The call would have to be made elsewhere. Walking around outside? Even worse. The Americans probably had phrenologists on staff who are trained to recognize people by the tops of their heads.

Pacing under the protective sunshades of the bustling West Taboor Market, Shwarma made the call.

To the liar, everything sounds like a lie. So when Shwarma finally reached someone from the CIA and the woman told him that terrorist attacks on US soil were the domain of the FBI, he assumed that she was just trying to get out of doing some work. But after hanging up and Wangling the FBI's number, he eventually got Agent Stephanie Gregg from the FBI's Honolulu office on the phone, and she assured him that yes, he had reached the correct agency.

"In that case," said Shwarma, "And as I've told your colleague at the CIA, we, the Shadow Holy War And Radical Militia Cooperative were the ones who masterminded and executed the recent attack on the Port of Honolulu, Hawaii, United States.

"I'm sorry, did you say the *port* of Honolulu?" asked Gregg.

"Yes. The port. A container ship—"

"The port is the jurisdiction of Customs and Border Protection," Gregg said. "You have to call them."

"Are you saying the FBI is not interested in defending your country?"

"Of course I'm not saying that, sir," Gregg said. "But in this case, CBP is the agency that will investigate."

"I'd like to speak with your supervisor, Stephanie," Shwarma said. He stopped at the edge of the market and turned around.

"Of course, sir. May I place you on a brief hold?"

"Make it quick," Shwarma griped.

Two floors above Agent Gregg and ten cubicles over, the phone beeped on the desk of Special Agent Jones Wallace. "Wallace."

"Sir, I have a Wahiri Shwarma on the phone. He is claiming responsibility for an attack on the port of Honolulu two weeks ago."

"What attack? There was no attack at the port. Even if there was, that's a job for the fruit sniffers at CBP."

"That's what I told him, sir. He wanted to talk to you. Should I put him through?"

"No, don't put him through. Transfer the call to CBP."

"Yes, sir." Gregg tapped a button on her phone. "Mr. Shwarma? Are you still there?"

"Yes, Stephanie, I'm here."

"I'm going to transfer you. Please hold."

The phone clicked and changed tone slightly. A stilted voice said, "Welcome to United States Customs and Border Protection. If you know your party's extension, you may dial it at any time."

Shwarma did not know any of the extensions of course, but he hit "1" in the hopes of being connected to the top-ranking person in the agency.

The phone connection went dead. *Boopboopboop*.

How typical, how perfectly American, for this to happen. A great stroke of fortune comes their way and they fumble it through their fat fingers because of institutional bureaucracy and sub-standard phone tree technology.

Shwarma looked up from his phone. A dozen people were around in the market. He felt the urge to yell to them, "America has done me and my nation a great harm! I shall exact revenge!" but of course he didn't because, as noted above, there were only a dozen people within his yelling range and a dozen is simply not enough.

He swiped away the CBP's phone number and Wangled one more. A final tap, and the phone connected.

"Hawaiian Now News what's news to you," Kyle Kang answered rotely.

This is more like it, Shwarma thought. "I have news of a biological attack on Hawaii and the government's efforts to cover it up."

"Please hold, sir," said Kang.

Another click. "Hawaiian Now News what's news to you, news desk."

"America has done me and my nation a great harm! I shall exact revenge…"

CHAPTER 44

- Improvise, Make do.

When the *Monkey Fist* left Honolulu Harbor on Wednesday afternoon, Jeff felt like a real fisherman. He had taught Izzo the googan a few things around the boat and he was leaving a twisted mess of land-based fuckups behind.

The land disappeared like the headache it was. Slowly. Gradually. Gone before you realize it.

Tasha stepped out of the pilothouse and called down to the crew. "We're coming up on the beds. Stow the gear."

Jeff looked up and scanned the reddening west. There. There it was again, the size of a pea held at arm's length. The Chinese mining platform. That must be the Yang Shi. Inspector Han Li was probably there right now, accepting the praise of his superiors for recovering their rhodium.

How did the Chinese know he had it? *How*? Jeff couldn't figure it out. Li said the rhodium was stolen, but Jeff had found it wedged in a discarded net, stirred up from the bottom of the ocean.

Li had showed a photo of the rhodium as if it was a scientific specimen. The Chinese actually had possession of it at some point. A third party must have stolen it. Perhaps some time after the Chinese mined and catalogued the lump of metal, this person, probably a rogue Chinese miner, tried to steal it and escape the platform by sea. But with the obviously competent Chinese security forces closing behind, the thief must have panicked and jettisoned the rhodium overboard where it somehow became tangled in the discarded net. The thief probably met the bottom of the ocean, as well. Weeks, months, years later, the net was storm-swept into the prop of a fishing boat, where Jeff found it, fair and square.

But when Jonny K sent an unencrypted text to the shady mineral buyer Mr. A, the vigilant Chinese authorities intercepted a photo of their missing rhodium (They were presumably alerted by some kind of facial recognition software adapted for rocks), and from there it was just good old-fashioned detective work. Inspector Li put a tail on Mr. A and followed him straight to the Intercontinental.

Another possibility was the XRF technology, still fairly unclear to Jeff. What was the range of those scanners? If they could sniff out rhodium from two inches, what about two meters? Two miles? Across a city? Do they work underwater? Should have asked more questions. How do those mining robots work, exactly? Again, Jeff imagined them as shovel-based. Whatever they looked like, it was obvious that the Chinese possessed some pretty advanced technology.

As if the "how" mattered. The rhodium was gone. Jeff was never going to see that $72,000. Money that would've paid for Rahim's passage to Hawaii 7.2 times over. For once, Jeff was grateful he had not been in contact with Rahim. The disappointment of his little brother when he heard of Jeff's failure would have been more than he could take.

Jeff forced his gaze away from the distant platform and turned his face north, into the wind.

The fish were out there.

Just hold on, Rahim. A few more weeks, brother.

"Jeff, you coming?" Kai said.

Usually, the crew took their mandated mineral bed break on deck, but Jeff turned to see his crewmates filing down the stairs to the galley. "Coming where?" he asked.

"Izzo brought some DVDs. Have you seen *Kill Zone 4*? We're going to watch."

Over the last few weeks, Jeff had worked his way through the *Monkey Fist*'s entire film library, from *Avengers* to *Zoolander*, including the first three installments of the *Kill Zone* franchise. (Which Jeff ranked in Star Wars order: 2, 1, 3.) Any new material was welcome.

Izzo brought about four dozen DVDs, their cases packed snugly in a cardboard box. Tommy was perusing it as Jeff entered the galley.

"Why do you have so many fucking movies?" Tommy asked.

"They're a dollar ninety-nine at the pawnshop," Izzo answered as he slid *KZ4* into the DVD player.

Jeff's attention was drawn to the colorful movie jackets as Tommy continued to run a finger over their spines, now and then offering a brief review. "Sucked. Sucked balls. Great stunts. Funny."

Tommy's hand moved. A flash of something familiar. The unmistakable aquamarine and blazing orange.

"Wait," Jeff said, reaching for the box. It was.

The logo.

Ocean Heat.

The training videos.

Jeff scrabbled to pull the disc from its slot and stared at it in disbelief.

Back in Shwarma's apartment, Shwarma had insisted that, in the interest of research into the American culture and psyche, Overseas Stealth Agent Program trainee Jefir Zaqq must watch Season One, Disc One of the American television action drama *Ocean Heat* (tagged with a Property of King Abbas College Library sticker) *repeatedly* in the weeks he spent waiting for an exfiltration route to the US to come together. At first, Shwarma would watch with Jefir and Rahim, then present an analysis/lecture on the episode's themes that would run nearly as long as the episode itself. After about a week of this, Shwarma generally left the brothers alone with the DVD in order to encourage "individual reflections" on the show.

It was safe to say that Jeff was quite familiar with *Ocean Heat.* But it wasn't the disc itself that caught his eye. It was what was scripted on the DVD case right below the show's wave-on-fire title logo, and above Tim Braddock's blow-dried waves: Season Two.

Season Two?

There was more?

"Let's watch this!" Jeff squawked.

"Fuck that," said Tommy. "Watch it later." *Kill Zone 4* was beginning. "*Ocean Heat* was the shit back in the day, though," he said smokily. "It's not the humidity…"

"It's the heat, baby!" Kai and Izzo chorused back.

"Have you all seen this?" Jeff flashed the DVD around to his crewmates. Kai and Izzo nodded. They agreed that *Ocean Heat* was indeed the shit back in the day, but they couldn't be persuaded into a rewatch just then. On the screen, a missile was already inbound.

Jeff examined the back of the *Ocean Heat* case. Season Two, Disc One. Six episodes.

Episode 1: "North by Northeast."

Episode 2: "The First Thing a Thief Steals is the Truth."

The first thing a thief steals is the truth?

It was almost midnight and the crew was getting ready to call it a day. As the *Monkey Fist* slid over glassy sea in the thick tropic night, Tommy sidled up to Jeff and said, "Thanks."

"Yes," Jeff said. "For what?"

"Last week," Tommy said. "Tasha wouldn't say it, but we were fucking going under if you didn't cut that net when you did."

"Yes. You're welcome, boss."

"I'll cover your watch tonight," Tommy said. He smiled and flicked his cigarette into the water. "Now we're even."

After the rest of the crew retired to their bunks, Jeff retrieved the *Ocean Heat* DVD in the dim galley. He slipped it into the player and waited impatiently as it spun up. The FBI silently warned him that video piracy is a serious matter.

When the menu appeared, Jeff worked the DVD remote to Episode 2 and hit play. The rocking theme song and title sequence were largely the same as they were in Season One: Shot of Heaton Barbary walking down a cold and greasy-looking street in Philadelphia. Jump cut to Barbary on a sun-drenched beach. Hollywood sign. Surfers. Car burnout. (Different car than S1.) Close-up of a grinning Tim Braddock as Heaton Barbary. Barbary shooting a basketball against light defense on an outdoor court. The ball swishing through the net. A black-clad figure riding a wheelie on a motorcycle. (Motorcycle also new. Now yellow.) Close-up of Bailey Brett-Houston as Rhonda Mix shaking her blond hair out of a motorcycle helmet. Another car burnout. Barbary firing his pistol. Glassy skyscrapers. A business-suited man picking up the phone. Close-up of Harold Pane as Cool Landerman. Barbary running. Waiter setting a viscous green drink in front of Barbary, who is comically wary of it. Car burnout. Ocean Heat logo. Created by Alexander K. Prentiss.

In Act I of "The First Thing a Thief Steals is the Truth," Barbary comes to the aid of a mysterious woman. When the woman disappears, along with some valuable museum pieces, the FBI dispatches rookie Agent Kenny Hsu, who specializes in Asian artwork, to question Barbary. When Hsu delivered the line, "The first thing a thief steals is the truth, Mr. Barbary," Jeff paused the DVD. It was him.

Decades younger, but unmistakably the same person. "Inspector Han Li of the People's Republic of China Ministry of Security," the man who had walked out of the Intercontinental with twenty-five point two-three ounces of rhodium in his pocket not two days ago, was an actor, an imposter. A thief of the truth, indeed.

Jeff quickly zapped to the end credits to see that the part of Kenny Hsu was played by a man named Alex Chen.

For the rest of the trip, Jeff's various personal problems and strict attention to Don't-Get-Killed/Mangled-On-Boat were pushed aside in his mind to make room for Alex Chen, rhodium thief.

In Season One of the training videos, Barbary had a run-in with a similar character, actually. A smooth-talking con-man who's MO was calling bars posing as a police detective on a counterfeiting case. He'd tell the bar that a known counterfeiter had passed through and most likely left some phony cash behind in the register. The con said he'd be right over to collect the evidence. He showed up, flashed a badge and carefully filled out a white-pink-canary form printed on city letterhead that indemnified the bar from a criminal conspiracy investigation and included instructions on how to recoup their $_______ in 5-10 business days. He left with the white and yellow copies and several thousand dollars in "counterfeit" bills. When the con struck the Riptide, Barbary's favorite watering hole, and the real police grumpily threw up their hands, Barbary had to team up with a local crime boss to track down the con-man.

In his short time in America, Jeff had had a number of bosses already. The deck boss Tommy was hard-working, but lacked the social skills required to hatch and execute a counter-theft team-up.

Tasha had, if anything, too much social skill and because of that Jeff wasn't sure he would be able to adequately explain himself when Tasha would start asking questions like *where*, exactly, did Jeff find this rhodium? and you did *what* to a guy in Zazaristan? and *who* is Rahim? and *why* is he in danger? and *how* could you leave him behind, you *stupid, stupid idiot*? Jeff had given a few half-truths to Tasha already, which probably added up to one full lie and he resolved to try to make that the limit.

Anyway, the choice here was clear. His boss at Pateena. Jonny K. He was a savvy businessman and his questionable recycling practices made him, if not a criminal, crime adjacent. Jonny was in the room when Chen made off with the rhodium and shared in the loss. Jonny was well-known and well-liked and he could probably make some of his calls to get close to Alex Chen and reclaim what was Jeff's, although Jonny would most likely demand another transaction fee in return. And what's another five percent? Jonny would help Jeff.

The *Monkey Fist* was working the western tip of the Molokai Fracture Zone, hundreds of miles beyond cell phone range. Jeff couldn't call Jonny K, let alone drop by the Intercontinental to ask for his help. But time was probably an important factor in tracking down Chen. As a slippery criminal, he must be moving on from Honolulu soon, if he wasn't gone already. The days were ticking by. Jeff knew how to use the ship's radio, but only for listening to chatter from other fishing boats and raising the Coast Guard on Channel 16 in emergencies. If there was a way to patch the radio through to a person on land, Jeff didn't know how to do it, and neither did he know a way to ask Tasha how without lying about his reasons.

It was settled. As soon as the *Fist* finished her trip and Jeff (hopefully) got paid, he would send some money to buy time from Shwarma and then go straight to the IC to enlist Jonny and his persuasive baseball bat to deal with Chen.

And not a moment too soon. With Jeff's mind bent on revenge upon a character actor, he had zoned out at the bait cart and only noticed the hooked gangion that Izzo had dropped on the deck when it lightly tickled over the meaty side of his flip-flopped foot and harmlessly shot overboard.

Back to work. The fish freezer wasn't going to fill itself.

The *Monkey Fist* sailed on.

CHAPTER 45

• Maintain a tight focus.

According to the most recent data made available by the office of United States Customs and Border Protection, over twenty million tons of cargo pass through the port of Honolulu, Hawaii each year.

Clothing. Electronics. Home furnishings. Robots with varying levels of self-awareness. All of it (and then some) pumped like so much life-giving blood into every last capitalist capillary of early twenty-first century America.

As any CBP officer would tell you, not all of this cargo is strictly legal, in the classical sense of the word. Some of it is. Some of it isn't. Some of it falls somewhere in the middle, just slightly more than arm's-reach from both the light and dark extensions of the human condition.

CBP refers to this sort of cargo as "gray material."

An interesting side note: The term "gray material" was first coined on Tim Braddock's eponymous podcast in 2016. Most readers would recognize Braddock from his role as ex-Detective Heaton Barbary in the television action drama *Ocean Heat*, which ran on CBN from 1993-1999.

The Tim Braddock Podcast, and *Ocean Heat* for that matter, were widely enjoyed by, and had excellent penetration among, the Pan-Pacific smuggling community. Who knows how these things work?

On one episode of the podcast, Braddock conducted an interview with ex-Special Forces operator-turned fitness instructor Tony Leland. In the course of their discussion, Braddock and Leland covered a wide range of topics, from Leland's experiences with counter-terrorism, to what defines a "pull-up," to the college football playoff system. Braddock, as was his habit, compared almost all of it to plot devices of various *Ocean Heat* episodes.

From the podcast transcript :

> *LELAND: Back in those days, the cartels moved a lot of material through shipping ports in Central America, but there ain't a lot of black and white down there, you gotta look for the gray—*
>
> *BRADDOCK: In Season Three, we busted some cartel guys smuggling coke hidden inside bags of dog food. The dogs would smell the drugs and go crazy, but everyone thought it was the food they were after.*

> *LELAND: Yeah. So anyway, that's the game. Staying one step ahead. It's a lot like creating a strong core through muscle confusion.*

When the listening smugglers heard Leland's use of the word "gray," they took it to mean the *color* of the trans-oceanic shipping containers wherein inspecting authorities like the American CBP found the most contraband. It remains unclear if this was actually the case. Leland's meaning of "gray" was ultimately left in question, as it were.

Nevertheless. Smugglers, being of a superstitious and cautious nature, decided to eschew the use of gray containers for a time. There were plenty of other choices, after all. Red, blue, black, yellow, green. In business they call that a low friction decision. Minimal risk, abundant substitutes. The smugglers didn't really have a name for it, but they figured they'd just go easy on the gray containers for a while, why the fuck not.

Whatever it's called, it worked for a time. Smuggler's loads lost to seizure ("LOLOs") went down slightly as Customs and Border Protection agents continued to search containers as they always had, taking no special note of color. Eventually however, some CBP quant became aware of the smuggler's "Ship in gray, money away" tendency and word came down to field agents to increase efficiency by searching gray containers *less frequently*.

Soon after that, the smugglers caught on to the fact that the few gray containers they still used were LOLO'ed far less often. And thus, they began using gray containers *even more.*

Until CBP caught on, and in a short period made dozens of seizures from gray containers.

Of course, this development was not lost on the smugglers, who countered by once again shying away from the use of gray containers.

And so on.

As one would expect, this gray container/gray material correlation dilemma became a knot of a problem for cop and criminal alike. Despite their opposing legal philosophies, both parties ultimately arrived at the same conclusions: 1. We are losing this battle. 2. The problem is beyond our solving. 3. Extraordinary measures must be taken.

Coincidently, and perhaps predictably, the feds and smugglers each commissioned bids from the West Coast's brainiest universities and private software developers to create proprietary algorithms that would calculate the best way to "untangle this fucking monkey fist," as a CBP official colorfully described it in a well-remembered memo.

As it happened, some grad students from ██████ University had recently developed some software code as an application for harness race handicapping, and were able to quickly adapt the so-called "Trot" program for shipping container-based game theory. The students were the first to fill the order of an anonymous bagman acting on behalf of the Yakuza, who the students would almost invariably characterize in later interviews as a "very chill dude."

Soon after the initial sale to the Yakuza, one of the enterprising students took the opportunity to sell the Trot software's intellectual property rights *again*, this time to a private equity firm run by his uncle (also a [redacted] alumnus), who then repackaged it as "SeaVenge Logistical Solutionscape" and sold the software to the Federal government for use by the Big Six. (NSA, FBI, CIA, Homeland Security, ICE, CBP.)

In very short order, the code was hacked and stolen by at least four of the Smuggling Big Six (The Yakuza, Blue Lightning, Rozzu, The Kane Brothers, Manila, Los Gatos), making Trot/SeaVenge Logistical Solutionscape the de facto industry standard.

Not surprisingly, since everyone ended up with virtually the same program, analytical and anecdotal evidence on both sides of the legal fence showed that no version of the software could provide any significant advantage in the concealment or detection of gray material.

The lesson learned was that one must keep one's fucking eye on the ball in this world and not go down any meaningless sidetracks. Now, where were we?

CHAPTER 46

keep it brief.

After closing the almost-case of the Sand Island Tiny Home Container Maybe Stowaway, Customs and Border Protection Officers Kazumi and Porter had spent the last three weeks training on some new software.

On their first morning back in the field, Captain Benito called them into his office.

"Did you two see the news?" He plinked a finger against his computer monitor. The screen showed a news story headlined, "CBP Drops Ball on 'Biological Attack' Suspect."

"I saw it," Kaz said. She read the story about how a group called SHWARMCO had claimed responsibility for the release of a "bio-toxin" at the GossCo port by a single agent. She had figured this development was what Benito wanted to discuss and she had brought the original report that she and Porter made.

"Captain, that case was a fat zero three weeks ago. No victim, no ID of a suspect, four or five conflicting accounts. We closed it that day."

"I know," Benito said. "But it's back open. The Commissioner called me this morning. He likes to be the one calling the press, not the other way around." Benito picked a file from his desk. "Here's a signed warrant. I talked to a Margot Carlene from GossCo this morning. She's expecting you. Get down to the port and find something. Witnesses, DNA, prints, anything. The forensics team and the media are meeting you down there."

"The media?" asked Porter.

"Yes, Porter, the media," Benito said. "The Commissioner wants to show people we're on top of this. He made me send both forensics trucks. Let the media shoot pictures of whatever they want and the more the better, but do *not* talk to them. No comment. The Commissioner will make a statement soon. No comment."

Kaz and Porter took their orders and thin file and headed back to Sand Island.

In the SUV, Porter said, "Do you think this SHWARMCO thing is the same as the stowaway case? That guy threw his shit at someone, he didn't release some biological w—Oh. I see it now."

Kaz said, "It doesn't matter what he used. The SHWARMCO claim confirms the guy is real and that he did, in fact, assault someone and illegally enter the country. He's still out there. Hopefully, we'll pull some prints and DNA off the container today."

Porter said, "Do you expect the prints to match anyone we have on record?"

"Doubtful. But now they'll be in the system in case he runs into trouble again."

"Why do you think SHWARMCO waited so long to make the claim?" Porter asked.

"Because the weight is the wait," Kaz replied. "Write this shit down, man."

Porter scribbled the note as Kaz drove on through Metro Oahu.

Just after they crossed the Sand Island bridge, Kaz and Porter spotted both of CBP's boxy forensics trucks pulled to the shoulder across from the main gate of the GossCo port. The news vans of Channels Two, Four, Five and Thirteen were parked haphazardly behind. Two of the crews were already set up and shooting b-roll of the CBP trucks and the chain link-fenced port.

Kaz slowed and waved for the forensics teams to fall in behind her as she drove up to the gate.

A GossCo security guard stepped out of the gatehouse to meet her. "Can I help you, Officer?" he said.

"We're here to meet with Margot Carlene," Kaz said. She glanced into her side mirror to see the trucks lining up behind her. "And gather some evidence for an investigation."

Seeing the CBP on the move, the news crews were scrambling. Guys with cameras and boom mics were hustling toward the gate.

The guard said, "The media can't come in."

"No problem," Kaz said. "Remind me where Lot X is, by the way?"

The guard pointed. "East end of the port. Follow the signs."

"Thanks," Kaz said. "Tell the media our investigation will start there. I'm not allowed to make any comment to them myself, you see."

"That's funny, my boss told me the same thing," the guard said. "I'm not telling them anything. Go ahead on through, Officer." He walked back to his little hut and raised the gate arm.

Kaz shouted, "LOT X? OVER ON THE EAST SIDE OF THE PORT? THANK YOU OFFICER!" She glanced back at the news cameras to make sure they caught it and drove on through the gate.

Two walls of GossCo's 2nd floor Conference Room A were almost entirely glass. The view over the port and wastewater treatment plant stretched to the ocean in the distance. The other walls were studded with dozens of floating shelves that held 1:500 scale models of GossCo cargo ships. An intricately detailed model of the entire island facility, complete with tiny trucks on a truncated bridge to nowhere, was displayed in the corner. A large tray of pastries and donuts, artfully arranged by color into the GossCo logo was displayed at the center of the long table. At the far end of the table sat Margot Carlene and Steve Doyle. It was casual Friday, so Doyle wore a white GossCo golf shirt with his laminated employee ID clipped to the sleeve. Margot wore a double-breasted Loro Piana suit the color of a cloud five minutes after the sun goes down and you must be fucking crazy if you think there was a badge clipped to it.

Everyone exchanged cards and sat down. Kaz laid a folder on the table. Porter flipped open his laptop.

Doyle's secretary Suzy opened the door. She carried a coffee service tray with a French press and two ceramic GossCo mugs to the table and set the tray between Kaz and Porter. She immediately left the room.

Margot said, “Agents, as I told Captain Benito from your office, GossCo is very well aware of the story reported by Hawaii Now News. We understand your concerns from a law enforcement perspective. But as you saw in the OSHA report dated July eighth, the incident in question was nothing more than an accidental spill. We are aggressively working with the newspaper’s attorneys to have them issue a retraction. GossCo has conducted an internal investigation and as a precaution, reviewed security procedures both here in Honolulu and with our international partners. I’m not sure any further investigation is needed.”

“We like precaution as well, Ms. Carlene,” Kaz said. She pushed the coffee tray aside and flipped open her file. “Is the security guard Trent Calvin around today? We’d like to talk to him about what happened.”

Doyle glanced at Margot, deflecting the question her way. She said, “Mr. Calvin is enjoying some paid vacation time as he continues to recover from his unfortunate, but accidental experience. But you have his written statement, which I’m sure is an accurate description of what transpired.”

Kaz said, “When you spoke to Captain Benito, I’m sure he told you that CBP was seeking a warrant to search container 5138008, a KozyHome Lucky Seven tiny home that was placed under CBP quarantine by Officer Porter the same day as the ‘accident?’” She slid a court-signed warrant from her file across the table to Margot.

Margot wrinkled her nose and pushed the warrant to Doyle, giving him the OK for him to sign. Doyle signed the warrant and slid it back to Kaz.

Kaz stood up and walked to the model island. "Mr. Doyle, I recall the container was left in Lot X. Show me where that is on this cool model." She prodded one of the tiny trucks. Surprisingly, it wasn't glued into place. "How often do you get to play with this?" she asked.

Margot smiled, not bothering to hide it.

"It's not a toy," Doyle grumped. He stood and walked to the corner windows. "Lot X is over—What is going on over there?"

Kaz joined him at the window. A couple hundred yards away, the forensic trucks had located the still-quarantined KozyHome in Lot X and were unrolling crime scene tape. "CBP forensics. They're collecting prints, physical evidence. It's going to take all day."

"No, not that," Doyle said. "What are the TV trucks doing there?"

There were four news vans on the other side of the fence in the Coast Guard softball field parking lot. Men were setting up tripods and cameras on the van's roofs in order to peer into the port and see what CBP was so excited about.

Margot joined Kaz and Doyle at the window. The North Shore Toyota NewsDrone Thirteen wobbled skyward and darted out over the port.

Kaz said, "First amendment stuff."

"As long as we're talking about the Constitution," said Margot, "I'd like to petition the government for a redress of grievances."

This time Porter smiled a little.

"Petition away, Ms. Carlene," Kaz said. "I'm listening."

"These media people are getting the wrong impression, Officer Kazumi. That yellow tape says, 'crime scene.' It should read, 'Alleged crime scene, or better yet, 'investigation scene.' I'd like to go down there and give a statement clearing up any misconceptions."

"You can read that tape from here?" Doyle said, squinting.

"You must know that I can't stop you, Ms. Carlene," Kaz said. "If you want to talk to the media, go ahead."

"Please call me Margot. And I was hoping that you and Officer Porter might join me. A joint statement to show we're united in our goals."

"Our goals?" Kaz asked.

"Life. Liberty. The pursuit of happiness," said Margot.

"That's the Declaration of Independence," Porter said.

"In other words, Officer Kazumi, we both want this case to be over with," Margot said.

"Fair enough," said Kaz. "But I'm not sure we would agree about what 'over with' means."

Margot said, "Truth. Justice. The American way."

"Superman," said Porter as he picked up the French press.

"I like to think of myself as a reasonable person, Officer Kazumi," Margot said. "I can hold two thoughts in my mind at once. Initially, the only evidence available suggested that an accident happened on the dock. Now, with this 'claim' by SHWARMCO and any forensic evidence you may find today, we may learn that there really *was* an unticketed person on that container ship. If that proves to be the case—"

"You want to get in front of it," Kaz said.

"Where else would I be?" said Margot. She stepped closer to Kaz. "Where do you want to be, Officer Kazumi?"

Kaz said, “I’m the back of the line, Margot. I sweep up the mess when someone up ahead of me gets run over. Don’t leave me a bigger one than necessary.”

Margot said, “If you think cleaning the mess at the back of the line is dirty business, try stopping the mess before it even happens.”

Kaz said, “The pay sounds better.”

Margot chuckled.

The women stared out the window together. Another news drone shot into the air. Doyle was showing Porter something on the island model.

Margot said, “I’m thinking of getting into the lifestyle space full-time.”

“I think you’d be good at it, Margot.”

One hour later, Margot had conjured up an impromptu press conference. She stood in Lot X flanked by Kaz and Porter, who were ordered by the Commissioner to convey a “CBP presence” for the invited cameras, but also ordered to say nothing more than, “We cannot comment on an active investigation.”

Margot gave her CBP-vetted remarks and told the gathered news crews that GossCo was committed foremost to safety and transparency. And that last month, on July 8th, GossCo employees made US Customs and Border Protection aware of a potential border violation at a GossCo facility. At the time, evidence was lacking and CBP had declined to investigate further. Margot made a point of saying that GossCo had, in the name of caution, decided to use the uncertain events of July 8th as an opportunity for training and to launch a comprehensive internal investigation of their industry-leading supply chain integrity.

As a result of these exercises, Margot informed the media, some inefficiencies have been smoothed both here and abroad. No price is too high to pay, no detail too small to overlook, if it secures the safety of GossCo's most valuable asset, their dedicated employees.

She smilingly gestured to Officers Kazumi and Porter and pledged GossCo's full support to the brave Customs and Border Protection officers working on the case.

She shed a few questions about SHWARMCO, advised viewers to stay abreast of the latest developments via GossCo's official ZoopZap account, and bid everyone a good afternoon. She stepped away from the clutch of microphones and walked away to a waiting car while reading an irate, all-caps text message from Heinz Gossler about GOSC's stock price taking a six-dollar hit.

CHAPTER 47

• Paint don't rest/rust.
(Unclear. Confirm with Tommy ASAP.)

Shwarma wove his Yamaha around and through traffic.

The news story had referred to SHWARMCO as the Shadow Holy War And Radical Militia *Company,* not Cooperative, but otherwise the basic facts were correct and Shwarma was pleased with the response. According to the article entitled, "CBP Drops Ball on 'Biological Attack' Suspect," an unknown person or persons released a biological agent at the GossCo shipping facility on Sand Island, south of Honolulu, Hawaii. The office of United States Customs and Border Protection acknowledged that "an incident" happened and were conducting an investigation. GossCo spokesperson Margot Carlene characterized the incident as "an accident."

Whatever stunt Jeff had managed to pull off over there, it would have to be enough. And the rest would be up to Shwarma, as usual. Another job intervention. Seemed like that was all he did these days. Wave and coax attention here, resources there, non-refundable real estate deposits over that way. And when a slack-jaw like Jefir Zaqq starts to actually amount to something, just when things were actually starting to advance, the kid goes native and starts holding out.

Zebar wasn't at his post at the Dapper when Shwarma walked in at 10:30, followed by Rahim, who had been told to tag along, stand attentively near Shwarma, answer to the rank of "lieutenant" when spoken to and otherwise keep his mouth shut.

Hallazallah was in Taj's chair. Rizwan stood nearby, working his phone. Mr. Talmahani sat in his own chair, watching a football chat show. A single customer in the waiting area attended to a cup of tea, a cigarette and the newspaper in equal measure.

Mr. Talmahani looked away from the screen. "Shwarma. It must be ten-thirty." He slid out of the chair and gestured Shwarma into it.

Zebar appeared from the back room and delivered a steaming half-cup of tea to his father. Mr. Talmahani took a quick sip with his steadier left hand before setting the cup on the astroturfed counter at the base of the mirror. He snapped his barber's cape. It sounded like a firecracker. Maybe Taj could cut a sharper beard these days, but nobody snapped the cape like Sami Talmahani.

As the cape settled over him, Shwarma glanced to his right. Hallazallah had his eyes closed and was possibly sleeping as Taj worked his wizardry. "Bashir," Shwarma said. Hallazallah didn't move. "Bashir. Good morning." No movement.

"Can I help you, sir?" Rizwan asked, looking up from his phone.

"Thank you, but no, Rizwan. I was just greeting my friend Bashir."

"Sir, Wahiri Shwarma is here," said Rizwan.

"Good morning, Shwarma," Hallazallah said, without opening his eyes.

Mr. Talmahani was assessing Shwarma's chin. "What are we doing this morning?" he asked.

"Don't take too much off. Just a trim," Shwarma said.

Talmahani selected a plastic guard and with a bit of effort, snapped it onto his clipper.

"Bashir," Shwarma said as the clipper buzzed alive. He had to get down to business. The longer he sat in this chair, the more time the doddering elder Talmahani would have to mess up his beard.

Before the clipper got too close, Shwarma looked around. The customer in the waiting area had finished the newspaper and was now playing a game of Golden Golf Tee. He favored a power game, one where the entire arm is drawn back before the palm is thrust forward across the trackball. At the door, Zebar and Rahim were watching football highlights.

Shwarma said, "Rahim! Wait for me outside, Lieutenant."

The top plays of the day were being shown. A dude headed a curving corner kick into the net.

"Rahim!" Shwarma hissed.

"Sorry, what?"

"Wait outside. Lieutenant. I'm about to discuss operations above your paygrade."

Rahim arched an eyebrow, but made for the door.

Hallazallah watched Rahim go. “Surely that wasn’t necessary, Shwarma,” he said. “You can speak freely in the Dapper. What is said here is held in confidence. These are barbers, after all. Besides, I’m sure there’s nothing you could say that my old friend Sami Talmahani hasn’t heard before.”

Mr. Talmahani nodded. Hallazallah’s barber Taj seemed to be so engaged with managing just the right angle of Hallazallah’s beard that he didn’t make any acknowledgement, but it was clear that his mind was on his work and little, if anything, else.

“I believe in security,” Shwarma said. “Compartmentalization. I believe you will find that my men know all that they need to know, but no more.” He reached into his jacket and pulled out a folded paper. “I have here an interesting news article relating to what we spoke about in my office last week.” He unfolded the printout of the news story and handed it to Rizwan, who handed it to Hallazallah.

Hallazallah read silently.

He refolded the paper. “Interesting,” he said, “But very basic.”

“What details would you like to discuss?” Shwarma asked. He shot a glance at Taj, who was bobbing his head to the unheard rhythms of his earbuds. “What you have just read is proof of what I told you the other day. One of my men, Agent One, a proud son of Zazaristan, has executed, on the orders of the Shadow Holy War And Radical Militia Cooperative, a biological attack inside the borders of the US. He then evaded capture by the Americans and slipped quietly into their foolish midst, where he stands ready to strike again. At your command.”

Hallazallah handed the paper off to Rizwan. "First thing, the 'Shadow Holy War whatever' is far too long a name. I see what you're doing there Shwarma, but these things are best kept short. Brevity. Second, tell me again why would this agent follow my command? Why are you giving up control of him? Why not continue to handle him as you wish?"

Shwarma swallowed the advice about the name. He asked, "Does it matter who controls him? I imagine my wishes are quite similar to your own. An attack on the United States, an attack that originated from Quudia."

"You said he was from Zazaristan," Hallazallah said. "Tell me what you meant about the attack coming from Quudia. Are you carrying the water of those people?"

"No, not at all," Shwarma said. "Quite—"

"Hold still," said Mr. Talmahani. He buzzed some off the right side of Shwarma's beard to even things out a bit.

Shwarma paused, then went on. "Quite the opposite. When I deployed Agent One, I sent him through Quudia. I designed this route with purpose."

This was technically true, but the purpose was solely that Shwarma's old schoolmate Hamid worked at the port as an Assistant Export Deputy and could provide intel like the fact that shipping container tiny homes were poorly secured and the exact locations in the Quudia Logistics Hub where containers bound for the West could be found.

"And what was this purpose?" Hallazallah asked.

"To create a trail back to Quudia, should Agent One be discovered. And through my contact at the port, I can tell you that it has worked. The American authorities have already turned their eye to the Quudis looking to place blame."

Shwarma knew this because he had received a text from Hamid late on Friday.

I was 🔥d.

When Shwarma tried to call him, it went straight to Hamid's voicemail. "Hamid El-Qami. *Garden of Delights* is available in paperback and e-book." Shwarma would try him again after this meeting with Hallazallah.

He continued, "Bashir, I have an active agent in play in America. Ready to execute. Any action he takes will fall on the heads of the Quudis. His cover is secure. His transportation has already been handled, which is, as you must know, the most difficult and costliest part when it comes to these kinds of things. Which brings me to the matter of price. Full command over Agent One: A hundred botcoins."

Hallazallah looked to Rizwan, who furiously scribbled out the day's botcoin-zazar exchange rate on a notepad and showed it to his boss.

Hallazallah laughed. "Good one, Shwarma."

"I'm quite serious, old man. This is a bargain. Agent One is worth twice that."

"Why not ask for two million, then?"

Shwarma said, "If you must know, I am expanding my business and I need capital at the moment. I will provide the handling of Agent One, Bashir. I will act as a buffer to you both. If One doesn't know you, he can't be made to name you if he's apprehended. Likewise, you have deniability if he fails, but the credit if he succeeds."

"Succeeds in what?"

"As I said, I am just the handler," Shwarma said. "I was given the impression that you were some sort of idea man when it came to operations. The planning will be up to you, I'm afraid."

"It will be simple," Hallazallah said. "Martyrdom."

"You got there very quickly," said Shwarma. "I was expecting something more… detailed. How were you planning to go about claiming credit, for example?"

"As I told you, there's very little Westerners fear more than they fear the unknown. It's sometimes better if the attack goes unexplained."

"Yes," Shwarma said. "So. Do we have a deal?"

"I'll think about it."

CHAPTER 48

• pain of loss. broken chain across.

Jefir's failure to slip into the US undetected had prompted a full "review" of GossCo's Pan-oceanic Shipping Route Security Controls. Disappointingly for Hamid, the review had nothing to do with *A Garden of Delights*.

The review became a study and the study became a report and the report became an action item and the action item was entered into a computer and the software that GossCo used to quantify actionizations bottom-lined that there was an 86% probability that firing the employee who signed off on KozyHome container 5318008 before it left Quudia, one Hamid S. El-Qami, would yield optimal value.

The software emailed Hamid's boss[3] and an hour later, two blouse-booted port security guards were escorting Hamid off the property of the Quudia International Logistics Hub Port.

When Shwarma finally reached him on the phone, Hamid sounded very upset. He said, "I got a FedEx today that was a big box full of the stuff that was in my locker."

"Was everything in it?" Shwarma asked. "I'll bet the Quudis helped themselves to whatever they wanted."

"They gave me a very detailed receipt," said Hamid. "It said, like, 'Calvin Klein CK One Fragrance. Frosted glass bottle. Pump Atomizer. Clear liquid. Approximately 200 sprays remaining.'"

"Quudis be uptight," said Shwarma.

"No Quudi ever got me fired!" Hamid shouted. "I'm mad at you, Dub. You told me this wouldn't happen."

"Again, Hamid, I'm sorry. It wasn't my fault. Our end was fine. Jefir screwed up the entry."

Hamid was quiet.

Shwarma said, "I'll make it up to you, Hamid. Why don't you move here? To Taboor City. You can work with me at my company."

"No thanks."

By themselves, the words are light. Like a bullet. It was the speed of the delivery that did the damage.

The long awkward pause afterward didn't exactly tickle either. Shwarma said, "Well. If. There's anything I can do… I'll just…"

"Don't call me anymore, Wahiri."

Shwarma had to think fast. "Wait! Hamid! Don't hang up! Let me send you a few botcoins."

"Don't give me your charity."

"No, no. This is for ah… another job. To make up for your lost income."

"I'm lucky they didn't arrest me or kick me out of the country. No more jobs, Dubs."

"That's just it though!" said Shwarma. "The job is *don't* help Jefir or his brother Rahim if they try to contact you. They were talking about sending Rahim to Hawaii. Jefir has been saving his money in America and I have a feeling he might try to arrange something with you directly."

"Is that the same Jefir who left a 5-star review for *Garden*? He called it 'evocative' and 'powerfully eponymous.' I'm not sure he knows what 'eponymous' means."

"I think he knows!" Shwarma said, way too quickly. "I think he was trying to say that the name of the book is, you know, very, very apt. A powerful garden of delights."

"That's not what the title poem is about, but whatever," said Hamid. "Why are you even worried about Jefir coming to me anyway? I don't work at the port anymore, remember?"

"Jefir doesn't know you were fired. He might still try to contact you for help. Do *not* answer the phone if you see him calling. Just for doing that, I'll send you… twenty botcoins."

It was almost everything Shwarma had at the moment. But he couldn't lose Hamid. Wouldn't let that happen. Almost as important was not losing Rahim. As long as the boy was around, everything still worked. If he or Jefir learned that Shwarma's access to the port via Hamid was lost, and therefore Rahim wasn't getting to Honolulu anytime soon, the kid would probably bolt.

Twenty botcoins was a lot, but if Shwarma played this right, it might just buy everything.

"Twenty botcoins?" Hamid asked.

"By the end of the week," Shwarma hedged.

"Can you do it by tomorrow? I'm going out of town."

"Where are you going?"

"Just… around. It's not like I have a job to get to."

"By yourself?"

"No, me and some guys from cricket. So, tomorrow, Dub? By noon?"

Shwarma hit mute on his phone. He took and let go a long breath. "I'll send it tonight."

Shwarma took down Hamid's new email and then, feeling as though a high point had been reached, quickly got off the phone before Hamid repeated his request for Shwarma not to call anymore.

Shwarma put the phone down and sat at his desk.

Jefir had made his choice and didn't leave much for Shwarma. But there's always an out. Sometimes it's only big enough for one person, but it's always there.

The sun was setting over H Street. Shwarma flung open his laptop. It's so much easier to lie in print. The words flowed out.

To: jeffzachary262@wmail.com

From: mohammad.mohammad54321@zmail.zaz

Subject: Breach

Jeff,

Shwarmco has been the victim of a COMPUTER ATTACK. I had plans to upgrade our system last week, but as you know cash flow has been slow and I was FORCED TO DELAY the installation.

Some or all of our data, including unencrypted communications have been COMPROMISED BY BASHIR HALLAZALLAH. Apparently, he has electronic sophistications that rival those of the West.

I believe you met Mr. Hallazallah a couple months ago, the night you KILLED HIS SON and you will not be surprised to know that he appears to be an eye-for-an-eye sort. We must assume Mr. Hallazallah has read your ill-advised messages to and from Rahim. HE KNOWS WHO YOU ARE, where you are and Rahim's true identity.

Of course, you are safe. But I CANNOT PROTECT RAHIM here in Taboor City any longer. It is only a matter of days before Hallazallah finds him and exacts his revenge.

The best course of action is to spirit Rahim away to Hawaii immediately. I have many contacts to negotiate with at every step along the route. They all demand their fees up front and the short timeline adds cost at every turn. SEND 40 BOTCOINS IMMEDIATELY TO SAVE RAHIM.

Wahiri Shwarma

The email message pinballed across the globe at the speed of light, but fell dead into the ocean off the coast of O'ahu, several hundred miles short of Jeff's cellphone, which rested darkly in the side pocket of his backpack.

Shwarma opened another new message window. *Think about this, old man.*

TO: bulacan4life@hotmail.com

FROM: wahiri.shwarma@shwarmco.zaz

Subject: Justice

Bashir,

I know where Jefir Zaqq is.

Wahiri Shwarma

Send.

Now Jeff would be forced to pay up in order to save his brother's life. With the stakes raised, and power tilted back in Shwarma's favor, he assumed Jeff would suddenly find the "lost" rhodium and send the full payment. And in the unlikely case that Jeff was actually telling the truth these last few weeks, if he actually *didn't* have the funds, Shwarma would simply turn to Hallazallah. The warden certainly had the means and would gladly pay for the identity of his son's killer and the opportunity to exact revenge.

Either Jeff would pay to protect his brother's life or Hallazallah would pay for Jeff's. And if the timing worked out for Shwarma, both! Now *that's* a double or nothing.

CHAPTER 49

• Every Work is in-Progress.

505 H Street had architectural flair, but the walls were fairly thin. Tycanni's slick brochure failed to mention that part. And Shwarma's meeting with Hallazallah needed to be held out of Rahim's wall-pressed earshot. Even Shinni's seemed risky. The café was busy morning, noon and night. Too many roving eyes and ears. Also, Shwarma still owed Shinni for last week's tab, and after sending Hamid twenty botcoins, he needed every bit of cash he could get his hands on.

Which is why he was meeting Hallazallah in the back corner of the bookstore, where it was quiet as a tomb and for a few blessed minutes nobody would be reaching into his pocket.

Shwarma was flipping through some YA when Hallazallah clomped down the aisle toward him. "I got your email," he said.

Shwarma tried to look just engrossed with the book. He held up a finger as if to say, *A moment, please.*

Hallazallah snatched the book and jabbed Shwarma in the throat with it. "What do you know about the man who killed my son, Shwarma?"

Shwarma's eyes were watering. He coughed and rubbed his throat. He rubbed his fingers together as if to say, *It'll cost you, asshole.*

"I expected nothing less, from you," Hallazallah said. "Was it a million zazars that you wanted the other day for your agent? I'd pay twice that for Jefir Zaqq's life. Two million zazars. You'll get it when Zaqq is dead and not before. Tell me what you know."

Shwarma had recovered, but his voice was a bit reedy when he said, "Jefir Zaqq. Is in Honolulu, Hawaii. He is Agent One."

Hallazallah's thick hand snapped onto Shwarma's neck. He drove him back into the shelf at the end of the aisle. A few books clattered to the floor. From her chair in the window, Bina shouted, "Quiet! I'm trying to read!"

Hallazallah squeezed Shwarma's throat. "You knew this whole time?" he seethed. "And you kept it from me? You even sent Zaqq to America. How can I avenge Bash now?"

Shwarma's vision was going dark. He grabbed a fistful of Hallazallah's beard and tugged in desperation before he passed out. The grip on his neck loosened in stalemate and then let go. Shwarma let go as well. He heaved a few deep breaths and shook his head. "I didn't know Zaqq killed your son until he was already in Hawaii. He owed me a debt and I had to wait until it was settled. But now, Bashir, please be my guest to collect yours."

Hallazallah said, “Just yesterday, you were calling this man your trusted operative. Now you’re selling him out? I didn’t think you had it in you, Shwarma.”

“He’s betraying me. Holding back funds. The Americans have corrupted him. You know how they are.”

Hallazallah nodded. “But being in America is the problem, isn’t it? How am I supposed to reach Zaqq if he’s thousands of kilometers away?”

“His brother isn’t. He’s here in Taboor.”

“Ah. Is that how you controlled him? A brother?” Hallazallah asked with something that sounded like appreciation. “Tell me how to contact Jefir Zaqq. He’s going to martyr himself in the United States in the name of Bash Hallazallah. If he refuses or fails, I’ll even my score with him through the brother.”

There was something missing. Shwarma was expecting another ask. “Don’t you want to know who the brother is, Bashir?” he said.

“No need,” Hallazallah replied. “I have no quarrel with Zaqq’s brother. For now. If the time comes that I need to know how to find him, I trust you’ll tell me. And if not, I’ll just even my score with you.”

Shwarma said, “It won’t come to that, I’m sure.”

“Time will tell,” Hallazallah said. “For now, how do I reach Jefir Zaqq? Or should I say Agent One? I need to let him know that he has a new mission.”

Shwarma said, “For Zaqq’s contact information, it’ll be a hundred thousand. Don’t mention my name in the message. Say you got his contact by intercepting an unencrypted message from his brother Rahim.”

"Rahim?" Hallazallah asked.

"Yes, like my lieutenant, Rahim Lotfi."

"If you're going to dictate what to say in the message, I think I should have to pay less. Ten thousand."

"If he knows you talked to me, he's gone forever and the brother with him. Fifty thousand," Shwarma insisted. "I cannot take less."

Hallazallah frowned. "Fifty." From his pocket, he pulled out a folded stack of zazars. He riffled through them, counting out a few bills. He added a worn, pink card and handed it all over. "Fifty thousand. And a Dapper gift card for a free Number Three. Certainly more than the life of Jefir Zaqq is worth."

Shwarma said, "He made his choice." He stuffed the cash in his pocket quickly. "Jeff Zachary two-six-two at Wmail dot com."

CHAPTER 50

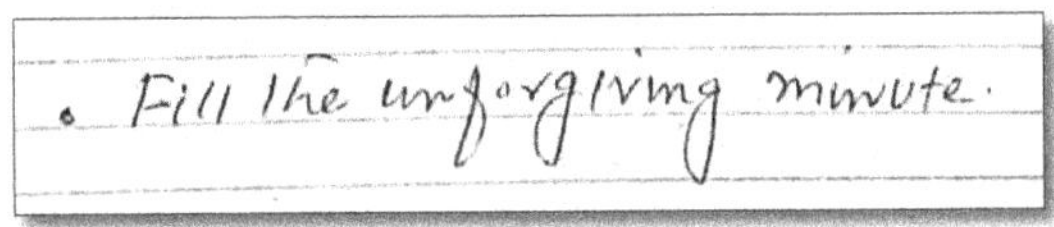

When the *Monkey Fist* returned to cellular range, Jeff powered up his phone and Wangled Alex Chen.

Wanglepedia reported that Alexander Hansen Chen, born January 22, 1964, was an American actor. Chen was born in San Anselmo, California and attended Yale Drama School. He is best known for his role as FBI Agent Kenny Hsu in the television series *Ocean Heat*. He now lives in Pearl City, Hawaii.

Wanglepedia has an EDIT button. Jeff clicked it to try to add, "rhodium thief," but he couldn't get it to work.

He exited the internet and checked his email. One from Shwarma.

Computer theft? Bashir Hallazallah? His blood ran cold in the warm night.

There was a second message. From bulacan4life@hotmail.com.

> You cannot hide in the arms of your Western whore, you infidel-loving fool. Your life belongs

to me now, payment for the life you took. You have one week to plan and execute a public attack martyring yourself in the name of Bash Hallazallah.

If you refuse to settle our account, I shall accept payment for your life from your brother Rahim, here in Taboor City.

Bashir Hallazallah

The terrifying threat on his life, on *Rahim's life* shot through Jeff like electricity, but he was powerless to do any more than pace the deck. Distant lights spangled the dark slash of O'ahu. Never had the *Fist* seemed to chug so slowly over the last few miles to Honolulu.

Jeff didn't want to believe it. But he rarely got what he wanted. This was no bluff. He had to get Rahim out of Taboor City ASAP.

Land looked to be no nearer than it had a minute ago. Jeff checked his watch. He would gladly send Shwarma every cent he had, although it would be nowhere near the $40,000 he required, and not until Pawn1[2] opened up the next morning, in thirteen hours and forty minutes.

One hour and fifty-two minutes later, the *Fist* was docked at the fish market. Jeff tugged on the line and the barrel of gray ice rose out of the freezer hold.

Izzo rested on his shovel. "This job sucks," he said. "I don't know how you do it, Jeff."

"I'm an ocean person," Jeff said. He picked up his shovel. There was at least one more barrelful of ice and fish body parts left.

Izzo grinned. "Is that why you like *Ocean Heat* so much? How many times did you watch that on this trip, anyway?"

"Three."

"You want the disc?" Izzo asked. "I'm getting more into documentaries these days."

"Yes," Jeff said. "Thanks, Izzo."

"Thanks for helping me clean out the hold. Man, this job sucks."

Working together, Jeff and Izzo finished shoveling out the slushy ice. Jeff hurried to wash up and change before Tasha returned with the pay envelopes. She distributed them by rank, and Jeff noticed that she slipped two envelopes to Kai, one marked "K" and the other marked "H."

As Izzo wandered off, Jeff caught Tasha as she started to climb the ladder to the bridge. "If it's alright," he said to her, "I'd like to get off the boat here instead of going back to the marina with the rest of you."

On the first rung, Tasha was still shorter than Jeff. She yelled past him, "Tommy! Are the jobs all done?"

"All done," Tommy said, while riffling through his envelope.

"K. No prob," Tasha said. She glanced at the DVD in his hand. "*Ocean Heat.* That was the shit."

"Yes," said Jeff. This shit was going to be his proof to Jonny K that Alex Chen was a thieving charlatan. He glanced over his shoulder at the lights of Honolulu.

Tasha stepped down to the deck. "Is everything alright with you, Jeff?"

"Yes, everything's alright. I just have someone… to meet here in the city." The Intercontinental was only ten blocks away.

Jeff hadn't opened his pay envelope. The corner of it poked from the pocket of his plaid pants. Tasha's eyes flicked over it. "You owe someone money, Jeff? Are you in trouble with Jonny K?"

From atop her three-legged stool of intuition, confidence and rhythm, Tasha always seemed to know.

"No!" Jeff exclaimed. And this was technically not a lie, not even a half-truth. He was in trouble with a Zazari warlord, but he and Jonny K were cool. In fact, the two were allies against the C-list celebrity who had swindled them out of $75,690 in precious metal posing as an agent of the People's Republic of China last week and *that's* why Jeff had to get to the IC right away. The sooner he could explain to Jonny K that Alex Chen has the rhodium, the sooner they could get to work recovering it so Jeff could fund Rahim's escape from Zazaristan. Also, Jeff knew Tasha would be delivering the week's pay to Jonny at the IC soon. He wanted to get there before she did. For one thing, the sooner he and Jonny could get to Chen, the better. After being at sea for days, helpless, every minute seemed to matter. And something also told him that Tasha would not be terribly impressed with his life choices as of late and it would be best if his dealings with Jonny K were kept sealed in their own compartment.

"OK," Tasha said, her brow slightly knitted. "I'll see you later."

"See you later."

Tasha climbed the ladder. Jeff bid his crewmates farewell with a quick 1-2-3-Monkeyfist, then he stepped off the boat and started running.

The questions washed up on the shore of his brain on a tide of pumping blood. Did Chen act alone? Was the actor living in Hawaii as some kind of con artist? How did he know about the rhodium? Was he partnered with Mr. A? Could Chen in fact *be* an agent of the Chinese government? An agent who spent some time undercover in the Los Angeles-based entertainment business in the 1990s? Would knowing Chen's true identity even help recover the rhodium? Would Jonny K agree to help get it back? And while it was true that Jonny had banned Jeff from the IC, that was with the understanding that "Inspector Han Li" was really a Chinese agent. Now that Jeff had proof that the thief of the rhodium was a harmless imposter that posed no further threat, surely Jonny would allow him back. And if it came down to it, if it meant getting his money back quickly and rescuing Rahim, Jeff would even volunteer to assist Jonny with the job of going to Pearl City to recover the rhodium from Chen. It's not like he'd never corkscrewed a guy who had it coming.

He dashed across Kukui Street and through the Intercontinental's parking lot. He could hear the dull thump of music from inside the building. He slipped in the front door a few paces ahead of a group of nurses.

The lounge was busy. Jeff twisted sideways to slip past a few parties waiting for tables near the hostess stand. Brad was working behind the bar and every stool was occupied. A woman was performing "Dancing Queen" on the karaoke stage. Jonny K was nowhere to be seen.

Jeff began to pick his way through the crowded tables toward Jonny K's office.

"What's up, Jeff?"

Brad had appeared out of the crowd and positioned himself directly in Jeff's path. He extended his arms out to make himself a barrier. "You can't be here, bro. Jonny said."

"Yes," said Jeff, trying to slip past. "I know. But—"

"Sorry. You gotta go."

"But I just need to talk to him for a minute," Jeff tried to edge past.

"Not here." Brad sidestepped to stay in front of Jeff and put his hand on Jeff's chest.

Jeff brushed Brad's hand aside. "He will want to see me. I—"

"Get your hand off me, bro," Brad said, giving Jeff a push.

"You get your hand off!" Jeff said, swatting Brad's hand away.

"Calm down, Jeff." Mikey from Pateena was suddenly at Brad's shoulder. Nep2ne and Chuck had also gotten off their barstools and stood in Jeff's path. "What's this about?"

"I have to talk to Jonny," Jeff said.

"He's banned," said Brad. "The *luna* said so. He can't be in here."

Mikey said, "Jeff, you want me to tell Jonny something?"

Jeff said, "No, I just—"

"K-den," said Mikey. "You gotta go. Out. You can talk to Jonny at the shop."

Jeff craned his neck, trying to see past the men to Jonny's office.

"Let's go," Mikey said. "Now."

Jeff allowed himself to be steered back to the front door and a moment later he was out in the parking lot, peeing on the grill of Brad's truck.

Feeling a little better, he walked around to the side of the building. Jonny's El Camino was parked in the alley. He was there. Jeff approached the sliding glass door that accessed Jonny's office, but it was reflective to the outside and Jeff couldn't see in. He knocked and cupped his hands to the glass, but there was no response. The door was locked and/or braced with the baseball bat.

Jeff didn't have Jonny's phone number, but even if he did, he realized that in his hurry to change clothes and get off the boat, he left his cell phone in his other pants.

He resigned himself to wait by Jonny's car until the man came out.

Twenty minutes went by. A shaft of yellow light spilled from the back door of the IC and the dull music amplified. A pair of barbacks stepped out onto the loading dock and sparked up cigarettes. Jeff hustled over and without comment, slipped past them and through the brick-propped fire door.

In the back hallway of the Intercontinental, Jeff made for Jonny's office. The door was locked. He knocked. No answer.

"Go Your Own Way" was blaring and the crowd roared in a way that could only mean the performer had just blown out a thundercloud of blazing green pot smoke.

Jeff edged to the end of the hallway to see the karaoke stage.

Jonny K was there.

With Alex Chen.

Sharing a single microphone. Jonny's bald head was beaded with sweat, his eyes clenched tight as he air-guitared the crescendo of the solo while Chen did some crowd work.

Jonny K and Alex Chen knew each other?

Jonny was involved in the theft.

Jeff realized it was he, and he alone, who had been had. In this world of crews and bands, he was a solo act the whole time. Shame and anger will not burn hotter than they burn inside the heart of a nineteen year-old man. It's not the humidity, it's the heat, baby.

Jeff glared at Jonny K. The journal explicitly said, "A single man, PROPERLY MOTIVATED, can change the course of the world," but it also *implicitly* discouraged say, charging a karaoke stage to tackle a three-hundred pound nightclub owner in front of a roomful of people. Revenge grows in the dark, not under spinning disco lights. Jeff tore his eyes from the stage and turned away to walk back out of the club before he could be spotted.

The nurses had congregated in the back of the room where they had carved out a makeshift dance floor. One of them grabbed Jeff and pulled him into their circle. One of them said something about a mustache.

Jonny's eyes opened for the final chorus and out of habit, they flashed to the group of wahine. They widened with alarm when he spotted Jeff Zachary in the midst of them, trying to wiggle his way out. He knew the *Monkey Fist* had returned to port that evening, but he had counted on his warning to Jeff to stay out of the IC to take a stronger hold. Now here the kid was, seeing Jonny and Alex Chen together. Why does everyone insist on choosing the hard way?

Jonny handed the microphone off to Chen, who at first thought, *Finally,* before realizing that Jonny was stepping from the stage to intercept the kid from the rhodium scene last week. Not a bad actor, the kid. He really seemed to be upset. That part, his emoting, was believable, but his dialogue was too rushed. Jonny was smart not to give the kid too many lines. Not that the script was set in stone. When Jonny had first hired Chen to act in the interactive micro plays that the eccentric club owner liked to stage from time to time for his own amusement, he made it very clear that the performers must never, *ever* break character and therefore some improvisation was going to be required. It was one of the things that drew Chen to the role of Chinese Ministry of Security Inspector Han Li in the first place, along with immediate cash payment, free drinks and high-quality weed.

Jeff was just one nurse away from freedom when a strong hand grabbed the base of his neck.

"What's the haps, Jeff?" said Jonny. "Aloha, ladies! Coming through! Next round's on the house!" he called out. The women whooped as Jonny hustled a grimacing Jeff down the back hall, his piercing grip only stronger now.

Quietly, close to Jeff's ear, Jonny said, "Didn't I tell you to bag, bruddah? You remember any of this? I said it would be trouble if we were seen together." He quickly unlocked his office door and shoved Jeff inside. "Now we got trouble." He shut the door, muting Chen's mellow voice and the clamorous room.

Jonny invited Jeff to sit by pushing him while kicking him in the back of the knee, making Jeff collapse face first onto the couch.

Jonny walked around his desk and bent to pick up his bat from where it lay on the sliding door track.

"Don't you have enough?" Jeff said. "You had to take what was mine, too?"

"I didn't take shit," Jonny said with a wave of the bat. "I bought that rhodium."

"You didn't pay me anything!"

Jonny took a step closer. "You know about distressed property, Jeff?"

"What?"

"You should," Jonny said. He sat on the edge of his desk. "Because you are one. Distressed property is when you can pay someone less because they're in trouble."

"You should pay those people *more*," Jeff said.

Jonny smiled. "That's funny. See, that's how I know you're not from around here, bruddah. I never pay more than I have to. But I still always get what I want."

"You stole my rhodium! Where is it?" Jeff demanded.

"The rhodium's long gone, bruddah. I sold it a few days ago in Maui. I used the money to upgrade the Pateena website."

"I needed that money!"

"I paid you a thousand dollars for that shitty toaster just the other day." Jonny flicked the bat toward Jeff's toaster, high on a shelf across the room. "What happened to that money?"

"I—"

"And I could've jacked you for the rhodium whenever. But I didn't. Straight robbing motherfuckers is no good for the brand. People have to trust you." He pointed the bat at Jeff. "Plus, you were off the grid and I can always use a clean guy. I didn't have to give you a job at Pateena. But I did. I wanted to keep you around."

Jonny glanced at the DVD, still clenched in Jeff's hand. "That's why I hired that idiot Chen. So you wouldn't know it was me that ended up with the rhodium." He jabbed the bat. "Even though I *told* you not to come back here, you did anyway. With your *Ocean Heat* DVD. And so now you know it was me. And *that* is def not good for the brand. You gotta go, Jeff. Sorry, bruddah."

"I needed that money," Jeff said again. "You told me I'd get sixty thousand dollars!"

"I tell wahine my wai o kaunu tastes like coconut water." Jonny sprang forward and gave Jeff's kneecap a swift rap with the bat. "People believe what they want." He turned back to his desk as Jeff tried to rub away the stinging ache. Jonny put down the bat and pulled a black pistol from the top drawer.

The office door banged open. Alex Chen ushered a giggling pair of nurses inside, saying something about a private party. He noticed Jeff on the couch and said, "Ah, there you are, young fellow. We never met after the performance last week. You were excellent by the way. The dialogue was a bit rushed. You must never do that. Is that Season Two of *Ocean Heat* you have there?" Chen removed a sharpie from his blazer and uncapped it as he stepped toward Jeff. "Perhaps someday I will be asking *you* for *your* autograph," he chuckled. "How should I make this out?" He reached for the disc.

"Chen!" Jonny barked. "Get out."

Chen looked around to see Jonny behind his desk, holding the gun. "Sorry!" he exclaimed. "Were you rehearsing? Apologies, Jonathan, apologies. This is Lori, by the way. And Jenn."

"Lauren," one of the nurses said. "Jean," said the other.

Jeff hoped his knee wouldn't buckle as he surged up from the couch. He grabbed a fistful of Chen's jacket and shoved him flailing toward Jonny's desk. He dodged past the nurses, using them as human shields for only the briefest of moments, bolted out the office door and down the back hall.

His knee throbbed a complaint when he landed on the asphalt below the loading dock, but held up well enough as Jeff once again ran for his life.

But where? And with what? He had the clothes on his back, a couple thousand dollars in an envelope in his pocket and a DVD. Everything he owned was in his backpack, tucked in his bunk on the *Fist*. Clothes, phone, journal. The journal! He had to get back to the *Monkey Fist*. Fast.

One of Jonny's employees, Brad the bartender—who never showed up with that champagne, now that Jeff thought about it—knew that Jeff lived somewhere at the marina and it would be a fairly simple deduction for Jonny to figure out exactly where, if he hadn't already. Jonny would get in his El Camino and drive to Sand Island, where he would lie in wait to kill Jeff Zachary, who doesn't legally exist, by the way, on the bloodstained deck of the *Monkey Fist* then motor out into the dark sea to dispose of the nameless corpse like a barrel of spent consumer goods.

The *Fist* was compromised. But Jeff had to get there first. What other choice did he have? As the world's greatest cross-country coach says: Run faster.

He ran across the short bridge over Nu'uanu stream and crossed North Beretania street to cut through Aala skate park. Behind him, headlights swung into the parking lot. A horn blared.

Jeff didn't slow, didn't turn. He'd outrun this, too.

"Jeff!" Tasha called.

Jeff stopped.

CHAPTER 51

• TBH = To be honest.

Tasha was driving on North Beretania Street, about three blocks from the Intercontinental, when she saw her plaid-pantsed third mate running across the street. His ragged speed suggested he was running *away,* rather than *toward* something.

Jeff veered off into the trees of Aala Park. Tasha turned into the skatepark lot after him, honked and called out the window.

He stopped running and came back cautiously, using the truck's cab to shield himself from view of the street.

Tasha said, "Everything all right, Jeff?"

"No," said Jeff. "No. I have to get back to the boat for something. I have to hurry."

"Get in," Tasha said. "I'll drive you."

"No." The light at the River Street intersection changed. Jeff glanced to the street. "No. You can't be seen with me. I'm sorry. I'm watching your back, Captain."

"What did I say about calling me that?" Tasha said. The dimples flashed in the light of the dash. "And what are you talking about? Seen by who?"

"Jonny K. I have to go, Tasha. I'm sorry," Jeff turned.

Tasha knew when people say, 'I'm sorry' in that way, it usually means something to the effect of, 'Please show yourself out.' Jeff started to run, but Tasha spun the wheel and tapped the accelerator. The nose of the truck lurched into Jeff's path and dove to a stop.

"So, goodbye in the skatepark?" Tasha asked. "You never did tell me your story, Jeff." Jeff glanced up at the street again. "Give me the last part, at least," she said. "What just happened? What did Jonny do? I'm on my way to see him right now to give him the week's take." She tapped the satchel on the seat next to her.

Jeff said, "Jonny stole something from me. When I went and tried to get it back, he put a gun on me. I ran out, but I'm afraid he might follow me back to the *Monkey Fist.* I need to get back to the marina." He scanned the street once more, as if expecting to see Jonny's gold El Camino any second.

Tasha shook her head. "I knew it was going to be something like that. I'm sorry Jeff, I should have warned you better to stay away from him."

"It's not your fault, Tasha."

"Let me help."

"No. If you drive me back to the marina and Jonny shows up there and sees you helping me, you might get hurt, too. I just have to get my things and go. Thank you, Tasha, Thank you for everything." Jeff turned to run.

Tasha reached out the window and snatched a handful of his t-shirt. "Get back to the boat and get your stuff. I'll keep an eye on Jonny and text you if he's coming your way."

"I left my phone on the boat," Jeff said.

"What are you waiting for? You better hurry back, then," Tasha advised.

"Goodbye, Tasha."

He pulled from her grasp and Tasha watched his back disappear into the trees at the edge of the basketball court. "Laters, Jeff."

Tasha pulled her truck behind Jonny K's El Camino in the side alley of the IC and switched it off. Jonny was coming out of his sliding office door carrying a Styrofoam to-go cup and his baseball bat.

Tasha got out. "Where are you going, Jonny?" She held up her satchel. "I've got the trip money."

"Give it to Brad," Jonny said. He dropped the bat in the El Cam's bed and reached for the door handle. "I've gotta go. Hey, do you know where I could find Jeff? I heard he lives at the marina."

"I don't know," Tasha said. "Haven't seen him since he left the boat."

Jonny said, "Move your truck, Tasha. I gotta get out." He got in the car and the big block 454 roared to life.

Natasha Hale doesn't sing backup. Let's get it straight.

Squeezing the monkey's fist on her keychain, Tasha silently mouthed her singing mantra: *The gauge of the age is the rage on the page is the cage of the wage. The stage*. She said, "I was hoping we could… sing a few together tonight."

The El Camino's engine shut off.

CHAPTER 52

• Determine who likes what.

Jeff had only been to this part of Honolulu once, but he knew if he followed the Waolani Stream north until it crossed Wyllie he would only be a block or two from the address Tasha had texted him, 88 Burbank Street.

88 Burbank turned out to be a small white house that shared a backyard with the apartment complex that Jeff had watched Tasha go into the night Brad drove them home from the IC. Tasha's truck was in the driveway. The house was lit.

Jeff knocked and the dot of light coming through the door's peephole flashed off for a second. The door opened and music flowed out. Tasha was barefoot. Her hair was wet.

"Come in," She wore loose, floral-patterned pants and a t-shirt with a surfboard on it.

Jeff stepped inside, carrying his belongings in a plastic bag. Tasha's hair smelled like ginger. Jeff looked over his shoulder. "I thought you lived in that other building."

"That's where that perv Brad *thinks* I live," Tasha said. "Even this place isn't really my house. My friend Haole Jan owns it, but she's in Kiribati all summer. I look after it and she only charges me a hundred a week."

Haole Jan was into vinyl, self-help books and artwork about dogs. Her house smelled of hippies and fresh-cut lime. She had an Apple computer.

"Did you get what you needed from the boat?" Tasha asked, walking into the kitchen.

"I hope so," Jeff said. He set his bag down and followed. "Thank you for letting me stay here."

"Sure." Without asking, Tasha fixed Jeff a gin and tonic. "You were right, by the way," she said, giving the drink a quick stir with her finger, also without asking. "Jonny was leaving the IC to look for you when I got there."

"And you were able to stop him?"

"Yes," said Tasha, making a face. "We sang "Go Your Own Way," "The Chain," "Leather and Lace," which was extra gross, then "Gold Dust Woman," "I Don't Want to Know," "Don't Stop," and he let me sing "Songbird" solo at the end. He was pretty high by the time we finished and I don't think he ended up going out to look for you tonight."

"Thank you, Tasha."

She picked up a half-full glass of her own and gave a clinky wave. "Code of the sea," she said. She moved to the living room and sat heavily on the couch.

Jeff sat on the other end. He fished the piece of lime out of his drink and ate it. "But why for me? Why not the code of the sea for Jonny? He owns the *Monkey Fist.* He's our boss. Your boss."

"I never told you how he came to own the *Fist*, did I?" Tasha asked.

"No," said Jeff.

"Until about a year ago, I owned the *Monkey Fist.* I'd been fishing with my uncles since I was a kid and I got my captain's license when I was twenty. I worked as a mate on bigger boats until I saved up enough to make the down payment on the *Fist.* Last year, my crew was Tommy, Hemi, Kai and... Dave. Remember when I told you about Dave? The guy who fell off the ladder?"

Jeff nodded.

Tasha sipped her drink. "When that happened, Dave got a concussion, a *minor* concussion, Jeff, I still have the medical report. And Hemi had to put a few stitches in his leg. That's it. No big deal. I paid him for a few weeks after, until the doctor said he was fine, but he never came back to work. He's a mountain person. Anyway, he started hanging around the IC a lot, drinking and playing Golden Tee all day and I think Jonny talked him into suing me for his injury so Jonny could swoop in and buy the *Fist* cheap. Dave hired Jonny's lawyer and long story short, my paycheck got garnished, which is *way* worse than it sounds, btw and basically I lost everything I had. I had to declare bankruptcy, and the morning, the very *morning* the *Fist* was repoed, Jonny bought her from the bank." She drank another splish. "Yes, he hired me back as captain but only because he knew I would take less if he paid me in cash. And it's not like he could do the job himself. He took my boat, Jeff."

Side one of *Tea for the Tillerman* ended and Tasha got up to flip the record over. "But I Might Die Tonight" began.

"So you're in trouble with Jonny now, too?" she asked.

"That's not the whole story," Jeff said.

"I think it's time you told me."

"Yes," said Jeff.

Jeff told Tasha that his name was Jefir Zaqq. He told her that he and his brother Rahim used to sell rainbow melons together in the East Station Market in Taboor City, Zazaristan. He told her that a misunderstanding with a local warlord named Bashir Hallazallah over an American ten dollar bill forced him to kill the warlord's son ("in self defense") with a corkscrew. He told her that he met a man eating an ice cream bar that night and that the man's name was Wahiri Shwarma. He told her that Shwarma protected him from the vengeful Hallazallah. He told her how Shwarma let him and Rahim hide out in his tiny apartment for weeks as the warlord searched the brothers' old neighborhood, the market, Mrs. Khan's shop. He told her how Shwarma had eventually arranged safe passage out of the country using the connections of a Quudi poet named Hamid for the price of fifty botcoins. He told her that he didn't understand most of *Garden of Delights*. He told her that Shwarma made him watch *Ocean Heat* every day on DVD. He told her how he said goodbye to Rahim in the back of a van at midnight on the coast of Quudia. He told her that he set out to cross the Pacific Ocean that night in a KozyHome Lucky Seven tiny home with only a full backpack, a half-full journal and an empty five-gallon bucket. He told her how he ended up in Honolulu Harbor and how he evaded capture at the GossCo port. He told her that yes, he was the stowaway that the CBP officer was seeking the morning that they met.

"I know this part," Tasha said.

He told her how he paid his debt to Shwarma and his plans to bring Rahim to Honolulu. He told her about finding a piece of rhodium worth $89,566.50 the same night the huge tuna almost pulled them both overboard and the prop got fouled in the net. He told her that Shwarma was demanding more and more money. He told her that he was a terrible employee at Pateena. He told her that Jonny K promised to help him sell the rhodium, but then double-crossed him with the help of the actor Alex Chen, the guy from *Ocean Heat* Season Two.

"Jeff, that dude's photo is on the wall of the IC," said Tasha.

"It is? Where?"

"Near the front door. You didn't recognize him?"

"I was looking at the gun, mostly."

He told her he was sorry for not heeding her advice to stay away from Jonny K. He told her that he finally figured out that Jonny K must have cut the digital photo of his rhodium that he "sent to the buyer" and pasted the image into the "Chinese document" that Chen flashed along with his gun. He told Tasha that the rhodium was gone, but he still needed to pay Shwarma 400 botcoins by next week to protect Rahim's identity from Bashir Hallazallah, the Zazari warlord he mentioned earlier, and that the alternative to all this was publicly sacrificing his own life in the name of the warlord's dead son.

"Complicated lives," Tasha said. The final piano notes of "Tea for the Tillerman" faded away.

During "Longer Boats," while Jeff was telling her about Taboor City, Tasha had pivoted on the couch to rest her feet on Jeff's lap. She withdrew them now and got up to put another record on.

Norah Jones joined the two of them there in Haole Jan's living room on Burbank Street in Honolulu, Hawaii.

Tasha sat back down on the couch and put her feet right back where they were before.

CHAPTER 53

• It's not the humidity, it's the heat, baby.

The Intertropical Convergence Zone, or ITCZ, lies around the equator. There's not much to it. It's mostly just glassy water, still as a puddle. The hot, thick air feels like it would be too tired to move. But it happens all the time. Every day, in fact. Uneven heat on the water's surface will create wisps of wind that stir up tiny capillary waves, weaker than the surface tension of the surrounding water. These diamond-shaped ripples give more purchase to the wind. And then a little more. And then the wind usually stops and the tiny capillary waves die out. But other times, when the air can muster enough strength or passion or courage or conviction or whatever, all it needs is six knots (6.9 mph). A measly six knot wind will catch, form a true wave and send that wave rolling out of the ITCZ.

Now, do not confuse wave and water. The wave moves, the water does not. The water is lifted by the surge of the wave's passing energy, then drawn back down, creating larger and larger gravity waves with crests and troughs. The wider the troughs, the longer the fetch, and the longer the fetch, the more time the wind has to gather momentum and drive its power into the next crest and the higher the wave becomes. This feedback loop goes on and on and on until the wind-driven waves, forty, fifty-foot breakers, literally tons of water, explode like liquid thunder on the shores of Hawaii all night long.

"Yes!" said Jeff.

CHAPTER 54

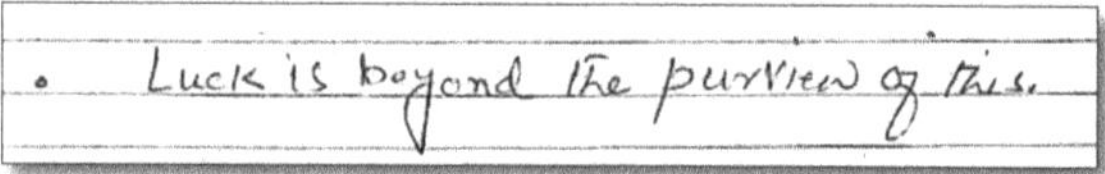

Haole Jan had a Pateena pancake batter dispenser. It was painted in B's blue-green, spangled with tiny metal Scottie dogs from the boardgame Monopoly and it had a ceramic Chihuahua glued to the rim, his pinched stance and nervous mien suggesting slim purchase on a narrow ledge. Tasha squeezed off six pancakes onto the countertop griddle.

"I was thinking about water last night," she said. "After we talked."

The pancakes had mooshed-up bananas in the batter.

"Do you know anything about fluid dynamics?" she asked. "I learned this when I was getting my captain's license. A body at rest in a fluid is acted on by a force pushing upward called buoyancy, equal to the weight of the fluid the body displaces. When there's heat in the water, buoyancy decreases and therefore more water is displaced. Do you want melon?"

"Yes," said Jeff.

Tasha handed Jeff a spatula. "Flip those pancakes when they're ready." She moved down the counter and began to filet a light green melon. "That's just like your plan. Like you." She cut the melon into cubes.

Mooshed-banana pancakes do not bubble when they're ready like a normal pancake. "I don't get it," Jeff said. "Am I the body or the water?" He probed the edge of the first pancake with the spatula.

"You're the body. Jonny K is the water."

Jeff flipped the pancake. Perfect. He quickly worked through the other five. In the training videos, Heat Barbary once flipped a pancake into the air and caught it in a pan behind his back, but after repeated slow-mo viewings of the culinary stunt, Jefir and Rahim agreed that the initial launch angle of the pancake was way, way, *way* off and besides, the camera cut to a close-up of the pan when the pancake landed. A cheap, but effective deception. "What are you, then?" Jeff asked.

"I'm the heat, baby." She slid him a bowl of melon.

CHAPTER 55

• A good mini-donut is still a donut.

After breakfast, Tasha emailed Jonny K to let him know that she was going to quick-turn the *Fist* in order to head out again the next day. There were reports of bluefin schools near the US EEZ and north of Kiribati.

Tasha glanced at Jeff, cleaning up the dishes in the kitchen. She added to the message: "BTW, did you find Jeff last night? Let him know we're sailing tomorrow." Send.

Tasha then made a phone call to Haole Jan. They talked for a few minutes. Jan wanted to assess Jeff's aura, so the call became a LiveZoop. Fortunately, Jan saw that Jeff's chakras were aligned and he was exuding strong vastu energy, which she could tell even through the computer screen. Tasha left the two of them chatting and left for the marina. On the way, she sent a short text to CBP officer Matthew Porter using Jeff's pawnshop phone.

"Good morning, Officer Porter! Nice to see you again," Tasha said, as she climbed down the ladder from the pilothouse later that morning. She walked to the rail. "What brings you back to the *Monkey Fist*?"

Porter and Kaz stopped at the edge of the pier.

"A serious matter of national security, Captain Hale," Porter said. "Remember when I told you, the last time I was here, that CBP could search every inch of your boat? We're here to search your boat."

Kaz said, "I'm Officer Sue Kazumi, Captain. We have a warrant." She held up a tri-folded paper. "May we come aboard?"

"I know who you are, Officer Kazumi. I saw you on ZoopZap last week at that press conference over on the cargo dock," Tasha said. "And technically, it's not even my boat, but yeah, come on aboard. Grab yourselves a couple muffins."

A box of six muffins was on the same deck hatch, right where Porter remembered.

Kaz and Porter stepped onto the deck and Kaz handed over the warrant. Her business card was clipped to the top.

Tasha scanned it and the terms "Probable cause" and "credible tip" and "text message" and "digital evidence" jumped from the page.

Tasha signed, took the card, and handed the warrant back to Kaz. "What's this about?" she asked. "Is there anything I can do for you?"

"This regards the events of July 8th. Officer Porter was looking for a stowaway that day," Kaz said.

"I remember," Tasha said, "Did you catch him yet?"

"Jeff Zachary," said Kaz. "How long have you known him?"

"Jeff? You think Jeff is the guy?"

"We received a tip this morning that made him a person of interest. Do you have a picture of him?"

"Of his face? I don't think so." Tasha took out her phone and scrolled through some photos. "This is his fist," she said.

"How long have you known him?" Kaz repeated, briefly examining the photo.

Tasha said, "Let's see... These guys come and go so much. But Jeff's been with me a few weeks now. One of my old mates, Claude Ohanu… You met Claude that day, Officer Porter, remember? Claude bagged after that trip and the very next day Jeff showed up. I needed a fourth guy, so I didn't ask a lot of questions. Jeff's been with us ever since. He's not here now, but his bunk's downstairs if you want to check it out. Top one on the left."

Porter went below.

When he was gone, Kaz picked out a lemon-poppy seed muffin. "Do you have a knife or something I could use to cut this?" she asked.

Tasha said, "Just a minute." She climbed down the cabin steps. "Everything OK, Officer Porter?" she called out.

Porter was pulling on rubber gloves. "Fine," he answered.

Tasha retrieved a knife and fork from the galley, returned to the deck, and handed them to Kaz.

"Thank you," Kaz said. "When's the last time you saw Jeff Zachary?"

"We finished a trip last night," Tasha said. "He left the boat, said he was going to the Intercontinental. Haven't seen him since."

"Please call me if you see him again," said Kaz. She speared a bite of muffin.

"Sure thing," Tasha said. "Can I ask you something, Officer? What's Margot Carlene like? I saw you with her at that press conference. Do you follow her on ZoopZap? I follow her on ZoopZap."

Kaz made a face and was silent.

"Sorry," Tasha said, "Are we done talking about Jeff?"

Kaz swallowed. She said, "For now, yes. We just need to find him. As Officer Porter might say, Margot is… efficacious. Efficacious is the word."

Tasha laughed. "You call her Margot? Do you know her?"

Kaz said, "We met that day. We talked for almost an hour while the news crews set up. She's really into interior design. Really into."

"She has amazing style," Tasha said, "I'd love to ask, just, how does she do it?" She picked a muffin and tore off a piece. "I know she's a big corporate boss and I'm a fishing boat captain, but I feel like we're both just women in business. I think she would be a great mentor or life coach or whatever." She popped a hunk of muffin into her mouth.

Porter appeared from the cabin. He was holding Jeff's journal in his rubber-gloved hands. "Tell us about Jonny Kalawai'a," he said.

Her mouth full, Tasha said, "Jonny Kalawai'a's my boss. He owns the boat."

"I found Zachary's diary, Kaz," Porter said, waving the book.

"On a boat it's called a log," Tasha said, swallowing.

"Log," Porter repeated. He opened it and began to gingerly turn pages. "It starts out like some sort of self-help guide. Some of it's possibly in code. But at the end, Zachary documents his whole operation."

"What operation?" Kaz said.

"The attack on the Sand Island Port," Porter said. "All of it." He showed a page to Kaz. "Zachary documents everything about his work as a courier between a high-ranking member of the House of Quud and one Jonathan Kalawai'a, a Hawaiian businessman who owns the Intercontinental Poke Restaurant and Karaoke Lounge as well as…" Porter flipped a page, "… the *Monkey Fist*, the *Monkey Fist Too*, various businesses, and a golden Chevrolet El Camino. Kalawai'a trafficked Zachary into Sand Island via GossCo cargo ship in order to smuggle untaxed precious metals into the country, including a piece of rhodium worth $100,000. Zachary records arriving in the US on 8 July and"—Porter made air quotes—"defeating port security. He delivered the rhodium to Kalawai'a on 30 July and has been maintaining cover as a fishing mate on the *Monkey Fist* after taking the place of a Claude Ohanu. He works the boat with Captain Tasha Hale and her crew, who Zachary describes as"—more air quotes—"incurious fishermen."

Kaz looked at Tasha.

"Can't say I like that, Jeff Zachary," said Tasha.

"Does all this surprise you, Captain Hale?" Kaz asked.

Tasha said, "The part about Jeff surprises me, yes. He's a cool guy and a good fishing mate. The other stuff, about Jonny K? Sounds legit. The IC is on the corner of Kukui and Nu'uanu."

Kaz thanked Tasha for her help and they finished their muffins as Porter bagged up the rest of Jeff Zachary's worldly possessions. As the officers left the boat, Tasha heard Porter saying, “Zachary also wrote about how Kalawai’a dumps a boatload of industrial waste in the ocean every Friday night.”

CHAPTER 56

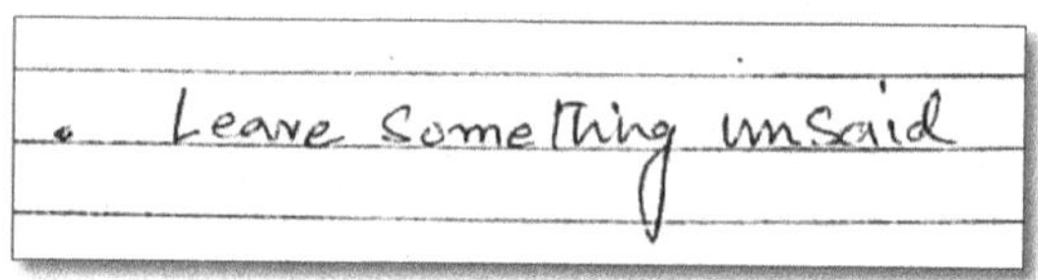

Margot Carlene's man Geoffrey answered the call. "Carlene."

"Margot?" Tasha asked. She sat inside the bridge of the *Monkey Fist*. Kaz and Porter had driven off five minutes ago.

"This is Geoffrey," Geoffrey said.

Tasha said, "May I please speak with Margot Carlene? This is Captain Natasha Hale."

"What is it regarding, Captain? And who gave you this number?"

Tasha said, "United States Customs and Border Officer Susan Kazumi gave me the number. And I need to speak with Margot about an opportunity. To enter the home furnishings and lifestyle space."

Geoffrey said, "I will give Margot the message, Captain Hale. Thank you for calling."

"Wait!" Tasha said. She slid off the captain's chair and stepped out of the pilothouse and into the warm breeze. This bullshit needed to be aired out.

"A window is closing in the next few hours, Geoffrey," she said. "And then the opportunity will be lost. And it's the kind of opportunity that has to come *to* a person, as opposed to the kind where a person has to dial *out* on their own phone if that person was ever worried about her phone records being reviewed in the future. You know how it is, Geoffrey."

"Is that the message?" Geoffrey asked. "I will pass it to the appropriate person. I have it memorized. Have a good morning, Captain."

"No, that's not the message!" Tasha said. "Wait, you memorized that? Say it back."

"I need to speak with Margot about an opportunity. To enter the home furnishings and lifestyle space. A window is closing in the next few hours, Geoffrey. And then the opportunity will be lost. And it's the kind of opportunity that has to come *to* a person, as opposed to the kind where a person has to dial *out* on their own phone if that person was ever worried about her phone records being reviewed in the future. You know how it is, Geoffrey."

Tasha said, "That. Is. Impressive. Geoffrey, you're not… a robot are you? You're a real person, right?"

"Yes, Captain. Very much so."

"Prove it. Quick, who's the best Van Halen singer?"

"Diamond David Lee Roth."

"Why does orange juice taste so bad after brushing your teeth?"

"I don't know."

"OK," Tasha said. "You check out. Do you work for Margot, Geoffrey?"

"I do. I am her personal assistant and social media coordinator."

"Do you write the Zoops of the Day?" Tasha asked.

"No. I post them for her sometimes. But I have written one."

"What? Which one?" Tasha asked. "Which Zoop was yours?"

"Find something you love and hang on with three hands," said Geoffrey.

"Solid," said Tasha. "I like what you did there."

"Thank you, Captain."

"You're welcome. Keep up the good work. Hey, Geoffrey, remember when I said a minute ago that a window was closing? If Margot wants this opportunity, she needs to know about it soon. Today soon. Like now soon."

"Please hold, Captain."

Tasha paced the deck outside the pilothouse.

"This is Margot."

"Margot Carlene," Tasha tried to say in a way that was a cool blend of matter-of-fact statement, freaking out, and boss energy.

"Yes. Who is this?" Margot asked. In sotto voce: "Geoffrey, I'll meet you downstairs."

Tasha said, "Margot, my name is Captain Natasha Hale. I follow you on ZoopZap. I admire your style. I dig your vibe." Tasha stopped herself. A long moment passed. The wait is the weight.

Margot said, "I recall Geoffrey saying something about a window of opportunity closing? And the home furnishings and lifestyle space?"

"Of course," Tasha said. "This afternoon, the owner of Pateena, Jonathan Kalawai'a, is going to be arrested on federal charges and he's going to be facing a huge fine and a ton of legal fees. You should call him, soon, before he's in custody, and offer to buy Pateena. Offer whatever low price you want."

Margot said, "The idea being that he will reject my offer, but when he soon needs the cash after being arrested, he'll come back to me."

"Yes! Yes! I knew you would get it. Because then he'll be a distressed property."

"Yes, thank you, Captain Hale, I understand."

"Please, call me Tasha. Can I give you Kalawai'a's cell number?"

"Why are you doing this, Tasha?" Margot asked. "Is this dude your ex or something?"

"No," Tasha said. "Oh, no. No. I'm just calling because I thought this would be a great opportunity for you. 'Opportunity doesn't knock,'" she recited, "'It just stands behind the door like an unsuspecting dolt.' That was your Zoop of the Day a few weeks ago."

Margot paused. "Are you that unsuspecting dolt, Tasha? Somehow I doubt it. Let me ask again: why are you doing this?"

"OK. Jonathan Kalawai'a took my fishing boat," Tasha said.

"Define 'took.'"

"He forced me to sell it," said Tasha.

"And now you have the chance to force a sale from him," said Margot. "And then what, Tasha? I just get this great tip for free and then we go our separate ways?"

Tasha said, "When you get the call back from him, get him to throw my boat, the *Monkey Fist*, into the deal. Then lease it back to me. At a reasonable rate."

"I'm not interested in getting into the fishing business," said Margot.

"It's just business," Tasha rejoined. "And catching fish. But for you, Margot, it'll be catching a pound of hundred dollar bills in your Saffiano handbag every week when we meet up for drinks after a trip."

Tasha watched a seagull glide past. The graceful rats of the seas, they were.

"What time will Kalawai'a be arrested?" Margot asked.

"I don't know," Tasha said. "But soon. Today."

"What's stopping me from just snapping up Pateena and cutting you out, Tasha? You already told me everything I need to know."

"I haven't told you the best part yet."

"Oh no? Why not?"

"Because the best part will cost you a fishing boat."

Pressing the END button was scarier than the night the net got snagged in the prop.

CHAPTER 57

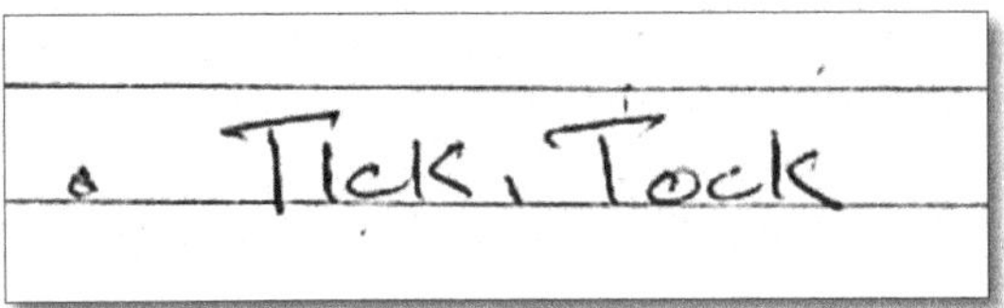

The bartender at the Intercontinental told Kaz and Porter that Jonny K had just left to go to Pateena. The guy at Pateena said Jonny K had just left to go to the Intercontinental.

By the time Kaz and Porter found Jonny Kalawai'a's home address on Kaneohe Bay, the sun was setting and Jeff Zachary's fingerprints found on the *Monkey Fist* had been matched to those from the KozyHome. The CBP wanted to hear what Kalawai'a might have to say about aiding and abetting the federal fugitive Jeff Zachary, human trafficking, tax evasion, racketeering, and various health code/OSHA violations at the IC.

They drove until the paved apron of Honolulu gave way to a single black ribbon. Then up and over a mountain, green in the headlights and black beyond. The road narrowed, and narrowed again. The pavement eventually ran out and the road became dirt the color of day-old blood. It ended at a chained gate. Kaz stopped the SUV and killed the lights.

The night was a riot of chirping coqui frogs. A light south wind blew off the ocean, clacking through the palm fronds. Kaz and Porter stepped over the chain and approached the modest bungalow on foot.

Beyond the house, the moon-speckled ocean came into view. An El Camino was backed up to a dock that extended almost a hundred feet into the water. At the end of the dock, a ski boat was tied up, its stern lightly aburble. Fleetwood Mac was playing over the boat's speakers.

Kalawai'a was at the helm of the boat. A thin teenager ratcheted down a wide strap that encircled a half-dozen large barrels, then turned and tossed off the boat's lines. Jonny K jammed the throttle ahead.

Kaz drew her weapon and ran toward the dock yelling, "Stop! Stop where you are!" but between the frogs and the boat's engine and "I Don't Want To Know," Kalawai'a didn't hear as he roared off across the glittering water.

CBP's marine unit was fifteen minutes away at the Marine Corps Air Station. By the time they arrived, Kalawai'a was long gone. His last heading was north-north-west. The *Monkey Fist Too* was too small to appear on the Air Station's radar, but she was also too small to venture safely into the high seas offshore. Kalawai'a couldn't have gone far, whatever he was doing. Were those barrels in his boat full of industrial waste, as Zachary's journal said? Or was he rendezvousing with another smuggler? Whatever the case, it would prove the journal credible and the stiff fine for ocean littering might be the least of Mr. Kalawai'a's problems.

A 41-foot CBP Coastal Interceptor Vessel slowed to touch the end of Kalawai'a's dock and Kaz and Porter stepped aboard. The boat's pilot curled away to the north-north-west.

"Anything on radar?" Kaz asked him.

The man adjusted the gain on his display. "On a night like this, we'd have to be within a couple miles. If he's running lights, we'd see him first."

"Kill our lights," Kaz said. "Did you bring the NVGs?"

"Yes, ma'am," said the pilot. One of his two crewmen handed Kaz and Porter intensifying night-vision goggles.

The pilot made the Interceptor dark and the CBP vessel cruised into the calm night. The crew flipped on their goggles and began scanning the green horizon. The pilot began making wide, sweeping turns to cover as much area as possible.

After about fifteen minutes stationed on the port bow, Porter started to feel a little queasy. The seas were relatively calm, but the boat banked hard and looking through the goggles did something weird to his equilibrium.

He flicked the NVGs up and took a few deep breaths. He rubbed his eyes and waited for them to adjust. After staring through the bright goggles, the night was newly dark. Except for a small cloud of green smoke blooming in the indeterminate distance. Not so close that Porter could make out the lasered "JK," but it was pretty close.

"There," Porter said.

Kaz's head snapped around. "Go quiet," she ordered the pilot.

The pilot killed the engines, then cocked his head. "Is that… "Gold Dust Woman"?" he whispered.

The following morning, at Honolulu's Federal Detention Center, Jonathan Kalawai'a used his one phone call to reach his attorney Charlie Keawe, who readers would recognize as Mr. A.

It was Saturday morning. The call from Jonny K, Keawe's biggest client, forced him to skip rehearsal for his community theatre production of "Beauty and the Beast." Keawe was playing the clock.

When he arrived at the DC, Keawe was handed a file and shown to a small room where his biggest client sat on a bench, manacled to a steel ring set in the floor. "Tell me I'm walking out of here, Charlie," Jonny said.

"As always, Jonathan," Keawe said, "there is good news and bad." He took a seat on a small folding chair set in the center of the room. "You are not walking out of here. Not today, anyway. Not with me."

"What's the good news?" Jonny asked.

"That wasn't the bad news. The bad news is you're stuck like a pig on the ocean littering charge. The fine will be half a million, at least. You have that kind of cash? If not, this is the State we're talking about. They'll just start taking stuff you own. Your house, liquor license, the IC, your boats, whatever they want. They don't screw around. Why were you dumping all that stuff in the ocean?"

"Tell them it was Finer's idea."

"Finer is fourteen years old. His uncle bailed him out this morning. I heard he was not happy."

"Who is? Tell them I was building an artificial reef. Sea turtles."

Keawe scoffed. "The permits to build an artificial reef probably cost more than the littering fine," he said. "I'd keep that plan to yourself. I advise you to just pay the fine."

Jonny rubbed his bald head and said, "What's the good news?"

"The good news is that everything else, the trafficking case, the tax stuff, all of it, will go away if they can't find this Jeff Zachary, who allegedly wrote this journal that implicates you. It sounds like they have no idea where he is."

"I hardly know that asshole. He did a little work for me. Why did he write all that bullshit?"

"Doesn't matter," Keawe said. "One way or the other, you're connected to him. But fortunately, the journal itself isn't proof of anything unless Jeff Zachary himself turns up. Do you know where he might be?"

"No," Jonny said. "But I have a guess. Call Pateena. Ask for Mikey."

Keawe pulled out a yellow pad.

Mindful that Keawe would be billing him time-and-a-half because it was the weekend, Jonny K gave his lawyer a few quick instructions, including his username and password for the GPS app that tracks the *Monkey Fist*, then sent him on his way.

Keawe left the Detention Center and made two calls. One to Mikey at Pateena. One to Margot Carlene.

CHAPTER 58

- obviously, you must ally with some at some point.

It had been almost twenty-two hours since Tasha hung up on Margot. 994 paces of the deck.

Her phone rang.

"Did you get my fishing boat?" she answered. Might as well play it out to the end.

"Yes," Margot said. "And I feel like I can smell it already."

"You get used to it," said Tasha. Her legs felt a little wobbly. She sat down cross-legged on the deck. "So." She muted the phone and hyperventilated for a second. Unmute. "You're ready for part two. The good stuff. What did you pay for Pateena, can I ask?"

"No, you can't ask. But not much. The Pateena brand alone is worth five X what I paid, not to mention the rights to the work. You were right. Kalawai'a laughed off my first offer and hung up, but this morning his lawyer called back and admitted that his client needed the cash fast. I think the lawyer just wanted to be sure he was going to be paid first."

"Congratulations," Tasha said. "You own a hot interior design brand."

"And a fishing boat," Margot said. "You were saying something about the good stuff?"

"Yes," Tasha said. "A friend of mine needs to create a video."

"What is he, some kind of wanna-be influencer?"

"No, just the opposite. This guy needs to disappear. But in a public way."

"I'm trying to get out of the disappearing business."

"I know. Look, here it is," Tasha said. "My friend is not just a friend. His name is Jefir Zaqq. You know him as Jeff Zachary, the Sand Island Stowaway."

"Are you kidding right now?" Margot asked.

"No," Tasha said. "He's in trouble and he needs help. We can help him."

"What do you think I'm trying to do here, Tasha?" Margot said. "I just wanted to get into the lifestyle space. I'm so done with cleaning up other people's messes. Do you think I like being the one-who-does-the-disappearing? I do not."

Tasha didn't say anything. A seagull could be heard squawking in the moment that passed.

"I saw him that morning, you know," said Margot. "In the security office at GossCo. A crane's camera caught a perfect shot of him looking up after he fell out of that container. I made that disappear."

"Good. He probably had that terrible beard then," Tasha said. "He's been rocking a 'stache ever since."

"He has the face for it," said Margot. "Did you know there's a keyboard shortcut on security camera systems for "Delete Recorded History? It's just control-shift-delete."

"A man invented that. I'd bet my boat on it," Tasha laughed.

Margot laughed too.

Tasha said, "You already helped Jeff once. He needs you again."

"I was helping myself then," Margot said.

"You can still do both," Tasha said.

"By helping your friend Jeff Zachary disappear? You think I can do that?" asked Margot.

"Yes," said Tasha. "Yes, I do."

"And how is this 'the good stuff'?" Margot asked.

"I'm a fisherman," Tasha said. "I have to go out and chase the fish. I'd save a lot of time and diesel fuel if the fish would just tell me where they were going to be and at what time. If I knew the where and the when ahead of time, that could be very valuable."

Margot said, "What are you saying? You have some valuable knowledge of the future? Concerning Jeff Zachary? What's so valuable? Is he getting arrested, too?"

"No!" Tasha said. "No, Jeff can't be arrested. He just has to *appear* to, well, to die, to one certain person, who doesn't even live in the US, by the way. Jeff's just going to disappear."

"Who is this person?"

"You don't need to know. I'll give you his ZoopZap handle."

"I checked you out on the Zap, @CaptainTasha69," Margot said. "You zap a lot of the zoops from @HaoleJanFL_U_RF, I noticed. She creates some great content."

"I prefer creators to disappearer-ers, yes it's true. No offense. But Haole Jan is the shit."

"Do you know her? IRL?"

"I live in her house, girl."

Margot said, "Why am I not surprised?"

"I should hook you two up. You'd like her."

"First things first," said Margot. "I can see a way to do this Zachary thing, but I need to be miles away from it, literally and figuratively."

"No prob," Tasha said.

"Tell me what you need from me first."

"Access to the location, that's it. I was thinking back at the GossCo port? Someplace public, someplace important, but controllable. Spin it however you want afterward, but Jeff has to be gone."

"What are you bringing to this party?" Margot asked.

Tasha said, "A 99-foot tuna boat. A crew of three guys who know how to keep their mouths shut. Jeff Zachary himself, and a place to stash him outside the country."

Margot made a few taps on her keyboard. "I can arrange a sixty-minute window on the GossCo offshore mining platform in the EEZ this coming Monday. I also have a GossCo Security uniform that very, *very* badly needs a washing, and a handgun that used to belong to ████ ██████."

"OK. Wow. I'll figure out the rest, I guess," Tasha said.

CHAPTER 59

- Condsider that Someone is struggling more than you.

To: mohammad.mohammad54321@zmail.zaz

From: service@botcoin.bot

Subject: You've got Bot!

Jeffzachary262 sent you 3.55871 botcoins!

Message from jeffzachary262:

Please accept this. It is truly everything I have left. I was once told that I wouldn't need money where I'm going anyway. I have been in contact with Hallazallah and we have reached a solution. Use the money as best you can to keep Rahim safe. Keep Rahim safe. Keep Rahim safe. Keep Rahim safe.

Jeff was about to press SEND on the Botcoin machine at Pawn1^{2} but Tasha grabbed his wrist.

"Jeff, just let me help pay," Tasha said. "Please. I can get eight or nine thousand. Another couple thousand on credit cards. Are you telling me your brother can't disappear from Zazaristan for less than ten grand? You said you only paid five."

"He's not just getting on a plane. It's difficult to travel without documents. When I came, it took weeks to plan," Jeff said. "I had to wait for the best opportunity. Even then, it was dangerous. I almost got caught."

He gently pulled his hand from hers and hit SEND. "Thank you, but I can't let you lose everything again. Anything less than the full forty thousand will probably end up wasted. Mr. Shwarma has a lot of hands to take care of. If any one of his contacts isn't happy with their share, everything falls apart. But I have to try."

"Are you happy with your share?" Tasha asked.

He took her hand again. "Yes," said Jeff.

CHAPTER 60

• The hero melon flies but the hero melon never hits the ground.

Bashir Hallazallah didn't ZoopZap.

The app was pre-installed on his phone of course, but he never created an account. Rizwan had to set it up for him.

"Tap where it says, "Join Zoopstream," Rizwan said.

They were sitting in Hallazallah's truck, parked across the street from 505 H Street.

An image of Jefir Zaqq appeared on the screen. Hallazallah had studied the face for hours on the ID card left behind in the square that night.

"Zaqq!" He barked at the phone.

"He can't hear you, sir," said Rizwan.

"Why is this fool holding the phone like that?" Hallazallah asked. Before Rizwan could explain about portraits and landscapes, Zaqq started to say something.

"My name is Jefir Zaqq. It is 0700 hours on Monday, twelve August. I am under a GossCo offshore mining platform in the United States Exclusive Economic Zone in the Pacific Ocean north of O'ahu, Hawaii. My vest is packed with ten pounds of Semtex plastic explosives. At 0745, I will be hiding under this platform's helicopter pad, near the northwest support leg, when a group of corrupt American executives arrives. I will destroy the pad as they land and cause the helicopter to crash. I'm doing this for my brother. Bash Hallazallah, Taboor City, Zazaristan."

Zaqq tilted the phone down to show ten yellowish bricks strapped to his chest. He then pointed the phone up, to follow a long ladder that disappeared into a web of struts and catwalks.

The phone rustled as Zaqq stuffed it under a strap of his vest. The view became a close-up of a metal rung. The rungs began scrolling down the screen. Zaqq's softly ringing hand and footfalls and his heavy breathing were the only sounds for several minutes of the video. The surface of the ocean grew further and further away while the main deck of the mining platform grew closer. When almost two hundred rungs had passed, Zaqq stopped climbing.

"In the name of Bash Hallazallah, I do this," he said, his breath ragged.

He climbed a few steps more. The mining rig's main deck came into view. Zaqq stepped onto the platform and the camera swiveled right and left. The structure looked like an unfinished building, all exposed I-beams and concrete columns.

"Show me your hands!"

Zaqq swiveled back to the left. A uniformed security guard stood about five meters away. The guard had his handgun drawn and aimed straight at the camera on Zaqq's chest.

Zaqq didn't say anything, but the video started to wiggle. The phone was moving.

"Don't touch that!" the guard yelled. He took a step forward.

The phone was in Zaqq's hand. "Bash Hallazallah," he said. The camera flashed over his face, then turned away to frame the guard again. Small puffs of smoke blew from the guard's weapon. *Crackcrack Crackcrackcrackcrack.*

Zaqq screamed and the video lurched wildly, showing sky, water, sky, platform, guard, sky, Zaqq, the underside of the platform rapidly falling up.

The phone hit the water and a small red slick could be seen ribboning through the sun-dappled bubbles around Zaqq's dark body. A second later the video went black.

"What was he screaming on the way down?" Hallazallah asked.

"I am... something?" said Rizwan. "I couldn't understand. He might have just been screaming in fear or pain."

"Let's hope," Hallazallah said.

Hallazallah made Rizwan replay the video a few times. They couldn't make sense of Zaqq's last words and concluded they were an unintelligible death scream. The replays also allowed timing of the length of his fall. It lasted just over two seconds. About seventy meters, according to Rizwan's quick research, enough to kill a man, even if he wasn't riddled with bullets.

Hallazallah smirked. He hoped it was the fall, rather than the bullets that killed Zaqq. That he knew at least one long moment of terror.

"A better fate than he deserved," Hallazallah said, finally. "But Bash's name will live in the minds of the infidels." He picked a paper bag containing two million zazars in cash off the floor of the truck. "I'm going in to pay Shwarma."

"Would you like me to come with you?" Riz asked.

"I would hope you think that I can still handle Shwarma alone," Hallazallah said.

"Of course, sir," Rizwan apologized.

Hallazallah took a few bills from the bag and nodded toward Shinni's. "Get me a chicken kebab while I'm upstairs."

The men got out of the truck and entered 505 H Street. Rizwan joined the back of the café's ordering line and Hallazallah headed upstairs to the 3rd floor.

"Sir," Rahim said. "Bashir Hallazallah is here."

"Send him in," said Shwarma. "And close the door, Rahim."

"What does he want?" Rahim whispered.

Shwarma shrugged. "I'll find out, don't worry, Mr. Lotfi."

He tried to give Rahim an encouraging look. Hallazallah just showing up at the office like this could be a problem. Shwarma tried to deal with the man only when Rahim wasn't around. Neither one of them should get too close to the other. If Hallazallah knew Rahim was actually Jeff's brother, he would cut Shwarma's best employee down like a blade of grass. And if Rahim knew that Shwarma was selling Jeff out over a few missed payments, then obviously that would affect Rahim's employment as well.

"Bashir!" Shwarma said. "What a pleasant surprise. Have a seat." The door clicked shut.

Hallazallah sat down. "Shwarma. Have you seen it?"

"Seen what?" Shwarma asked. "The cricket match? I felt it was just average."

"No. Your boy Jefir Zaqq. It was on ZoppyZop."

"I'm not sure I understand," Shwarma said.

Hallazallah took his phone out and hit play. He turned the screen so Shwarma could see the final minutes of Jefir Zaqq's life and hear his screams extinguished by some deep blue ocean halfway around the globe.

"What did he say at the end, there?" Shwarma asked.

"I believe he said, 'I am a loathsome coward."

"Yes, we believe what we want, don't we?" said Shwarma.

Hallazallah tossed the bag of cash onto Shwarma's desk.

Shwarma took the money out, did a quick count, and put the cash in his desk drawer, on top of the $3,500 Jeff sent two days ago, which now looked like it was going to be the last of it from Agent One.

Hallazallah pushed back his chair, stood up and left the office.

Rahim was standing in the middle of the outer office. "I know what he said."

"What?" said Hallazallah. He stopped.

"I know what Jefir Zaqq said at the end of the video. And it's ZoopZap, you fuck."

Hallazallah said, "Rahim, is it?"

"Yes. Rahim. Rahim Zaqq."

After a moment, Hallazallah said, "Ha. I can't believe I didn't see it." He reached for his pistol.

Rahim held a riverstone paperweight the size of a medium lime and he fired it at Hallazallah.

The stone went a centimeter high and it skipped off Hallazallah's forehead. Stunned, the old man took a step back. Rahim rushed him and lowered his shoulder into Hallazallah's midsection as he raked down on the gun with both hands to knock it to the floor.

Hallazallah weighed nearly twice as much as Rahim. He barely budged as the kid bounced off him and sprawled backwards. Like a cat, Hallazallah pounced. He had a knee on Rahim's chest and a hand around his throat. Before Rahim could get his hands up, a giant fist smashed his nose once, twice, three times. He saw fat red stars, his ears roared and his throat was filling with blood.

BLANGBLANGBLANG!

Hallazallah let go and slowly raised his hands. The sensory world returned to Rahim.

"Get off my lieutenant and get out of my office, old man." Shwarma stood in the doorway of his office holding an AK-47. He quickly bent to pick up Hallazallah's pistol. "I think you got what you came for. Go."

Hallazallah pushed himself up and slowly turned to face Shwarma. "Think hard about this, Shwarma," he said. "Whose life in this room is worth more?"

"Shut up," Shwarma said. "Get—"

"PUT DOWN YOUR WEAPON!" Rizwan yelled, bursting in the door. He sprayed the ceiling above Shwarma's head with 7.62 mm bullets. Real bullets, not like the three blanks Shwarma just spent from his Property of King Abbas College Theatre Department prop gun.

Shwarma dropped to his knees as his security deposit on the office, in the form of plaster dust, blew away in the evening breeze.

"Sir, we should be going," Rizwan said nervously. "The gunshots. This is not our neighborhood."

"This won't take long, Riz," Hallazallah said. "I just have to get something I left in Mr. Shwarma's office, now that he won't be needing it." He stepped into the office and disappeared from sight. Rizwan kept his rifle trained on Shwarma and Rahim. A pool of blood was growing in front of Rahim.

"Rizwan!" Hallazallah called out. "Come in here. I'm stuck!"

Rizwan's eyes widened with question, but he responded without. He crossed the outer office while keeping Shwarma and Rahim covered.

Hallazallah's ample thighs were pinched in the narrow gap between Shwarma's desk and the wall and he was bent over under the arched ceiling in such a way that left him without the leverage to free himself. Rizwan tried to nudge the desk with his hip. The desk wouldn't move.

"Push from the end!" Hallazallah growled.

Rizwan said, "I think it's screwed to the fl—"

Shwarma leapt to his feet and pulled Rahim by the shirt sleeve. They tumbled out the door and were halfway down the fire escape before Rizwan got to the hallway.

Thirty minutes later, another bleeding Zaqq brother who had just gotten his ass kicked by a guy named Bashir Hallazallah sat in Shwarma's living room.

"I'm sorry about Jefir, Rahim," Shwarma said. "I don't know how Hallazallah discovered his identity. I didn't know his group was so technically savvy. Are you sure you never used that email?"

"No," Rahim said, through a wet towel.

"And for the record," said Shwarma, "I don't believe Jefir was really acting on behalf of Hallazallah as some kind of true believer. Your brother would never be turned so easily. There's only one reason he would do that. It was to protect you, Rahim. I believe it was all he ever wanted."

"All he wants," Rahim said.

"Well, yes. We believe what we want, don't we?"

Rahim took the towel from his face, "Do you want to know what he said at the end of the video?"

CHAPTER 61

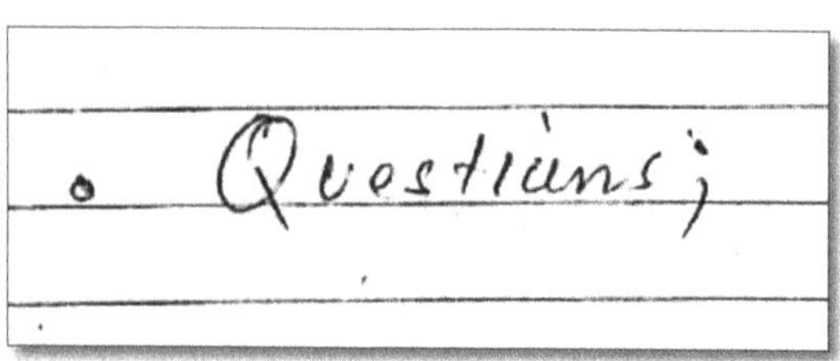

"Why did you scream, 'I am the hero melon' in Zazarish at the end?" Hemi asked. He was taking off Trent Calvin's GossCo Security Uniform. (Margot had collected the foul clothes from the dock that morning, sealed them in a bag and stashed them in the storage unit she rented in Pearl City under the name "Laura Ashley" because you never know.) Tasha had washed the uniform three times, but it still stunk.

"Yeah," said Tommy. "What the fuck?"

The crewmates sat around the table with Jeff in the galley of the *Monkey Fist.* Jeff was still wet. There were streaks of red across his neck and arms.

"You speak Zazarish, Hemi?" he asked. Why did you never tell me?"

"You never told me *you* speak it," Hemi replied. He pulled on a t-shirt.

"Yes," Jeff said. "Well. 'I am the hero melon' is a message to my brother Rahim. I was letting him know that I would be OK."

"Are you OK?" Kai asked. "That line jerked hard before it snapped."

"It was scary," Jeff said. "And it knocked my wind out. But better than hitting the water at full speed. Hemi was right."

"Physics," Hemi said. "Including the weight of the vest and ten Proteinsanity bars, Jeff is 158.5 pounds. The height of the platform deck is about 205 feet. Acceleration of gravity for one point five seconds of freefall created a force of 1,378 newtons, distributed across three semi-ductile fishing lines with enough combined tensile strength to absorb no more than 1,200 newtons. The lines stretched and slowed him down enough before snapping at the weak upper knot point to create a survivable impact—"

"Then I fucking nailed him with a red paintball from that catwalk platform," Tommy said. "Center of the chest from fifty feet away. Ha!"

Tasha came down the stairs. "Shut up, none of this is funny."

Tommy said, "What about the part where we pulled this crazy shit off while everyone working on that platform was in a mandatory corporate OSHA safety meeting?"

"That's ironic and stupid," Tasha said, "But not funny." She stopped behind Jeff and wiped a little red paint off his neck. "We're coming up on where we left the GPS buoy," she announced. "Let's grab it and get out of here. Kiribati's set in the nav, but it's a long run to get there. Haole Jan said we can use all three of her yurts for a few days before we head back, but Jeff can stay in one as long as he wants. He has to bag Honolulu for good."

In Honolulu, Jonny K wanted Jeff dead. A federal human trafficking charge is never good for the brand, but if Jeff disappeared, so would the charge. And if Jonny didn't get to him, Customs and Border Protection was now on Jeff's trail as well. Kaz and Porter had been looking for him that morning at the marina, observing the *Monkey Fist* as Tasha Hale and her remaining crew, Thomas Coughlin and Hemi and Kai Tuigamala loaded their large cartons and barrels aboard the boat and sailed out of the harbor.

Jeff had wanted to stay in Honolulu. Most do. But some don't. Some get into their boats one blue-sky morning and set out to see the next island. There are more islands out there, that someone reasons. Perhaps bigger, perhaps smaller. Perhaps just a dull and mossy nub, perhaps a swelling green glade, vast and beautiful and just over the horizon. Just another day or two away. Maybe three days. Maybe more. No one can say. Just as reason tells there must be more islands out there, reason also demands that some of these islands must lie beyond where the water and wind run out.

The tiny island of Kiribati juts from the Pacific Ocean 1,600 miles south of Hawaii. Haole Jan ran some kind of artist's retreat/eco-tourism yurt campground there. Her three yurts were named "Flowing Love," "Uniting Realms" and "Freedom." Kiribati has a great fruit market and its azure seas hold more fish than even Tasha could catch in a lifetime.

"I call dibs on Flowing Love," Tommy said. "Is Haole Jan going to be there?"

"Why are you asking, Thomas?" Tasha said.

"Yes, why, Thomas?" Kai repeated, grinning.

"Fuck off. Haole Jan is the shit," said Tommy.

Tasha was smiling too, which made Jeff smile.

"She asked about you, too," Tasha said. "But she won't be there. She'll be in Honolulu this week. Margot saw some of her designs on my ZoopZap and they're having a meeting. Now, get on deck and haul up the GPS so it seems like we're out here fishing."

Tommy climbed up to the main deck, followed by Hemi and Kai.

From the foot of the steps, Jeff heard Tommy say, "Who the fuck are these guys?"

Tasha put a hand on Jeff's shoulder. "Stay down here," she said. She hurried past him up the stairs.

A twenty-foot ski boat was pulling alongside the *Fist*. The *Monkey Fist Too*.

Four men were aboard. Mikey, Chuck, Nep2n and B from Pateena.

Tasha appeared on deck. "What are you doing way out here? What do you want?"

The men signaled for her to cut her engine.

"Fuck you, Mikey!" Tommy yelled above the engines and wind. He flipped the double bird. He glanced over his shoulder to see that Hemi and Kai were behind him.

Mikey swerved a little closer alongside. Chuck, Nep2n and B drew blue-painted weapons.

"What the hell?" Tasha shouted. "What do you guys want?"

"Jeff Zachary!" Mikey called back. "Is he with you?"

"No! Haven't seen him in days!"

Jeff crouched on the stairs, listening.

Mikey said, "We're gonna check. It's what the *luna* asked. We're coming aboard, just to be sure. Cut your engine."

"You guys are out too deep in that little boat!" Tasha shouted. "Get back to Honolulu! If we see Jeff, we'll let you know!" She turned to Tommy. "Get us out of here."

Tommy climbed to the bridge. When he hit the throttle and the *Fist* pulled away, Mikey signaled and the Craftsmiths fired a volley of bullets over her bow.

It was only a matter of time, Jeff thought. He crept down the stairs back to the galley.

"What the fuck, Mikey?" Tasha yelled.

"Cut your engine!" Mikey shouted again, accelerating to keep pace. "We're coming aboard!"

Tasha signaled to Tommy. Tommy cut the engine and in the relative silence of the open ocean, Tasha called, "Be cool, Mike! But whatever. Make it quick. Then you guys can take the rest of the day to do some wakeboarding!"

Jeff's grip tightened on the 12-inch knife he'd taken from the galley.

Mikey slowed *Monkey Fist Too*'s engine to match the inertia of the larger boat.

Tasha beckoned Hemi and Kai close and said quietly, "Tie these clowns aft. We'll dump them in the drink. They can decide to look the other way about Jeff or swim home."

Mikey brought the boats hull-to-hull briefly. Nep2n and Chuck stood side-by-side, poised to climb aboard the larger fishing boat, but the boats skipped apart.

Tasha called to them, "We'll tie to your beam!"

Kai was already carrying a coil of line to the rail. He tossed the end, landing it on the *Too*'s deck between Nep2n and Chuck. He pointed to a sturdy midbeam cleat. "Tie a bowline there."

Nep2n and Chuck looked at one another, each hoping the other knew what to do. The wakeboard ropes all had loops already made into the ends. The boats drifted about ten feet apart and their end of the line slipped from the deck and into the water.

Kai pulled it back and tossed it again, this time landing it closer to Nep2n. "Tie a bowline there," he repeated, pointing.

Nep2n glanced at B, wordlessly asking for cover, then holstered his handgun in one of *Monkey Fist Too*'s port cupholders and picked up the wet line.

Kai said, "Rabbit comes out of the hole, sees fox, goes around tree and back down hole."

Nep2n followed the directions and tied off. Hemi and Kai hauled on the line and the boats clunked together in the rolling seas.

In the dim cabin ladderway, Jeff wished he still had Zoey, not this ridiculous blade.

Kai hitched *Monkey Fist Too* to the *Monkey Fist*'s rail. "Tie us up at two points!" Tasha barked. She looked at Mikey, who was still at the wheel of the ski boat. "In captain school, they tell you, always tie up at two points. Safety first."

"You be cool, Tasha!" Mikey snapped. "We're going to come aboard for two minutes. K said to check the cabin. Then we'll be out."

"Don't forget to look in the pilothouse," Tasha said. "We could totally hide a dude up there." She waved a hand up toward Tommy to catch his eye.

Jeff crouched on the stairs like a sprinter in the blocks.

Mikey nodded to Chuck and Nep2n. Nep2n picked up his pistol and reached for the *Monkey's Fist*'s rail to pull himself aboard.

Tasha jabbed a finger up and Tommy pushed the throttle full ahead. The *Fist* reared from the water and jerked the smaller boat out from under Nep2n's feet. He was left dangling from the *Monkey Fist*'s gate post by one hand.

Jeff was knocked sideways, but he caught the OSHA-regulation handrail to keep from tumbling down the stairs.

Monkey Fist Too lurched sideways, securely tied at the beam, then swung stern-first and smashed into the hull of the *Monkey Fist*. Chuck and B stumbled back and fell. Holding the control console, Mikey managed to keep his feet, but just barely. He pulled his pistol from the larger of the console's starboard cupholders and fired wildly.

Jeff ran up the stairs toward the gunshots.

Tasha, Kai and Hemi were standing at the edge of the stern deck. They scrambled and dove behind the pilothouse as the gunshots rang out. Hemi got to his feet and looked around for a weapon. Margot Carlene said the [illegible] [illegible] gun must follow Jeff into the water immediately after use. Margot was cleaning out her storage unit in advance of her pending career change and the Sig Sauer P365 no longer sparked joy, apparently.

Hemi grabbed a long gaff from the bulkhead. Tasha dropped to her belly and peeked around the corner. Nobody had managed to board her boat, but twenty feet updeck, she saw Nep2n's stubborn left hand gripping the post as he was being dragged across the water. His right hand flashed up into view, fired two shots from a blue pistol, and disappeared. Tasha stayed low and scooted forward; the abrasive, non-slip surface of the deck rubbed her bare knees raw. Kai followed on his belly. When Tasha was about a body length from the gate, she reached back and Kai passed the gaff up to her.

Tasha didn't gaff Nep2n's hand, didn't even smash the white knuckles with the handle. She pushed the thick and gleaming hook through the gate slowly, so Nep2n could get a nice look at it, then she yanked it back through air.

The hand disappeared. The volleys of gunfire stopped. Simultaneous cries from the *Too*: "Nep!"

The bullet had felt like a hot string pulled through the fist of Jeff's chest. Dark blood burbled. The black-on-black fireworks again. Faster this time.

"Cut them loose, Kai!" Tasha yelled. The boats were still tied beam-to-beam. The ski boat twisted and bucked, being dragged alongside the bigger boat.

Kai duckran to the rail where the boats were tied. With a deft yank at an innocuous loop, the hitch dissolved. Unburdened, the *Monkey Fist* surged ahead. *Monkey Fist Too* rocked steady and drifted away. Nep2n's head bobbed in the *Fist*'s white wake, growing smaller by the second.

The Craftsmiths were all looking back for Nep2n and didn't notice that the *Too* was still securely bowlined to the stern of a powerful fishing boat with a hundred feet of rapidly tightening line.

Tasha stood up. "Have fun wakeboarding! You dicks!" she yelled.

Firing the guns was too much. Someone could have gotten hurt. Tasha decided she would let these Pateena a-holes float on the open water for little while until they agreed to get their stories straight about the rogue wave that swept over *Monkey Fist Too* before they were rescued by Tasha and her crew, a crew which definitely, for sure, did not include Jeff Zachary.

Tasha walked to the stern rail with Hemi and Kai. They watched as the last of the line's slack was taken up and it sprang from the water in a wall of spray.

The *Monkey Fist* slowed as her little sister vessel was yanked sideways, still tied at the beam. The deck of the *Too* lurched to an angle and Mikey was launched overboard immediately. Chuck got dumped in as well, but he managed to cling to the tilted hull. The boat was being dragged sideways and B fought to keep his feet while trying pull Chuck back aboard. A small, gushing wave had formed ahead of *Monkey Fist Too*, and water was pushing over the gunwale, filling the deck up to B's knees.

"Jeff!" Tasha yelled.

"Are we sinking them?" Kai asked Hemi.

"No," said Tasha. "Just swamp them a little." She turned back toward the pilothouse. "Jeff! Hide in the engine compartment! Jeff!" She left the rail and walked back to the cabin stairs.

"We can't tow that fucking boat forever!" Tommy yelled down from the bridge. The small wave grew, snapping at the *Too* like a wild animal. B was pulled into the water. Chuck disappeared under the boat.

The *Monkey Fist*'s engine whined in protest. The line between the boats hummed with tension.

Tasha returned to the stern holding a blood-spattered 12-inch galley knife. She watched wordlessly from the rail until the *Monkey Fist Too* had completely disappeared into the sea's roiling maw.

Then she cut the line.

And the *Monkey Fist* sailed on.

EPILOGUE

The body of Jefir Zaqq, proud son of Taboor City, Zazaristan, was commited to the deep. Run easy, Jef. Your name hasn't been spoken for the last time.

Finer's uncle was not happy. Stories about Finer's uncle must wait for another time, but he was known around Honolulu as sort of a *luna*'s *luna*. He did not appreciate Jonny K getting his brother's only son jammed up. Finer's uncle moved some weight around and most of it landed on Jonny K. Between the bounties and bribes, the fees and fines, Jonny ended up forced to sell his liquor license, then the Intercontinental Lounge itself, then his house, then the El Camino and ultimately, the last 8-track copy of *Rumours*.

Using the $500,000 Heinz Gossler paid her to quietly "disappear" the bloody mining platform video from Jeff Zachary's ZoopZap account, Margot Carlene formed a partnership with Janine Garabedian that would go on to become Flurf.com.

The unexplained disappearances of the Pateena Craftsmiths raised the value of their extant work to the point where Tasha was able to completely buy back the *Monkey Fist* by selling some of the boat's (now vintage!) Pateena-branded galley equipment via ZoopZap auction.

Despite what he felt was due justice served to Jefir Zaqq, Bashir Hallazallah never fully recovered from the death of his son. He moved from Taboor City and began spending more and more time in the foothills of the Pir Mountains.

Though not as upset as Finer's uncle, Jama Tycanni was pretty pissed at Shwarma. The expensive millwork on the third floor of 505 H Street was all shot up and the shooting did no favors for the West Taboor property values. Tycanni forced Shwarma's eviction, but managed to negotiate with him a very reasonable price for the windowless albatross in South Taboor.

A NOTE FROM THE PUBLISHER

Thank you for reading this edition of *The Honolulu Situation* by Mark A. Henry. We at Operation Dodecahedron welcome the feedback of influential people like yourself. Please provide your honest rating and review on Amazon and/or Goodreads to help Mr. Henry improve his craft, but also please be kind. He is an artist. You know how they are.

Get some free stickers in the mail!

Email your address to: freestickers@operationdodecahedron.com

ACKNOWLEDGEMENTS

If writing a book is building a ship, writing a second book is building a ship in a bottle.

Hard and painstaking, appreciated by a very few. And the very few are very likely weirdos.

Here's to you all. My brothers, my sisters, my band, my crew, my loose passel of weirdos so powerful, we dare not speak its name.

It's readers, actually.

Thank you. Thank you for using some of our shared time on this earth together. Thank you for the words of encouragement and words of critique. It is my sincerest endeavor to use them both skillfully and carefully as I venture forth into what may come.

My girls: Kerrie and Madi and Emma.

My parents and brother: Roland, Ailene and Kraig Henry

The Horsemen of the Tropocalypse: Nathan Auclair, Heath Burdick and Todd DiBattista.

And Maura McGurk, Paul Klee, Allison Bright Rose, Larry Tressler, Brian Grouhel, Kathryn O'Donnell, Paul Bourdolous, Sean McCallum, Avner Landes, the *Beyond the Zero* Podcast, Jane Gordon Julien, Audrey Beattie, Andrea Barton, Lisa Piquettte and Patty Muldoon.

Meghan, Ernio, Kaitee and Nora from the River Bend Bookshop and Seth, Liz, Lina, Emma and Jonathan at Curiosity & Co.

APPENDIX A

Article Talk Read Edit View history Search Wanglepedia

Ocean Heat

From Wanglepedia, the encyclopedia of the internet

Ocean Heat is an American television action-drama series created by three-time Emmy Award-winning television producer Alexander K. Prentiss. *Ocean Heat* starred Tim Braddock as Heaton Barbary, an unjustly fired Philadelphia Police Detective who moves to Malibu, California to become a private investigator. The series ran from September 23, 1993 to May 12, 1999 on the American television network CBN. *Ocean Heat* consistently ranked in the top 20 U.S. television programs in the Nielson ratings, regularly drawing ten million weekly viewers. In 1997, Braddock was nominated for Best Actor in a Drama Series, but did not win.

Season 1 (1993-94) [edit]

No. overall	No. in season	Title	Directed by	Written by	Original air date
1 2	1 2	"It's Not the Humidity, It's the Heat, Baby"	Alexander K. Prentiss	Alexander K. Prentiss	September 23, 1993
In the pilot episode, Detective Heaton Barbary is fired from the Philadelphia Police force and accepts the invitation of an old friend to visit Los Angeles. When the friend ends up dead, Barbary must team up with a yoga instructor to infiltrate a ring of party drug suppliers. Meanwhile, some old debts from Philadelphia must be paid. *NOTE*: This episode originally aired as a two-hour pilot film, but subsequently was shown as two separate episodes.					
3	3	"A Bird in the Hand"	Alexander K. Prentiss	Alexander K. Prentiss	September 30, 1993
When his new neighbor's valuable macaw goes missing, Barbary hunts down an eccentric wildlife trafficker.					
4	4	"The Sun Also Rises"	Alexander K. Prentiss	Bradley West & Milos Garabedian	October 7, 1993
A day at the beach turns deadly when a beautiful life guard is accused of murder.					
5	5	"Friends Like These"	William Titus	Alexander K. Prentiss	October 14, 1993
Barbary teams up with an underworld figure to pursue a conman. Guest starring George Mitchell.					
6	6	"Sour Grapes"	Lawrence Levine	Benny Torres	October 21, 1993
During a visit to wine country, Barbary suspects a vintner of being the front for a smuggling operation.					

Made in USA - North Chelmsford, MA
26323_9781736344675
11.02.2023 0528